Scam on the Cove

John Marks

Black Rose Writing | Texas

First printing

ISBN: 978-1-68433-284-7
PUBLISHED BY BLACK ROSE WRITING
www.blackrosewriting.com

Printed in the United States of America
Suggested Retail Price (SRP) $21.95

Scam on the Cove is printed in Plantagenet Cherokee

For Ellie, Gabe, and Grace.

Scam on the Cove

Prologue

She knew the drill. But this was the first time she'd do it for real, carrying cash and an underwater pistol. The latter accessory gave her pause. It was supposed to be just for show, though that couldn't be the reason for the dart-shaped projectiles loaded inside its chambers.

Trying to calm herself, she refocused her thoughts on the overall dive profile. It should be no big deal after all the scuba training. Just twenty minutes of bottom time at max depths of fifty to sixty feet. A closed-circuit rebreather equipped her for much more, and she'd have the added assurance of continuous communication topside with the divemaster who had trained her.

He'd also taught her how to use the gun.

His eyes swept the horizon one last time.

"Listen," he said, "if you don't want to do this, we can just..."

She rolled over the side of the boat, hit the surface of Lake Huron, and sank into the frigid freshwater of a vast blue world. Her destination was one of many historical objects preserved in these waters, a small steamer, the *EJ La Way*, whose final voyage nearly a century before had come up a mile short of Drummond Island's Chippewa Point—on the lake's bottom.

The dive began as it always had during her training. The only factor that varied was visibility, which ranged from five to fifty feet depending on weather and water conditions. Today it was about thirty. A large light attached to her head added some focus and color within that range. More importantly, the glow could be seen at a much greater distance by another diver, whom she would soon meet for the first time.

The edge of the debris field came into view. She stopped and looked north, toward Canada. In this vast expanse of water, the international border was only a couple hundred yards away.

From the distant depths a light emerged, right on time, coming from that direction. The beam grew brighter and bobbed erratically for a while before it stopped moving. Then it vanished. She counted slowly in her head. Almost exactly at the count of ten the light rapidly blinked on and off four times. Following another similar interval, it turned on and stayed on.

Now it was her turn. She shut off her light, counted to ten, and then clicked it on and off three times. After another ten count, she turned it on and left it on.

Still hovering at the edge of the debris field, she placed a hand on her hip to reinforce the location of the gun and looked back to confirm that she still had in tow a length of crystal-clear PVC tubing. It was stuffed with cash. Dead presidents stared back at her through the transparent tube, prompting the thought, *What the hell am I doing?*

She swam forward.

A blurry outline of the *EJ* appeared ahead, listing slightly to port. Soon, the details of the vessel's algae-covered remains came into focus. She sometimes wondered what it was like for sailors on board that day, April 19, 1929, when a chunk of ice gashed the vessel's hull and took her down to the bottom. It was no doubt a violent end. From cargo hatch to bow the vessel was collapsed and split open, and most of its upper decks and cargo were left scattered in a large debris field off the port side.

She scanned the site for tourists.

"It's clear," she said into her mic. Her speech was garbled by a mouthpiece that wouldn't let her lips move, but somehow her trainer always understood.

"All right, let's get it done," he replied.

She finally reached the meeting place. It was the site of one of the more prominent artifacts in the debris field, a large galley stove. Just beyond it hovered the other diver.

She stopped on the opposite side of the stove and looked up. The water above him was still. His scuba gear, like hers, was fitted with a rebreather that recycled his air and produced no bubbles. Originally designed for stealth military operations, the device made them much like the surrounding marine life—silent underwater and undetectable on the surface.

She dropped her gaze and saw behind his mask a serious game face. Hers, she thought, probably looked just as she felt, uncertain and scared.

He promptly raised a length of clear PVC tubing and extended it over the stove, but not within reach. She unhooked hers and likewise extended it partway toward him. His contained layers of pills of different colors, shapes, and sizes.

Where are the liquids? she wondered.

As if reading her mind, he raised his other hand, which held a large—but opaque—dry bag. Continuing to read her reaction, he extended both items close to her and shrugged with a look that said, "It's all I had to haul it in."

She paused over the merchandise, unsure of what to do, and then, despite the cover of her dive mask and the wall of water between them, she turned her head away and whispered, "Half his drop's in a dry bag. I can't see inside it."

Several interminable seconds passed before her trainer replied, "Okay, just do the deal."

She turned back and, in one fluid movement, released the tube of cash above the stove, snatched the items from his hands, and pushed off.

Chapter 1

Traverse City, Michigan, four months later.
Harlan Holmes used to be an ex-cop turned private eye. These days, he was an ex-private eye turned assistant manager of this place, the TC Fitness Center, which appeared beneath the buzz and flicker of fluorescent lights struggling to boot up as he flipped a long row of switches a few at a time.

He often questioned the owner's decision to call the facility a "fitness center." It certainly wasn't one for those who liked to be pampered with steam baths, saunas, and hand-holding personal trainers. It was more like a gymnasium—a barely renovated warehouse cluttered with exercise equipment—for muscleheads who preferred a no-frills workout environment or couldn't afford any better.

Harlan glanced at a clock and then out the front window. It was 5:28 a.m. He had two minutes to turn on the cardio machines and unlock the front door for them, a wave of early-bird gym members coming at him from the parking lot. Their silhouettes trudging through the morning twilight reminded him daily of the zombies from the old movie, *Dawn of the Dead.*

After unlocking the door, Harlan seated himself behind the counter. The zombies bottlenecked in front of him at a sign-in sheet, on which they signed their names beneath a five-hundred-word pre-injury release clause intended to shield the gym from liability for any mishaps on the premises.

"When the heck are they gonna get an electronic card reader for this place?" one complained.

"After they build the indoor pool," Harlan answered without looking up from the morning paper.

He was reading an article that appeared on page three, just beneath the fold: "Traverse City Man Released on Parole." Off to the side was a photo of the parolee, Tank Lochner, towering over a police officer whom he'd just assaulted. It had happened a couple years ago at the side of a road in a small town up north.

The cop's body cam guaranteed Tank's conviction, though it was not surprising to see him getting out on the short end of a two-to-five sentence. As the video clearly showed, the cop had become verbally abusive over a simple parking violation despite Tank's best efforts to cooperate—that is, until he lost it.

Harlan's thoughts turned to a part of the story that had never received much media attention: his part in the story, as Tank's friend and apparent employer at the time of the assault. The relationship proved problematic because, under Michigan law, a PI is responsible for the acts of his employees.

At Harlan's license-revocation hearing, he argued that Tank was not actually on the job at the time of the assault; indeed, Harlan didn't even know where the man was or what he was doing when it happened.

But that didn't matter to the administrative law judge. Her hostility to Harlan's defense was fueled by his own behavior during the case he was investigating at the time for a client whose son had gone missing in northern Michigan and was later found dead. The client had retained Harlan initially to find his lost son—and subsequently, to find his son's killer.

What Harlan didn't know going into the case was that his client was an old-school mobster of Chicago lineage. And what he didn't learn until it was almost too late was that the mobster was hell-bent on assassinating his son's assassin.

Solving the case and avoiding his client's endgame, however, became the least of Harlan's concerns. What ultimately did him in were the insights he gained along the way about his client's underworld activities.

The state police and attorney general wanted to know all about it, as did the judge who presided over the administrative hearing. At the close of the case, she revoked Harlan's PI license for as long as he might take to come clean with everything he knew about his former client's racketeering.

That was two years ago. Harlan was now fifty-five. If he fulfilled the judge's condition and rolled over on the mob, he'd be deep-sixed before seeing fifty-six.

"Harlan, may I borrow that?" asked a woman approaching the counter.

He continued staring at the paper, not reading a word.

"Please, Harlan, I'd like something to read while I'm on the spin bike."

He looked up and extended the paper to her. She was one of the younger zombies, a tax attorney, who certainly could afford more, but chose this bare-bones gym over a full-service fitness center. In recent weeks her pretty face had become gaunt and her smooth body ripped from the latter phases of a bodybuilding regimen that consisted of intense cardio workouts, high-repetition weight training, and a severely restricted diet.

The woman had begun walking away when he overheard her say to another member, "Oh my gosh, look at this. That thug's getting out of prison today."

"He sure is," Harlan said under his breath. He looked up at the clock. "In thirty minutes, Tank Lochner will step through the front gates of the Ionia Correctional Facility, a free man."

His next thought he kept silent. *And his first stop after leaving I-Max will be the TC Fitness Center.*

Chapter 2

Harlan's knee popped loudly as he rose up from a crouched position beside a treadmill. He had a spray bottle in one hand, and a rag in the other, tools of his current trade used to clean up the sweat of gym members who sometimes forgot to do it themselves. Or just left it for him.

Turning from the machine, Harlan nearly tripped over one of several cast-iron weight plates that had been left lying on the floor. "Rack your damn weights," he complained to the lifters who'd created the hazard.

Every Tuesday morning these three met for a big bench workout. And, every time, they trashed the place. Two of them worked construction but were between jobs. The third worked afternoons as a deputy sheriff. They were the gym's most impressive lifters and seemed to think that this status placed them above some simple rules of courtesy posted on the wall.

"Sure, man," one replied. "We'll take care of it."

They didn't. They returned to their workout as Harlan turned toward the front desk. And that's when he realized that everyone else in the gym had stopped what they were doing to look, or in some cases gape, at someone—a gigantic someone.

Tank Lochner was standing by the front counter, watching.

Harlan caught himself glancing down at the rag and spray bottle still in his hands. He looked up in time to see Tank's expression turn sad. It felt like a reversal of roles that had played out over the years since Harlan visited his friend in prison and saw him bound in shackles.

Both men quickly dismissed the awkward moment with a handshake that led immediately into a full embrace. It swallowed Harlan whole, not because he was by any means small at an even six feet, 190 pounds, but because Tank was just so much bigger—six inches taller and a hundred pounds heavier, at least.

After the greeting, Tank glanced again at the rag and spray bottle, which Harlan had placed on the counter. "Aren't you supposed to be the manager here, Boss?"

"Assistant manager, like everyone else who works here."

"Same job you have in mind for me?"

Harlan nodded. He had lined up the job for Tank at the fitness center some time ago, when Tank's parole hearing was coming up. The prospect of a job waiting for Tank on the outside pleased the parole board, but now Harlan sensed that his friend had no desire to join the ranks of assistant managers at this dive gym.

Tank looked at his watch and then into space. It was 8:45 a.m.

"You got somewhere you need to be?" Harlan asked.

There was no response.

"Listen, Tank, I've arranged to get off work soon. What do you say we go out for a bite to eat and talk about the new job?"

"No time, Boss."

"Why?"

"Got another meeting to go to."

"Where?"

"Northport."

"About what?"

"A real job."

Harlan could tell from the terse answers and lack of eye contact that this wasn't something Tank wanted to discuss. Obviously, he had kept news of this job prospect a secret to this point, even though Harlan had been the only friend who visited regularly while he was in prison.

And there was something else Tank had kept from him. A week earlier Harlan had offered Tank a ride home upon his release from prison, but Tank declined the offer and then became evasive when Harlan asked what he'd do instead for transportation.

"So tell me something, Tank. How'd you get here?"

"I drove."

"In what?"

"Check it out," Tank said, nodding at the front window.

Harlan looked at the vehicle parked out front. It was a shiny Jeep Grand Cherokee still plastered with dealership window stickers.

"Shoulda seen the looks on the faces of those guards," Tank added, "when that sweet ride pulled up in front of I-Max, just when I was gettin' released, and a dealership guy hops out and asks for a *Mister* Lochner."

"That's yours?"

Tank smiled. "Uh huh. First time I ever had a new car that was actually new."

Harlan returned his attention to his guest. "Well, c'mon already, tell me how you got it."

"Signing bonus."

"From your new employer?"

"Yeah, but actually he's an old employer."

"Who?"

After a long pause, Tank answered, "Jimmy 'the Leg' Dillon."

Harlan forgot where he was for a moment. "What? Have you lost your mind, Tank?"

Again, many gym members stopped what they were doing to look.

Tank shrugged, as if the news required no further explanation.

Jimmy "the Leg" Dillon was a one-legged bookie who, until a couple years ago, had run an illegal sports book from the back room of a bar near Traverse City. He was also one of Tank's prior employers, the one right before Harlan. Jimmy had employed Tank as a *bagman*—a guy Jimmy turned loose on gamblers whose delinquent markers required special collection efforts.

"Is Jimmy back in business?" Harlan asked.

"Yeah, but not as a bookie."

"Says who?"

"Well... Jimmy."

"And you believe him?"

Tank didn't respond.

Harlan stepped close and glanced around before whispering through his clenched teeth, "Dammit, Tank, start talking to me here."

"Okay, look," Tank replied defensively, "Jimmy says he's gone straight, for real. He's running a fishing business up in Northport. You can check it out for yourself. It's online and everything. Jimmy's Charter Fishing. And he wants me to join him. That's all."

Harlan recalled the name of the bar that used to serve as a front for the old gambling operation—*Jimmy's* Pub.

"*Jimmy's* Charter Fishing, you say, huh?"

Tank nodded.

Harlan glanced again at the car out front and said, "Must be catching a lot of fish."

"He says he's doin' good."

Harlan shook his head. "No offense, Tank, but what do you know about fishing?"

Tank had to stop and think before answering, "Well, my old man took me a few times when I was a kid."

"What kind of setup did your old man teach you? Worm on a hook?"

"Yeah, I guess... and a bobber."

"How about a USCG captain's license, Tank? You got one of those?"

"A USDA what?"

Harlan sighed deeply and said, "So Jimmy hasn't told you what the job is."

"I guess that's what the meeting's for."

"You still have my phone number, Tank?"

"Sure. Got it programmed right here in my brand-new smartphone."

Tank pulled the phone from his pocket. "Check it out, Boss. This thing can do practically—"

"Where'd it come from?" Harlan asked.

"It was in the car, with a little note from Jimmy telling me the password and stuff, and saying that it's mine, cost-free, for a whole year. Unlimited data, the note said."

Harlan eyed the device. It was contained in a clear waterproof case, the kind that someone working on the water might have. But he remained certain that whatever that work might be, it wasn't fishing.

"Listen, Tank, when you learn of the illegal antics that Jimmy has in mind for you, call me so I can come get you. Then ditch that phone and the car. You hear? Just walk away from whatever he proposes."

The silence that passed between them was interrupted by a crash and a shout—"Yeah, baby! That's what I'm talkin' about. Two solid reps."

It came from one of the three lifters whom Harlan had confronted earlier, the biggest one, who rose up from a bench now surrounded by weight plates strewn all over the floor. The bar that he had just slammed back into the rack had four 45-pound plates on each end. Those weights and the 45-pound bar totaled 405 pounds. He had pressed that weight twice in a single set.

"Hey, Boss," Tank said as he began to unbutton his shirt, "can I get in a quick workout before I leave?"

Tank was already on his way to the bench area before Harlan could answer.

"You boys mind me workin' in for a couple sets?" Tank asked upon arriving at the bench being used by the three big lifters. He spoke loudly enough for others in the gym to hear. Once again, many of them stopped what they were doing and watched.

"We're almost done here," the biggest of the three said. "How 'bout just using one of the other benches?"

"Appreciate it," Tank said, ignoring the suggestion. He then removed his outer shirt. Beneath it was a compression t-shirt stretched to its limit over a massive torso that had been made crazy ripped from two years of pumping prison iron. Over those two years, Tank had also grown his hair into a lengthy mullet, which he tied back with a rubber band before lying back on the bench and settling beneath a bar still loaded with eight 45-pound plates.

The second biggest of the three guys stepped toward the bench.

"Whadaya think you're doing?" Tank complained.

"I... I was just gonna give you a lift off... and a spot."

"Don't need either."

"What about some warm-up sets?" the smallest guy said.

"What the hell you think *this* is?" Tank answered as he yanked the bar from the rack.

Ten repetitions later—the last as easy as the first—Tank returned the bar to the rack. Harlan expected to hear a loud slam, there being no spotter to help set the bar down, but that didn't happen. Tank eased the bar into the rack, as gently as one would place a sleeping infant into a crib.

And then he jerked himself up into a seated position and pointed at a wall, the one with the gym rules on it. "You boys see number eight over there?" he growled. "The rule right after the one that says, 'Rack your weights?'"

Tank glared at the biggest of the three and added, "Well?"

"It says, 'Don't slam the weights,'" the guy answered.

"Then why the hell did I just hear you slammin' weights a minute ago, after your lame-ass two-rep set?"

There was no answer, just a blank stare.

Tank turned to the other two and bellowed, "Two more wheels, boys!"

"T-two more 45s?" the smallest guy stammered.

Tank rolled his eyes. "Don't make me repeat myself, Spanky. And after you add those plates, slap on some bigger collars."

With the added plates and collars, he'd be lifting an even 500 pounds, about twice what the biggest of the three guys himself weighed.

The iron masses on its ends caused the bar to arch and bounce over Tank's body as he yanked it from the rack, lowered it to his chest, and pushed it back up. His form throughout was perfect, as it was for seven more repetitions, the last only slightly slower than the first.

Again, he set the bar gently into the rack.

After he rose to his feet and retrieved his shirt, Tank leaned toward the biggest of the guys and began speaking, this time too quietly for onlookers to hear. The other two lifters drew near and listened. Harlan studied Tank's stern expression and tried to imagine what the ex-bagman turned ex-con might be saying.

The huddle eventually broke, and Tank headed for the door. Upon reaching it he stopped, turned, and stared back at the three guys, the gym's most impressive lifters, as they scurried around racking not only the weights they had strewn about, but also those that had been left on the floor by others.

Chapter 3

Harlan left the gym later that morning and returned home to his studio apartment for a much-needed nap. Fitful thoughts of Tank's whereabouts, however, wouldn't allow it. They led him instead to his computer, where he typed "Jimmy's Charter Fishing, Northport, Michigan," into a Google search.

Tank was right. There was a website for the business. It included numerous photos of Jimmy and his employees posing with satisfied customers holding large, dead fish. According to contact information, the business operated out of a marina on Shotgun Landing, just south of Northport, on the east coast of the Leelanau Peninsula.

Only thirty miles away, Harlan thought after opening a map online. He moved the cursor up the computer screen, northbound on M-22, and stopped it on Shotgun Landing. After a long pause spent staring at the word—Shotgun—he tried to confirm a suspicion he had about its origin.

Various images of the map revealed nothing about the area's geographical configuration that might explain the name, and nothing else he could find online explained it either. However, he did come across another business, named Shotgun Landing Marina & RV Sites, with the same address and phone number as Jimmy's fishing business. Photos on its website again showed Jimmy and his same crew, posing this time with happy campers and sailors.

Harlan leaned back in his chair and reflected on the one occasion when he had met a man sometimes called by the name "Shotgun."

Giovanni Cruzano.

AKA *Shotgun* Gino.

About a year before, the man had dropped by the fitness center along with one of Harlan's former clients, Angelo Surocco, the Chicago wiseguy whose case had cost Harlan his PI license. On this occasion, Angelo came by to ask Harlan if he might have time to join them for a little tour of the Traverse City area. Harlan thought it an odd request—suspicious, actually, considering the source—and managed to cut the conversation short. He recalled the exchange that turned them away.

• • • • •

"Ole Gino here retired from the life a little while back," Angelo said, "and he's looking for things to do while he lives out his years here in northern Michigan."

A broad smile deepened the wrinkles in Gino's face.

"He retired from... *the life*?" Harlan said.

"Yeah, you know. The life. Like mine. It's what Shotgun Gino used to do too."

"Shotgun?"

To this there was no reply, other than the annoyed expressions of two elder mobsters, who seemed to think that answers to such questions were unnecessary.

Behind them stood a younger man who was never introduced. His stoic manner and enormity made any explanation of the life he was leading unnecessary as well. He slowly shook his massive head. Beneath it he had no neck, just a quarter-ton body insulated with at least a hundred pounds of surface blubber.

• • • • •

Still at his computer, Harlan wondered now as he had then where that tour of the town would have taken him. He knew full well what the life of Giovanni Cruzano had entailed before his purported retirement. Like Harlan's former client, Cruzano was once a Chicagoland capo; in fact, he and Angelo reported to the same underboss. They were dinosaurs even back then, living a Mafioso version of life outside the law that had been on the decline for decades.

Harlan left the computer and went to the kitchen for some lunch. While making it he clicked on the TV to check the news.

"Glad to be with you on this Tuesday, October third. It's twelve o'clock noon for our viewers on the East Coast, and I'm Jamal Maris continuing with our live coverage of breaking news."

"All day long there's nothing but *breaking news* with this guy," Harlan murmured.

"Joining me now is our own senior military analyst, General Emma Kay Synar. Welcome, General."

"Thanks for having me, Jamal."

"Well, you know the story, General, of the mass murder that happened just under two hours ago on the coast of Lake Michigan. Some are saying it was an act of terrorism, but you think not. Tell us why, General."

"What?" Harlan shouted at the TV. "Mass murder on the coast?" He thought about the several states with shorelines along Lake Michigan and said, "Where exactly?"

"That's right, Jamal. Bear in mind that this massacre happened nowhere near a major population center, where terrorists are more apt to strike, but in a remote area of northern Michigan."

Harlan stepped closer to the TV, stared at it, and asked, "Where in northern Michigan?"

"But General, isn't a small community like the one involved here just the kind of place where an act of terrorism could strike the greatest fear in the psyche of everyday Americans? I mean, think of the impact, General, of terrorists attacking a sleepy little community like Northport, Michigan."

"Northport?" Harlan shouted. "What the hell happened there?"

"Perhaps, Jamal. But let me just say—"

"Sorry to interrupt, General, but for the benefit of viewers who might just be joining us, I'd like to make it clear here that a fishing boat with several people on board was entirely blown out of the water by a massive explosion occurring just off the shore of this quaint community in the heart of mid-America. And on the heels of that blast, General, a man on shore was gunned down and another man with him may have suffered the same fate. How do you explain events like these?"

Harlan planted a hand on the counter to steady himself. With his other hand he grabbed his cell phone, and then realized he never got the number for Tank's new phone.

He returned his attention to the TV. The general was still advancing her opinion.

"I'm just saying, Jamal, that before we jump to any conclusion about this being an act of terrorism, I'd like to know more about the victims. For example, if they were all associated with one another in some way, that might explain some motive other than terrorism. Terrorists usually kill indiscriminately."

Harlan tried to imagine the terrorist theory and a coincidence of that kind of lightning strike with the timing and purpose of Tank's visit to the very area that it hit.

Shit.

He didn't believe in coincidences.

"Excuse me, General," Jamal Maris said. "We're getting additional information... more breaking news... along the lines you suggest. News of uh..."

Jamal Maris was looking at a laptop computer while pressing a fingertip on his earpiece, apparently trying to hear more clearly someone speaking to him through it.

"It's a report, General, saying that these victims may indeed have been associated in some way, with a fishing business right there on the coast, a business that goes by the name of... uh..."

"For God's sake, man, spit it out!" Harlan shouted. "What fishing business?"

"Do we have a name?" Jamal asked, looking directly into the camera, and thus, it seemed, directly at Harlan. After a short pause, Jamal answered his own question. "We do. It's a small business that operates out of a private marina near Northport, Michigan... named Jimmy's Charter Fishing."

"There you go, Jamal," General Synar said. "That's just the kind of association that might..."

"Hold on, General. There's more. I'm told that we have someone live on the scene, right there at the marina, from an affiliate station in Traverse City, speaking with a woman who may have captured everything on video."

Chapter 4

Harlan drove his old pickup truck north on M-22, along the Leelanau coast, passing between close-up views of a placid Grand Traverse Bay to his right and, to his left, a rolling landscape of vineyards, cherry orchards, and stretches of forest that exploded with the colors of autumn.

To the stunning panorama, however, he was oblivious. Foremost on his mind were thoughts about Tank's welfare. It had been nearly three hours since the mass murder and still there had been no call from him. It was hard not to imagine why. The big man was last seen by Harlan, and by viewers of a video now gone viral, running down a pier toward Lake Michigan under sniper fire.

The shots fired at Tank were the finale to an assault on Shotgun Landing that began a few minutes after 10:00 a.m. that morning. Among the witnesses were the owners of a small yacht, a retired couple who'd rented a slip at the marina for an autumn getaway. This morning they were adding some footage to a videotaped journal of their vacation when, in the background, they happened to record a massive explosion not far offshore.

A zoomed-in replay on cable news showed the sudden disappearance of a fishing boat at the spot of the explosion—a thirty-foot bowrider that belonged to Jimmy's Charter Fishing. According to a talking head on TV, the bomb must have been quite sophisticated to have instantaneously obliterated a boat of that size. Survival of anyone on board, the head said, was unimaginable. Names had not yet been released, but anyone who checked Jimmy's website, as Harlan did, might guess them to include the boat's skipper, Paul Russo, and his first mate, Chase Banwell.

After the blast, the massacre continued onshore. Harlan had

replayed that segment of the recording several times on YouTube, including a few times in slow motion, before he got on the road. Now he couldn't stop himself from replaying it in his head.

• • • • •

"Jimmy!"

The shout boomed from somewhere onshore seconds after the explosion on the water.

A frenetic pan of the camera froze at a point near the videographer, where a man was down, but not out. He struggled to rise as another man beside him—Tank Lochner—reached down to help.

And then came the characteristic crack-thump sound of a sniper's bullet traveling at supersonic speed. Jimmy's body convulsed a split second before the thump and then went limp.

Tank realized long before the videographer what was happening. She continued recording his reaction—his sudden sprint toward the water and the crack-thumps of two more sniper shots following him.

The second shot clearly was intended for Tank. It blasted through the lid of an outdoor grill just as he passed it, producing a deafening clang that finally alerted the videographer to what was causing his panic. The video portion of her recording became chaotic as she fled in no discernible direction. The audio portion, however, captured two more shots, which the videographer's husband, who froze throughout the ordeal, said he saw hit the surface of the water right where Tank had jumped in.

• • • • •

Harlan slowed his pickup as he began passing between tightly parked vehicles on both sides of M-22. At the entrance of a dirt drive stood a sign for "Shotgun Landing Marina & RV Sites."

The last vehicle on the right shoulder was a media van. Harlan parked beyond it, got out, and slammed his door shut. Every sound he made, however, was muted by the whir of a Coast Guard helicopter buzzing the treetops overhead.

Chapter 5

A few more vehicles were parked along the entrance drive. After hiking by the last of them, Harlan paused to take in the crime scene ahead, where the driveway dead-ended into a small marina. It bustled with police activity along twin piers that were crowded with boats. Overlooking the scene, up high in the surrounding bluffs, were Shotgun Landing's rental RV sites. They were filled with luxury mobile homes, including one with an "Office" sign out front.

Harlan's access to the marina was blocked by a state police car turned sideways and, in front of it, two state troopers whom he readily recognized, Detective Riley Summers and her partner, Sergeant Frank Tice. Harlan had a lot of history with these two, going back to his days on the force. Not all of it was good.

Only Frank smiled as Harlan approached.

"Who'd you two piss off to get stuck working the perimeter?" Harlan said as he stopped before his former colleagues.

Riley's expression changed from indifference to displeasure. "The captain took this one himself," she said.

Harlan scanned the area beyond the officers and the police-tape barrier they enforced. Amidst the investigative activity onshore and a search-and-rescue operation on the water he soon spotted the man, Captain Martin Nash, at the tip of the southernmost of the two piers.

"Can't imagine why Marty would pull his top detective from this one," Harlan said.

"Yeah, right," Riley replied, rolling her eyes with obvious ire. A high-profile homicide investigation should have been hers. Harlan had reason to know why this one wasn't.

"So, Shotgun Landing *does* in fact belong to Shotgun Gino Cruzano," he said.

"Like you're just finding that out now," Riley scoffed.

Harlan turned his attention to Frank, wondering if he might be more forthcoming. Frank nodded and said, "The captain took a personal interest in Gino Cruzano long before all this happened."

"Marty's had him under surveillance?"

"Yeah, him and his marina."

Harlan glanced at Riley. She avoided eye contact, so he continued with Frank. "Who's been assigned to spy on Cruzano?"

"Some of the newer recruits who—"

"That's enough, Frank," Riley admonished.

Harlan shrugged and said, "I'm just curious is all, Riley. Why put newbies on a badass gangster from Chicago?"

"Because of all the stunts you pulled on us old-timers two years ago, Harlan Holmes, when you were working for that other badass gangster from Chicago."

Harlan recalled the trouble he'd caused them during his work on the missing-person-turned-homicide case for his wiseguy client. Riley, Frank, and some other veteran officers involved with the police investigation had made the mistake of extending professional courtesies to their former colleague, unaware, as he was for a while, of the vigilante justice that his client was pursuing and very nearly accomplished.

Harlan turned to scan the area behind him, inland, as he thought about the crack-thump sounds of the sniper fire that he had listened to earlier on YouTube. He had played the recording several times to get as good an estimate as he could of the time delay between the crack of the sniper's bullet breaking the sound barrier and the thump of the gun's muzzle that followed. His crude estimate of the interval placed the shooter anywhere between one and two thousand meters from the videographer. There were many elevated locations, most to the southwest of where he stood, that might provide a sniper positioned at that range a clear line of sight.

With his back still to the officers, Harlan could hear Riley calling Captain Nash to inform him of Harlan's arrival. By the time Harlan turned back, Nash had already begun walking toward them, his gaze fixed on Harlan, who in return watched his former boss struggle to hurry his stocky body up the hill between them.

No doubt the moment he arrived would be awkward. Four years ago, Nash was the one who announced that Harlan, among others, wouldn't survive a departmental downsizing, though his job would. It was given to Riley Summers, who at the moment resumed avoiding eye contact with him. *Survivor's guilt*, Harlan thought as he recalled his last assignment on the force—training her do his job.

Since the layoff, he and the captain had not spoken, even after Harlan had applied when the department started hiring back many of the officers who'd been let go. The captain responded to Harlan's application with a standard rejection letter, and he never returned any of Harlan's phone calls seeking a real explanation.

And that was *before* Harlan got himself into trouble with the case he worked for the Chicago wiseguy. Now he wanted something else from the captain. It wouldn't come easy. Apparently, a simple hello wouldn't either.

"Hi, Marty, how's it going?" Harlan said, striving for a tone of civility. And then he waited as the man labored through his last few steps.

Despite the autumn chill in the air, several beads of sweat streamed down the captain's plump face as he struggled for a breath and then, finally, to speak. "Cut the shit, Holmes, and just tell me what the hell you're doing here. Looking for your bagman friend, Tank Lochner?"

"You mean *alleged* bagman, don't you, Marty?"

"Oh, that's right. At his trial for beating the crap out of that cop, everyone else he ever messed up was too damn scared to testify about him being a leg breaker for that low-life bookie, Jimmy 'the Leg' Dillon."

A glance from Riley confirmed the obvious. This was not getting off to a good start.

Harlan tried again. "Look, Captain, you're right. The man made some bad choices in the past. But he's done his time. And I'm just here as a friend, hoping to find out that he's okay."

The captain stepped forward. His eyes narrowed. "Do you actually expect me to share information I've learned during the course of an ongoing investigation?"

"Well, Captain, I was just thinking that—"

"There may have been a time when you had that kind of access," the captain said as he gave Riley and Frank an angry glance. "But those days are long over, Holmes, especially on a case I'm running."

Harlan paused before responding, "Okay, Captain," and then he gave Frank a nod and Riley a long look. Finally, she was able to sustain eye contact with him. It had been a while since they worked together, but when they did, they came to know each other well and could sometimes communicate without speaking. He tried to connect with her that way on this occasion, and then he turned and walked away.

"Hold on, Harlan," Riley said.

He stopped and looked back. "What?"

"You have information. I can tell. Something that might help with the captain's investigation."

"Maybe."

"No, Harlan. You do. I know you. You don't ask for a favor like this unless you have something to offer in return."

"Okay, I do. But the captain doesn't want to talk with me. So, what's the point?"

Harlan resumed walking away.

"Dammit, Holmes," the captain said. "What have you got?"

Harlan stopped again and turned. He slowly walked back, but deliberately stopped halfway before responding, "A missing friend. What have *you* got?"

The captain closed the distance between them, literally meeting Harlan halfway. The two locked into a stare. After a long pause, the captain said, "Do you really think I wanted to boot your ass off the force four years ago?"

"What?"

"You heard me, Holmes."

Harlan was taken aback. The departmental downsizing was the last thing he expected the captain to ever talk about with him. And what he seemed to be saying about it made no sense. "But, Marty, you were my boss, the one who fired me."

"It was either you, or her," he replied, glancing at Riley. "And I was told it had to be you."

"Who told you that?"

"My boss's boss."

"The head of the department?"

"You have no idea how political the process was. I wanted no part of it. Picking and choosing among good cops—men and women who were like family to me—whose careers we were gonna trash. I told the brass I wouldn't do it, that I was just gonna retain those with most seniority and hold my nose through the whole stinkin' mess. But they wouldn't let me do that in the higher ranks. To this day, I don't know what their reasons were for wanting you out."

Harlan looked at Riley. Her look back said that the captain was speaking the truth.

He turned back to the captain and said, "You say it was political, Marty. Was it about gender? Did they think it'd be politically incorrect to choose a guy over one of our few female detectives?"

"You think they'd ever admit something like that? All I know is that you were one of my best detectives. Unorthodox sometimes, maybe a lot of the time, but you were good. So was Riley. Merit had nothing to do with whatever they were thinking."

"But, Marty, when you started hiring us back, I applied, and it was you who—"

"Because I was told to put you on deck for the next opening."

"By your boss's boss again?"

"That's right. And don't ask me why."

"Okay… but later another detective slot *did* open up. I heard about it. Why didn't you—"

Realization stopped him short.

"That's right," the captain said, "because by then you were in bed with Chicago mobsters. Or so it seemed to some. I knew you weren't. Riley and Frank told me how you got blindsided by those crooks. But you know damn well that it was too late after that."

After that debacle, Harlan thought, he wasn't even eligible for private investigation anymore. He paused for the noise of the Coast Guard chopper flying low. When it passed, he said, "I saw Tank Lochner this morning, after his release from I-Max."

"Where?" the captain asked.

"TC Fitness."

The captain didn't ask for more details about Harlan's current workplace. Apparently he knew what had become of one of his best detectives, as did Riley. She returned to avoiding eye contact with him.

"What was the purpose of the visit?" the captain asked.

"To talk about a job at the gym, I thought."

Harlan waved off the captain's next question and summed up the details of what he had learned from Tank that morning about his new job prospect and his seeming oblivion to its likely unlawful objectives, even after having already received a signing bonus in the form of a $50,000 Jeep Grand Cherokee.

"I saw the Jeep just a few minutes ago," Harlan said, looking back at the entrance drive. "It's parked up there, about halfway to the road on the north side. You can't miss it. It still has the stickers in the window."

The captain took a few steps away and made a call on his handheld radio. After dispatching an officer to check out the vehicle he turned back and said, "I appreciate that, Harlan. And I don't see any harm in telling you what we know about your friend. Just the same, I'm asking you not to repeat it to anyone."

Harlan nodded.

"We're pretty sure he took a round," the captain said.

Harlan shook his head. "I watched that video over and over, Marty, and there was no sign of him getting shot. The one to the grill clearly missed. And from what the guy on the yacht said, there was no way to tell about the two that hit the water after he was under."

"It was the second shot, Harlan, to Jimmy 'the Leg.' The one that finished him. We think it went through the man while Lochner held him."

"But he never reacted like he was hit."

"Maybe so, but there's blood—a lot of blood—splattered all the way down the pier where he ran."

Harlan glanced beyond the pier, out at the search team on the water.

"Are you looking for his body out there, along with the guys on that boat?"

"Yeah."

"Why? He could have come to shore after swimming away underwater."

"Because the guy on the yacht kept watching. He didn't run. He froze right there and watched Lochner go under—and never come up."

"How long did he watch?"

"He was still there when my first unit arrived."

Chapter 6

Harlan returned up the entrance drive and slowed when he reached Tank's Jeep and the state trooper examining it. The officer paused when their eyes met. "Aren't you the one who gave us the tip on this vehicle?" he asked.

"How'd you know?" Harlan replied as he stopped.

"Saw you talking to the captain."

"Marty and I go a long way back."

"I know. I've heard quite a bit about you."

"Good stuff?"

"Not so much."

Harlan smiled and then resumed walking.

"Hold on, sir, please."

He stopped again.

The officer held out an iPad and said, "Maybe you can explain something to me. It's the name that came back when I ran the check. It's not quite what I expected."

"Tatanka Cikala Lochner" was the name on the screen.

Harlan explained what Tank had once told him about the name. "It's Lakota Sioux for *Little Buffalo*. When he was born, I guess he looked like one. But if you ever meet him, don't call him that. He's a full-grown buffalo now, and he prefers the name 'Tank.'"

"So, he's Sioux Indian," the officer said.

"Actually, no. There's not a drop of Sioux blood in him."

"Then how'd he get the name?"

"His mother was fascinated with Native Americans. She collected their crafts and artwork. I guess she picked up some of their language too."

"I get that," the officer said, "parents sticking their kids with names they find amusing."

Harlan looked up from the iPad at the nameplate on the officer's chest. It read, "Sgt. Zeppelin Reed."

"Don't tell me," Harlan said. "Your parents were into World War I German airships."

The officer's eyebrows scrunched together. "No, not that. It's a reference to..."

"I'm kidding," Harlan said. "Led Zeppelin was one of my favorite rock 'n' roll bands back in the day."

The officer responded with a smile that made him look even younger than he probably was, late twenties at most. Enthusiasm for the job was written all over his face. It reminded Harlan of himself, thirty years ago, in what now seemed like someone else's life.

Harlan returned to his pickup truck, climbed in, and just sat there staring at a part of the landscape ahead that he'd earlier surmised might have been the position of the sniper who shot at his friend. "That son of a bitch," he muttered to himself, or so he thought, until there came a response.

"What's the matter, Boss?"

"What the hell?" Harlan shouted as he spun in his seat and reflexively reached for a sidearm that he no longer carried. After he turned, his surprise changed to bewilderment at the sight of his lost friend reclined in the rear seat of the truck, looking back at him like nothing had happened.

"What took you so long?" Tank complained.

Harlan ignored the question as he leaned over the seat for a closer look. Tank was pressing his right hand against his left shoulder. Beneath it was a bunched-up jacket drenched in blood. Harlan grabbed the hand and lifted it up. "Let me see that."

Tank shrugged. "It's not so bad."

"It's not so good either."

Harlan retrieved a first aid kit from his glove box, climbed into the backseat, and began doing what he could to treat the injury. "Where'd you come from, Tank?"

"I was out in the woods, waiting for you. Knew you'd come looking."

"Why didn't you just call me on that new smartphone of yours?"

"Because it fell in the lake, along with me. You're not gonna believe what happened to me, Boss. I was just standing there by the shore, talking with Jimmy, when all of a sudden—"

"I know what happened, Tank. It's all over the news, man, including a video of you dodging sniper bullets."

"Except for this one, still in you," Harlan added as he pressed his thumb into a hole that began at the tip of Tank's shoulder. He watched Tank's face as he made what should have been a painful probe into his deltoid muscle. There was no reaction, even when Harlan pressed his thumb against the metal jacket of a fully intact bullet, about two inches long, that had turned sideways after crashing into Tank's upper arm bone.

"This thing should've torn through your shoulder, just like it should've blown a big hole through Jimmy before it got to you, but it didn't…"

"What is it, Boss?"

"What was Jimmy wearing?"

Tank shrugged his shoulders, causing Harlan's thumb to pop out of the bullet hole. Blood oozed from the wound until Harlan slapped his bare hand over it.

"I dunno, Boss. Just clothes, I guess."

"It took two of these rounds to stop an old one-legged man, when either one should've ripped him open."

"You thinking he had on some body armor? Maybe under his shirt?"

"Maybe. Something must've slowed the bullets that hit him, and the one that went through him and into you."

"That would mean he was thinking something like this could happen."

"We can talk about this later, Tank. Right now, we need to get you some help."

Tank's smartphone was sticking out of his shirt pocket. Harlan stared at it, pondering a difficult question: Should he keep Tank under wraps long enough to make sure he'd done nothing he could be arrested for? After deciding he should, he grabbed the phone and asked, "What's the password for this thing?"

"I'm telling you, it went underwater with me for as long as I could hold my breath."

"It was in a waterproof case, Tank. It's fine."

Chapter 7

Harlan had completed a phone call to an old friend, Dr. Bree Cornell, and was taking Tank south on M-22 to see her in Traverse City.

"Who's Dr. Cornell?" Tank asked.

"Someone who owes me a favor."

"She works at a hospital?"

"Kind of."

"What's that supposed to mean?"

"An animal hospital," Harlan replied as he glanced in the rearview mirror. Tank was still reclined in the backseat. For the first time since their reunion, the man looked concerned.

"You can't be serious, Boss. Why not a hospital for people?"

"We can't check you into one of those, not with that gunshot wound and your face being all over the news."

"Why? I didn't do anything wrong."

"You sure about that?"

"Hell yeah, I'm sure."

Harlan wasn't, at least not yet. "Tell me what you know about Shotgun Landing," he said.

"Didn't even know it existed until Jimmy set up the meeting."

"How about Gino Cruzano?"

"Never heard of him."

"*Shotgun* Gino? The owner of *Shotgun* Landing?"

"No, I'm telling you. Who's he?"

"Someone you don't want to be on the wrong side of."

"You think he had something to do with Jimmy and his guys getting whacked this morning?"

"I don't know what to think, Tank. Why don't you tell me what happened out there? Start at the beginning, when you first arrived."

"There's not much to tell, Boss. I was running a little late. Guess I almost held up the guys. They wanted to shove off at 10:00 a.m. sharp, Jimmy said, and I got there just a few minutes before."

"What guys?"

"The ones on the boat. Jimmy wanted me to meet them before they left, you know, because I was the new guy on the crew."

"The crew?" Harlan said skeptically.

"Well, yeah, there was the skipper, Paul Russo, and the Banwell brothers, Chase and Miles. I already knew those three from back when Jimmy ran his old pub and… uh… his bookie operation. They were all writers in Jimmy's wireroom back in those days."

"The guys who took the calls from players placing bets?" Harlan asked.

"Yeah, but that's not what they were doing these days. Pauly was working as a real skipper on that bowrider. He had one of those licenses you asked me about this morning. That… uh…"

"United States Coast Guard captain's license?"

"That's it. He had a plaque right there by the boat's steering wheel sayin' so. I could tell he was real proud of it."

"And the Banwell brothers, what new jobs were they doing for Jimmy?"

"Don't know. They didn't say."

"Was there anyone else on the crew?"

"Just one more. A guy I never met before, named Sully. He was on the wheel when they shoved off."

"That's all you got of his name—Sully?"

"Yeah, like the nickname of that guy who landed the plane on the Hudson. That's what they all called him."

"And was that everyone on the boat, just those four?"

After waiting through Tank's silence, Harlan caught his eye in the rearview mirror and added, "What about fishermen, Tank?"

Tank looked away.

"Well," Harlan pressed, "was there anyone onboard who *wasn't* part of the crew? Someone who was expecting to go fishing?"

"I guess not, Boss. But they had fishing poles all lined up on deck, like that's what they were going out to do."

"I'm sure that's exactly how it looked," Harlan said, shaking his head. "Was there anyone else you remember seeing?"

"Sure. There was that couple on the yacht, the ones making the video, and… oh yeah, when I got there, the first person I met was Sam Boadle. She was up at the front counter in the office RV when I walked in."

Harlan thought for a moment. The name sounded familiar. "I think you once told me about Sam. Isn't she the one who used to tend bar at Jimmy's Pub? The one who managed the place?"

"That's right. And now she's the manager for Jimmy's Charter Fishing."

Harlan sighed deeply. "Okay, tell me if I have this right. The woman who used to run Jimmy's Pub—the front for his bookie operation—is now up front running Jimmy's new charter fishing business. And the boat for the business she oversees shoved off this morning fully equipped to go fishing, but on board there were no fishermen—just a crew of mostly guys who used to book illegal bets in the backroom of Jimmy's Pub."

"Yeah, Boss. That pretty much sums things up."

"Didn't any of this make you suspicious?"

"I guess not."

"Seriously? You've been in the joint for two years, and you can't tell when somebody's running a scam?"

"C'mon, Boss. You got the advantage of hindsight here. It would've been blowing things out of proportion for me to accuse my old friends of doing something wrong when I first got there."

"Oh, I see. You didn't want to blow things out of proportion. So you waited until someone blew that fishing boat out of the water, whacked Jimmy, and then started shooting at you. And that's when it first dawned on you that maybe things weren't what they appeared to be at Jimmy's Charter Fishing."

"That's not quite right, Boss. I actually started getting suspicious a little before all that happened."

"Okay, let's hear it," Harlan said, shaking his head. "Tell me what happened before all hell broke loose."

"Not sure I want to. Think it'll just make you more upset with me."

"C'mon, Tank, tell me. What else did you learn and ignore?"

After a long pause, Tank said, "After I met the guys, one of them stepped aside with Jimmy and me and asked Jimmy if he really had to make the trip."

"Which guy?"

"Chase Banwell."

"Was he not feeling well?"

"No. It was more like he just didn't want to go. Like he didn't see the point."

"Of what?"

"Of going wherever it was they were headed."

"And where was that?"

"I don't know."

"What'd Jimmy say?"

"That they'd find out when they got there."

"Wherever that was."

"Yeah."

"And what were they gonna find out?"

Tank didn't respond. Harlan took that to mean he knew more. "I asked you a question, Tank."

He remained silent.

"You think the questions are gonna get any easier when you're dealing with cops and prosecutors? Now tell me. What—"

"After Chase went back to the boat, Jimmy kind of told me something," Tank said, "about the line of work they were into, besides fishing."

"And what did he *kind of* say they did, *besides fishing*?"

"He didn't want to be specific until we got back to the office, but I could tell by the way he was talking that they were into… uh… trafficking something… some kind of contraband, I guess."

"C'mon, Tank, let's have it. Tell me exactly what he said. His words, not yours."

Tank did so reluctantly.

• • • • •

"We'll talk details inside," Jimmy said as he turned his attention away from the boat leaving shore.

"C'mon, Jimmy, just tell me now."

Jimmy's head spun like it was on a swivel as he checked to make sure nobody else could hear. Then he leaned toward Tank and spoke barely above a whisper. "Truth is, we've been making peanuts moving certain cargo on the Lakes since last spring. But a little while back I got us into a new product line, one that's a lot more lucrative. Not all the guys know about it yet. Those that don't are gonna learn about it soon, seeing it firsthand."

"Seeing what?"

"Something that's gonna make us rich, big man, come this winter when we drop a huge stash we got up north."

"How much money you talking, Jimmy?"

"Millions."

"Did you just say…"

"Ten million gross, give or take," Jimmy added, smiling broadly. "And I want you personally to handle the deal."

"Me?"

"Hell yeah, you. You're the best damn bagman on the planet, big fella. Nobody can be trusted more to bring home that kind of cash. And rest assured, you'll get a fair share of it."

• • • • •

Up north, Harlan thought, *that could be anywhere above the 45th parallel.* He glanced into the rearview mirror and asked, "Did Jimmy specifically use the word *gross* to describe the payday? Ten million dollars *gross*?"

"Yeah, give or take, he said. Why would that matter, Boss?"

"Because it sounds like he had some expenses or maybe a cut owed to someone else, leaving a *net* amount for him and his guys."

"Like he had a lender or a partner?"

"Or maybe someone he answered to. Are you sure he didn't say anything about Shotgun Gino Cruzano?"

"Nothing about anyone else," Tank answered as he rose up in the backseat.

"Get back down," Harlan said. He was angry. Tank should have heeded his earlier warning, but the man always had to do things his way.

"Listen, Boss, I just want you to know that—"

"Dammit, get the hell back down and tell me exactly what kind of contraband Jimmy's been moving on the Lakes."

They were coming into Traverse City and traffic was picking up.

"I really don't know," Tank said as he slid back down into the seat. "After Jimmy said that stuff about me moving his stash, I started doing what you told me to do this morning. I tried to hand him the keys to my new car and walk away. Next thing I know, Jimmy and I are in a big argument. He tells me that I owe him after causing his book to close a couple years ago, you know, because of all the heat he caught after his ex-bagman got busted for assaulting that Yooper cop. I told him that I don't owe him shit—that I could've took a deal and rolled over on him. But I didn't do that. I did the time, man."

Tank paused before adding, "And right then, when I'm telling Jimmy where he can shove my new job, that boat blows up right in front of us, with... w-with three of our old buddies on board."

The shake in Tank's voice was uncharacteristic. In the rearview mirror Harlan saw something else he'd never seen him do. Tank was fighting back tears. The bullet lodged in his shoulder he could handle without emotion. But apparently the loss of his friends he couldn't.

Harlan took a deep breath and said, "You know, Tank, I've been feeling nothing but sorry for myself since all that shit came down on us two years ago and messed up our lives. Losing my PI license after losing my job as a state trooper—it just seemed so unfair. But I know you've had it a lot worse these past couple years in a maximum-security prison. And now, here you are on your first day out, and you witness this... this massacre... and almost get killed yourself. I'm sorry I've been busting your chops over it. I guess that's my strange way of telling you I care. Just don't ever want to see you locked up again."

"I appreciate that, Boss. You think I can sit up now?"

"Sure. We're here."

Chapter 8

Harlan pulled the truck around to a rear parking lot, where Dr. Bree Cornell stood waiting outside an employee entrance to the clinic. She was an attractive blonde whose hooded tunic and cropped jeans custom fit her tall, slender body.

"I must say, Boss, I like your choice of animal doctors. And you say she hired you once for some infidelity surveillance?"

"A few years back."

"What kind of guy would cheat on her?"

"The kind who hides five million in assets overseas before filing for the divorce."

"And you figured it out?"

"That's why she's willing to do this, despite the risks."

"You mean the kind of trouble she could get into for treating a human at her animal hospital?"

Harlan nodded as he pressed a button to unlock the truck. Dr. Cornell opened a back door and poked her head inside.

"I really appreciate this, Doctor," Harlan said.

"Appreciate what?" she replied. "We still haven't seen each other for going on three years."

Without introduction, she grabbed Tank's chin and began turning his head while shining a tiny flashlight into his eyes from different angles. "Can you walk?" she asked after releasing his face.

"Sure."

"All right then. Follow me."

• • • • •

Harlan had been waiting in the truck for a couple hours when Tank emerged from the clinic's back door wearing a medical scrub shirt. His left arm hung bent in a sling over his chest, but not for long. As he approached the truck, Tank pulled his arm out of the sling, it seemed, to make a point of using his left hand to open the door. After getting in, he held something out in his other hand.

"Check it out, Boss," Tank said as he handed him a clean bullet. "What do you think? Maybe a seven-six-two NATO sniper round?"

Harlan shrugged and then returned his attention to the empty sling hanging from Tank's neck. "Did the doctor tell you to keep your arm immobilized in that?"

"Yeah, to keep the stitches from busting. I just told her to put in a few extras and call it good."

"What about painkillers?"

"Left those behind. Told her to give 'em to a sick dog."

"So, you're all better now," Harlan said, raising his eyebrows.

"Got that right. Ready to go after the son of a bitch who put that bullet in me. What do you say, Boss, you in?"

"And just who would we be going after?"

"I figure you'll sort that one out. Then I'll take it from there."

"First, how about you sort out something for me," Harlan said as he picked his cell phone up from the console between them. It was already cued up online to the YouTube recording of the massacre and paused at the point he wanted Tank to see. "Watch this closely. It's the few seconds between the first round Jimmy took and the second one that finished him."

After viewing it, Tank shrugged. "Okay, what about it?"

Harlan rewound the recording and said, "Watch again. Jimmy's saying something to you between the shots."

There was a long silence after Tank watched it again. "Well," Harlan said, "do you remember what his last words were?"

Tank nodded his head slowly. "He was telling me he was sorry."

"About what?"

"At first I thought it was about the argument we were having, that maybe he was sorry he blamed me for putting his old book out of business."

"But that wasn't it."

"No. He was apologizing for what just happened. The explosion on the water."

"What were *his* words, Tank, as best you can remember?"

"He said… 'I'm sorry, Tank, for getting our guys killed.' Something pretty close to that, anyway."

"And that was all he—"

"Hold on, Boss. There was more. I remember it now, exactly. He said, 'Promise me, big man, that you'll get to our other guys before they do.' And then I asked, 'What other guys, Jimmy?' And that's when he took the next round."

Chapter 9

"No way, Boss, I won't go to the cops," Tank objected after Harlan pulled out of the clinic's parking lot and announced that they were going to state police headquarters.

"They can protect you, Tank."

"Maybe they can, but they won't. I just finished doing time for beating the crap outta one of their own. Remember? And even if they would, protective custody would be like more lockdown for me. And I won't do another minute of that."

"I'm telling you, Tank, based on what you've said, I think we can convince the police that you've done nothing wrong. In fact, I know the lead investigator on the case, and I think he'll trust me if I vouch for you. The cops need to know everything you've told me. And you need their protection from what by all appearances are professional assassins."

"The hell I do, Boss. You can just drop me off anywhere you want. I'll handle it myself. I'm a professional too. Like Jimmy said, the best bagman on the planet. I'll get 'em without you, before they get to anymore of my friends."

"This isn't like collecting on gambling markers, Tank. You don't even know who you'd be tracking. Hell, you don't even know for sure who these other friends of yours might be, let alone where they might be, though I'll bet you know as well as me the state they're in if they didn't see this massacre coming."

Tank leaned into Harlan's space, clenching his teeth as he said, "You may be the best friend I've ever had, Boss, but I'm telling you right now, if you don't pull this truck over in five seconds, I'm gonna punch you out and take over that wheel."

Harlan pulled over. He looked at Tank. The man's hands trembled and, staring ahead, he looked ready to explode. "Easy does it," Harlan said. "Try taking some deep breaths."

As Tank's breathing slowed, his hands relaxed, but his stare did not.

"How 'bout we go to my apartment, Tank. Grab something to eat and just chill for a while. We can talk about this later, when our heads are clear."

• • • • •

It was after dark when they turned onto Harlan's street. Parked a couple blocks ahead, under a streetlight in front of his apartment complex, was a car that didn't belong in his working-class neighborhood—a cherry-red Range Rover Sport with oversized wheels.

Harlan made a quick right into another apartment complex that came up a block ahead of his. "Hold up," he said as Tank began opening his door.

"What is it, Boss? Don't you live here?"

"No. I'm in the next set of apartments, the one with that car out front."

"What car?"

"The hundred-thousand-dollar Range Rover with two guys in the front seat, one with shoulders broader than yours and… and…"

"And what, Boss?"

"No neck."

"You know them?"

"Sit tight, Tank. I'll be right back."

Harlan got out and worked his way through the backyards of several apartments to an opening flanked by bushes. He crept around one until the rear of the Range Rover came into view. It had an out-of-state plate that at the bottom said, "Land of Lincoln." In the plate's lower-left corner was another obvious clue to the residence of the car's owner—the image of the angry-faced, long-horned mascot of the Chicago Bulls.

He crept further toward the street, bringing into view the back of the neckless man's closely shaven head. Harlan recalled the time he met Shotgun Gino Cruzano at the gym, along with a soldier who stood behind him, the enormous guy with no neck and no hair—from Chicago.

"What'd you see?" Tank asked when Harlan returned to the pickup.

"Pretty sure a couple of Cruzano's guys."

Tank's eyes widened. "And you said we didn't know who we're tracking. The fools came to us. How should we take 'em?"

"Slow down, Tank. They're not here for a hit."

"How do you know?"

"Because they're sitting out there directly under a streetlight, right in front of my place, in a luxury SUV that practically shouts, 'Look at me.'"

"Well, what do you think they want?"

"Let's find out."

Chapter 10

Harlan was crouched down by the same bush that he had previously used for cover while spying on the Range Rover. This time he was going to make an appearance, after Tank made his.

The old pickup truck completed a turn three blocks down the street with Tank behind the wheel and his foot, by all appearances, barely on the gas pedal. The vehicle crept along at walking speed as it closed in on the Range Rover, fallen leaves crunching beneath the slowly turning tires.

The entire time, Tank rested his wrists on top of the steering wheel and extended his hands, wide open, toward the windshield. Harlan had told him to do this so the guys he approached could see that he held no weapon.

Harlan had also told him to stop at least three car lengths in front of them. But he didn't.

"What are you doing, Tank?" Harlan murmured as he peered around the bush.

Tank brought the truck to a stop with a low-impact head-on collision into the Range Rover. Then he backed up to the instructed three-car-length distance and remained behind the wheel with the engine still running. If they showed guns, he was supposed to floor the gas pedal.

They both stepped out, hands empty.

Harlan, approaching slowly from behind, could see more clearly that the neckless passenger was in fact the soldier who had accompanied Shotgun Gino the day they met at the gym. The driver, however, was someone he'd never seen, at least not among any of his mobster acquaintances. He would have remembered this one as the shortest wiseguy he'd ever seen, made to look even shorter as he stood beside the enormous soldier.

It quickly became obvious that the little guy was in charge, and he seemed unaccustomed to people deliberately taunting him.

"Shit, man, look at this fucking dent in my new car. You got any idea who I am, asshole?"

The front door of a house down the street slammed shut.

Harlan continued his approach as Tank took his time opening his door. He then eased out of the truck but left the engine running and the door open for a means of escape, if needed. "Oh, yeah, I got an idea of who you are," Tank said as he straightened up his massive frame—chest out, shoulders back—and placed his hands on his hips. "You're a guy far from home in *my* town, on *my* street, who thinks I actually give a shit who he is."

The little guy took a couple steps back, away from Tank, and replied, "Listen you... uh... you—"

"Hey, wait a second," the big guy said to the little one. "I've seen this guy, today on TV. He's the one who dove off that pier when—"

"Shut up, Eddy," the little guy said. "I'll handle this."

"Handle what?" Tank said.

"You, tough guy. What the hell is your name, anyway?"

"What the hell is yours?" Harlan said as he came up behind them.

Both men wheeled around to face Harlan. "Gino Cruzano," the little guy said. "What's it to you?"

"No you're not," Harlan replied.

"Hey, that's him," the big guy said, "the guy we're looking for, the one your dad and I met that time when—"

"I told you to shut the hell up, Eddy."

The big guy went silent and dropped his head.

"So, you're Harlan Holmes," the little guy said.

Harlan nodded. "But you're not Shotgun Gino Cruzano."

"No shit. I'm his son—*Sawed-Off* Gino."

Harlan averted his eyes and summoned the will to stifle a reaction. But Tank didn't. He burst out laughing.

Sawed-Off turned. "What's so damn funny?"

"Oh, just a little something between us," Tank answered, flashing a grin, first at the big guy and then at Harlan.

Harlan could no longer take it. He and Tank had been through a grueling day, and at this moment the stress of it seemed to reach a breaking point. He began laughing so hard, tears welled up in his eyes.

"Enough with the laughing!" Sawed-Off shouted.

After he settled down, Harlan turned his attention to the big guy and reached out to shake his hand. "Apparently you already know who we are."

"I'm Eddy Chub," the big guy replied as his mitt swallowed Harlan's hand. "Glad to see you again and get to meet you this time."

"Did you say Chub?" Tank asked.

Eddy nodded.

"I've heard that name somewhere," Tank said, scratching his head. "Oh, yeah, Nick Chubb. Standout running back for the Georgia Bulldogs. Any relation?"

"No, for me it's just a nickname."

"Really? How'd you come by it?"

Like that isn't obvious, Harlan thought as he looked both behemoths up and down. The two were about the same height, but Eddy had Tank by at least two hundred pounds, much of it subcutaneous flab.

Eddy shrugged and looked down again, his expression sullen. "I've been called that all my life, ever since my grandpa raised me. He used to say I looked just like some kid on an old TV show, 'The Little Rascals,' who they all called Chub because… uh… you know, he was kind of overweight, like me."

Tank placed a hand on the bigger man's shoulder and said, "Tell me something, Eddy Chub, why are you so glum?"

"Because the fat slob fucked up," Sawed-Off said.

Tank glared at Sawed-Off. "I didn't ask you. Why don't you let the man talk for once?"

"He's right," Eddy said. "I messed up, real bad. I lost his dad, Mr. Cruzano."

"What do you mean, you lost him?"

"I'm his bodyguard, and he was at home when, you know, that boat blew up today and the shooting started. At least that's where I last saw him and Mrs. Cruzano before it happened, when I left to go somewhere. And then, when I got back to their house, they were both gone."

Sawed-Off couldn't contain himself. "Tell them just what the hell you were off doing when my mom and dad went missing. Go ahead, Eddy, tell 'em."

"Truth is, I was at a meeting, one that Mr. Cruzano lets me go to every week. It's a support group for people who are like me, you know, having trouble with their body weight. We talk about it and try to help each other."

"Yeah, that's right," Sawed-Off said. "You're at some fat-ass anonymous meeting, talking with other fat asses about how fat your asses are, leaving my parents all by—"

"Hey, cut the guy some slack," Tank said. "Takes courage to face down something like that and try to get some help. Don't you listen to him, Eddy."

"Hold on, all you guys," Harlan said. He turned to Sawed-Off Gino and eyed the little man. "Are you saying that your dad, Shotgun Gino Cruzano, might be a victim in all this?"

Sawed-Off nodded.

"And you didn't come here to ask me the whereabouts of my partner here, Tank Lochner?"

"Look, man, I've only watched the video of that massacre one time. Never even caught his name. Why would I want him?"

"Then why are you here?"

"Because I have to find my parents. Alive or dead, I have to know what came of 'em. Whatever that may be, all I know is it happened here, in your town, where I hear you're the best PI who'll work for a guy like me."

"You mean a wiseguy like you?"

Sawed-Off nodded.

"And some other wiseguys from Chicago told you that?"

"Yeah. They say you're a stand-up guy."

Harlan shook his head. "Listen, Gino, they're telling you that because I never rolled over on them. But that's only because I value my life."

"All I know is you can be trusted. Why that's so, doesn't matter to me."

"Does it matter to you that I haven't done private investigation for two years? I don't even have a license to do it anymore."

"You think I give a shit about any of that? I want you on this, Holmes. And I'll pay you more than you've earned on any job you've ever worked. A hell of a lot more."

Harlan took a deep breath and said, "Let's talk about this inside."

Chapter 11

Tank looked across the kitchen counter, stunned by the voracity of the man's appetite. "Slow down, Eddy. The food's not going anywhere."

On top of the counter was a collection of every finger food in Harlan's kitchen: crackers, cookies, sandwich fixings, and the like. Eddy had just scarfed down his third peanut butter sandwich and was chugging a chocolate milk chaser.

Harlan and Sawed-Off Gino also stood at the counter, talking as they grazed, though Sawed-Off could report nothing more about the events of the day than what anyone could have learned from cable news. He'd been estranged from his parents since they moved to Michigan nearly two years before, and his only contact with Eddy Chub since then were the few minutes they'd spent waiting for Harlan outside his apartment this day.

But ignorance didn't stop the junior wiseguy from trying to dominate the conversation with a theory he'd already spun to explain the massacre on Shotgun Landing and the disappearance of his parents. By this point, he was repeating himself.

"It's the start of a war, man, and we just got blindsided."

"You keep saying that," Harlan said. "But what makes you so sure?"

"The way it went down at the marina. That was mob style, I'm telling you. And I'll tell you something else about whoever did that…"

Harlan raised a hand to halt the rambling. "No offense, Sawed-Off, but what I'm hearing from you is a lot of speculation. I'd like to hear from Eddy. He's the last person we know of who saw your father today."

Eddy looked up from a tall glass that he had just refilled with chocolate milk. Residue from the first glass stained the space between his nose and upper lip. "Where do you want me to start?" he asked.

"At the beginning," Harlan said, "from the day Shotgun Gino moved to this area."

As Shotgun's only soldier since that day, Eddy knew a great deal about him. He explained how Shotgun had retired from a life of crime in Chicago and settled himself and his wife into a quaint home on Suttons Bay, about twelve miles south of Northport. The man, however, was not idle in retirement. He bought some coastal property outside Northport and on it built a business where he rented marina space to recreational mariners and provided related coastal services. Eventually he added luxury mobile homes to his rental offerings, and thus came to call his business Shotgun Landing Marina & RV Sites.

Eddy paused his account for a long swig of chocolate milk, which grew the stain beneath his nose. After he set down the glass, he continued, "But no matter how hard he worked that business, I could tell that Mr. Cruzano was restless."

"Why?" Harlan asked.

"Because he was missing the action."

"And by action, you mean what?"

Eddy glanced at Sawed-Off Gino, who nodded and said, "Just tell him."

After a pause, Eddy said, "His marina business was all straight and narrow. No action. Nothing... you know..."

"Illegal," Harlan said.

"Yeah. I don't think Mr. Cruzano realized how much the action meant to him until he tried to walk away from it."

"So, he decided to get back into it."

Eddy nodded.

"When?"

"About a year ago, around the time we first met you at the gym, actually."

"That would have been last fall."

"Right. It was when his new marina business was shutting down for the season. That's when it really hit him."

"What did?" Harlan asked.

"That he had nothing going on in his life. Nothing to look forward to. And it was really getting him down, making him more than just sad. It looked to me like he was suffering real depression, just like I've seen in some members of my support group."

"Depression?" Sawed-Off said. "No way. Not my old man."

"I wanna hear this," Harlan said, again holding up a hand. "Go ahead, Eddy."

"Well, I decided to talk with him about it, the way I would with people in my group. And I convinced him to get some help."

"What?" Sawed-Off said. "You sent my old man to a shrink?"

"No. He didn't want that. We just went to his regular doctor, ole Doc Kimble."

"Who the hell is he?" Sawed-Off asked.

"You mean *she*," Eddy amended.

"Whoa, back up," Harlan said. "Did you say you went with him to see this doctor?"

"That's right," Eddy said.

"But you didn't actually go in with him during the visit."

"Oh yes I did, Mr. Holmes. Right into the examination room with him and the doc. You see, Mr. Cruzano had never experienced the kind of feelings he was having, and he needed help talking about it."

"Oh, c'mon," Sawed-Off said.

"I'm telling you, Gino, that's what happened, and it was the right thing to do. Doc Kimble said she's been struggling with semi-retired life herself, for going on twenty years, and really understood what was happening with him. They had a good talk."

Sawed-Off rolled his eyes.

"What'd she say?" Harlan asked.

"Same as I said, that he was depressed. Eventually Doc Kimble started talking about treatment options. Mostly about the different kinds of drugs she could prescribe. At one point she asked about Mr. Cruzano's insurance, whether he had a good prescription plan, which he does, a real good one. Doc said that was important because she wanted to prescribe an antidepressant that would cost a fortune without it, unless... uh..."

"Unless what?"

"Unless you get it outside the country, in a place like Canada or Europe, where they don't have broken health care systems and drug prices all out of whack."

Harlan reached for the carton of chocolate milk and poured some into Eddy's glass. After topping it off, he asked, "And this exchange was significant?"

Eddy nodded. "Especially when Mr. Cruzano started asking Doc Kimble questions about what happens to people in our country who don't have good insurance and can't afford prescriptions they need. Doc told him about people who suffer, some who even die, because they don't get the treatment they need. All kinds of people—old people, children, even babies—who fall through the cracks. And not just poor people. Sometimes being in the middle class, she said, is the worst, because they don't qualify for public assistance and what insurance they might have isn't worth shit with the huge deductibles and copays."

"Okay, Eddy, but why was this information significant?"

"Because it's what gave Mr. Cruzano the idea for a way to get back into the action. I could see it in his eyes. The more Doc talked, the more excited he got. At some point he cut her off and said he was good to go—that he felt cured of his depression and didn't need any drugs."

"And the idea he had, Eddy, what exactly was it?"

Eddy shrugged and said, "Smuggling pharmaceuticals into the country, and getting them to people here in the United States at prices they can afford, or at no charge if they can't pay."

"Seriously? Doesn't sound like a very profitable business model."

"The man's already well off, Mr. Holmes. He didn't do it for the money. He had a different kind of need—to do some good."

"Yeah, right," Sawed-Off scoffed as he shook his head. "There ain't no way my old man becomes a charitable bootlegger."

"Why don't you just shut up, man," Tank interjected. "All you been doing is interrupting Eddy's story here."

"Because that's what it is, a lame story. He's talkin' out his chocolate-coated face about my old man being some sort of Robin Fucking Hood."

"But that's basically what he was trying to be," Eddy replied as he slid a forearm across his mouth, smearing the chocolate across his jowl. "He told me himself. He felt like it was time for him to give something back after all the years of taking from people. And being able to do that *and* get back into the action, too, well, that made him happier than I've ever seen him."

"Oh, come on, Eddy, cut the shit," Sawed-Off said.

"Why is it so hard to believe?" Tank said. "People change, especially as they get old. Isn't that right, Boss?"

Harlan raised his eyebrows. "How would I know?"

"Not my old man," Sawed-Off insisted. "Do you have any idea how he got the name Shotgun?"

"Don't know that either," Harlan said.

"It's just as well," Sawed-Off said. "It's not something you wanna think about while you're eating."

"All right," Harlan said, turning his attention back to Eddy. "Tell us about this action he got into. How'd he get it started?"

"What I know about the launch is kind of sketchy, Mr. Holmes."

"That's okay, Eddy. Tell us what you can."

"Well, I know that Mr. Cruzano found his Canadian source through a capo in upstate New York, some guy with Ontario connections to a Calabrian faction up there, I think. And Mr. Cruzano brought on a guy named Jimmy 'the Leg' to run things on the US side. Never did catch the guy's full name."

"By US side, you mean Shotgun Landing?"

"There, and some other locations on the Great Lakes."

"Where?"

"I dunno. That guy Jimmy put the network together. I guess he used to be a bookie with a pretty good crew of guys who needed work."

"How many locations?"

"Just a few, as far as I know. It was supposed to be a small operation, at least that's what Mr. Cruzano said when he cleared it with some of the families."

"What families?"

"Well, his own in Chicago, first."

Harlan looked at Sawed-Off, who paused before he said, "I guess he did come to us. It was last winter when I heard about it from the boss's consigliere. He was fishing for information, seeing if I knew anything about a gig my dad might have going, something on the Lakes come the spring. I told him I knew nothing about it, except that it wouldn't surprise me. I knew when my old man left the life that he wouldn't be able to go totally legit."

Harlan turned back to Eddy and asked, "What other families?"

"Basically, those in every major city on the lower Great Lakes."

"Like Milwaukee, Detroit, Cleveland, and on down the line?"

Eddy nodded and said, "Thing is, though, Mr. Cruzano was pitchin' it as a small operation that really wasn't gonna affect them anyway. I guess he was just playing it safe."

"Are there really many wiseguys left in those places? I mean, it's not the 1970s anymore."

"More than you might think, Mr. Holmes. I've heard that Detroit still has around fifty made guys. They're just not as obvious as they used to be, with all the legitimate business that most of 'em do these days. But they're still in the game. Maybe even more into it than back when their kind ruled the Great Lakes region."

"What makes you say that?"

"Cuz they're like the last of the dinosaurs, only they *know* they're going extinct. And they don't like it."

"Sounds like you may have attended some of the meetings Shotgun had with these guys."

"Are you kidding? I went to all of them. Mr. Cruzano wanted to show some muscle, and I'm really the only soldier he has left."

"What'd you hear?"

"They all seemed to be cool with the plan, as long as it was just pharmaceuticals on a small scale and the trafficking didn't go through high-profile places on their turf, you know, like airports and bridges or any of the locks."

"And Shotgun assured them he'd keep to those terms?"

"Yeah. He told them there'd be no recreational drugs, just pharmaceuticals. And the trafficking would be done only on the big water with just a few fishing boats. No big boats. And no air or land transport. From Canada through to US dealers, everything would be done in small boats."

Harlan sighed deeply as he recalled what Jimmy had said to Tank that morning about the "new product line" they'd recently begun moving and the huge transfer of it that was supposed to make them rich come winter.

"I'm gonna ask you again, Eddy, and I want you to be straight with me. Did Shotgun Gino stay to the terms: only pharmaceuticals, in small quantities?"

After a long silence, Eddy answered, "From what I've seen, it's only been pharmaceuticals. But maybe the quantities haven't been so small."

"What do you mean?" Harlan asked.

"I've seen the stash, Mr. Holmes. It looks kind of like a Walgreens. Maybe two or three Walgreens."

"Like a real pharmacy?"

"Yeah, a big one in somebody's basement."

"Whose basement?"

Eddy stared into his glass of chocolate milk, reluctant to answer. "It's okay, Eddy," Tank said. "You can trust me and my boss."

Eddy nodded and said, "Doc Kimble's basement."

"Really?" Harlan remarked. "The old doctor who's been semi-retired for twenty years?"

"Yeah. Mr. Cruzano recruited her to run the distribution side of the operation."

"Hold on," Harlan said in disbelief. "You're telling me that ole Doc Kimble has been working for Shotgun Gino Cruzano, dealing the man's drugs out of her personal residence?"

"That's right. I was kind of surprised too, when she agreed to do it. But she has her reasons, including some of her own patients who can't afford the meds they need."

"Where's her house?"

"Eastport."

"East-what?" Sawed-Off asked.

"East*port*. It's east of Northport, straight across the Grand Traverse Bay. I'm not sure if it's a real town. You won't find it on any maps. But that's what the locals call it."

He's right, Harlan thought. *It's due east of Northport. Relative to Jimmy's location, it's not up north, where Jimmy said he kept his new product line.*

"How the hell do you know all this shit?" Sawed-Off asked, shaking his head. "Meetings with bosses up and down the Great Lakes. A safe house in some phantom town with a drugstore inside. Why would my dad bring *you* in on all this? You're nothing but a fat-ass bodyguard."

Eddy's face turned red and his eyes bulged. "Enough with the jabs about my weight!" he shouted as he slammed a fist on the counter. Vibrations from the blow toppled a jar of peanut butter, which fortunately was plastic. It fell to the floor and rolled straight toward the pantry, as if scurrying for cover.

"That's right, Eddy, you tell him," Tank said as he joined Eddy on his side of the counter. Together they formed an eight-hundred-pound mountain, the span of their shoulders as wide as the kitchen counter was long. And from the look of their twin stares at Sawed-Off, the mountain was volcanic.

"I'll tell you why your old man let me in on all this," Eddy said. "Because I'm the only one who's been there for him. You sure as hell haven't, not after you ran him out of Chicago."

Sawed-Off bumbled for a reply. "But, but that's not what—"

"Bullshit, Gino, and you know it. You couldn't stand being in his shadow any longer. So you turned his whole crew against him, everyone but me, and forced him into retirement."

"That's not how I see it, Eddy. Age was catching up with the man. He was making mistakes. Everybody saw it happening, including you."

"What I saw was a man who wasn't ready to be old. He was trying to hang on, while you did everything you could to break his will. It's been two years, but I'll bet you remember the last thing you said to him."

"What, he told you that too?"

"He did, Gino, about you saying he was a useless old man who needed to get out of the way or do you the favor of dying."

"He *was* useless. Worse than useless. He left town owing us money. The cheap bastard."

"Wait a minute," Eddy said. He paused before continuing. "It was *you* then, of course—always complaining about money. *You* were the Chicago captain demanding a cut of your dad's take from his new business."

"Damn straight it was me. But the boss sided with him. Said I'd inherit my due when the old man dies... Shit... like I'm even gonna be mentioned in his stinkin' will."

"Hold on," Harlan said. "What are you two talking about?"

"It came out at our Chicago meeting," Eddy said. "An underboss said there was a captain wanting a percentage. He didn't say who it was, but I should've known."

"Yeah, you should have," Sawed-Off said.

"What I want to know," Harlan said, "is why you're here looking for him. You're not very fond of him, obviously."

"Because he talked me into it," Sawed-Off replied, pointing at Eddy.

Chapter 12

After the heated exchange, Tank and Eddy stepped aside, into an area of the studio apartment furnished with a couple overstuffed chairs. They each took one and began speaking quietly among themselves.

Back in the kitchen, Harlan's meeting with his prospective client continued.

"Here's your first week's pay, in advance," Sawed-Off said as he pulled an envelope from his pocket.

"Didn't say I was taking the job."

"Count it before deciding not to."

Harlan took the envelope to the other side of the kitchen. He stopped by the refrigerator. On the front of it, held in place by a magnet, was his work schedule at the gym that week. He stared at it, but his mind was elsewhere.

Ever since he lost his PI license, he'd been telling himself that he didn't care—that he wanted to move on to something new anyway.

Two years of lying to myself while cleaning up after gym rats, he thought. *My punishment for once taking on a client who turned out to be a mobster.*

Now he could work for another one—one who couldn't care less about the lack of state sanction.

And if the licensing board ever found out?

So what, Harlan thought, glancing around at his cramped, single-room apartment. *What more could they take from me?*

His thoughts turned to the state troopers he'd met that afternoon and how they'd react if they learned about him taking on this case.

But if I turn it all over to them, what good would that do? Tank's already said he won't work with cops. And these Cruzano guys sure as hell won't.

Concerns from within kept coming. An investigation might reveal that Shotgun Gino himself was the one behind the Northport massacre, perhaps after discovering that Jimmy had gone rogue on him with some new product line. Then what? Would he turn his client's father over to the police?

But I wouldn't be doing this for Sawed-Off anyway, Harlan thought. He looked across the room at the person for whom he'd really be working, Tank. *He's not gonna let this go, not after what he's been through today, and he'll need help.*

And there was one other factor that helped tip the balance. It was the work schedule affixed to the fridge. The words on it finally came into focus. Harlan was supposed to open the fitness center the next day at 5:30 a.m. And the same time the next day, and the next, and...

The hell with that, he thought, as he snatched the schedule from the fridge and crushed it in his hand. On his way to the sitting area, he tossed it in the trash.

Harlan handed the envelope to Tank and said, "This is what Sawed-Off is offering as our weekly salary. Tell me if you think it's enough."

The amount, however, really didn't matter. Harlan immediately turned to Eddy and went to work.

"What'd you do today after that support group meeting?"

"I went back to Mr. and Mrs. Cruzano's house."

"And they were gone."

"Yeah."

"Any sign of forced entry?"

"No."

"Foul play?"

"No, sir."

"Any sign that they may have left in a hurry?"

After a pause, Eddy nodded his head slowly. "The garage door was open and the car was gone. And the door leading into the house from the garage was unlocked. I've never seen the Cruzanos leave things open that way."

Eddy paused again before continuing. "And upstairs, in the master bedroom, the TV was left on. Cable news. That's when I first learned about the hits at Shotgun Landing. It was around noon, and that guy, Jamal Maris, was talking about breaking news the way he always does about stuff that's not at all new. Only this time, it really was."

"What'd you do next?"

"I called Mr. and Mrs. Cruzano's cell phones, but only got their voicemail."

"Is that something Shotgun Gino usually does—let his calls go?"

"Not mine, unless there's some reason."

Harlan imagined what that reason might be if indeed the man didn't order this morning's massacre, and if he wasn't himself one of its victims. In that case, he'd probably be on the run, incommunicado, not trusting wiseguys from any family, not even his own. They'd turned their backs on him long ago. He'd have to hide from everyone, including perhaps the two here now—one of them an estranged son—claiming to have his best interests in mind.

"And then what'd you do, Eddy?"

"I drove to Eastport, to Doc Kimble's house, on the off-chance they might be there and to check in on the doc. She wasn't answering her phone either. On the way, I called Sawed-Off and told him about what happened." Eddy looked toward the kitchen and added, "Thought you'd at least give a shit about your mother, Gino."

"You got nerve, fat man," Sawed-Off shouted back, "talking to me like—"

"All right you two," Harlan interjected. "Give it a rest. Tell me what you saw at the doctor's house, Eddy."

"Nothing, really. Nobody was there."

"You let yourself in?"

"Yeah."

"How?"

"With a key she hides outside and her security password. It was part of the deal when she became Mr. Cruzano's distributor, that we'd have access to the pharmaceuticals."

"What about the pharmaceuticals, Eddy? Did you check them out?"

"Sure, I went down into the basement. Everything seemed to be in order."

"Where'd you go when you left the doctor's house?"

"I drove up the peninsula to check out Shotgun Landing. But I turned around when I saw the cops still there. On my way back, Sawed-Off called and told me he was on his way. He said we were going to check out a PI he'd heard of, you, and that he'd meet me at your apartment. So I drove to your place, here. Tried your door, but there was no answer. Then I just waited for whoever got here first, you or him. The two of you got here at nearly the same time, him about five minutes before you."

"Is that your Buick parked on the other side of the street?"

Eddy nodded.

"Speaking of cars," Tank said, "we have a little transportation issue, Boss."

"What are you talking about?" Harlan asked.

"There's only ten grand in this envelope, not nearly enough to get you the new vehicle you're gonna need for this job."

"What the hell?" Sawed-Off complained. "Ten large a week isn't enough? You expect me to buy him a new car too?"

Tank rose from his chair. "You saw that piece of shit truck I was driving earlier, didn't you?" he asked as he walked to the kitchen counter.

"Of course I did. You fucking hit my car with it."

"Well, then you understand the situation. You know that my boss can't be seen in that thing while he's working for important guys like you and your dad. People won't take him seriously."

"Then just lease one and charge it back to me as an expense."

"I don't think that's very cost efficient."

"I don't give a damn what you think. I'm not buying him a new car."

Tank stopped a few feet short of the kitchen counter. "A new car won't be necessary," he said, smiling at Sawed-Off. "I know of a used one that'll be just fine."

"Okay, maybe we can work that out."

"The Range Rover."

Sawed-Off's eyes bulged and his mouth fell open. "Are you outta your mind? That's my car. I haven't even had it a month."

"He's just gonna use it 'til the job's done."

"Answer's still no. Hell no."

Tank stopped smiling and said, "And if he finds your folks alive and well, he gets to keep it."

"But that car c-cost... me..."

Tank stepped into the little man's space and stared down at him. "That *is* what you want, right? Your folks back alive and well?"

Sawed-Off nodded his head slowly.

"I'll take those keys now."

Chapter 13

"Looked like you and Eddy Chub had yourselves a pretty serious conversation last night," Harlan said as he turned the Range Rover from a paved road onto a dirt one.

"Yeah, I feel some connection with the guy," Tank replied from his reclined position in the passenger seat, eyes closed. "His situation is a lot like mine was back when I was a bagman—you know, the guy brought along for muscle who nobody figures has a brain."

"What were you talking about?"

"His weight problem and how he might deal with it. I told him about the diet and training program I did in prison and how it got me all lean and chiseled."

"And Eddy's going to do that too? Carve a lean, mean bagman out of all that blubber?"

• • • • •

A while later Harlan stopped the car and scanned the area. According to the GPS monitor, they'd arrived at Dr. Kimble's address, but all he saw in every direction were trees.

"We there?" Tank asked as he opened his eyes and sat up.

"Supposedly."

Harlan got out of the car and paused. All he could hear was the sound of a stiff autumn breeze ripping leaves from tree branches. And all he could see through those branches, other than sky, was the edge of the sun peeking over the eastern horizon.

"We should have gotten Eddy's phone number," Tank said as he joined Harlan. They had arranged to meet Eddy at the doctor's house first thing in the morning and assumed that the address was all they needed.

A lull in the breeze created an interval of dead air during which, Harlan thought, there might be some other sound, a faint one, coming from the direction of the rising sun. He took off that way.

"Slow down, Boss," Tank said, chasing after him. Harlan stopped abruptly to listen again. As Tank caught up he said, "Where are you—"

"Quiet, Tank. Listen. You hear that?"

"Hear what?"

"That."

This time Tank heard it too. "Sounds like a person ahead in those woods, calling out, maybe for help."

They pushed ahead through ferns and low-hanging tree branches at a slower pace, studying the landscape, and then stopped when they met back up with the dirt road. Beyond the opposite shoulder stood a perfectly straight row of bushy arborvitae shrubs. *Those aren't wild,* Harlan thought. And then he heard it again, this time clear enough to make out the call.

"Doc Kimble! You out here?"

"That's Eddy Chub," Tank said.

"And that's a two-track," Harlan said, pointing at a gap in the row of arborvitae shrubs.

They ran down the two-track road, which soon became a paved driveway to a sprawling ranch-style house that seemed better suited for an upscale urban neighborhood than these remote woods. Parked in front of the house was Eddy Chub's Buick. And coming around the side of the house was Eddy, a hand cupped to his mouth, about to shout again until he saw them. "Expected to see you guys in your new Range Rover," he said instead.

"How long you been here, Eddy?" Tank asked.

"About a half hour."

"But we weren't supposed to meet for another half hour."

"I woke early and couldn't get back to sleep, worrying about the doc now, too, and what we might've gotten her into. She's still not answering calls. And there's still no sign of her here."

"You looked everywhere?"

"Inside and out."

Harlan finally caught his breath after the short sprint and said, "Show us the stash, Eddy."

• • • • •

A stairway led down into what seemed like a black abyss, until Eddy flipped a panel of light switches and suddenly there appeared a spacious, unfinished basement. Its configuration matched the footprint of the entire house. Within it was row after row of fully stocked shelves.

The two big men silently followed as Harlan walked up and down the aisles studying the underground pharmacy. Its organization was meticulous, most of it alphabetical by syllable-heavy generic names on labels that included specific warnings and dosage instructions. There was a separate area for some of the more common drugs, which were organized by brand names and corresponding generics. Another area was dedicated to drugs that required refrigeration.

Without exception, every bottle, box, and package looked ready for direct delivery to end users.

Tank broke the silence. "It's like you said, Eddy, just like a real pharmacy."

"No, he said two or three pharmacies," Harlan corrected. He estimated that the shelves covered about 2,500 square feet of floor space. In some of the extra space there was a desk and, behind it, a file cabinet. Neither were locked. He rummaged through the drawers but found only office supplies. Whatever records the pharmacist might be keeping, he thought, were probably on the computer, which sat on the desk, powered off.

"Tank, watch your head," Eddy said. Tank ducked as Harlan looked up. The two big men were looking nearly eye level at something protruding from the low ceiling—a dark bulb the size and shape of half a softball.

"What is it?" Tank asked.

"A security camera," Eddy said, "like the ones in real drugstores that they hide under those bulbs in their ceilings. We installed a bunch of them down here."

Harlan looked around and saw several more and then reached for the one in front of them and unscrewed it. Inside was a camera, pointing straight into his face. A tiny green light on the back indicated that it was running.

"We triggered its motion detector," Eddy said.

"Who could be watching us?" Harlan asked.

Eddy held out his smartphone. "I could be, on this. It's been vibrating in my pocket since we got down here."

"Could Doc Kimble be getting some kind of alert too?"

Eddy nodded.

Harlan returned to the desk and found a Sharpie and some paper. In big block letters he wrote down his phone number and a note: "Dr. Kimble, I'm Harlan Holmes. I've been hired to find Mr. Cruzano. Please call me."

He then held the note up in front of the camera.

Chapter 14

Harlan's cell phone rang soon after he displayed the note.

"Dr. Kimble?"

"What are you doing in my house, Mr. Holmes?"

He smiled at the camera. "Came here to talk to you. What are you doing *not* in your house?"

"Watching you on my laptop."

"From where?"

"That's none of your business. Let me talk to Eddy Chub."

Harlan put the phone on speaker and held it in front of Eddy. "Hey Doc," he said, looking into the camera. "Are you okay?"

"I'm fine. Just scared out of my wits is all, seeing what happened to Jimmy and his men all over the news."

"Why didn't you return my calls, Doc? I've been worried about you."

"Because I didn't know who to trust, until I saw you with that guy you're with now—one of 'em they've been showing on TV."

"Tank? What makes you trust him?"

"He's the one those assassins tried to shoot after they got Jimmy, isn't he?"

"Yeah."

"Well, in that case, I figure he can't be on the side of whoever was shooting the gun."

"You got that right, ma'am," Tank said. "And my boss here, Harlan Holmes, he's cool too. Maybe we shouldn't be in your house the way we are, without you being here to let us in. But we're on your side, just looking for your boss, Mr. Cruzano. We're doing it for the family. Will you help us?"

"What kind of family?" she asked.

"Not the kind you might be thinking, ma'am. I mean *real* family. His son, Gino Jr., hired us to find him."

"Sawed-Off? The one Mr. Cruzano says is good for nothing?"

"Can't argue with that, ma'am. Junior's a first-rate asshole, if you'll pardon my French. But, yeah, he's the family we're working for."

After a pause, she said, "Okay, sit tight. I'm not far from you."

• • • • •

Fifteen minutes was all it took. Her car stopped abruptly behind Eddy's and out of it she charged, a scrawny old woman whose wild grey hair and deeply wrinkled face made her look like a female version of Albert Einstein.

Harlan tried to make eye contact as she blew past him on her way to the front door.

"Inside," she said without looking back.

By the time they joined her she had lit a cigarette and was pacing the front room.

"Are you really a doctor?" Harlan asked.

"Of course I am," she answered, smoke dribbling out of her mouth as she spoke. "Why would you think otherwise?"

"Oh, I don't know. Maybe because you're a drug dealer?"

"That's not quite what's going on here, Mr. Holmes."

"Okay then, why don't you tell us what *is* going on here."

"First tell me *your* story," she said as her pacing came to a halt in front of Tank. She stared up at him expectantly.

"My story?" he replied. "About what?"

"About what the heck happened yesterday. The massacre at the marina—what was it all about?"

"I really don't know, ma'am," Tank said as his head dropped. "The people who got killed there, they were my friends. But I hadn't seen them for two years because I was, well, away."

"In prison is what they've been saying on the news, Mr. Lochner."

"That's right. I'm an ex-con. But I don't commit serious crimes."

"No, you just beat up police officers."

Tank sighed deeply. "I'm telling you, ma'am, they were my friends. And I don't know who did that to them, or why."

Dr. Kimble stuffed her cigarette butt into a potted plant and asked, "The man you were talking to, the one who was shot dead beside you, was he really your friend?"

Tank nodded.

"Did you know him, Doctor?" Harlan asked.

She didn't respond.

"Were you working with him?" Harlan pressed.

"You already know I was."

Harlan gestured for her to sit in a chair as he seated himself in one next to it. "Please, Doctor, sit down and tell us what's going on here, from the beginning, when Eddy Chub brought Giovanni Cruzano to your office to treat his depression."

Dr. Kimble paused before sitting down, and then paused again before providing a brief account of the meeting. It was the same as Eddy's. She recalled how their conversation had somehow digressed from the subject of Gino's depression to the challenges faced by many patients who can't afford needed prescription drugs, and then, during that exchange, a moment when Gino seemed to experience what she described as "a sudden change in affect."

"Do you mean he suddenly felt better?" Harlan asked.

Dr. Kimble nodded.

"Would that have been right after you told him about how much cheaper drugs are in countries like Canada?"

She fidgeted in her chair, glanced at Eddy, and said, "Look, I'm not inclined to say anything further about Mr. Cruzano. He's my patient and, as I'm sure you know, Mr. Holmes, there are laws protecting patient privacy that doctors must follow."

"Really," Harlan said, smiling. "There are laws requiring you to conceal information about the drug trafficking that you and Mr. Cruzano have been engaged in since… oh… when would you say, Doctor, maybe a few months after you cured his depression by planting the idea?"

"You make it sound like I initiated it. That's not at all what happened. I didn't even know what he was thinking at the time."

"Then when did he bring you into the operation?"

"Oh, c'mon," Dr. Kimble snapped. "*Drug trafficking. The operation.* You make it sound like we're hard-core criminals, when in fact we've been doing a lot of good."

"In that case, you should have no problem talking about it."

"What I have a problem with is you, Mr. Holmes. Before questioning me, aren't you supposed to tell me that anything I say can and will be used against me?"

"I'm not a cop. And I have no intention of turning you in. My only concern is the whereabouts of Mr. and Mrs. Cruzano. I'm certain that their disappearance has something to do with the drugs stashed in the basement of this house. So tell me—"

"His wife is missing too?"

"Yes."

A long pause followed. During it, Harlan noticed for the first time a slight tremor in the woman's left hand. She caught him looking at it and covered it with her right hand before asking another question.

"How old would you guess I am, Mr. Holmes?"

Harlan shrugged. "Close to eighty, maybe."

"You're being kind, detective. Truth is, I turn ninety next month. I was married once, but couldn't have children. My husband passed away twenty years ago. Since then, I've watched the rest of my family and most of my friends join him. Sometimes it feels like my patients are all I have left."

Harlan realized that the woman was explaining her reasons for what she'd been doing in the basement of her house, before she'd discuss the details of what exactly that was. He leaned back in his chair, letting her decide when she would do that. Eventually, she did.

"A few weeks after his first appointment, Mr. Cruzano came to see me again. I assumed that it was still about his problem with depression. But it wasn't. He talked instead about arrangements he was making to smuggle pharmaceuticals into our country and distribute them to patients here on a pay-as-you-can basis. I couldn't get over how direct the man was, like he was talking about the start-up of an ordinary business. And, just as directly, he asked whether I might be willing to help him run it."

"How?" Harlan asked.

"By heading up the distribution side of things."

"And you agreed to do that?"

"Not at first. As I could see him coming around to the question, I began shaking my head no. But in my mind, I wasn't saying no. I found myself thinking about the many patients I have who could benefit from what he was describing. So I started asking Mr. Cruzano questions, trying to get a sense of his supplier."

"What did he say?"

"That he could get pharmaceutical-grade meds of just about any kind at prices near product costs."

"From Canada?"

She nodded.

"And you believed him?"

"I did a week later, when he came back to my office with a batch I'd asked him to get for me, including some meds I take. I had a pharmacist friend of mine check them out. He said they were the real thing. And I confirmed that he was right by taking the ones I use."

"You experimented on yourself?"

She reached into her purse, pulled out a bottle of pills, and handed it to Harlan. "Yeah, with these," she said. "They're meds for a problem I have with tremors. You wouldn't believe the kind of hoops I had to jump through to get my insurance to help pay for them. A month supply retails for forty thousand dollars. Mr. Cruzano got them for a fraction of that."

Struck by the woman's nerve and that of any others she might have on board, Harlan asked, "Has your pharmacist friend been helping you manage the stash in the basement?"

"He and I go a long way back," She replied, nodding slowly. "He's damn near as old as me. And he's in the same boat. No family any more. Friends dropping like flies. Nothing left to lose."

She looked away before adding, "And sick and tired of seeing our patients suffer because our country's health-care system is so screwed up."

"Is it just you two, or are there more?"

Still avoiding eye contact, she replied, "There are eight of us, so far. The rest are downstate providers in urban areas like Flint and Detroit. But none of us take a dime for what we do. And as far as I know, Mr. Cruzano doesn't either."

"And you and these dealers—excuse me, you said *providers*—give the meds away to patients who don't have insurance and can't afford them, correct?"

Returning her stare to his, she answered, "In some cases, yes. But most of the time my *providers*, Mr. Holmes, charge what our patients can reasonably afford to pay. We also have some patients who pay full retail prices, and sometimes even more."

"Why would they do that?"

"Because they have the resources, and they have reasons for not wanting a paper trail about certain problems they're having."

"Like..."

"Like opiate addiction or erectile dysfunction. Some people are ashamed of that sort of thing or don't want a spouse to ever find out. If they have the money, they'd rather pay through the nose for the meds than get them through prescription plans that require documentation."

"Do you keep track of the patients you're treating and the meds you're treating them with?"

"We have a system, yes. But we keep their true identities out of it."

"How do you manage to—"

"That's enough questions about my patients, Mr. Holmes. If you want information that might get you somewhere with your investigation, move on."

"All right, fair enough," Harlan said. "What can you tell us about the supply side of the operation, Doctor? Who's been smuggling the drugs into the country?"

"I only knew one guy who was involved with that. I mentioned him before, the one killed yesterday. The name 'Jimmy' was all I knew him by. I wasn't even supposed to meet him. He was just supposed to leave the drugs in the kitchen here at the house at times when I was out. But one time he was running a little late, and I walked in on him. Surprised the heck out of me, there being no car out front."

"How'd he get here?"

"By boat. My property goes about a quarter mile back, all the way to the bay, which means he was hiking the drugs all that way through the woods on those crutches he used. I asked him why the heck he didn't just drive a car here. He said he couldn't because everything on the supply side had to be done on the water."

"Per Gino?"

She nodded and said, "So after that, we started meeting at the shore, and I helped him carry the stuff to the house. It was unreal, two old farts like us hauling illegal drugs through the woods that way."

"From the looks of things downstairs, you hauled large quantities, or small quantities frequently."

"Lately it's been both, on account of a disruption in supply that Jimmy said would last all winter."

"So the stash downstairs is supposed to get your patients through to spring."

"Yes."

Dr. Kimble turned her head and stared off, as if deep in thought.

"What is it, Doctor?"

"Sometimes he'd stay and have a cup of coffee with me and chat a little."

"Jimmy?"

"Yes. It was just idle conversation, but he was good company. A nice man. Not what I expected of an illegal drug courier."

Still looking lost in thought, she asked, "Mr. Holmes, what will you do if you catch up with the people who killed him?"

"Turn them in to the police, of course."

Tank cleared his throat. The doctor and Harlan both looked at him as he glared into space and said, "What's left of 'em."

Chapter 15

After their visit with Doc Kimble, Harlan and Tank drove around the bay to a state park located at the northern tip of the Leelanau Peninsula. They parked their car at the precise point on the coast where Lake Michigan and the Grand Traverse Bay run together. In the distance they could see the iconic Grand Traverse Lighthouse. Sam Boadle had insisted on this time and place when Tank called her the prior evening to arrange a meeting.

Harlan looked at his watch. It was five minutes later than when he last checked it; ten minutes later than the time before that.

"She'll be here soon, I'm sure," Tank said.

"What could she possibly have to do here for Jimmy?" Harlan asked.

"I didn't ask, Boss. All she said was that it's something he asked for in his will."

"Why her? Why not family?"

"Well, I guess that's what *she* is. I didn't know that until we talked last night. I always thought Jimmy was a loner and she was just one of his employees."

"What's the relation?"

"Turns out, he was her uncle. Married into her family before she was born and became her godfather after. Then he divorced the aunt and became estranged to everyone, until Sam tracked him down about ten years ago."

"Is that when he hired her on at the old pub?"

"I think so."

"And you're sure that she'd play it close to the vest with the cops, the same way she would if he was alive?"

“There she is,” Tank said, as an old Pontiac Grand Prix pulled into the parking lot.

Sam parked alongside them and got out of her car as they got out of theirs. Her movements were impeded by skin-tight jeans and spiked heels that stabbed into the parking lot’s gravel surface. Tucked under her left arm was a bright orange Nike shoebox. As she approached, she tilted her unsteady body sideways to shield the box from a stiff wind coming off the lake. The steady current of air pulled back her long brown hair, exposing sharp facial features.

After he gave her a big hug, Tank introduced Sam to Harlan. Her stern expression was offset by eyes puffy and red from what must have been a recent cry.

“What’s in the box?” Tank asked.

“Jimmy,” she bluntly replied.

“Jimmy?”

“Yeah, his ashes. I had him cremated this morning.”

“And you put ’em in a shoebox?”

“Just temporarily, until I dump ’em into the lake.”

Harlan couldn’t stop himself from asking, “How did you get that done so fast, Sam? He passed just yesterday.”

She shrugged. “Cops were done with the body last night, and I had it sent straight to Trazuski’s Funeral Home in Traverse City. You remember Lou Trazuski, don’t you, Tank?”

“Oh yeah, Deadman Lou Trazu. One of Jimmy’s regular players back in the day. If I’m not mistaken, I saw Deadman more than once about some markers of his that were growing big and old.”

“I’m sure you did,” Sam said. “I told Deadman Lou last night that I wanted Jimmy incinerated first thing this morning. He gave me some line about a forty-eight-hour waiting requirement. I told him, like hell, you’ll have it done first thing tomorrow, or I’ll be sending my collector straight away. He says, what collector? And I say, the one who just got outta I-Max today. Then he doesn’t say a word, and I wait a while to let him think about it. Then I say, see you tomorrow at 9:00 a.m., Deadman.”

Harlan thought to ask whether a permit might be required to spread ashes on the shore here, at Leelanau State Park. But he was fairly certain she wouldn't know, and absolutely certain she wouldn't care.

"You mind being the pallbearer, Mr. Holmes?" she asked, extending the shoebox to him. "I'm gonna need a little help getting down to the water."

After Harlan took the box, Sam hooked arms with both men and they all headed slowly for the lakeshore. As soon as they got underway, she said, "Tank says you have some questions for me, Mr. Holmes. Go ahead, let's get to it."

"Now?" Harlan asked, thinking this was already a bizarre way to conduct Jimmy's interment.

She didn't respond.

"Okay, what can you tell me about Jimmy's operation?"

"Not much. Start-up was last spring—for the fishing business, that is, which was all I ran."

"As the front for something else, though, right?"

"Obviously."

The last remark begged the question, *Obviously what?* But Harlan let that go for the moment.

"Who worked for the fishing business, besides you?"

"Paul Russo and Chase Banwell, just like the website says. Pauly skippered the bowrider. Chase was his first mate."

"Tank says two other guys were with them yesterday. Chase Banwell's brother, Miles, and some guy they called Sully."

"Yeah, but they were more like regular customers—not really employees—along with another regular named Randall, who wasn't there yesterday."

"Three *regular* customers, you say? Miles, Sully, and this guy Randall?"

"Uh huh."

"How regular?"

"Well, Miles alone used to be the customer more often than the rest of our customers combined. That's why we eventually brought on Randall and Sully, around mid-July, so Miles wasn't always the regular. That was getting kind of suspicious, as you might imagine."

Harlan nodded uncertainly and said, "Why'd you wait until then to get more help?"

"Because that's when things really started picking up."

"Do you know why?" Harlan asked, recalling what Doc Kimble had said earlier about the need to stockpile meds for the winter.

"Nope."

Recalling also whom Tank had seen at the boat's wheel the day before, Harlan asked, "Do you know why that guy Sully, one of your regular customers, was skippering the boat yesterday?"

"Because Sully always did whatever the hell he wanted—that jagaloon."

"Jagaloon? What does that mean?"

"Means I couldn't stand the little prick. Nobody could, except his buddy Randall. After a while, he was the only one who'd work with Sully."

"Are you saying that Sully eventually skippered the boat when Randall was the regular customer?"

"That's right, and he never bothered getting the captain's license, like I told him to."

"And when Miles was the regular…"

"He'd go out with Pauly and his brother Chase," Sam said, "the way they always did from the beginning."

"So having those three and Sully on board yesterday was not the norm."

"It was the first time I'd ever seen it."

"I take it you don't know where Randall was."

"No idea."

"Do you know the full names of these two newer guys, Sully and Randall, or anything about them, like where they're from?"

"No. They weren't from Jimmy's old book, like the other three were."

"How'd Jimmy meet them?"

"Don't know."

"Do you know where the bowrider went when any of the regular customers were taken out fishing?"

"No, nobody ever told me, and I didn't ask. All I can tell you is that they went out northeast from the marina and came back the same way, usually a few days later."

"How many days later?"

"A few, you know, like three or four."

"Did they ever bring back any fish?"

"Not a single one, ever," Sam said. "But I think they must've brought something else back, because after they returned, that day or the next, Jimmy always made a trip too, alone, in the bass boat."

"To deliver whatever it was?"

"I assume."

"Where was he going with it?"

She shrugged. "Due east somewhere is all I can tell you."

"Due east out of the marina at Shotgun Landing?"

"Yeah."

"Toward Eastport, then."

"I guess."

They stopped at the shoreline, unhooked arms, and Harlan turned to face her directly. He stared into her still-irritated eyes and asked, "Are you sure that you never once heard any of the crew say anything about where they were going? Never heard them mention the name of a town? Or maybe a person?"

After a long pause, Sam replied, "Well, maybe a person."

"What'd you hear?"

"The Banwell brothers were talking one time in the office, when I was in the supply room. They must not have known I was there. I clearly heard one of them, Chase, I think, say something about a guy named Iggy. I'd never heard of a guy by that name, but I know that's the name he used."

"What was he saying about him?"

"I don't remember exactly. But I know he was worried because they were running late. And he said something like, 'We need to see Iggy before dark.'"

Harlan paused over the name. He'd heard it used somewhere before, but not as the name of a person. "You said they headed northeast out of the marina, right?"

"Uh huh."

"Toward the Straits."

Sam nodded and then gave the shoebox a long look. Harlan extended it to her, but she raised her hand and said, "You mind doing it, Mr. Holmes? Could you wade into the water a little way and dump Jimmy in?"

"Seriously?"

"Well, yeah, that's why we're here."

"Don't you think Jimmy would've wanted this done on the open water, off the coast?"

"Why would it matter? It's all the same lake."

Harlan shrugged and set the shoebox on the ground so he could remove his shoes and socks and roll up his pants. After wading into the frigid water, he opened the box and tipped it upside down. About six pounds of what seemed more like sand than ash, grey in color, poured from the box and into the water. He turned his head to avoid inhaling some wafting particles of the deceased.

Sam took the shoebox from Harlan when he finished and looked inside. "Still a little bit of him in there," she said, "stuck to the sides." She held the box over the water and smacked it a few times. As more dust sprinkled out, she casually said, "Got me some sweet cannabis back in my car, gentlemen. Whadaya say, should we go blow a doobie in memory of Jimmy?"

"What the hell, Sam," Tank said, "you smoke pot?"

"Not as often as I'd like. It's expensive. But what's in the car I got for free as part of my inheritance."

"From Jimmy?" Harlan asked.

"Yeah. I came across it going through some of his stuff. I'm telling you boys, it's some potent shit."

"May I see it?" Harlan asked.

"Sure," Sam replied, "unless you're gonna smoke it with your eyes closed."

Chapter 16

They stood in the parking lot beside the open trunk of her car, Sam rolling a joint as Harlan examined the Ziploc storage bag. Printed on the bag was the leafy image of a cannabis plant followed by the warning: "*For medical use only as per the Controlled Drugs and Substances Act (S.C. 1996 c. 19).*"

Harlan had Googled the parenthetical citation to the consolidated laws of Canada earlier that day when he saw the same label on bags of medical marijuana at Doc Kimble's house. Apparently, Jimmy had helped himself to some of the goods they were trafficking.

"How much of this did he have?" Harlan asked.

"Just a few bags," Sam said as she fired up the joint. "But I'll tell you what, it goes a long way."

She blew on the lit end before hitting the joint hard. Then she passed it to Tank, who explained himself before taking a turn. "It's that sniper shot to my shoulder, Boss. Still giving me some trouble."

"Sure it is," Harlan said.

Harlan took the joint when Tank was done and passed it directly back to Sam. As she reached for it, he asked, "Did you suspect that Jimmy was trafficking in some kind of contraband all along?"

She took a deep drag and, without exhaling, replied, "Sure. Just wish I knew it was this reefer."

"Did anything make you suspicious besides the regular customers who never fished?"

She nodded, still holding her breath.

Harlan waited for her to exhale.

"What else?" he asked when she finally did.

"The way Jimmy was acting lately, all jittery and uptight. That's not like him. Nothing used to rattle him. Remember, Tank, that deadpan face he always wore no matter the situation?"

"Sure, he got that from his gambling days. Man had no tells."

"Well, he had 'em in the end."

"Can't imagine that," Tank said as he put out the roach and held it up. "You mind if I keep this, Sam? In case my shoulder flares up again?"

"Hold on," Harlan said, struggling with the vagueness of what he was hearing. "What exactly are you saying, Sam, about this change in Jimmy?"

"I'm saying there came a time when he was flat scared, Mr. Holmes."

"When did you first notice this?"

"The first time I noticed him wearing body armor under his jacket."

"And when was that?"

"Late July."

"After he took on the new hires? Those guys, Sully and Randall?"

"That's right."

"And when the pace of his business picked up?"

Nodding, Sam added, "And then there was the time more recently, while he was doing some of that business, when he looked like he was gonna shit bricks."

"What business?" Harlan asked.

"I dunno. Some deal I accidentally walked in on."

"Tell us about it."

"There's not much to tell," Sam said. "Few weeks ago I went up the coast after work to smoke a little weed and look out at the water, like we're doing now. On the way home I caught a wicked case of the munchies. So I stopped at the marina cuz there's always something to eat in the break room. Except when I get to the office, some guy I've never seen before is right inside the door, in my face. He starts making a ruckus about me being there and won't let me back out. I can see he's got a gun, so I yell for Jimmy. But when he comes out from the back office, he's all speechless and freaked out, completely useless. Hell, I was the one who ended up talking the guy down to get me outta there."

Tank's eyes widened.

Harlan asked, "Did you see anyone else, Sam? Anyone in the back office with Jimmy?"

"No, but I figure there must've been, and that the dude at the door was on lookout. But I don't know for sure."

"You said this happened a few weeks ago. Can you be more specific?"

Sam paused before answering, "I remember exactly. It was the night we had that weather bomb blow in from the lake, out of nowhere."

"The night of the pop-up storms?"

"Might've been pop-up storms down your way in Traverse City, Mr. Holmes. But up here it was damn near a hurricane. People lost boats. I remember coming to work the next day and seeing the bowrider missing. Asked Jimmy about it, and he said the boys took it out for a run and got caught in the storm but managed to get through."

"Did you and Jimmy ever talk about the run-in you had with the guy in the office?"

"No. My job was not to know about that side of the business."

"Do you remember what the guy looked like?"

After a pause, Sam answered, "This may sound strange, but the guy was so into my face that the thing I remember best was the color of his eyes. They were so blue, like a perfect sky on a clear day."

"Anything else?"

"Nothing distinctive. He was just an average-sized white guy, I guess."

"What color hair?"

"I dunno. I'm not even sure he had any. He was wearing a wool cap."

Harlan pulled out a notepad and added some notes to those he'd taken during his interview with Doc Kimble earlier. He continued writing after asking Sam to describe Randall, the one other guy whom Tank had never seen.

When the interview was over, Tank asked, "What do you think, Boss?"

Harlan paused for a look at the lake, in the direction of the Straits. "I think we need to see Iggy."

Chapter 17

"Who's Iggy?" Tank asked as Harlan pulled their car out of the parking lot.

"Get out your cell phone and see for yourself," Harlan said.

"What am I looking for?"

"A map of northern Michigan. Zoom in enough to see Northport."

After tapping at his phone, Tank said, "Okay, got it."

"Now start scrolling, like you're traveling by boat in the direction that Sam said these guys went, northeast, across the Grand Traverse Bay and onto Lake Michigan. Keep going northeast past Sturgeon Bay and then tell me what your headed for."

"The Mackinac Straits?"

Tank was referring to the waterway that joins Lakes Michigan and Huron and runs between Michigan's Upper and Lower Peninsulas. Over the waterway, connecting the peninsulas, stretches the five-mile-long Mackinac Bridge.

"That's right," Harlan said. "Now, look at the northern side of the Straits, just east of the bridge along the Huron coast. You might have to zoom in some more to see it."

"St. Ignace?"

"Yeah, I think that's Iggy."

"The guy who the Banwell brothers were talking about when Sam was listening?"

Harlan nodded.

"Is a city?"

• • • • •

The two had driven all afternoon, stopping only once at Harlan's apartment to grab some food and do something about Tank's appearance. Two people, Eddy Chub and Doc Kimble, had already recognized him from media coverage of the prior day's events at Shotgun Landing. That had to stop if he was going to accompany Harlan any further.

As they approached the Mackinac Bridge, Tank looked at the mirror on the visor. "It doesn't really match my hair," he said as he stroked his new mustache and goatee. Harlan had created the make-shift disguise at the apartment with some spy items left over from his PI days.

"That's why I wanted you to shave your head."

"But I'm telling you, Boss, I spent two years in the pokey growing my hair out like this. I can't just cut it off."

"It's a damn mullet, Tank. Nobody's worn their hair that way for decades."

"So what? I like it."

"Well, we still have to do something about it. Between that big hair and your freakish size, your identity is unmistakable."

"What do you have in mind?"

"You'll see when we get to St. Ignace. For now, put on those costume glasses I gave you."

"Oh, c'mon, Boss. These things are ridiculous. They make me look like Clark Kent."

"Just put 'em on, will you, before we get to the cameras on the bridge. And try not to look so damn big."

"How am I supposed to do that?"

"I dunno. Maybe slouch down in the seat a little."

Ten minutes later they exited the interstate for St. Ignace, the first stop north of the Mackinac Bridge and last bit of urban life before entering the boreal forests of Michigan's Upper Peninsula.

Along the city's three-mile stretch of the Huron coast were countless shops selling fudge, t-shirts, books, jewelry, antiques, and just about anything else that might appeal to the downstate tourists who'd squirreled away a few extra bucks for their annual up-north vacations.

Harlan waited in the car outside one of the clothing shops while

Tank went inside to make himself look more like one of those tourists. A few minutes later he emerged with his lengthy mullet tucked under a "Pure Michigan" baseball cap and his near-perfect physique hidden beneath a matching, oversized hoodie that bunched up around his waist.

Tank hopped into the car and asked, "What's the plan, Boss?"

"Thought we'd look for Miles Banwell."

"Why him?"

Harlan retrieved a newspaper from the backseat. "Take a look," he said as he handed it to Tank. On the front page was an article about the prior day's massacre at Shotgun Landing. Accompanying the article were photos of those captured on the amateur video, including Tank.

As Tank reviewed the article, Harlan returned to what he'd been doing while Tank was shopping—reviewing photos of Miles Banwell on Facebook, looking for a good headshot.

"Oh, I get it," Tank said, looking up from the paper. "The video never got a good shot of Miles, so people around here won't know who he is unless they saw him some other time when he might've been in St. Ignace working for Jimmy."

"That's right," Harlan said. "That makes him our guy."

Harlan showed his phone to Tank for a look at a photo he'd downloaded.

"Oh yeah, that's Miles all right," Tank said. "One of Jimmy's favorite writers back when he ran the book. We used to call him Old Style Miles cuz of the way he did everything by hand. No iPads or iPods for Old Style. Not even a calculator when he crunched the numbers."

Harlan rolled his eyes. "What is it with you guys and these names?"

• • • • •

They drove along the three-mile strip and stopped at businesses that operated directly on the water providing boat rentals, ferry services, and the like. Such places, Harlan thought, were the most logical candidates for a front to a drug-smuggling operation on the Lakes. His approach was direct. He just walked into each establishment, looked for someone who seemed to be in charge, and told a sad story about Miles Banwell.

"His family is worried sick. He's been missing for days. Last known to be on a fishing boat that was supposed to dock somewhere along the coast here in St. Ignace…"

As he spoke, Harlan studied their responses. A co-conspirator, of course, could be expected to deny knowing Miles, but the denial might be betrayed by a look or a gesture. Harlan studied those he questioned for such a reaction, but repeatedly there were none, even when he followed up with further details intended to provoke one.

"Thing is, he was far from home, the Traverse City area. And we're pretty sure he came out this way to do something other than catch fish…"

When they ran out of logical candidates for a front, Harlan and Tank each took a side of the street and walked the entire three-mile stretch, making the inquiry at the rest of the businesses along the way.

Harlan was long frustrated with the effort by the time most of the shops had closed. He was also hungry and decided it was time to eat. No doubt Tank would also be up for a meal by now, he thought, as he scanned the area looking for him.

"Hey Boss, I'm over here!"

Tank had crossed over to Harlan's side of the street and was up ahead, peering into a shop window. Harlan stepped out to the curb to get a look at the sign out front: "Jimmy's Souvenirs."

He hurried toward it.

A sign on the door said that the shop was closed for the day; another in the window said it would close next week for the season. Harlan couldn't recall having seen any other businesses giving notice of seasonal closure. *It's too early,* he thought. Tourism would continue strong in the weeks to come as the brilliant colors of autumn remained in the northern forests, and it would continue strong well into deer hunting season, which wasn't until next month.

Harlan joined Tank at the front window. Both men pressed against the glass with their hands to the sides of their faces to shield away the outside streetlights. A sole ceiling light inside shone down on a cash register and something on the wall behind it.

"Check it out, Boss, on the wall there," Tank said.

Harlan pressed closer and squinted. It was an old Stroh's Beer 3-D wall hanging with the trademarked crowned lion and the logo "Stroh's is spoken here."

"How cool is that?" Tank added.

To Harlan, the wall hanging looked like a piece of old plastic junk left over from a bygone era. But he could see that it meant something to Tank, who stared at it like it was a piece of vintage art stirring his soul.

"What's so cool about it?"

"I think I've seen that before."

"I'm sure you have," Harlan said. "They started brewing Stroh's Beer in Detroit over a hundred and fifty years ago. There's a lot of old memorabilia like that in this state."

"I mean that particular one, Boss. I've seen it before, I'm sure. You got binoculars?"

"No. What might you see if I did?"

"A few holes in the lion's ass."

"What?" Harlan asked, jerking his head from the window.

Tank slowly turned, smiled at Harlan, and explained, "The exact same memorabilia used to hang on a wall behind the bar in Jimmy's Pub. One time a couple drunks playing darts decided to see who could put one into the lion's ass first. I personally eighty-sixed those fools myself after they dissed the bartender."

"And they hit the lion's ass?"

"A few times, and in some other places."

Harlan's thoughts turned to a succession of businesses: Jimmy's Pub, Jimmy's Charter Fishing, and maybe…

"No wonder the guy's book back in Traverse City got busted."

"What do you mean, Boss?"

"He's got no semblance of an imagination when it comes to naming businesses that are supposed to be fronts for his illegal activities."

Chapter 18

They returned to the St. Ignace strip the next morning and parked a few doors down from Jimmy's Souvenirs. While waiting for the shop to open, Harlan probed Tank for more information about the incident involving the abuse of the Stroh's wall hanging: what exactly happened, when it happened, and every detail that Tank could remember about the people involved.

"Why all the questions?" Tank asked when the interrogation ended.

Harlan didn't answer. He was immersed in thought about various scenarios that could play out during an exchange with whoever might open the souvenir shop.

"You're working up one of your scams, aren't you, Boss?"

In fact, he was. Running a scam to get information used to come easy for him back when he was a licensed PI, but that was years ago. On this occasion, Harlan caught himself feeling unsure.

A gangly young man eventually approached the storefront, unlocked the door, and entered.

"You recognize him, Tank?"

"No."

"And you're sure you would if he used to work for Jimmy back when you did?"

Tank nodded.

"Okay then, stay in the car."

"Oh, c'mon, Boss. We're supposed to be a team."

"Stay here but keep your phone handy. If there's a connection to Jimmy, I'll probably call you in."

An old-fashioned storekeeper's bell clanged as Harlan entered the shop. The man who had opened the store stood behind a counter, alone, poking at the keys of the cash register hesitantly. Suddenly he smacked the machine on the side as he grumbled, "Dammit, open up."

For the sake of the business, Harlan thought, *he better not be running the place.*

"May I help you?" the clerk said as he looked up, his eyes wide and uncertain. Over his head on the wall behind him hung the Stroh's Beer decoration.

Harlan stopped at the other side of the counter and studied the man. He had missed a button around the midsection of his shirt and half of his collar was turned up. Above the wardrobe malfunctions, on one of his high cheekbones, was a teardrop tattoo, historically a staple for prison inmates. In that context, it could have any number of meanings about the crimes of its wearer, or it could have no meaning at all.

"My name's Harlan Holmes, young man. And you would be...?"

"Zane Hertz."

"Well, I'm pleased to meet you, Zane," Harlan said as he shook the man's boney hand. "I'd like to see the manager of this fine establishment to talk about—"

Harlan stopped himself abruptly, cocked his head, and began staring at the Stroh's wall hanging. Slowly he said, "What the... Could that possibly be..."

He stopped himself again and glanced back at the door through which he had just entered. Returning his attention to the wall hanging, he said, "The sign out front... it says *Jimmy's* Souvenirs, right?"

"Always has, as far as I know," Zane said, also glancing at the door and then once over his shoulder.

"Can I see that Stroh's Beer thing up there?"

"It's not for sale."

"I don't want to buy it. I want to see it, up close."

"Why?"

"To see if there are some dart holes in it—a few right in the lion's butt."

"There are," Zane said, looking curiously at Harlan. "How'd you know?"

"Please, young man, just let me see the thing, would ya?"

Zane retrieved a step stool and pulled down the wall hanging. Harlan smiled broadly as he examined the holes. "So, you wanna know how I knew, eh?"

"Yeah."

"Because the name of this store is just like the one for an old hangout of mine that used to be in Williamsburg, a place called Jimmy's Pub, where I last saw this thing and the guys who put these holes in it."

"You were there?"

"Heck yeah, I was there. Saw the two drunken fools who threw the darts at it. Man, they were really carrying on—until my buddy eighty-sixed 'em."

"The big bouncer?"

Harlan smiled. "So, you've heard this story."

"Sure, from my boss. He was tending bar there that night and he—"

"Whoa, hold on there, partner. Are you saying that your boss, here at this place, is the same bartender who one of those drunks took a swing at that night?"

"Yeah, he's— "

"Wait, don't tell me," Harlan said, recalling something Tank had told him about the incident. "It may have been some years ago, but I partied with that guy more than once, and I never forget a name. It was... Bo something... Bo Kitner!"

"Yeah, he's my uncle. He's the manager here these days."

"And the guy who owned that pub, Jimmy, does he own this place?"

"Maybe. I've heard Uncle Bo talk to a guy by that name on the phone a few times. It seemed like business."

"Man, talk about a small world. Here I am in St. Iggy, droppin' in to cold pitch my wares for next summer, and a prospective customer turns out to be Bo 'the Mojo' Kitner."

Zane flashed an awkward smile and said, "He told me about that nickname, but I've never heard anyone actually call him that."

"Oh man," Harlan replied, "when that pub got hopping, Bo could turn on the mojo and crank out the drinks. And he did it with style, flipping bottles and glasses around while making fancy cocktails. They called it flair bartending back in the day, and there was none better at it than Bo."

After a light laugh, Zane asked, "So tell me, Mr. Holmes, what are you selling?"

"Same useless tourist crap that you are, only I do it for a downstate distributor. Is Bo around?"

"No, he left town."

"When?"

"Couple days ago."

"Darn, I just missed him. Where'd he go?"

"Not sure. Business trip, I think."

"When'll he be back?"

"Don't know."

Harlan glanced again at the front door and said, "Your sign out front says you guys are closing shop next week. You think he'll be back for that?"

Zane shrugged and started poking at the keys to the cash register again.

"You have his number?" Harlan asked.

"What for?" Zane responded. He stopped poking at the register, but didn't look up.

"You know, to talk to him about my wares, and maybe some about our glory days."

Zane still didn't look up.

"You okay?" Harlan asked.

"I'm fine," Zane said as he finally picked up his head, though there was a long pause before his expression eased. "I'll get you that number."

Zane's attention had returned to the cash register by the time Harlan finished keying the phone number into his contact list.

"Well, I guess I'll be going now."

"Uh, huh," Zane murmured.

About halfway to the door Harlan stopped, turned, and asked, "How 'bout some of our other buddies from back in the day? Is Bo in contact with any of them?"

Zane stopped messing with the cash register and answered, "Like who?"

"Oh, I dunno, maybe Pauly Russo and the Banwell brothers, Chase and that other one, the guy they called Old Style Miles. If memory serves, they fancied themselves as expert anglers, though my sense was that their tales of fishing exploits weren't much rooted in fact, if ya know what I mean."

Zane's eyes widened as he asked, "Who a-are you?"

"Well, like I told you before, I'm—"

"Cut the shit, man. You're no pitchman for a downstate distributor. That name you said before, Harlan Holmes, is that supposed to mean something to me?"

"No, but those other names obviously do. And I'll bet you recognize the pictures of Pauly and Chase that they've been showing on the news."

Zane's eyes darted around the room until they locked onto a back door for employees only. He had the look of someone about to run.

"Easy, friend. I'm no threat to you."

"How am I supposed to know that?"

"Would you recognize the big guy they've also been showing on the news?"

"The one who ran from the sniper?"

"Yeah. He's the bouncer who saved your Uncle Bo's ass that night. And he and I are working together right now, tracking down that sniper and whoever else helped light up that marina the other day."

"So you're after the guys who killed my Uncle Bo's friends?"

"That's right. Puts us on the same side, don't ya think?"

"Maybe… if it's true," Zane said.

Harlan speed-dialed Tank on his cell.

"Lose the costume and come inside."

Chapter 19

Zane and Tank quickly discovered something they had in common besides a genuine connection with Bo Kitner. Both men were ex-cons. Zane had done his time in Jackson State Prison for auto theft. Although it was a short stint, he still had trouble adjusting to life on the outside after his release a few months back.

"Biggest problem was finding a real job," Zane said from behind the counter, where he had remained after Tank joined Harlan on the customer side.

"I can relate," Tank replied. "Nobody's hiring thieves and thugs these days, except my boss here and your uncle. What's Bo got you doing, anyway?"

"Just helping with the shop."

"That's it?"

Zane nodded slowly before answering, "Uncle Bo's been looking out for me, you know, making sure I stay out of trouble."

"How about Bo himself?" Tank asked. "Has he been staying out of trouble?"

Zane glanced at a display of souvenir back scratchers before responding, "I sometimes wonder."

"About what?"

"What he's been doing to pay me a whole helluva lot more than he should for selling this junk."

"Whatever that might be, he's been doing it with those guys who got whacked in Northport, don't you think?"

"And maybe with you, too, Tank. I mean, shit, man, you were right there with them when they got it."

"For less than ten minutes is all," Tank said. "Like I said before, I just got outta the joint that morning. How about telling me what those guys did here."

Zane shrugged as he answered, "Mostly just a lot of coming and going."

"Coming from where?"

"The few times I saw, they came in from the south and headed out going east. But I don't know where from or to."

Must have been their outbound trip, Harlan thought.

"What'd they do while they were here?" Tank asked.

"Usually just tie off at our dock and gas up and go. Sometimes they'd stay longer, overnight on occasion, right here in the store. I asked Uncle Bo about them, but he just told me to never mind and stick to doing my job. So I did. I never had much conversation with any of them."

"Sounds like you might've been suspicious of these guys right from the start," Tank said. "Why's that?"

"Because they weren't fishing."

"How do you know?"

"I helped them gas up a few times. Never saw a single fish. Never even caught a whiff of one."

"That's it? Just because you didn't see any fish you thought—"

"And because of what I *did* see."

"Like what?"

"Like the briefcase."

Tank and Harlan shared a glance.

"One of them always brought it along," Zane continued. "It's actually Uncle Bo's briefcase. I know because it used to be my dad's. Dad gave it to him just before he died. It's real fancy. All aluminum attaché, dual combo locks, and engraved with Dad's initials. Same initials as mine—ZDH. Never understood why he gave it to his half brother rather than me."

"What'd they do with this briefcase?" Tank asked.

"Whoever brought it would always give it to Uncle Bo, and he'd go off alone with it into his office. Few minutes later, he'd come out with it and give it back to them, locked tight."

"Like he'd put something in it for them to take?"

"I guess."

Tank rested his hands on the counter, leaned toward Zane, and said, "You know, you remind me of Bo."

"How's that?"

"The way you notice things. Bo's like that too. All those years bartending made him real observant of people and able to figure out things about them by the way they behaved. How's he doing these days, anyway?"

"He's either dead or on the run," Harlan interjected.

Following a long sigh, Zane said, "Most likely dead."

"What makes you think that?" Harlan asked.

"Because the briefcase is nothing compared to some other things I've seen around here."

"What else?" Harlan asked.

"Some real crazy shit, Mr. Holmes. I wouldn't know where to begin."

"How about with the first crazy thing?"

Zane paused before he reached under the counter. And then, slowly, he brought out a hammer, stared down at it in his hand, and replied, "That would've been the day we had the big storm."

Harlan wondered first about the hammer before recalling Sam Boadle's account of her run-in with a blue-eyed stranger, also on the day of a big storm. "You mean the weather bomb that slammed this area last month?" he asked.

"Yeah, it hit us hard here in the Straits. Cars blowing off the Bridge, boats capsizing… all kinds of chaos… including a dumpster getting blown through the front window of the shop."

Zane set the hammer on the countertop as he continued. "Uncle Bo was here trying to secure things when it happened. He called me, and I came in to help. And just as we're nailing down the last of the boards, those guys showed up."

"Who?"

"Sully and Randall."

"In the middle of the storm?"

Zane looked up from the hammer, took a deep breath, and recounted the events of that evening.

• • • • •

"Did you hear that?" Bo asked.

Zane thought he did, over the howling wind. Someone was pounding on the back-alley door.

They rushed to the back of the store and, as soon as Bo flipped the dead bolt and turned the doorknob, Sully and Randall, soaking wet, blew into the shop.

Zane helped Bo close the door against the driving gale before they turned to their visitors.

"What the hell is *that* for?" Sully shouted.

The hammer Zane had been using was still in his hand.

"We were just fixing some storm damage is all," Bo said. "Where'd you guys come from, anyway?"

"The lake, man," Sully said. "Damn near lost the boat out there. Could use another line or two to make sure it stays on the dock."

"The bowrider? Why did you take it out in the first place?"

"We didn't know all hell was gonna break loose," Sully said. "Forecast was just for a little rain."

Bo stepped closer to them and, in hushed tone barely audible over the raging storm, said, "That's not what I mean, Sully. I'm asking why you took the boat out, *period*."

Sully cleared his throat and shot a passing look at Zane before answering, "Well… you know, Bo…"

"What I know, Sully, is that we're all supposed to be on the same damn page. And as I recollect, there's no fishing scheduled until next week."

"I… d-don't understand," Sully stammered. "There… must be some mistake."

"So, you guys thought we were on for today?"

Sully's stare went blank.

"Well, if you did," Bo said, "you must have brought the briefcase. Let's see it."

After a long, uncomfortable silence, Bo asked, "Does Jimmy know about this trip?"

Sully nodded.

Bo pulled out his cell phone and started for his office, leaving Zane alone with them. They stepped closer to him, Sully first, saying, "Time for you to lose that fucking hammer, stock boy."

• • • • •

"That jagaloon," Tank grumbled after Zane had finished.

"What?" Zane said.

"He's talking about Sully," Harlan explained. "We're learning that he was a real jerk. What about Randall? What's he like?"

"Not as mouthy as Sully, but a real jerk in his own way," Zane said, "and a helluva lot bigger. Built like Tank, minus a couple inches and twenty or thirty pounds. Carried himself like he was Sully's goon."

"What do you mean?"

"He was always following Sully's lead, like he did when Sully made that stock boy remark to me. Randall was the one who got in my face after Sully said that."

"Did he have anything to add?"

"Just a look that he always gave me."

"What kind of look?"

"The kind that made me think I better not lose the hammer."

Chapter 20

They went into an office at Jimmy's Souvenirs while Zane remained up front to serve a customer. Tank was browsing through some things on Bo's desk as Harlan paced the office, reflecting on the events of a particular day, the day of the storm.

According to Sam Boadle, that day was not business as usual for Jimmy. He had dealings with a blue-eyed stranger who seemed to be standing lookout for a backroom transaction that made Jimmy, a once cold-blooded gambler, nervous to the point of speechlessness. And later that same day, according to Zane Hertz, the two newbies on Jimmy's crew, Sully and Randall, were forced off the lake by the storm and sought shelter from longtime crew member, Bo Kitner, who was surprised by the unscheduled visit.

Were the newbies moving some of Jimmy's new product line, purchased by him earlier that day? Harlan wondered. And did Bo find out about it?

His thoughts shifted to what Tank had reported seeing a month after the night of the storm, minutes before the bowrider blew. Sully was on board along with three longtime crew members: Paul Russo and the Banwell brothers, Chase and Miles.

Harlan stopped pacing, turned to Tank, and asked, "What was it Jimmy said that day, when Chase Banwell asked about the purpose of the trip?"

"The day of the massacre, right before it happened?"

"Yeah."

"That he'd see when they got there."

"Were the Banwell brothers tight?"

"Sure, real tight. Don't think I've ever seen one without the other."

"So, one wouldn't be likely to keep the other in the dark about a multimillion-dollar deal he had coming up in the winter."

"I can't even imagine that."

"And Paul Russo was the one with the USCG captain's license," Harlan said, "on a plaque you saw by the boat's steering wheel, right?"

Tank nodded as Harlan continued. "But Sully, who Sam Boadle said had no license, was the one on the wheel that day, taking the other three to wherever they were going to see the new product line."

"That's right, Boss. Saw that myself."

And only three of the four on the boat had been confirmed dead, Harlan recalled from recent media accounts, the two employees—Paul Russo and Chase Banwell—and a presumed customer whose identity remained unreleased.

Of course, the media was also reporting virtually no chance of survival for anyone on board. *Unless one of them was the saboteur, who knew when to jump ship*, Harlan thought, *working with the sniper onshore whose job was to take out two more old timers, Tank and Jimmy himself… Wonder where Randall was that day.*

Tank had continued rummaging through Bo's desk as they spoke.

"Find anything?" Harlan asked.

"Nothing interesting, Boss."

"I didn't either," Zane said as he stepped into the office. "And I searched everywhere in here."

"What made you do that?" Harlan asked. "All the crazy shit you mentioned earlier?"

Zane nodded.

"What else besides the unexpected visit from Sully and Randall?"

"Stuff that happened two days ago."

"When all hell broke loose at the marina?"

"Not exactly then; it was a little later, when it hit the news," Zane said. "I was here in the office watching it on TV. They were talking about a terrorist attack near Northport. This was before the video came out showing the boat that blew up and the shooting onshore. So I wasn't thinking too much of it at the time, when my phone rang. Caller ID said it was Uncle Bo. I was expecting him to say something about why he was running a little late for work that day. But when I picked up, it wasn't him."

"Who was it?" Harlan asked.

"Some other guy, named Eddy. He's all worked up about—"

"Hold on," Harlan said. "Eddy who?"

Zane paused before answering, "I had the same question. I asked him..."

• • • • •

"Eddy who?"

"Don't fuck with me, Hertz. You know damn well you're talking to Eddy Chub—Gino's guy."

"What? I don't know *you* or any guy named *Gino*. Where's my Uncle Bo? And what are you doing with his phone?"

"Oh, we got your uncle right here, little nephew. And your story better line up with the one he's telling us, or you'll never see him again."

"My story about what?"

"About the cargo that Jimmy's been running behind my boss's back."

"You mean the Jimmy who owns this souvenir shop?"

"Of course, dumb shit."

"Look, man, I've never talked to that guy in my life. And I don't know nothing about any cargo he's running."

"Oh c'mon, Hertz. There's no time for this shit. If Jimmy didn't tell you about the new product that he's moving out of Shotgun Landing, then your Uncle Bo must have."

"I'm telling you, I have no idea what you're talking about. Never even heard of a place called Shotgun Landing. I'm just a fucking stock boy."

"Is that so? Well, I'll tell you what, Hertz. I'm gonna send a guy over to see you in person about this. And he better like your answers, or I'll be coming next, after I'm done with your uncle. You understand?"

"Yeah, of course, man... I-I'll be here. And I'll answer whatever questions your guy has. Can I talk to my uncle, please?"

The call ended.

Chapter 21

They remained in the office at the souvenir shop while Zane dealt with more customers up front. Harlan had returned to pacing the room, this time as he listened in on Tank's side of a phone conversation with a material witness who might just have become a suspect.

"Well?" Harlan asked when the call ended.

"Eddy says he never made that call, Boss. Says he doesn't even know of these guys in St. Ignace."

The latter claim of ignorance, Harlan thought, lined up with Eddy's earlier assertion, during his initial interview, that he knew little about the launch of Shotgun Gino's pharmaceutical business. *Assuming he wasn't lying then too.*

"What do *you* think?" Harlan asked.

"That someone's trying to frame Eddy."

"So you believe him."

"In fact I do, and I think he can prove it if he has to."

"How?"

"Remember the support group Eddy told us about? The one he goes to because of his weight problem?"

"Sure. He said he went to one of their meetings on the day of the massacre, leaving Gino and his wife without him when they went missing."

"Well, Eddy says the meeting was scheduled for 10:30 a.m. that day and lasted about an hour. That would place him with his support group when the call was made to Zane from Bo's phone."

Harlan thought about the timing of events that morning. Tank had said that the bowrider shoved off at 10:00 a.m. sharp, and that the explosion happened just offshore only a few minutes later. Media coverage of it began forty minutes later, around 10:45 a.m., according to the talking heads on TV whom Harlan saw later that day. And Zane had said that the guy claiming to be Eddy Chub called early in the news cycle while the talking heads were still speculating about it being a terrorist attack.

"Okay," Harlan said. "You think there are people who may have seen Eddy at this meeting near Traverse City, 150 miles away, when Zane got the call from a guy using Bo's phone?"

"That's right, Boss. And the guy threatened to come here to the store himself, like he was real close."

"That's what he *threatened* to do over Bo's phone," Harlan said skeptically, "which he could have been using from practically anywhere in the state, including Traverse City, if he had nabbed Bo the night before or early that morning."

"I thought about that, Boss. But Eddy says he never left the meeting. So he couldn't have been calling on the phone, unless he did it right in front of everyone."

"How could we ever corroborate that?" Harlan countered. "If that group even exists, I'm sure it's anonymous, and whoever runs it wouldn't tell us about who was or wasn't present at one of their private meetings."

"What do you mean, Boss, if it even exists? You think Eddy would lie about something like that?"

"Okay, let's say he's not. And let's say we could track down someone at the meeting who remembers seeing him there. That's still not gonna prove he didn't make the call."

"Why not?"

"Because none of them could credibly remember a negative—that the guy *never* got up and left the room for a few minutes."

"Oh, c'mon, Boss. Like the guy's gonna get up in the middle of a support-group meeting to make a call like that."

"All right, we're not going to sort this issue out right now," Harlan said. "What was it that Eddy said about Bo Kitner?"

"He had nothing to say about him. He doesn't know him."

"He's never even heard of him?"

"That's right," Tank said. "Eddy's got no knowledge of Bo

whatsoever."

Harlan sighed deeply as he thought about how incredible that sounded in light of the role he suspected that Bo played in Shotgun Gino's pharmaceutical business.

"But when I told Eddy about the souvenir shop," Tank added, "he had a theory about Bo's role in the operation."

"Oh, you don't say. What would that be?"

"Eddy thinks he was probably Shotgun Gino's banker."

"His banker?"

"Yeah, the guy who handled the money that Shotgun Gino gave 'em to buy the pharmaceuticals. Eddy says it would be Gino's style to separate things, so as few guys as possible had access to the money."

"Did you tell Eddy about the heavy-duty briefcase with combination locks?"

"I did, and he said the same thing that I'll bet you're thinking."

"Well, let's see," Harlan said. "Eddy thinks that when Bo took the briefcase from one of the mules and went into the office alone with it, he put purchase money that he'd received directly from Gino inside and locked it tight."

As Tank nodded, Harlan continued, "And the only person, other than Bo, who knew the combination to the locks on the briefcase was someone trustworthy who directly handled purchases somewhere down the line."

Tank nodded again.

"So the mules who carried the money between the two points would never have access to it," Harlan concluded.

"You got it, Boss."

"Why wouldn't Gino just drop the money directly with the trusted purchasing agent to begin with?" Harlan said, "or drop the briefcase with the money already inside, locked tight, with Jimmy right there in Northport, closer to home?"

"Eddy thought about that, too, Boss. He says that Gino's been under police surveillance since he moved to the Traverse City area, and he wouldn't want to lead the cops to either end of the operation—locations where the pharmaceuticals were being bought or delivered. So he handed the money off in between, to a guy who never came near the drugs."

Harlan thought about Zane's account of the bowrider's journey. He'd only seen it come in from the south and head out going east—its outbound journey toward Canada. Never did he see a return trip back to Northport when, presumably, it carried the pharmaceuticals.

"Sounds like Eddy Chub has some pretty strong powers of deduction," Harlan said.

"That's right, Boss. He's plenty smart."

Either that, Harlan thought, *or he's lying through his big chops.*

Chapter 22

The conversation stopped as Zane returned from up front. "What are you guys talking about?" he asked.

"The chronology of events on the morning of the Northport massacre," Harlan said. "It's important that we know precisely when things happened that day, including when you received the phone call from the guy claiming to be Eddy Chub. You said it came in shortly after the news of the massacre broke. Can you be more specific?"

"Sure," Zane said without hesitation. "It was 11:04 a.m."

"And you're so certain of that because..."

"Because it's still logged in my phone, and I've double-checked it since it came in."

Zane handed his cell phone to Harlan after pulling up its call history. The only incoming call that day was one from Bo's phone, logged in at 11:04 a.m., as Zane had said.

"Why'd you double-check it?" Harlan asked.

"Because I've done what you're doing, trying to make sense of everything that happened that day."

"So, there's more," Harlan said.

Zane nodded and hesitantly continued.

"Not long after I got off the phone with Eddy Chub, his guy showed up. I remember what time it was when that happened too, 11:30 a.m., because of what happened right as he came in."

"And what was that?" Harlan asked.

Zane took a deep breath before describing the experience.

• • • • •

The clang of the shopkeeper's bell coincided with the half-hour chime of a clock in the souvenir shop. Through the door came a visitor who couldn't possibly be the one he expected, or so Zane thought.

The man looked like a stereotypical nerd, the type lampooned in caricatures of geeky people, complete with jet black hair greased over to one side, glasses so thick they reduced his eyes to small dots, and pants hiked up high at the waist and ankles, revealing white socks that bunched up over his dress black shoes. The only thing missing, Zane thought, was a pocket protector. Instead, his pocket contained something shaped like a pack of cigarettes, only smaller.

"Sorry, pal," Zane said. "Like the sign says, we're closed. Besides, Halloween's not for a couple weeks."

"Oh, now you're a wise guy," the nerd said, as he flipped the bolt lock on the front door. "And here Eddy Chub told me I should be looking for a guy who just shit his pants."

"Y-you're… the guy?" Zane replied. "Hey look, man, I didn't realize—"

"Just shut the hell up and get your ass in the office, wise guy."

"Not by the desk," the nerd said as he followed Zane into the office. "Get over there by the TV. And turn it on to cable news."

"You want to watch TV?"

"I said cable news, wise guy. I want *you* to watch it. Now turn it on."

Zane turned on the TV and remained standing in front of it.

"Louder!" the nerd commanded as he joined Zane by the TV.

• • • • •

"It was bizarre," Zane said as he continued telling the story. "I was expecting him to ask me more questions, like the ones Eddy Chub asked about that guy Jimmy and whatever business he's into. But the nerd didn't seem to care at all about that. All he wanted to do was watch cable news."

Harlan and Tank shared a look before returning their attention to Zane.

"It's the truth, I'm telling you," Zane said, looking them in the eyes. "And it gets even stranger."

"How's that?" Harlan asked.

"Well, all they were talking about on cable was the Northport massacre, you know, speculating about it being some kind of terrorist attack on American waters. This was still before the video came out, so they didn't know any details yet, not even who might've been killed."

Harlan recalled that it wasn't until straight-up twelve noon that day when he watched Jamal Maris first break the news about those details and the video recording of them.

"And then the nerd turns down the volume on the TV," Zane continued, "and *he* starts telling me the details."

"At 11:30 a.m.?" Harlan said.

"Yeah. That fucking nerd started telling me facts that he said would come out as the media learned the story. Like the names of some of the victims—Jimmy 'the Leg' Dillon and the guys working his fishing business, Paul Russo and Chase Banwell—I remember him saying. And even you, Tank. That nerd knew your name, man, and how you just got outta I-Max that morning."

"You're shittin' me," Tank said.

"I swear, I'm not. I didn't know what to think, until that nerd told me that that's what happens to people like Jimmy and the other guys who fucked with his boss, Gino Cruzano. And then the nerd asked me if I'm one of those guys too. I started swearing up and down that I'm not, and the whole time that nerd was just smiling at me, like he was amused by me being scared shitless. Then he cut me off and told me what I have to do if I wanna live."

"And what was that?" Harlan asked.

"He told me that I have to run this shop for the rest of the week like nothing ever happened, and then disappear and never come back."

After a pause, Harlan asked, "Was that it?"

"Yeah. He just walked out after that. And ever since, I've been doing just what he told me to do, running the shop like usual."

Harlan still had Zane's phone and began scrolling through more of its call history. Since 11:04 a.m. that day, every call, and there were many, was outgoing—*from* Zane's phone *to* his uncle's.

"I take it that your Uncle Bo didn't answer any of these calls," Harlan said.

Zane's expression turned deeply sullen as he shook his head. "That's... why I think he's... he's..."

Tank placed a hand on Zane's shoulder and said, "We'll figure out what happened to him Zane. And whoever did it will pay. I promise."

It wasn't exactly what they'd been hired to do, Harlan thought, but finding someone involved in Shotgun Gino's business activities in Upper Michigan—alive—seemed a likely prerequisite to finding him.

"What'd he look like?" Harlan asked.

"Who?" Zane replied.

"The nerd."

"What, you've never seen a nerd?"

"C'mon, we need more than that," Harlan said. "His height, build, race—is there anything you can remember beyond the costume?"

"I dunno. Average-sized guy, I'd say. White. No distinguishing marks, as I recall."

"Could he have been Randall?" Harlan asked.

"No, definitely not him," Zane said. "He was way too small to be that goon."

And Sully was on the bowrider that morning, Harlan mused.

"Can you think of anyone else you ever saw on the bowrider who might have been the right size to be the nerd?" Harlan asked.

"Everyone else I ever saw was on the boat that morning, assuming Miles was on board like Tank says."

"Did this nerd say anything more about Gino Cruzano?"

"No. He just mentioned the name, the same way as that guy who called me on my uncle's phone, Eddy Chub."

"Or someone claiming to be Eddy," Tank added, shaking his head. "I'm not buying it, Boss. Eddy didn't make that call, and he didn't send that nerd. Somebody else did, trying to make it look like Eddy and Gino set up the hits at Northport."

But that was exactly what Gino might do, Harlan thought, if he found out that some of his crew had gotten into another product line behind his back. Or if he was in on it with them and decided not to share the profits.

"Where does your uncle live?" Harlan asked, returning his attention to Zane.

"I'll get you the address," Zane said as he pulled a key from his pocket. "This will get you in. It's a key Uncle Bo kept hidden outside his place."

"So, you've been there since all this stuff happened."

"Yeah, but there's no sign of foul play. You'll see. Only thing unusual is Uncle Bo's truck. It's still there, and he'd never leave without it—not on his own, anyway."

Chapter 23

"Bo, you in there? Open up!" Tank shouted as he pounded on the front door of a double-wide trailer. It was set up on an undeveloped lot off Cheeseman Road, two miles outside St. Ignace. Parked beside the trailer was the Ford F-150 pickup truck that Zane had described as Bo's only mode of transportation.

Harlan watched from the scraggly front yard until Tank stopped, turned, and shrugged.

Bo apparently liked his privacy, Harlan thought as he scanned the surrounding woods. Visible through a narrow gap in the trees, miles away, was the only sign of civilization—a segment of the Mackinac Bridge reaching for the tip of the Lower Peninsula.

Harlan tossed Tank the key and said, "You start inside while I check around out here."

His shoes became soaked with water as Harlan tromped through the soggy brush around the trailer's perimeter, checking windows and doors but finding no sign of forced entry.

He next checked the pickup truck. It, too, was locked and showed no sign of vandalism.

Near the truck was a hazmat marker partially obscured by brush. It warned of the Enbridge Line 5, a petroleum pipeline that had come under the scrutiny of environmentalists throughout the nation. Harlan imagined the gush of crude oil running through the earth beneath his feet and glanced in the direction it went. A couple miles south it would pump through sixty-four-year-old pipes lying exposed at the bottom of the current-whipped Straits of Mackinac. He wondered whether Bo Kitner's body might also be concealed somewhere nearby, beneath soil or water.

If they didn't break into the trailer, Harlan thought, *maybe they jumped him outside.* He tried to imagine where in the yard assailants might lie in wait. There were two doors to the trailer. Bo would have probably come out of the one on the side nearest the truck.

Harlan paced back and forth between that door and the truck, looking in every direction. *They'd have to get close if they were going to take Bo alive,* he thought. *And they probably took him alive to make him unlock his phone and question him about what Zane knew of the operation.*

Harlan stopped pacing. The best place to launch an attack up close seemed to be just beyond a corner of the trailer that poked into a grove of pines. He entered the grove and searched for traces that might have been left by someone passing through—footprints, trampled weeds, or broken tree limbs. He found none of that, but instead something that struck him as too obvious to be the trail of a hitman or kidnapper—a bunch of foil gum wrappers hung up in the needles of a fallen pine tree.

Looks more like the trail of a litterbug, Harlan thought, dismissing it to search elsewhere.

A half hour later, however, he returned to the gum wrappers, having found no trace of a trespasser anywhere else outdoors. There was something about Zane's description of the nerd that brought him back to the litter. The bulge in his pocket, Harlan recalled, where one might expect a nerd to have a pocket protector, he had something else.

Harlan pulled out his cell phone and called Zane.

"Did your uncle chew gum?" Harlan asked without saying hello.

"Mr. Holmes?"

"Yeah, it's me. I'm outside your uncle's trailer, looking at a bunch of gum wrappers on the ground. Might your uncle have made this mess?"

"I don't understand. Why would you care about some litter? I mean, shit man, you're supposed to be—"

"Dammit, Zane, would you just answer my question? Did Bo chew gum?"

"Not that I ever noticed."

"What about the nerd? Did you see him chewing gum?"

"Well... I... don't know. I was kind of scared shitless when I met him."

"You remember the bulge in his pocket? You said it was shaped like a pack of cigarettes, only smaller."

"Sure, I remember."

"Could it have been a pack of gum?"

"I suppose, maybe one of those big packs that holds lots of sticks."

Harlan ended the call and then used his phone to take some photos of the gum wrappers before returning to the trailer. Inside he found Tank seated at a kitchen table, playing Panda Pop on his smartphone.

"What are you doing just messing around?" Harlan complained.

"There's nothing worth looking at here, Boss. It's like Zane said, no sign of foul play."

"Have you been through everything? Every dresser drawer? Every shelf in every closet? The pockets of every shirt, jacket, and pair of pants?"

"Not when you say it like that, Boss. But that kind of search could take all day."

"Well, is there somewhere else you need to be?"

"Hell yeah, there is. I need to be out there catching that nerd and his crew."

"All right, Tank, I'm all for that. Lead the way."

Harlan stood motionless, arms folded, waiting.

• • • • •

Hours later Harlan's stomach grumbled as he sat at the kitchen table poking at the keyboard of Bo's laptop computer. They'd found a notebook containing Bo's internet passwords for everything he did online—banking, gaming, Facebooking, Tweeting, etc.—which allowed Harlan to advance their search into Bo's virtual world while Tank continued in the real one.

"Who's hungry?" came a shout from someone entering through the trailer's front door. It was Zane. He entered the kitchen carrying two large pizzas and a twelve-pack of beer.

Tank was not far behind. "Now that's what I'm talking about," he said.

Harlan and Tank hovered impatiently until Zane got out of the way. They each then dug out a slice and took positions, side-by-side, eating over the sink while Zane put the beer in the refrigerator and searched some cabinets and drawers for plates and utensils.

"You guys find anything?" Zane asked.

"Nothing," Harlan said through a mouthful. "Still at square one."

"Wish there was more I could tell you, Mr. Holmes. All day at the shop, I've been thinking about those guys who came and went with the bowrider, and I just can't come up with anything else about them."

"Are you sure you never heard them mention where they might be going when they left St. Ignace—the name of a town or person?"

"Like I said before, all I know is that they left here headed east."

That narrowed it to an enormous land mass—the entire eastern third of Michigan's Upper Peninsula—Harlan thought as he watched Zane place three beers in can koozies he'd found in a drawer.

Tank snatched his up, knocked it back, and slammed the can back to the counter, empty. "Appreciate it, Zane," he said, "but there's no point in leaving the rest in the fridge. I'll be right back with 'em."

As Tank went for more beer, Harlan grabbed his, raised it up, and—froze. "What's this?" he said, staring at the foam sleeve.

On it was printed an advertisement:

Chuck's Place
Easternmost Bar in the UP
Celebrating our 25th Anniversary on Drummond Island!

"Why, it's a can koozie, Mr. Holmes," Zane said, "you know, something my Uncle Bo, the former bartender, has around the house to—"

"I mean this place," Harlan said, "Chuck's Place, on Drummond Island."

"Well, I couldn't say. I've never—"

"The *easternmost* bar in the UP."

“What’s all the fuss about?” Tank asked as he returned with the beer.

The sound of a clock ticking seemed to slow as Harlan watched Zane stare into space, thinking.

“He went there last summer,” Zane said as his attention returned to Harlan.

“What for?”

“Something to do with Jeeps… a Jeep festival of some sort. I forget what he called it.”

“The Jeep Jamboree?” Tank asked.

“That’s it,” Zane said.

Harlan turned to Tank.

“Saw it on a t-shirt, Boss, in Bo’s closet. And on a brochure on his nightstand.”

Harlan scrambled off for Bo’s bedroom and found the items. Beneath the brochure’s caption, Jeep Jamboree, was a photo of a Wrangler Rubicon scaling dolomite boulders at a place on the island called Marble Head. A tourist magazine also on the nightstand showed more photos of Jeep and ATV enthusiasts at the event off-roading through woods and over rocky trails and creek beds.

Harlan returned to the kitchen with a stack of tourist information and dumped it on the counter.

“Sorry, Boss, I didn’t realize this stuff was somehow important to us,” Tank said as he looked over some of the information.

“I’m not sure it is,” Harlan said, “but it’s the only thing we’ve found that points to a location east of here. And the timing of this Jeep Jamboree might be significant.”

“Late July?” Tank said as he looked up from the tourist magazine.

“Yeah,” Harlan said, “right around the time when Jimmy’s business was going through some changes. The pace of things was picking up for him, and he had just brought on those new hires.”

“That’s when Uncle Bo went,” Zane said. “And he came back with a whole box of those can koozies. Gave ’em away at the souvenir shop, like he was advertising for that place—Chuck’s Place.”

“What did he tell you about the trip?” Harlan asked as he began working at the keyboard on Bo’s laptop.

"Not much that I can recall."

"Did he go alone?"

"I think so."

"Did he visit with anyone there?"

Harlan had found some information online about Drummond Island. It was a remote, eighty-seven-thousand-acre island off the easternmost tip of Michigan's UP mainland, tucked between two other likewise remote islands, St. Joseph and Cockburn Islands. These two neighbors, however, belonged to Canada.

"I'm pretty sure he met up with someone there," Zane said. "But I don't think he ever mentioned a name… just…"

"Just what?" Harlan asked.

"Just that he and a friend were gonna go to the Jeep thing."

"What kind of friend?"

Zane looked confused.

"A guy? A girl? A business associate? Who?" Harlan asked.

"I think he said some guy he knew there."

"That's it? Just some guy?"

Zane shrugged.

"Was he some guy associated with this bar, Chuck's Place? Maybe some guy Bo knew from back in the day when he tended bar at Jimmy's Pub?"

"I'm sorry, Mr. Holmes, but I have no idea. Uncle Bo never said."

Harlan turned to Tank and said, "Slow down on the beer. We have work to do."

Chapter 24

They were in a line of vehicles waiting for a ferry scheduled to depart at 1:40 p.m. from the village of DeTour. Harlan wondered whether the village name had something to do with how out of the way this place was and, even more so, the trip that the ferry was about to make from there—across a remote channel in the northernmost waters of Lake Huron to the easternmost place in the Upper Peninsula, Drummond Island.

"Check it out, Boss," Tank said, looking up from the tourist magazine they'd found the prior evening at Bo's trailer. "Says here it's the Gem of the Huron."

"We're not going to Drummond to see the sights, Tank. Why don't you put that magazine down and get back to those yellow pages I gave you?"

"Because I'm tired of looking at stuff like that. It's getting us nowhere."

Harlan let it go. After making the Drummond Island connection the day before, the two had stayed up late reviewing every local and business directory they could find online for the island and neighboring communities along the mainland side of the channel they were about to cross. The hope was that Jimmy's tendencies to name business fronts after himself and to hire guys from his old crew might produce a lead.

But the search yielded nothing, causing Harlan to question the wisdom of the current excursion into one of Michigan's most remote regions in search of some nameless guy for whom their only lead was a customized can koozie.

The gate at the dock finally rose and the cars ahead began moving forward. Harlan and Tank proceeded onto the ferry, where they and other passengers remained in their vehicles for the ten-minute crossing of DeTour Passage. Tank, still studying the magazine, began pointing out features of the mostly undeveloped island that were well within view even before they departed. He sounded like a tour guide.

"Look at that, Boss, right next to the dock on the other side. The world's largest dolomite quarry. Been operating since 1853."

"Listen, Tank, no offense, but I'm really not in the mood for—"

"Whoa, you feel that? We're moving."

"Well, yeah, we're on a ferry."

"That means we're now on the same waterway where the United States once took on the Brits during the War of 1812, after the Second Battle of Mackinac."

"Please tell me you're not going to keep this up for the whole trip."

"Oh, c'mon, Boss, lighten up, would you? There's so much interesting stuff here, like this passage we're on right now. There's a reason it's called DeTour."

"And I suppose you're going to tell me what that reason is."

"Sure. For centuries, it's been a channel for freighters and voyagers—maybe even the Vikings—to detour around Drummond Island and get to Lake Superior for destinations north and west, like Wisconsin and Minnesota and a big stretch of Canada."

"Oh, I see," Harlan responded sarcastically. "It's a channel used to *detour around* the remote place we're headed to."

"And check out the—"

"Oh shit, look at this," Harlan complained. "My phone's roaming cuz it thinks we're in Bumfuck, Canada."

"Mine's fine, Boss. Says in one of these brochures that some mobile providers don't have the right tower spacing to cover the island. That must be the problem you're having. Canada's right over there, next door. You must be roaming into one of theirs. That's gonna run you up some serious charges."

"Okay, Tank, enough idle talk. I need you to listen up so I can tell you about the play we'll be making when we get to Chuck's Place."

"The play? What do you mean?"

"You know, a scam. Something to make the locals cooperate with us."

"You're gonna try to trick 'em, Boss?"

"No, *we're* going to."

"Why do that? Why not just ask 'em straight up if they know Bo Kitner and whoever it was he visited on the island? Maybe slip 'em a bill for the name."

"It may be a large island, Tank, but not many people live on it. They probably all know each other and won't respond well to a couple strangers coming across like big-city bounty hunters tracking down one of their own."

"You might be right, Boss. Says here in this magazine that the population on the whole island is barely a thousand. What's the plan?"

Chapter 25

Their drive along Johnswood Road had taken them deep into the island's forested interior before they came upon a few cabins clustered around the establishment, "Chuck's Place Bar & Grill," and an enormous satellite dish out front—an adaptation, Harlan assumed, required in this distant place to cling to the grid. Among the few vehicles in the parking lot was a monster truck. Harlan parked alongside it, directly in front of the bar, where he had a clear line of sight through a window. Inside he could see two patrons shooting pool and a bartender whose head was down.

"Hold on, Tank," Harlan said after shutting off the engine.

"I understand the play, Boss. A basic good-guy/bad-guy hustle. I think these dorky glasses you gave me are finally gonna be worth wearing."

"Good, but just hang on for a second. We're gonna wait until this guy..."

The bartender looked up.

"All right, let's do it," Harlan said as he opened the door. After stepping out, he slammed the door shut, threw his hands in the air, and shouted, "I can't believe this mess you got us into! Just what the hell are we supposed to do now?"

"I'm sorry, man," Tank said as he chased after Harlan. "But I'm sure we'll figure something out."

Harlan stormed into the bar. "Beer," he said gruffly as he jerked a stool into place and plopped himself down in front of the counter.

The bartender shrugged. "Well, what kind of beer?"

"Don't matter. Whatever you got on tap. Just make damn well sure it's cold."

The bartender gave Harlan an irritated look that quickly turned into open-mouth dismay as his attention shifted from his nasty customer to the spectacled behemoth that followed him in.

With each of Tank's heavy steps the bar's old wooden floor struggled. Then, over the creak of buckling floorboards, there came a loud clank. Harlan glanced at the pool table. A player had miscued after catching a glimpse of the beast. The cue ball drifted aimlessly. Its path evidenced a slight lean to the table, which sat in the middle of the bar surrounded by mostly empty chairs and tables.

"What'll you… h-have?" the bartender asked as Tank joined Harlan.

"Oh, man, I'm so thirsty. I think I'll have me a big—"

"He'll have nothing," Harlan snapped as he turned to Tank. "Not until you figure out what the hell we're gonna do now."

The bartender shrugged as he reached for a tap to pour Harlan's drink.

"You're making too big a deal out of this," Tank replied.

"The hell I am. You convinced me to come to this godforsaken island, and now you can't even remember the name of the guy we're supposed to meet."

"I'm telling you, Harlan, we'll find a way to get ahold of my uncle and get the guy's name and number again."

"That's what you said when we got on that damn ferry thirty minutes ago, and you still haven't figured out what to do."

"Uh, excuse me, fellas," the bartender said as he slid a mason jar filled with beer in front of Harlan, "you're not gonna be causing any trouble here, are you?"

Tank sighed. "My apologies, sir. It's just that my good friend here has—"

Harlan slammed his mason jar on the counter after a big swig. "It's just that my damn *fool* for a friend here has put us in a bind," he said.

The bartender slid a mason jar filled with ice water in front of Tank. "Even so, you gotta let the man drink something."

Tank smiled at the bartender and extended a hand. "Thanks, buddy. The name's Zane Hertz."

"Glad to meet you, Zane. I'm Gerry Haley. What kind of bind did you get your grouchy friend into?"

Harlan rolled his eyes before taking another long drink.

"Truth is, I did kinda mess up. My uncle came home from a visit to this island not too long ago, all excited about it. Some guy here he knows showed him around the whole place, you know, Marble Head, Maxton Plains, the ATV trails, everything. This friend of my uncle knows all about the things to do around here. And I wrote the guy's name and number down on a piece of paper, but I lost the piece of paper."

Gerry shrugged and said, "Why don't you just call your uncle and get the guy's info again?"

Tank glanced at Harlan, who said, "Go ahead, tell him why you can't do that, how you managed to screw up your cell phone too."

Tank sighed deeply before confessing to the bartender, "I, uh, kinda dropped my cell phone in the toilet this morning, and I, uh, let it sit in there for a while because I'd just, you know, done my business and didn't wanna reach in for it."

"No shit," Gerry said.

"Oh, there was plenty of that," Harlan remarked.

"C'mon, man," Tank complained, "he doesn't wanna hear all that."

"You can say that again," Gerry said, frowning at Harlan. He then smiled at Tank before adding, "What about your backup? Don't you store your contact list in a cloud somewhere?"

"Only cloud he knows of," Harlan groused, "is the one he's got his fat head stuck into."

"It's none of my business, Zane," Gerry said after giving Harlan a stern glance, "but does this so-called friend of yours always treat you this way?"

"Not usually, but I guess I have it coming today, seeing as how I talked him into joining me on this trip. We're just a couple downstate city boys who don't know our way around up here and could use the kind of guide I promised him we'd have."

Gerry shrugged. "Well, there's not that many people on this island. Maybe I know the guy. What's he look like?"

"Don't know. Never met him. But you know what? I think you're right," Tank said, suddenly brightening. "I'll bet you or someone at this place knows him, cuz I think my uncle has something from Chuck's Place, and maybe he was with his buddy when he got it."

"Oh, yeah," Gerry said. "What's that?"

"A whole box of customized can koozies with the name of this bar and something about its twenty-fifth anniversary coming up."

Gerry reached under the counter and brought out two koozies. "You mean like these?"

"Yeah, just like those."

"Well, here, take 'em both. And maybe give one to your friend when he chills out."

"He just said his uncle brought home a whole box," Harlan complained before turning to Tank and adding, "Are you gonna tell this guy your uncle's name, or do you want me to?"

Tank smiled. "Now *that* I remember—Bo Kitner."

Gerry's eyebrows scrunched together as he murmured the name, "Bo Kitner… Bo… Nope, I'm afraid it's not ringing a bell." Then Gerry yelled across the room to a table server, "Hey, Candis, you ever hear of a Bo Kitner?"

"Bo Kitner, ya say, eh?"

"Yeah."

Her perplexed face suddenly beamed with recognition. "Yeah, you betcha I've heard that name before… but…" The perplexed expression returned. "But I have no idea where, wouldn't ya know."

"How 'bout right here, in this damn bar?" Harlan shouted.

"Don't you be hollerin' at me, you old curmudgeon," Candis shot back. "That's not helpin' one bit, that's for sure, eh."

"What's up with all the yellin' out there?" bellowed someone through a kitchen service window behind the bar.

Gerry leaned toward the window. "It's okay, Alene. Everything's under control."

Moments later a kitchen door leading into the barroom flung open. Through it busted a woman short in stature but big in attitude—armed with a plastic spatula. She strode directly up to Tank, pointed the utensil at his face, and bellowed again, "You causin' trouble in my establishment, buster?"

Gerry intervened. "He's actually a nice guy, Alene. It's the guy he's with who's annoying everyone."

"And just who the heck are you?" Alene said, turning to Harlan.

Harlan continued drinking his beer, looking off as though the woman wasn't even there.

"Hey, I'm talking to you. What's your—"

"Harlan Holmes."

"Well, I'm Alene Garth, and Chuck's Place is my place. And I don't tolerate customers yelling at my employees, you hear?"

Harlan snorted as he looked Alene up and down. "And just what do you think you can do about it?"

"Dammit, Harlan, stand down," Tank said. "These people have been nothing but nice to us, despite you being a total jackass. You start showing some respect to Ms. Garth, or you'll be dealin' with me. Get it?"

Tank shook his head and turned to Alene. "I can't tell you how sorry I am, ma'am. Let me just pay for my friend's drink, and we'll leave you good people alone."

"Not so fast, big guy," Alene said. "Back there in the kitchen, I heard most of what you guys were saying. Sounded to me like you were asking about a fella named Bo Kitner."

"We were. You know my Uncle Bo?"

"I know the name. Just can't come up with a face to go with it."

"Maybe if I describe him, that'll jog your memory," Tank said.

Alene began nodding slowly as Tank gave a detailed description of Bo's physical features. Suddenly her face showed recollection. "Now I remember," she said. "He's the guy who saved my butt a while back on a Buck-Off Wednesday."

"What kind of Wednesday?" Tank asked.

"On Wednesday nights, we knock a buck off the price of domestic beers. It always boosts business a little. But that was the Wednesday right before the Jeep Jamboree, and the island was crawling with tourists. You remember the night, Gerry? You were out sick, and Candis took the night off to take care of you. That made us seriously shorthanded when we got slammed."

"That's right," Candis said. "Now I remember, yah, sure I do. I heard about it the next day, how impossible it was to handle the crowd, until that guy Bo stepped in and got 'er done, with style."

"My Uncle Bo? What'd he do?"

Alene stepped closer to Tank. "Your uncle offered to help out behind the bar. Said he'd been a bartender for most of his life and that he'd do it that night for just the tips. We were so swamped, I took him up on it. And, man, he turned out to be something real special behind that bar. Churning out drinks while spinning bottles and flipping glasses around, like some kind of juggler. They had a nickname for him. It was... dang, I can't think of it now."

Tank smiled. "That's my uncle all right. Bo 'the Mojo' Kitner."

"Yeah," Alene said, "that's what they called him."

"Who's *they*?" Harlan asked abruptly.

Alene turned to him. "What?"

"*Who* had the nickname for him?"

"How about you ask a question nicely for a change?" Candis said, wagging a finger at Harlan.

Harlan took a deep breath and nodded. "You folks are right. I've been a real jerk here today. And there's no excuse for it. I'm sorry. Really, I am. It's just been a long day on the road. And I was looking forward to finally meeting this friend of Bo's who's supposed to show us around."

"Well, I don't know if he's the friend," Alene said, "but the one who called him Mojo is a guy named Bert... a stout fella who moved to the island not long ago, from Traverse City... Bert... uh..."

"Oh my gosh," Tank said. "Bert Brydges! I remember him from—"

Harlan gave Tank a not-so-gentle kick under the counter.

"Uh..." Tank continued, "his... name being on that piece of paper."

"Yep, that's his name all right," Alene said. "He and your Uncle Bo were here that night with another fella who comes here all the time... that guy who works for Bert..."

"Finn Ramsey," Gerry said, chiming in. "He's a regular here on Buck-Off Wednesdays. Never drinks, but knows how to have a good time. Every Wednesday night ole Finn comes in and rules on that pool table over there."

Tank's face beamed with recognition. "Oh, yeah," he said, "That sounds like—"

Harlan kicked him under the counter again.

"Uh…" Tank continued, "a guy who… knows how to have a good time."

"Bert and Finn are newer than most to the island," Gerry said. "Been running a scuba diving center out there on Maxton Bay for what, maybe a year?"

Alene shrugged. "Not sure. Maybe two."

Harlan cleared his throat and asked, "Can any of you tell us the name of the business, *please*?"

Candis smiled at him and said, "Now that's more like it, Mr. Holmes."

"No problem," Gerry said. "Just give me a second and I'll pull up Bert's website online and get you some contact information."

"There's no need to do that," Candis said. "It's right here."

Candis slid a placement off a table and handed it to Harlan. It was covered with advertisements for local businesses. As Harlan took it from her, he could see that she had circled one ad in green ink and put a smiley face next to it. He looked back at her and nodded. She winked in return.

Chapter 26

Tank took a turn driving while Harlan looked online for somewhere to eat on their way to Maxton Bay.

"How about this place at Four Corners?" Harlan asked.

Tank didn't respond.

"Something wrong?"

"Just wish we didn't have to scam those nice people at Chuck's Place."

"What else could we do, Tank? Tell them we've been hired by the mob to hunt down drug smugglers operating on their island?"

"I get your point. But the way you behaved in there, being so mean and all, just makes me feel guilty. Thing is, I don't think it was all acting on your part. You've been pretty moody lately."

Harlan didn't respond.

"Talking about it might do you some good, Boss."

"Might make it worse, too."

An extended silence became uncomfortable. "You're right," Harlan finally said. "I've had some things on my mind."

"Like what?"

"Like what the hell am I doing here? I'm a middle-aged gym manager playing private detective on a mass-murder case that might get real."

"You feeling unsure of yourself?"

"Are you kidding? Think about what happens if we find the guys who blew up that boat, murdered Jimmy, and probably did the same to Bo Kitner—unless he's among those who did the others."

"You think Bo's a suspect?"

"Why not?"

"And Bert Brydges and Finn Ramsey?"

"They were dealing with a lot of money and drugs, Tank."

"But I know these guys. We're all good friends."

"When's the last time you saw any of them?"

Tank shrugged. "Couple years ago, you know, before I got locked up."

"So, none of them ever visited you in prison."

Tank didn't respond.

"And I'll bet they never called or wrote."

Staring at the road ahead, Tank replied, "Doesn't mean they'd try to gun me down."

"Just the same, if we find one alive, we're not going to assume you're still friends. You understand?"

Tank nodded slowly.

"Back when you knew these two, Brydges and Ramsey, did either of them carry?"

"No," Tank quickly answered.

"How can you be so sure?"

"Well, maybe I can't be certain about Finn Ramsey. But I know for sure that Bert Brydges never carried a gun."

"Why's that?"

"Because I worked closely with him. He was my protégé."

"You were training him for something back when you worked for Jimmy?"

"Yeah, to do what I did for Jimmy."

"To be a bagman?"

"Sure. Colleting debts from deadbeat gamblers is not as easy as you might think."

"What, there's an art to it?"

"You could say there is. It's not just about busting people up when they don't pay. You gotta read the player. Figure out if he's bullshitting about needing more time. And you gotta weigh the pros and cons of doing something like breakin' a guy's thumbs. If that puts him out of a job, how's he ever gonna pay up? But if you don't bust his thumbs, is he gonna take you seriously? Those aren't easy calls to make."

"So, you were teaching Bert about how to make those calls?"

"Yeah, and I'll tell you what, the guy was a natural for the job. He'd been a club fighter until he joined up with Jimmy's book. A light heavy with a granite jaw. But he wasn't just a tough guy. He had a heart. It wasn't easy for him to mess up a player the first couple times he had to do it. That's what you want in a bagman. A guy who doesn't like hurting people, but will do it if he has to."

"Did you ever see him box?"

"Only when we sparred."

"And you say he could take a punch."

"He could take mine."

"You're kidding."

"Shit, Boss, I've never seen anything like it. The guy's hands are slow, see, so I was able to pound on his face at will. Every once in a while he'd go down, but he always got back up, usually smiling, like gettin' hit in the face felt good to him."

Chapter 27

"C'mon, man, I'm freezing just standing around out here," Tank complained as he rubbed his hands together. "How much longer 'til we make a move?"

Harlan took advantage of the last few minutes of daylight as he continued to peer between tree branches at a few cabins grouped together where Way Winx Road formed a cul-de-sac along Maxton Bay. They had parked their car about a half mile away and hiked through the woods along the shoreline to get to this spot. No doubt their vantage point made them trespassers on the property of the rustic resort next door.

Through its windows Harlan saw activity in only one cabin, the one with a sign out front advertising "Bertram's Scuba Adventures." The name also appeared on the side of a small utility dinghy tied off next door at the resort's marina.

"I'm still trying to get a fix on who she might be," Harlan answered.

He was referring to the only person they had seen inside the cabin, an attractive woman around age thirty whose short black skirt, high heels, and heavy make-up did not jibe with her actions. She'd been doing mostly housework for the entire hour that they'd been watching.

Between chores she sometimes paced. While pacing she sometimes smoked. Throughout, she frequently looked out the front window, as though she was expecting someone to visit, or perhaps return. Or maybe she was just hoping for one or the other.

She sure doesn't look like a housekeeper, Harlan thought. He turned to Tank and asked, "If she's Bert's wife or girlfriend, would he have told her about you?"

"I'm sure he would have. I was like a big brother to him when we used to work together."

"If you guys were so tight, why didn't you recognize the name of his business when you were checking the Yellow Pages earlier?"

"Because he always went by the name Bert. I never knew that was short for Bertram."

"And I take it you didn't know about his interest in scuba diving either."

"He never mentioned it to me," Tank said, shaking his head. "My guess is that he got into it after Jimmy closed the book. But I'm telling you, Boss, we were close. In his apartment, I remember he used to have a wall full of pictures, all of them family except for a couple of the two of us sparring, like I was just as important to him."

"All right, listen," Harlan said, "in five minutes I want you to call the number for the business. Keep an eye on this woman inside to see if she answers. I think she will. Be straight with her about who you are. And if you think she's someone close to Bert, go ahead and tell her what's been going on with you these past few days. But don't mention me or our client. Lead her to believe that you're on your own, looking for old friends, like Bert and Finn, just like Jimmy asked you to before he died. Your goal is to gain her trust and get inside."

"What will you be doing, Boss?"

"Slipping in through the back and getting a look around before I join you."

"Do you think she'll let me in?"

"Just be yourself, Tank. And take off the hat and glasses. Maybe she'll recognize you as a friend if Bert still has those photos on a wall."

• • • • •

Harlan peered around a corner of the cabin, watching as Tank ended the phone conversation and approached the front door. It opened upon his arrival. He stopped on the porch, exchanged a few words with the woman inside, and then stepped in.

After waiting another minute, Harlan picked the lock on the back door and entered the cabin's utility room. His attention was immediately drawn to some scuba equipment piled loosely on a washer and dryer. On top was an item he assumed was some sort of underwater breathing apparatus. It looked like something one might wear to masquerade as Darth Vader.

He paused at the sound of a woman clearing her throat toward the front of the cabin. She spoke loudly enough for him to hear her voice, though he couldn't make out what she was saying. Whatever it was, her tone seemed pleasant.

Beneath the Darth Vader mask was scuba gear that Harlan more readily recognized: a wetsuit, fins, mask, gloves, gauges, and a four-barreled, hinged-break pistol with words on one side engraved in what he guessed was Russian.

He opened the firearm and tipped it back. What slid out of the chamber was no bullet. It was more like a short spear, or long dart, about five inches in length with a blunt tip and finned tail—hydrodynamic design features that would enable it to cut through water when fired beneath the surface.

Above the washer and dryer were cabinets that contained more equipment, including clear PVC tubing constructed of transparent, heavy-wall plastic and thick endcaps. *Why clear tubing?* he wondered before pausing to imagine how a scuba diver might use it, perhaps to carry something that would be visible underwater to another diver.

Inside a cabinet on the opposite side of the room he found another item of interest. It had to be the briefcase that Zane Hertz had described—an aluminum attaché with dual combination locks and the engraved initials ZDH—unlocked and empty.

The conversation continued up front as he made a quick pass through a bathroom, a hallway closet, and two bedrooms. In the second bedroom he slowed to examine numerous photos that had been left lying on the bed, along with a large envelope.

Many of the photos were of the woman up front and a man with blue eyes and blond hair who looked a few years younger than her. Harlan didn't recognize the guy, but he understood immediately the significance of these superficially mundane photos of him and her coming and going from the same house, sometimes holding hands, and sometimes sharing a kiss and an embrace beside a parked car.

Harlan looked at the nightstand, where there was another picture of the woman up front together with a different man, one with brown hair and dark eyes, who looked a few years older than her. He fit Tank's description of Bert, Harlan recalled.

He had his hands pressed on the foot of the bed as he leaned over the photos when suddenly he felt the poke of cold metal behind his ear—followed immediately by the whisper of a woman's voice.

"Move, and you're dead."

Harlan remained stock still as a hand passed over every part of his body.

She whispered again, "Where's your piece?"

"Don't carry one," he whispered back.

"Bullshit."

Harlan tried to turn before responding.

"I said don't move."

"Okay, okay. I lost my license to carry a couple years back."

"What about your big friend up front?"

"He can't carry either."

"Why?"

"Because he's an ex-con."

"Terrific. What's your story?"

"I'm an ex-PI. Involuntary retirement. Now, how about letting me turn around?"

"Slowly."

He completed the turn and showed his hands. For a moment he looked beyond the gun pointing at him and saw only the woman. She was not at all what he expected. Her hair was as grey as his. She had it pulled back, revealing a face gently seasoned by years that her body had yet to concede.

She leaned toward him and asked, "Who are you?"

He didn't answer. His attention had returned to the compact Glock in her right hand, held steady. It was within reach. He was contemplating making a move for it when a hard left jab split his lower lip and rocked him back on his heels.

"Don't even think about it," she said.

He spit out a mouthful of blood and stared back at her, into eyes so dark they were nearly black. And before he could give it another thought, she did it again—another jackhammer left. This one split his upper lip and dropped him to his butt on the foot of the bed.

"For crying out loud, would you stop hitting me?"

"When you start cooperating. Now tell me who you are."

"I told you already. I'm a retired PI. Or was retired until a couple days ago."

He rubbed his forearm across his face, smearing blood on the sleeve of his jacket.

"Name's Harlan Holmes."

She grabbed a wool hat off a dresser and tossed it to him. "Try using this," she said.

"Thanks a lot," he grumbled.

"So, Mr. Holmes, what kind of case are you and that big guy up front working on?"

"That might be easier to explain if we join him and his friend."

Harlan started to rise from the bed—

"Get back down."

She kept the gun pointed at him but looked away.

"What's the problem?" Harlan said. "Let's just go up there and—"

He paused. From the look on her face he could tell. "You don't know her, do you?" he asked.

"I know who she is."

"But she doesn't know you."

"No, she doesn't."

Harlan reflected on the circumstances: the photos and the sudden appearance of another intruder who must have also been casing the place.

"It's the guy in the photo on the nightstand, her lover, or maybe ex-lover, Bert Brydges, who knows you," he said.

"Yes."

"He's your client."

She nodded.

"And you took those for him," Harlan said, glancing at the photos on the bed.

She nodded her head but stopped at the sound of friendly conversation coming from the front of the house.

"What's your name?" Harlan asked.

"Rosalina Cortez."

"Well, Detective Cortez, if Bert Brydges is the stand-up guy my partner says he is, you and I would seem to be on the same team."

Chapter 28

"I'm coming now," Harlan said as he finished a quick phone call to Tank.

"Why didn't you tell him about me?" Rosalina asked.

"I'll let you do that."

Despite the forewarning, their eyes bulged when Tank and the woman with him saw Harlan and his new acquaintance enter the front room.

"What the hell happened to you, Boss?" Tank asked.

Harlan wiped the wool hat across his busted lips before answering, "I had a little run-in with our new friend here, Ms. Rosalina Cortez."

Rosalina nodded at Tank and the woman with him.

"Looks to me like Ms. Cortez whipped your ass," Tank said, eyeing her up and down.

"Call me Roz, gentlemen. You too, Ms. Pierce."

"You know me?" the woman asked.

"I don't," Harlan interjected.

Tank stood up and said, "Meet Morgan Pierce, Boss. Morgan, this is Harlan Holmes. He's the PI friend of mine who I was just telling you about. Like I was saying, he went around back to check out the place and make sure everything is cool. Isn't that right, Boss?"

Harlan only nodded in response as Ms. Pierce stood to shake his hand. She had big hair, big eyes, and little in the way of a party dress that revealed much of her curvy body. A classic bombshell, Harlan thought, all dressed up with nowhere she could possibly be going on this largely uninhabited island.

"As for my boss's lady friend," Tank continued, "I'm not sure what to tell you, Morgan. I'm only meeting her now for the first time, just like you."

Morgan turned from Harlan to Roz and asked, "How do you know me?"

Roz glanced at Harlan before answering, "I'm also a private eye. Bert hired me to surveil you when he suspected you were having an affair."

"So you're the one who took those pictures."

Roz nodded.

"Well, just how long have you been sneaking around and—"

Morgan stopped herself. After a long pause she sat back down, put her face in her hands, and began crying. The others watched and waited for her to calm down. When she didn't, Harlan went ahead and asked, "Are you expecting Bert?"

"Not anymore."

"What do you mean?"

Morgan pulled something out of her purse and stared at it. It was a picture. Mascara ran with the tears streaming down her face and dripped on it. "I'm the one who was sneaking around and… and… ruined the best thing in my life."

Harlan leaned in for a look. It was one of the photos of her and Blondie.

"Bert slid it under the door at my apartment before he left," Morgan said, "along with a note."

"Before he left for where?"

She shrugged as her tears began flowing harder.

"When did you find it?"

"Why would that matter?" she said.

"Just tell us," Harlan said. "When?"

"A few days ago, Tuesday morning."

"What time?"

"Early."

"How early?"

"C'mon, Boss, ease up," Tank said. "She's been through a lot. They were gonna get married soon."

"I don't think it was light outside yet," Morgan answered.

"Do you still have the note?" Harlan asked.

She flipped the photo over. It was on the back.

"May I?" Harlan asked as he reached for it.

She gave him the photo. It was one of her kissing the young blond-haired man in front of a parked car. The note on the back struck Harlan as odd coming from a jilted lover. Apparently, this one put business ahead of displeasure. The note said:

Morgan,

The combo to the case is 3-7-9 on the left lock and 2-6-8 on the right. Make sure the guys get it.

Goodbye,

Bert

"I assume that's his handwriting?" Harlan said.

She nodded.

"And the combination he gave you is to the locks on that aluminum briefcase in the utility room."

Morgan stopped nodding.

"What briefcase?" Roz asked.

Harlan ignored the question and asked another of Morgan: "Who are the guys he wanted you to give this combination to?"

Morgan's eyes darted around the room, as she said nothing.

"C'mon," Harlan said, "Who are these guys?"

"Boss," Tank intervened, "you need to ease up, I'm telling you."

"Okay," Harlan said, sighing. "We'll talk about them later. Obviously, you've been close to Bert for some time. Can you tell us anything about where he might be or how we can reach him?"

Again, she didn't answer.

"How about his cell number?" Harlan said. "You can at least give us that, can't you?"

"Why should I?" she said.

"Please, Morgan," Tank said. "It's like I've been telling you. My boss and I are just here to help Bert stay clear of some bad people who—"

"I wanna hear it from the *boss*," she said, looking at Harlan. "Why are you asking about *my* Bert?"

She may have looked like a stereotypical party girl, Harlan thought, but that remark made him reevaluate.

"Do you know what almost happened to Tank on the same Tuesday morning that you found this photo?" Harlan asked.

She nodded.

"If we can," he said, "we're going to prevent that from happening to Bert. So please, tell me what you can about him and his possible whereabouts."

Morgan's tears slowed as she answered, "I came here right after I found the picture. Bert was gone. So was his car. He doesn't answer my calls. I don't know where he is or if he's… even…" She paused before asking, "Ms. Cortez, do you know if Bert is okay?"

"He's fine. At least the last time I saw him, he was. But he's not taking any calls, except mine."

"When did you last have contact with him?" Harlan asked.

"I haven't decided yet whether that's any of your business," Roz answered.

"Well, why is he taking only your calls?"

"Because I'm working for him."

"Doing what? I've done infidelity surveillance. Once you get the photos, the job's done."

"It *was* done," Roz said. "He's got me doing something else now."

"More surveillance?"

"Yes."

"Of Morgan?"

Roz sighed as she nodded her head.

"Why?"

"He thought she might be in danger and asked me to keep an eye on her."

"What kind of danger?"

"I don't know. He won't tell me. But even if he did, I wouldn't tell you."

"Why?"

"Because I just caught you breaking into my client's house and snooping around. You might be willing to assume that we're on the same team, Mr. Holmes, but I'm not saying anything further without consulting Bert first."

"It doesn't matter," Harlan said. "I already know."

"What do you know?"

"Well, for starters, I know pretty close to exactly when Bert contacted you for this second job you're doing for him."

"When?"

"Oh, it would have been the same Tuesday we're talking about—this past Tuesday—I believe sometime between 10:45 a.m. and early afternoon."

"All right," Roz said after a long pause. "How do you know that?"

"Because that's when the story of the Northport massacre went viral, and that's when Bert first realized that he and Morgan might be in grave danger."

"The Northport massacre?" Roz said. "How could that have anything to do with…"

Roz suddenly turned to Tank, her eyes widening, and said, "I don't believe anyone's mentioned your name yet, *Mr. Lochner*. But that's who you are: Tank Lochner, the guy all over the news dodging bullets at Shotgun Landing."

"In the flesh, ma'am."

Harlan could practically see Roz's wheels turning as she said, "You think that whoever tried to kill him that day is also after Bert Brydges."

Harlan nodded.

"And that Bert asked me to keep an eye on Morgan because he thought they might be after her too."

"That's right."

"Why?"

"Oh, I dunno," Harlan said with a shrug. "Maybe because they're drug dealers?"

Roz's eyes darted to Morgan and then back to Harlan. "Are you serious?"

"It's a long story, but that's the short of it. For quite some time, Bert's been working with some drug smugglers who've lately been getting whacked or going missing." Harlan looked at Morgan and added, "Though I'm not sure about the extent of her involvement."

Morgan looked at the floor before she answered, "Just a little."

"A little of what?" Roz asked.

"Drug smuggling, like Mr. Holmes said. But I only did the one dive and decided not to do it again. It scared the hell out of me."

Roz shook her head and threw her hands in the air. "A dive? What are you talking about?"

"You know, a scuba dive. I did one of the deals once, underwater, where I met a Canadian diver and gave him cash for drugs."

"Cash that some guys brought to Bert in that aluminum briefcase, right?" Harlan said.

Morgan went silent again.

"Hold on," Roz interrupted. "What kind of drugs was Bert Brydges dealing in?"

Morgan remained silent.

"Do you know anything about the guys Bert answered to?" Harlan asked. "A one-legged bookie named Jimmy or a guy named Shotgun Gino Cruzano?"

"A one-legged bookie? Shotgun who?" Roz asked, as Morgan shook her head.

"That might explain it," Harlan said.

"Explain what?" Roz asked, her eyes rolling in exasperation.

"How she could remain in plain sight and not get killed or kidnapped. She probably kept a safe distance from the guys who drew the fire."

"Look," Roz said. "I don't know who the hell you're talking about, but I wouldn't be so sure she's safe."

A long pause followed as Roz stared into space.

"What is it?" Harlan asked.

Roz didn't respond.

"You've been surveilling her for the last few days," Harlan said, "and you saw something."

She nodded slowly.

Harlan leaned toward her and asked, "Has there been someone

watching her, besides you?"

Roz stopped nodding and answered, "I think so. But he broke off the stakeout about thirty minutes before you arrived, and he's left the island."

"How do you know he's gone?"

"Because I was able to stick a tracking device on his car, and the last time I checked the signal, he was on the Mackinac Bridge heading south."

"You have a name or description? Or maybe one of your surveillance photos?"

"I've already told you more than I should. You get nothing more about this until Bert okays it."

"Oh my gosh," Morgan said, "maybe it was him."

"Who?" Harlan asked.

"I got a text today from someone saying he was Bert. I had my doubts about it. But I wanted to believe it."

"You think that the guy who was watching you sent you a text?" Harlan asked.

"Maybe."

"May I see it?"

Morgan tapped at her cell phone until she found the text and showed it to Harlan. It had been sent that day at 2:30 p.m. It read: "Morgan, it's Bert. We need to talk. Meet me at my place today at 5." The sender ID said, "Anonymous."

"This is why you're here today?" Harlan asked. "To meet a texter who blocked his number and told you he was Bert?"

"I know how stupid I must look right now. But I love Bert. I wanted to believe that I was going to see him."

Morgan walked over to the window and looked out, as if it still might be possible, and cried some more.

Roz moved close to Harlan to see the text, but he turned the phone away and said, "Maybe I should first ask my client if it's okay to share this—you know, because of the duty of confidentiality I owe him as his PI."

"C'mon, Harlan," Roz said as she flashed a smile, "just a quick look."

"How about you give me something?"

"Like what?"

"Morgan says she received that picture of her and Blondie early Tuesday morning. Do you recall when you delivered the photos to Bert?"

She paused before answering, "I hand-delivered them to him here, on Monday night."

"How'd he react?"

"Not surprised. We'd already talked about it on the phone."

"Did you get the impression that he was going to leave town right away?"

"Soon, but he wasn't specific. He insisted on paying for my services. I told him I'd bill him later, but he said he'd be long gone before the bill got here."

Harlan paused to think about timing. "Her affair might have saved his life," he eventually said, glancing at Morgan, "by prompting him to take off before they came for him."

Morgan began crying harder.

Harlan showed Roz the phone. She nodded as she looked at it.

"What are you saying, Boss?" Tank asked.

Roz answered, "The guy surveilling her was actually here for Bert, not her. He texted her only to confirm that she wasn't in contact with Bert and didn't know where he was."

"And after she confirmed that for him, he left," Harlan said.

"How did she do that?" Tank asked.

"By arriving here on time," Roz said, "and waiting for Bert to show."

"Dressed for seduction," Harlan added, "and pacing around nervously when he didn't come home."

Tank's head had been turning back and forth as the two detectives finished each other's thoughts. His gaze stopped on Roz.

"What?" she said.

Tank shrugged and replied, "Just checking to see if you two are done."

Chapter 29

"Well, I guess I'll be on my way," Roz said. "It's been nice meeting you all."

Harlan stepped between her and the door. "You can't just leave."

"I most certainly can. And I must. My client is in danger."

"Please wait," Morgan said. "Would you first tell me where Bert is?"

Roz sighed. "I'm sorry, Morgan, but I've already said too much here. Besides, contact with you right now might not be in Bert's best interest."

"But... but..."

Harlan interjected, "Well, it seems that he still cares about Ms. Pierce, or he wouldn't have hired you to look after her. The least you can do is tell the poor girl where the guy is."

Roz rolled her eyes. "Like you care about this *poor* girl's feelings."

"I'm just saying..."

"Okay, look, I'll tell her this much," Roz said, turning to Morgan. "He's in a safe place, right here on the island."

"What kind of place?" Morgan asked.

"A house where I sometimes hide domestic-abuse victims."

"You put the guy in a battered women's shelter?" Harlan said. He glanced at Tank and added, "a two-hundred-pound club fighter who used to work as a leg-breaker for a bookie?"

Morgan's mouth fell open. "My Bert used to do what?"

"That's right, a shelter," Roz said. "It's a place I use for my more typical clients."

"Victims of domestic abuse?" Harlan asked.

"Yes."

"What exactly do you do for them?"

"I help get the abusers out of their lives."

"How do you do that?"

Tank stepped between them. "You two can get acquainted later," he said. "Listen, Roz, I want to talk to Bert too."

"I'm sorry, but I have to think about what's in his best interest."

"You keep saying that," Tank countered, "like he can't take care of himself. He's a grown man, for crying out loud. Why don't you just call him and let him decide who he wants to talk to?"

Roz looked at Harlan. He raised his eyebrows and shrugged. She returned the gesture and removed her cell phone from her pocket.

While Roz stepped outside to make the call, Harlan went back to the utility room and retrieved a local map that he'd seen there earlier. On his return to the front room, he placed it before Morgan and asked, "Can you show me where you did that dive you mentioned?"

"Right there," she said, pointing at a spot in a narrow channel of water between Drummond Island's Chippewa Point and Canada's St. Joseph Island. "At the wreckage site of the *EJ La Way*."

"A sunken vessel?"

Morgan nodded.

"Is that where all the deals were done?"

"As far as I know."

"And the deal itself, did that involve exchanging a clear PVC tube full of money for drugs?"

"Yeah, so the Canadian guy could see the cash."

"And he had the drugs in a clear container too?"

"Most of them."

"You said you did this only once. Why'd you do it at all?"

Morgan glanced at the floor before responding, "Because I felt like I was losing Bert to his work. He was doing these drug deals on top of his usual business, and I wasn't seeing him at all. It was a way to try to stay close. He didn't like the idea, but I insisted."

"Why not get involved with his legitimate business?"

"Because I'm not a certified scuba instructor."

"But you know how to dive."

She nodded and said, "It was a mistake, though. I can't begin to tell you how scared I was when I rolled into the water with all that cash and that SPP-1 strapped to me."

"The SPP-1..."

"That's the pistol you must've seen in the back."

Roz returned, extending her phone as she said, "He wants to talk to you."

Morgan hurried across the room, but Roz, nodding at Tank, pulled the phone back and said, "Not you—him."

While Tank stepped outside with her phone, Roz joined Harlan. He looked up from the map. Her expression was subdued. "What's wrong?" he asked.

"I just got canned."

"Why would Bert take you off the case?"

"Apparently he has more confidence in Tank Lochner and *his* PI."

"But you're still needed, probably more than any of us. You have the GPS trace going on that guy's car. And you may have taken some surveillance photos that could be useful."

"Look, Harlan, before I say goodbye, I just want to apologize for busting your mouth the way I did."

"What? That? It's no big deal. Besides, I had it coming. The first punch anyway. I really *was* thinking about going for your gun. Now, the second one, that might have been a little much."

His attempt at a smile cracked a clot of dry blood on his lower lip, causing the wound to ooze more blood.

Roz returned a smile and said, "Let me go find something better than that wool hat to treat it with."

"No, I'd rather talk about how we're going to keep you on the job."

"What do you have in mind?"

He paused before answering, "Hiring you myself."

"Not sure you can afford me."

"My client can."

"Tank Lochner?"

"No, my client is..."

He paused to consider how she might respond to this bit of information—that his client was a Chicagoland mobster named Sawed-

Off Gino Cruzano.

"Boss!" Tank shouted, barging back in. "Bert just left that shelter of hers. He's on the move."

"Where to?"

"Mike's house."

"Who's Mike?"

Roz answered, "Blondie."

Chapter 30

"I appreciate your candor," Roz said, "so much that I'm going to do you a huge favor and pretend I never heard a word you said. Now, Harlan Holmes, you can get out of my car. I'm done with this case."

Roz had driven the two of them across the island to Bass Cove. They were parked in front of the same house where she had more than once caught Morgan on camera with her lover, Blondie, who at this point was known as Mike. On the way there, Harlan had spoken frankly about his mobster client and the case in the hopes that his honesty might make Roz willing to help.

It wasn't working.

Harlan opened the passenger door to Roz's vehicle, a Ford Edge, and paused. He glanced across the front yard. On the porch steps sat Tank. He and Morgan had come in her car and texted Harlan when they arrived that Mike wasn't there. *She must be inside with Bert,* Harlan thought, *and the Malibu in the side yard must be his.*

His thoughts returned to Roz and one more desperate shot at changing her mind—a veritable Hail Mary.

"My client's dad may be into some stuff that's illegal," he said, turning to look back at her. "But what's illegal is not always wrong, you know, like what that African American woman did back in the 50s when she wouldn't sit in the back of the bus."

"Are you even serious, Harlan? That was an act of civil disobedience done on behalf of oppressed people. There's no comparison here."

"Well, there kind of is."

Roz rolled her eyes.

"I'm telling you, Roz, there are people in this country who are systematically being denied access to health care, people who really need the kind of prescription meds that Mr. Cruzano..."

"Oh please, Harlan, just stop it. He's a criminal. And you're starting to sound like a complete idiot, like you actually believe his bullshit."

"What I believe, Roz, is that we've seen nothing linking the man directly to anything but his pharmaceutical operation. No evidence of him dealing in any of the other contraband—whatever it is—that seems to be at the root of all the killing."

"So, now you believe this guy Eddy Chub and the alibi he's feeding you. A minute ago you questioned it."

"He just doesn't seem like the kind of guy who could kill in cold blood. Ask Tank. He's a good judge of character, and he's gotten to know Eddy."

"Oh, I see. Your ex-con bagman thinks that the five-hundred-pound mobster with no neck has a soft heart beneath all the blubber."

"And so do I... I think."

"What if you're wrong?"

"Whoever the real bad guys turn out to be, if we find 'em, we turn 'em in."

"So you're asking me to distinguish between bad guys who deal in pharmaceutical drugs and *real* bad guys who deal in serious contraband and kill people."

"Yeah, there's a difference, considering the circumstances."

"And by circumstances, you mean a broken health-care system that some good-natured mobster is single-handedly trying to redress?"

"Basically, yes. Maybe if you talked with Eddy Chub, you'd see what I mean. Could you do that? Just stay with us until you've had a chance to talk to him, maybe by Skype or Facetime, so you can see the guy too? He's not as bad as you think. And this pharmaceutical operation isn't either."

"I don't know, Harlan. I've never been a proponent of situational ethics."

Harlan wasn't sure of what the term meant. It didn't sound good, but then Roz surprised him.

She looked up from her phone and said, "I just Googled this Dr.

Kimble you described. She looks for real."

"That's because she is," Harlan said. "I'm telling you, Roz, I spoke with her at length, and she corroborated everything Eddy Chub said about Shotgun Gino's motives. The man's not making any money on this venture; he's not even trying to, she says."

• • • • •

Roz entered the house ahead of Harlan. He stopped when Tank pulled him aside on the porch.

"I could hear some of that, Boss."

"Hear what?"

"Her yelling at you during your little lovers' quarrel."

"For cryin' out loud, man, what makes you think—"

"But you know what, Boss? I think things are picking up between you two."

"Are you kidding? She called me an idiot."

"Yeah, but at least this time she didn't kick your ass."

Chapter 31

Tank remained on the porch to keep watch as Harlan entered through a now unhinged door that Bert had apparently busted through to get inside.

A real lovers' quarrel was in progress in one of the interior rooms. Harlan paused before entering and listened.

"I don't know what else to say, Bert."

"Well, for starters, Morgan, you can stop making it sound like it was my fault."

"I'm not blaming you. I know I'm the one who messed up. But you made some bad choices too."

"You mean like trying to make some extra money for us to live on?"

"I mean like sending me off to live alone in that apartment while you worked practically 24/7."

"The apartment was for your own good, Morgan. I wanted you to have—"

"I know. Plausible deniability. You keep saying that. But while you were off doing scuba and dealing drugs, I was isolated."

"Isolated? Like hell. You were here, in this house, bangin' a little pretty boy because you were done with your ugly boyfriend."

"Please, Bert. That's not—"

"Okay, you two," Harlan said from the doorway.

They went silent as he entered the large dining room. Everything in it beneath the ornate chandelier was makeshift, including an old, beat-up card table and four folding chairs in the middle. Morgan and Bert sat across from each other at the table.

Roz stood leaning against a wall by a bare window, watching. She raised her eyebrows and shrugged as she looked over at Harlan. The couple had been carrying on this way right in front of her, but at this point had their heads down and were avoiding eye contact with each other and the two elders in the room.

Harlan pulled up a chair at the table and introduced himself to Bert, who eventually looked up but said nothing.

The man *was* ugly. Ten years of club fighting had left him with cauliflower ears, a disfigured nose, and a face that looked beyond its years.

After dabbing her eyes with a tissue, Morgan also looked up. The juxtaposition of her soft features with Bert's worn face explained much about his insecurity. She was way out of his league. Yet they'd been a serious couple for nearly two years, according to what she'd told Tank earlier.

"Where is this pretty boy, Mike?" Harlan asked.

Morgan answered, "Downstate was where he told me he was going, last time I saw him."

"When was that?"

"Probably the last time she came here to get him off," Bert answered.

Harlan raised a hand to stop Morgan from responding and said, "Enough with the arguing, Bert. Why'd you come here, anyway? To kick the guy's ass?"

Bert shook his head and answered, "Tank told me what Jimmy said before he got shot, about how he got into something other than the pharmaceuticals—something that'd deliver a big payday, come winter. Whatever it was, I think he got into it with the Grovers."

"Who?"

"The Grovers, you know, Sully and Randall... and Mike. It's what they called themselves, like they were in some kind of club."

"This guy Mike is one of them too?" Harlan said. "One of the guys Jimmy hired last summer?"

"That's right."

"What makes you think they were into the new product line with Jimmy?"

"What Bo told me."

"After the night of the big storm?"

"Yeah, a few days later. Bo called all pissed off cuz he figured out that Jimmy had something special going with these guys. But Bo said he got in Jimmy's ear and worked it out with him and the Grovers to bring the rest of us into the deal."

"Who do you mean by, *the rest of us*?"

"You know, Jimmy's regular crew, the ones he started with: me, Finn, Bo, Pauly, and the Banwell brothers, Chase and Miles."

"When were you guys gonna get brought in?"

"Last week, after Tank got outta the joint, cuz he was gettin' brought into it too, at least that's what Bo told me. He said that the Northport crew was gonna shove off on Tuesday, after they met Tank, and then the Grovers would show us the new product line a couple days later when the crew got to Drummond. But I called Bo on Monday, the night before they left, and told him I wouldn't be there on account of I needed to blow off some steam." Bert glanced at Morgan and added, "So Bo was gonna loop me in after the meeting. Course it never happened. Everybody on the old crew got whacked or went missing."

"Along with Sully, it would seem," Harlan added.

"Like hell," Bert said. "I'd bet the farm that he's very much alive. He was their leader. Fucking head Grover. Ain't no way he went down with the Northport guys. Son of a bitch took 'em down is what he did."

"Where did Mike fit into the pharmaceutical operation?" Harlan asked.

"Jimmy hired him to work right here on Drummond. I had to teach the little shit and his buddy Randall how to dive, while he was into another kind of diving after hours, down on her fine little—"

"Dammit, Bert," Harlan said, "would you just let me help you here?"

"I'm sorry, Mr. Holmes. I appreciate what you're doing. It's just that after seeing those photos Roz took, I can't stop imagining what went on behind my back."

Bert glanced curiously at Roz.

"She's working with me," Harlan said. "Now tell me about these new guys and this name you're calling them—the Grovers."

"Like I said, it's what they call each other. I don't know why."

"I do," Morgan said. "It has to do with their college days at Michigan State, when they were all members of an anti-frat."

"An anti-frat?" Harlan said.

"Yeah, Mikey told me about it. They were in with a group of guys—anti-frat boys—who lived off campus in a house in East Lansing, on Grove Street. They called themselves Delta Grove, like they were a fraternity. But it was a joke. Mikey said it was more like an animal house than a frat house."

"Is that what you called him? Mikey?" Bert said. "Maybe when the two of you were—"

"I'm not the only one who called him that," Morgan fired back. "You know damn well it's what Sully and Randall called him most of the time."

"How about telling us some full names for these guys," Harlan said, voice raised. "Mike who?"

Roz burst out laughing. Harlan shot her a look. "It's these names," she said. "I can't take it anymore. It's too ridiculous."

"What's ridiculous?" Harlan asked.

"I could tell you the full names they were using, without ever having heard them before."

Harlan cocked his head, confused.

"Mike Wazowski," Roz said. She began poking at her cell phone as she continued speaking. "That's Mikey's full name, am I right? And when they called him by his full name, they often shouted it—Mike Wazowski!"

Bert and Morgan shared a wide-eyed look as they nodded.

"Randall's last name is Boggs," Roz continued, without looking up from her phone until she finished tapping at it. "Sometimes they called him by that last name, Boggs, but most of the time it was Randall—and rarely, Randy."

"How do you..." Morgan said, her mouth remaining open as Roz continued.

"And then of course there's Sully, whose full name—James P. Sullivan—you only heard when he introduced himself to someone for the first time. And when he said it, he was full of pride, like the name had some family significance."

"Here's how I know," Roz said, before Harlan asked. She held out her phone for him to see. It was logged onto a website that described a computer-animated Disney/Pixar movie, *Monsters, Inc.*, and provided images for its lead characters, several monsters with the names Roz had recited.

"You watch Disney cartoons?" Harlan asked.

"I did when my son was eight years old, back when the movie came out. He's now twenty-five. That's about the age of the younger two Grovers, Mike and Randall, though it's hard to say for sure because of their disguises."

"They were disguised?"

"Those two especially well," Roz said. "To do the scuba diving, they must have had advanced hair systems."

"What do you mean?" Harlan asked.

"Systems that required shaving their heads and gluing on hairpieces. It gave them an authentic look. A lot better than Sully's, anyway."

"What was wrong with his?"

"Sully opted for a cheap toupee, which was a bad idea for the color hair he chose."

"A red head?" Harlan said, recalling Tank's description of him.

"Yeah, with a rug that wasn't much better than what a clown wears. And his freckles—oh my god—completely amateur. Looked to me like simple eye shadow dust flicked on by hand. Those spots on his face were never in the same place from one day to the next."

"But if Mikey's and Randall's looks were so much better, how do you know that they were disguised too?" Harlan asked.

"Oh, they were. I'm sure of it. Take Mikey's baby blues; nobody has eyes that pretty. Those were contacts, no doubt. I'll bet they all altered their eye color the same way. And all of them tried to color their eyebrows and what facial hair they had to match up with the color of the fake hair on their heads, but none of them had the match quite right."

"How do you know all this?" Harlan asked.

"Because I saw these guys. And because I used to be a beautician."

"You mean to say that before you became a PI, you styled hair and gave people manicures for a living?"

"You got a problem with that, Harlan?"

"No, of course not," he answered, reflecting on his last job. "I guess you never know what kind of prior experience will prove useful in our line of work. Are you absolutely certain about these disguises?"

"You can probably confirm this," Roz said as she turned to Morgan. "Was Mikey a true blond?"

"You mean… uh… below the waist?"

Roz just stared at her in response.

Bert leaned forward.

Morgan's eyes darted around the room, eventually returning to Roz. "Well… uh… no. He had dark hair down there."

"And I'll bet you got yourself a *real* good look at that!" Bert shouted.

The argument between them resumed. As he was about to intervene, Harlan noticed Roz gesturing for him to join her.

"What's up?"

Roz held her phone between them and showed him a photo. "It's the last one I took of the guy who was watching Morgan today. I think it's Randall Boggs, clean shaven with his hair dyed another color—its natural color, I'm guessing."

She scrolled back to another photo and said, "Here's one of him disguised. Focus on the structure of his face and the shape of his nose. You see that natural flare to his nostrils?"

Harlan nodded as Roz scrolled back to the first photo. The same features were apparent.

"There's one more you should see," she said.

It was a picture of a boat tied off to a dock. Harlan recognized it as the bowrider he'd seen in the video of the Northport massacre. "What about it?" he asked.

"It was here, at Bass Cove, when I took this picture."

"Where's the dock?"

Roz looked through the window and answered, "Out back."

Harlan reached for a light switch and flipped it down.

The darkness quieted the room as he returned to the window. He cupped his hands to the sides of his face and peered out until his eyes adjusted to the dark. "Where's the water?"

"You can't see it from here," Roz said. "There's a rise to the yard, and the trees are too tall. It's a couple hundred yards beyond them."

"What about you, Morgan?" Harlan asked. "Did you ever see the bowrider docked here?"

"No."

"I did," Bert said. "I followed her here once, and it was Sully who answered the door and let her in. But the only cars in the drive were Mike's and hers. So I checked down by the water, and sure enough there was the bowrider. I figured Sully and maybe Randall used it to get here."

"You followed me?" Morgan said.

"I sure as hell did. And later when I asked where you were that night, you lied to me. That's when I hired Roz."

"What made you think…"

"I had my reasons."

It looked like Bert was about to start back in on Morgan.

"Hold on," Harlan said. "Is that why you came here today, Bert? Because you once saw Sully and the bowrider here?"

"That's right, Mr. Holmes. The bowrider had no business being here that day. No pharmaceutical pickup was scheduled. At the time, I didn't know what to make of it. It wasn't until later, when Bo told me about the new product line, that I figured it out."

"Do you think they brought it here?" Harlan asked.

Bert nodded and said, "It's where Mike lived and the other two stayed when they were on the island. Whatever the new product line is, I'm sure it's somewhere around here."

Chapter 32

Roz left the dining room to begin searching the house for a multimillion-dollar stash of contraband. Meanwhile, Harlan took advantage of a lull in the lovers' quarrel.

"Okay, Morgan, earlier you mentioned that the last time you saw Mike, he said he was going downstate for some reason. When was that?"

"Tuesday morning."

"The day of the massacre?"

"Yes, before it happened, when I went to Bert's place after finding the photo he left for me."

"Was Mike there when you arrived?"

"No. He showed up about a half hour later."

"At what time?"

"Seven o'clock."

Harlan paused at her quick and specific answer.

"Exactly seven, Mr. Holmes. I know it was because I went there hoping to see Bert and at first was surprised when Mikey showed up. But then I remembered Bert's note about the combination to the briefcase and how he wanted me to give the guys the cash for the deal. And 7:00 a.m., sharp, was when they always met up at Bert's for that."

Harlan turned to Bert, who explained, "It was supposed to be the last pharmaceutical run for the season. Jimmy wanted it done before the Northport crew got here to see the new product line, so they could pick up the meds while they were here."

"Was Mike supposed to do the run with someone else too?" Harlan asked.

"With me," Bert said. "We always did it in twos—one on the boat, one in the water. It used to be Finn Ramsey and me before Jimmy brought on the Grovers. And then when they came along—for the uptick in pharmaceutical runs, Jimmy said—Mike was supposed to rotate in with me or Finn. That day he was gonna rotate in with me, even though…"

Something interrupted Bert's train of thought.

"Even though *what*?" Harlan asked.

"Even though his buddy Randall was on the island that day, and Mike liked partnering with him when he could."

"I thought Randall worked out of Northport," Harlan said.

"He did," Bert replied. "But he liked doing the dives more and sometimes worked it out with the Banwells so he could hang here on Drummond and work on this end with Mike. But for that last run, Mike specifically said that he wanted to do it with me."

"Even though Randall was here," Harlan said.

"But it ended up being Randall anyway," Morgan said, "with Finn."

"Randall and Finn?" Bert said.

"Where's Finn right now?" Harlan asked.

Morgan and Bert both shrugged. "I've been trying to get ahold of him since Tuesday afternoon," Bert said, "but he doesn't answer my calls."

"Try calling him right now," Harlan said.

Harlan then turned to Morgan and said, "Tell me everything you remember about that morning, starting with the first thing Mike said when he arrived."

"As I recall, the first thing he wanted to know was where Bert was. I told him…"

• • • • •

"Bert's not here."

Mike looked at his watch. "He hasn't forgotten about the run today, has he?"

When Morgan didn't answer, Mike smiled and stepped close. She could feel his breath on her neck as he spoke. It was a familiar move.

"Well, how long 'til he gets back?"

"Get away from me, Mike."

"What's the problem, baby? Wrong time of the month?"

Morgan snatched the photo from her purse. "Here's the problem," she said.

It was the photo taken at Bass Cove of the two of them kissing. Mike looked up from it and asked, "Where'd this come from?"

Morgan flipped the photo over. "That's Bert's writing. He slipped it under my door sometime before I woke up this morning, probably on his way outta here."

Mike continued studying Bert's note on the back of the photo. "Where's the briefcase?" he asked.

"Fuck you, Mikey. Why should I give it to you?"

"Dammit, Morgan, he told you to, right here in this note. And now I'm telling you to. Just give it to me."

"I'll think about it."

He looked out a window facing the drive where Bert's car was usually parked and sighed deeply. "You think he left the island?"

"That's my guess."

"And you have no idea where he's going or how long he'll be gone?"

"I doubt *he* has any idea. He's hurting right now. And it's all because of…"

"Who took the picture?" Mike asked.

"What?"

"The fucking picture of you and me kissing—who took it?"

"I don't know. Maybe he did. What the hell difference does that make?"

"Are there others?"

"Yeah, in the master bedroom."

She remained in the kitchen after Mike left; soon she heard him shout a random string of profanities from down the hall. Seconds later he returned to the kitchen carrying a large envelope. It looked like the one Morgan had seen before on the bed beside the photos.

"The loser may have fucked us all!" Mike shouted.

"He's not a loser, you conceited bastard."

"Oh, I see, you think the doofus is still your boyfriend."

"Well... I..."

"Do you have any idea what that dumb ass did? He went and hired a PI to spy on us."

"What are you talking about, Mike?"

He slammed the envelope on the counter. On it was written, "Bert Brydges." That side of the envelope must have been facing down on the bed when she saw it earlier. She hadn't turned the envelope over.

"If he took the photos," Mike said, "he wouldn't have put them in an envelope addressed to himself. He hired a fucking PI."

What Mike was saying made sense, Morgan thought, not to mention that the handwriting on the envelope clearly wasn't Bert's. "Okay," she said, "maybe he did. So what?"

"So what?" Mike shouted as he began pacing the room. He ripped open a stick of gum and stuffed it into his mouth. After tossing the foil wrapper to the floor, he immediately ripped into another.

"Don't you see?" he said before stuffing the second stick into his mouth. "Whoever's been spying on you and me could've seen what's been going on around here."

"You mean the drug smuggling?"

"Of course that's what I mean," Mike said, glancing around as if it were even possible that someone might overhear them. He reached for another stick of gum.

"But all the photos were taken at Bass Cove," Morgan said. "Nothing went on out there, other than me ruining my life for a fling with a complete jerk."

Mike stopped pacing. "I take it he doesn't answer your calls."

She shook her head.

"Well, he sure as hell isn't going to answer mine." As he said this, however, Mike unlocked his cellphone.

"Who you calling?" Morgan asked.

"Finn Ramsey."

"I've already tried him," Morgan said. "He doesn't know where Bert is and can't get through to him either."

"Yeah, it's me," Mike said into the phone. "You need to get to Bert's place. He's a no-show for our last run... Because I was screwing his woman, and he found out… What can I say, man? It's not like this island is crawling with tail… Okay, Finn, how about we discuss this later? Right now, I need you to step in for Bert on this run… Yeah, be here in thirty minutes."

After he ended the call, Mike made another. "Randall, hey, it's me. Bert Brydges is missing… He found out I've been banging his woman and blew town… She's right here, sobbing over the bonehead. Look, I need you to do the run… No, with Finn Ramsey… Uh huh, in thirty minutes… Don't worry about the other thing. I'll deal with it."

As he ended the call, Mike left for the utility room. Morgan followed and watched from the doorway as he began organizing the scuba gear. She then headed back to Bert's bedroom. After another long look at the photos on the bed, she dropped the envelope back beside them and turned for the door.

Mike was standing in the doorway holding an empty PVC tube. "Finn and Randall are gonna need that briefcase when they get here," he said.

Morgan held his stare as she responded, "I'll give it to them, but not because you're telling me to."

He tossed the PVC tube onto the bed and said, "I don't give a shit why. Just make sure you do it." Then he turned and began walking away.

"That's it, Mike? You're just gonna walk outta here like nothing happened?"

He didn't respond.

"Where the hell are you going, Mike?"

"I got urgent business downstate," he said as he continued walking. She followed. He stopped at the door, looked back, and added, "If you ever see your loser boyfriend again, make sure to tell him how much I enjoyed mixing my pleasure with his business."

Chapter 33

Harlan stood by the dining room window, looking out, as Morgan finished her story.

"Randall and Finn got there about a half hour later, like Mike told them to."

"Together?" Harlan asked.

"No. Randall got there first by a few minutes."

"What'd they do?"

"Collected the gear and money and took it out to the boat. Last I saw, they were on the bay, heading toward the channel."

As he continued looking out the window, his back to Morgan and Bert, Harlan saw a flashlight cut through the darkness. It stopped beside a pole barn near the tree line. Roz had apparently moved her search outside.

"So you never saw them bring the boat back," Harlan said.

"No, and now that you mention it, I never saw the boat again either."

"My Carolina Skiff?" Bert said. "It's gone?"

"I think so," Morgan answered. "It wasn't in the marina today. Just the dinghy."

"What about cars?" Harlan said. "You say Randall and Finn arrived separately. Are either of their cars still parked near the scuba shop?"

After a pause, Morgan nodded slowly and said, "Not Randall's, but Finn's car is."

"In the same spot as it was Tuesday morning?"

"I don't know. I didn't see where he parked when he got there."

Bert looked at his phone and then back at Harlan, who asked, "Still no call or text from him?"

"Nothing," Bert said.

"Did you ever see Mikey chew gum that way before?" Harlan asked, turning back to Morgan.

"Not that I recall."

"I did," Bert said, "when he was uptight, like he was the first few times I took him out for pharmaceutical runs. He was like a nervous chain smoker, only for him the fix was gum."

"What'd you see him do with the wrappers?"

"Same thing she saw. No matter how many times I told him to knock it off, he kept tossing them on the floor of the skiff. Most were ending up in the water. It's bad for the wildlife. But it's like he couldn't control himself once he started tearing into them."

Harlan thought about timing. It was shortly after 7:00 a.m. when Mike had left the island. Plenty of time to get to Bo Kitner's trailer in St. Ignace, where he could lie in wait, chain chewing gum, until later that morning when he'd do "the other thing" he'd mentioned during his phone call to Randall.

And he could have remained in St. Ignace to check out Zane Hertz with a call from Bo's phone claiming he was Eddy Chub, and later to make a personal visit to the souvenir shop as the menacing nerd. The nerd who carried something shaped like a pack of gum in his shirt pocket, Zane had said.

But Zane had also said that his hair was jet black.

"Morgan, was Mike still a blue-eyed blond when you last saw him?"

She looked surprised by the question, but then nodded.

• • • • •

Tank was in the driveway rummaging through the back of Roz's SUV when Harlan, Bert, and Morgan came out of the house. Leaning against the vehicle was a Remington bolt-action rifle.

"What's with the gun?" Harlan asked.

"Don't know," Tank answered. "Roz just said she needs it, along with a few other things that she asked me to get for her."

"What other things?"

"Some cartridges, a wire coat hanger, and this pry bar set," Tank said as he removed the tools from the SUV and placed them in a backpack sitting next to the rifle.

"She also has some wire snips back here," Tank added, "but I can't find 'em."

"I'll get them and take this stuff out to her," Harlan said. "There are some things I want you and these two to do, assuming they can get along well enough to work together."

Morgan nodded immediately. After a pause, Bert did too.

"Good," Harlan said, "because you two are the best witnesses we have to ID these Grovers."

Bert and Morgan pulled closer as Harlan began giving instructions.

"I want you two to go back to Bert's place and run some internet searches for the real names of these guys. Focus first on Randall Boggs. Roz is going to text you a photo that might be of him without his disguise. Try to get something on him from this anti-frat of his, Delta Grove, maybe from a website or Facebook page with photos that you can compare. If he's the age Roz estimates, he could've graduated three or four years ago, so he might not be a current member. And don't limit your search to Randall. Look for these other guys too—Mike and Sully—based on the way they're built, their facial structures, and any distinctive features you might remember, you know, skin blemishes, scars, that kind of thing."

Morgan's face flashed with realization. "What is it?" Harlan asked.

She nodded slowly and answered, "Something about Mike that's distinctive, but not about his face or skin."

"Oh, don't tell me," Bert said, "we're gonna hear more about what he has going on below the waist."

"No, not below his waist. Above it. Right above it. I'm sure you've seen it too, Bert, when he took off his wet suit."

After a pause, Bert said, "You mean his navel?"

"Yeah, isn't it the ugliest one you've ever seen?"

"Probably the only thing about the son of a bitch that's *not* pretty."

"An outie?" Harlan asked.

"A huge, twisted outie," Morgan said. "Yet he seemed proud of it, the way he walked around the house shirtless all the time so everyone could see it."

Harlan shared a glance with Tank, who shrugged before asking, "What about me, Boss? Should I go with them?"

"You'll take one of their cars and join them. But first I want you to do something with the front door that Bert busted through when he got here. Check inside for tools you might need, and fix it as best as you can." As he said this, Harlan removed a piece of paper from his wallet and handed it to Tank.

"That's the password information and name of the app that Roz is using to track Randall's car right now. Last she said, it was moving southbound on US 127, approaching Mount Pleasant. Download the app and keep an eye on it. If the car stops, try to get the address and any other information you can find online about where he's at."

"Got it, Boss. Anything else you want me to do?"

"One other thing. I'm going to ask Roz to text you some photos of Mikey and his baby-blue eyes. I want you to forward them to Sam Boadle and ask her if he might be the same blue-eyed guy who she ran into at Jimmy's Charter Fishing on the night of the storm."

After he sent them off, Harlan searched the back of Roz's SUV for the last of the items she'd requested. She had an impressive supply of PI gear stashed beneath the spare tire, including some tiny spy cams and GPS trackers of the same brands he once used.

Chapter 34

"What are you doing up there?" Harlan asked as he joined Roz. She was up in a tree next to the pole barn shining her flashlight along its roofline.

"Just making sure there aren't any others."

"Other what?"

"Security cameras."

Harlan spun his head. "Out here? Recording us now?"

"I don't think so. It looks like there's just the one inside."

"In the pole barn?"

"Pretty odd, don't you think? The only security device I can find on the premises is in an outbuilding."

Roz hopped down from the tree and directed him to a window as she pointed her flashlight through it. "Take a look."

"At what?"

"Here, try with this," she said, handing him a spy glass.

Harlan focused on the spot again and eventually saw it between two rags hanging on the far wall, a dark circle about the diameter of a number two pencil, the lens of a camera.

"Geez, Roz, how did you notice that?"

"Just being thorough."

"And you're sure it's the only one?"

"No. But I'm done looking. Let me see the backpack."

Roz removed the pry bar set from the pack and worked the thinnest bar between the window's bottom rail and sill. Then she inserted a thicker bar.

"You must have a lock-pick set in the back of your car," Harlan said, glancing back at a service door for the pole barn.

"The door's too close."

"To the camera?"

Roz nodded as she began working the hanger through the gap created by the pry bars. "It probably has a motion detector."

"Well, how do you know that this window is out of range?"

"I don't. I just know it's farther away than the door."

"So, right now, you have no idea whether that camera has been activated by what you're doing."

"True. But I haven't heard an angry homeowner shouting at us through a speaker yet. Have you?"

"Maybe there won't be a warning."

"Then we better be ready."

"Is that what the rifle is for?"

Looking over her shoulder at him, Roz said, "For a guy who once made a living doing this, you sure do ask a lot of dumb questions. How about telling me what you learned from Bert."

While Harlan explained what Bert and Morgan had told him earlier, Roz continued working the hooked end of the hanger toward an interior latch on the window's side jamb.

She paused when the hook reached the latch and said, "So you think Randall Boggs stayed on the island and killed Finn Ramsey while Mike Wazowski went to St. Ignace to kill Bo Kitner and deal with his nephew, Zane Hertz?"

"It all fits, don't you think? The way Finn went missing after going out alone with Randall for a dive. And the way Mikey chews gum and tosses the wrappers, just like whoever tossed the ones outside Bo's trailer and maybe showed up later at the souvenir shop as the nerd with a pack of gum in his pocket."

"Maybe."

"Well, given your experience as a beautician, you tell me. How hard would it have been for Mike to color his hair black to pull off the nerd disguise?"

"That would have been the easy part," Roz said. "All he needed was some colored hairspray or hair chalk. If it was jet black, the way Zane

Hertz described it, he might have used cheap costume stuff, or maybe simple shoe polish or hair mascara, though the thought of using that stuff makes the beautician in me cringe."

"Are you going to open that window?" Harlan asked.

Roz flipped the latch. But before sliding the window, she said, "So, your theory is that the Grovers were more than just a little upset when they learned that Jimmy had told his regular crew about a new product line and how they were going to share in its profits, come winter."

"Something like that," Harlan said.

"And if the Grovers were going to eliminate all those unwanted partners, they might as well get rid of Jimmy too... and maybe Shotgun Gino."

Harlan didn't respond. He still wanted to believe that Shotgun had nothing to do with the new product line.

"Your theory is short one Grover," Roz said, changing the subject.

"I know. The sniper."

"But I might be able to help you with that."

"Do you know something about a fourth, Roz?"

"I'll tell you inside."

Chapter 35

Roz rested the rifle on the window sill, leaned over it, and pointed it at the camera.

"What are you doing?" Harlan asked.

"I'm gonna shoot it out."

"Hold on, Roz. Think about what you're doing. Destroying the thing is bound to set off an alarm somewhere."

"I'm sure all it'll do is signal outage," she replied, "the same as it would if its battery simply died or it malfunctioned—which is what those Grovers will think as long as we haven't set off a motion detector."

"How do you know?"

She placed her right cheek against the stock and stared down the sights.

"Because that's what my wireless cameras would do."

After thinking for a moment about the brand, Harlan started for the pole barn's other window to see if he could determine whether this one might be the same or similar.

"Where you going?" Roz said.

"To look at it from another angle."

"You're not going to see it any better from over there. Now get back here, would you? I need your help."

"With what?"

"I want you to shine the flashlight over my shoulder, down the gun barrel, and illuminate my target."

He hesitated.

"C'mon, Harlan, get in here," she said, her finger still on the trigger guard.

After a quick look around at the darkened homes of distant neighbors, he stepped in close behind her—directly behind her due to encroaching bushes to each side of the window—and leaned over her with one hand on the sill beside her and his other holding the flashlight over her shoulder. As he aimed the light, his imagination strayed to the position of their bodies and what it was perfectly suited for, but for their clothing.

Looking for a distraction, Harlan turned his attention to the side of Roz's face. She was breathing slowly, in through her nose, out through pursed lips. It was the same technique he would have used to promote deep, diaphragmatic breathing and still himself for a shot requiring a high degree of accuracy, as this one did. The target was at least a hundred feet away, and it was as small as a ping pong ball if the camera behind the tiny lens was like one of her cameras.

Harlan sensed that the breath she then drew in was the one. If her technique remained the same as his, she would wait through the exhale for her natural respiratory pause—a three-to-five-second interval—during which she'd gently squeeze the trigger until…

"Hey, Boss," suddenly came a voice from behind, followed by the sound of a throat clearing.

"What the hell!" Roz shouted as she jerked up and slammed the back of her head into Harlan's face. The blow reopened his busted lips.

"Tank?" Harlan shouted through the flow of blood.

"Yeah, Boss. Sorry to interrupt. Can I have a word with you?"

Holding out his phone as Harlan approached, Tank said, "It's the password you gave me for the GPS app running on that guy's car. I can't get it to work."

Roz must have overheard. Before Harlan could take the phone, she said, "You need to capitalize the first two letters."

Tank pulled the phone back and tried again. "There we go," he said. A moment later he added, "Hey, check it out, the car isn't moving."

Harlan shared a look at the screen as Tank zoomed in, gradually revealing the exact location of the signal from Randall's parked car. It was coming from a residential area in East Lansing, Michigan, on Grove

Street.

"Looks like you have an address to work with when you get back to Bert's place," Harlan said.

Tank nodded as he stepped closer to Harlan. "You know, Boss," he whispered, "there are better ways to go about what you two were doing over there behind those bushes."

"What are you talking about? We were just trying to get inside the pole barn."

"Sure, Boss."

Chapter 36

What a mess, Harlan thought as he directed the beam of his flashlight around the pole barn's spacious interior. He surmised from the layer of dust and dirt that the eclectic collection of old junk inside belonged to Mike Wazowski's landlord—except, perhaps, something large in the middle of the room, on the floor, covered with a tarp that, unlike everything else, was spotless.

Roz flipped a row of light switches as Harlan removed the tarp. Beneath the bright lights there appeared three shiny new crafts that at first he thought were airboats, and then he thought might be snowmobiles, and then he decided were a combination of the two. Each had a huge fan mounted behind an enclosed hull that sat on a set of skis, about twelve feet long, running beneath the hull's outer edges.

Harlan separated one of the hybrids from the other two for a closer inspection. It slid along the floor with relative ease because of the material used to construct the hull—lightweight carbon fiber—which he recognized from a characteristic weave pattern on its surface.

Expensive and versatile, he thought, as he studied the enormous fan and outboard engine, wide skis, and rigid hull. Such design features would enable it to propel over virtually any waterway, whether its surface be water, snow, ice, or any combination of the three.

"I've never seen anything like that," Roz said as she joined Harlan.

"I have, something similar anyway. I think it's a modern-day version of what the locals here once called an aero sleigh."

"A what?"

"An aero sleigh—a mode of transportation used by some people on

Drummond Island a long time ago. Tank told me about it."

"Tank?"

"Yeah. Some tourist magazine he's been reading says the temp drops so low here in the winter that the North Channel freezes over in places, creating an ice bridge to Canada. Years ago, before snowmobiles were invented, some islanders started using these so-called aero sleighs to cross over the ice. Tank showed me an old picture of one. It was a much cruder craft in those days, but the concept was the same: a fan-propelled platform on skis."

"Interesting."

"Oh, but I haven't even told you the most fascinating part, Roz."

"And that would be…"

"The cargo that some aero sleighs hauled back from Canada *during the prohibition era.*"

"No way—liquor?"

Harlan nodded at a large map of Drummond Island on the wall behind Roz and said, "Looks like the Grovers might be aiming to bring back an old bootlegging tradition."

While Roz looked at the map, Harlan used his cell phone to search the web for information about the ice bridge to Canada across the North Channel. He quickly learned that in recent years the bridge had been popularized as the "Christmas Tree Trail" by winter sports enthusiasts who annually marked the safest route with evergreen trees. The route had also come under the close scrutiny of US Customs since the events of 9/11.

"It's too high profile," Harlan said, looking up from his phone.

"What is?" Roz asked.

"The ice bridge across the North Channel. I just Googled it and—"

"What about the False DeTour Passage?" Roz asked.

"Where's that?"

"Right here, by Bass Cove," Roz said, using the map to point out a channel of water on the southeast side of the island. "It's also right outside the window over there."

Harlan went to the window. It was the one Roz had opened earlier when she shot out the security camera. From that vantage point he could see, just barely, the water's rippling surface beneath the lights of the night sky.

So that's it, Harlan thought, recalling another of the lessons learned from the tourist magazine. It had told of *two* waterways that mariners might choose from to go around the island for northern destinations: DeTour Passage, which provided a direct route north along the island's western edge; and False DeTour Passage, the one before him, which meandered northeast around much of the island before returning west.

According to the magazine, False DeTour was the narrowest passage of water separating Drummond Island from Canada, and the decision to run the international boundary through it might have resulted from a border-drawing ruse played out two centuries ago by American surveyors while on board a vessel with British counterparts. As the magazine told the story, the lead British surveyor—while hung over after an evening of too many cocktails—was led to believe that the false detour was the direct one, which resulted in the drawing of a circuitous international border that essentially carved Drummond Island—the Gem of the Huron—out of Canadian waters and gave it to the United States.

Still staring out the window, Harlan recalled the proximity of the convoluted border and the land mass just beyond it, less than two miles away—Cockburn Island, Canada.

"Well?" Roz said.

Harlan turned from the window. "Well what?"

"Did that magazine say anything about an ice bridge forming over False DeTour Passage?"

"Not that I recall."

They both started tapping at their smartphones, Roz with both thumbs flying, Harlan with one finger hunting and pecking.

"What do ya got?" Roz asked.

"Hell, I got nothing. Haven't even hit search yet."

Harlan walked over and looked at Roz's phone. "Every link takes you to something about that Christmas Tree Trail on the North Channel," she said. "There's nothing about any ice bridge on this side of the island, except... wait... check this out."

The print was small. Harlan hesitated, but then pulled a pair of reading glasses from his pocket. He looked at Roz before putting them on.

"Go ahead," she said. "If it'll make you feel any better, I'll wear mine too."

The spectacled detectives stared down at the fine print on Roz's phone. It was a conversation among some bloggers discussing the adventures of one, referred to as "Snow Daddy," who boasted of having traversed False DeTour by snowmobile. The other bloggers were skeptical.

"Bullshit, Daddy. Nobody does False DeTour. It doesn't ice over. It's too close to the big water."

"It ices enough," Snow Daddy replied. "The window's in February. Around the middle for a couple weeks. You can make it if you ride flat out, so if you have to, you can hydroplane over the weak spots."

"You hydroplaned to Canada? Now I know you're full of it, Daddy."

"Don't know one way or the other. Never looked back."

Both detectives looked up from the phone, over the tops of their glasses, at the shiny new aero sleighs—machines equipped for more than hydroplaning. Much more.

"Come winter," Harlan recalled out loud, "that's when Jimmy said the drop would happen."

"Those sleighs might not be the only technology the Grovers are planning to use," Roz said.

"What do you mean?"

"There were a couple small drone copters, fully assembled, in one of the upstairs bedrooms. Toys, I thought, when I saw them. But now..."

"Equipped with cameras?"

Roz nodded and said, "For recon, I imagine."

Harlan turned to the map on the wall, focused on False DeTour Passage, and imagined its condition in the dead of winter. There'd be too much ice for boats, and too little for winter sports. "Surveillance by air would eliminate virtually all risk," he said. "Can't imagine anything going on out there anyway, assuming the Canadian side is as quiet as this side."

No sooner had Harlan completed the thought than Roz finished tapping at her phone. “Guess what the population of Cockburn Island is in the dead of winter?” she asked.

Harlan shrugged.

“Zero.”

His expression must have shown disbelief, until she held out her phone and showed him the Wikipedia website.

“We need to find the cargo,” he said, returning his gaze to the junk-filled pole barn.

Chapter 37

They were digging through a cabinet filled with an odd assortment of things when Roz came across a burlap bag. Harlan noticed her pause to study its contents.

"What is it?" he asked.

She turned the bag over rather than explain. Out of it spilled a pile of sports apparel and accessories that Harlan immediately associated with his own alma mater, Michigan State University.

Harlan stared down at the gear, sensing that it had some significance to Roz.

"You want to hear about him?" she asked.

"Who?"

"The one I mentioned earlier."

"The fourth Grover?" he said, looking up at her.

Her eyes stared back, but not into his, as she slowly nodded.

"Are you okay, Roz?"

She ignored the question and said, "You mentioned visiting Chuck's Place when you got to the island today."

"Is that where you saw him?"

"Yeah, along with the other three for the first time."

"When?"

"The first weekend after I took the case. I told Bert to make up an excuse to leave the island that weekend without Morgan—maybe tell her he was going to a bachelor's party downstate—so I could see what she'd do. That Saturday I followed her to the bar…"

• • • • •

Roz pulled into one of the few open spaces that remained in the parking lot as she watched Morgan approach the entrance to Chuck's Place. The clamor of satisfied customers poured out as the door swung open, and it could still be heard, though muffled, when the door closed. She decided to join them.

College football season was just getting underway, and a more than ample supply of beverages and widescreen TVs had drawn the crowd there that day, most in green and white garb, to watch their nationally ranked Spartans' home opener against the Western Michigan Broncos.

Something hushed the crowd, however—all except a small group of Broncos fans sitting at a corner table. Their distant cheer caught Roz's attention. She had just found a place to stand at the bar and glanced up at one of the widescreens. It was a few minutes into the first quarter and the Broncos had kicked a field goal to go up 3-0 on the heavily favored Spartans.

"Don't mean shit!" shouted the largest of four men at the table Morgan had joined. Rumbles of agreement came from the other three.

All four wore extreme fan gear and had painted their faces half green and half white. Most extreme among them, to be sure, was the foul-mouthed big guy. He wore an inflatable Spartan football helmet over his painted face, a green spandex body suit over everything beneath his neck, and a giant, bright-white "S" on his chest.

Roz eventually ordered a soft drink and sipped on it and a refill until halftime. All the while, she kept her focus on a mirror behind the bar, where she could watch Morgan and her companions as the game and their consumption of beer progressed.

It was a good first half for Spartan fans. After the Broncos' field goal, the Spartans scored twenty-seven unanswered points: three touchdowns, three extra points, and two field goals. And, upon every one of those scores, two of the men at Morgan's table took a turn chugging full schooners of beer to chants from the other two of "Grover! Grover! Grover!"

Roz had no idea what the term meant, and their varied use of it throughout the first half was nonsensical. "We're in the Grove zone, baby!" was one use of the term Roz overheard when the Spartans advanced the football inside the Broncos' twenty-yard line. Another use began when the Spartans took over the line of scrimmage late in the half. One of the men repeatedly shouted, "Grove it down their throats, Sparty!" as his team pounded the football up the middle, eating up yardage and building time of possession.

The most obnoxious use of the term, however, occurred during a break in the action. It was halftime and Roz was returning from the bathroom when it happened. While stuck in a bottleneck of patrons in front of the men's room, she suddenly felt a large hand grab her butt and squeeze hard. She spun around and froze at the sight of the man who had assaulted her—the large, foul-mouthed Spartan fanatic from Morgan's table. As if feeding off her shock, he leaned in toward her, close enough for her to smell the beer on his breath, and spoke through the mask of his inflatable helmet—

"You're looking mighty fine for a woman who's fightin' age. How would you like to go somewhere quiet for a taste of young Grover?"

Forgetting the job she was there to do, Roz impulsively drew back her fist and was about to unload when there came a shout—"Make way!"—followed by two of the other Grovers who pushed their way in front of her to gain access to the men's room, one of them puking everywhere. Roz jumped back to avoid flying barf and nearly fell when she collided with another patron. She regained her balance in time to catch only a glimpse of her assailant disappearing into the men's room with his two buddies.

• • • • •

Harlan had returned his stare to the pile of fan gear still on the floor of the pole barn, struggling to focus on what Roz said next because her story, thus far, had evoked a troubling memory of his own. At this point, she was explaining how she later learned that her assailant was the one they called Randall, but she never caught the name of the fourth Grover and would not be able to identify him based on what she'd seen of him in costume that day.

"Harlan?" Roz said when she finished.

His mind had drifted somewhere else by this point, and his fists and teeth had become tightly clenched, though he didn't realize it until she said with a raised voice, "Harlan, are you okay?"

He slowed his breathing to calm himself.

"Did my story stir up something inside?"

He nodded.

"A memory of a similar experience suffered by someone in your life?"

"My daughter, during her freshman year in college. It still pains her to this day."

"And, it would seem, her father," Roz said as she placed a hand on his shoulder. He wasn't sure where the tremble he felt was coming from—her hand, his shoulder, or perhaps both.

The exchange reminded him of something Roz had said earlier about the nature of her PI practice. "These clients of yours who've suffered domestic violence," he asked, "what exactly do you do for them?"

"I'll tell you later, after we find whatever it is these Grovers are planning to aero sleigh to Canada."

Chapter 38

They both checked the time. It was straight-up twelve midnight.

"We've been over every square inch of this damn pole barn," Roz said as she sat down on the side of one of the sleighs. "What do you think, Harlan, should we start tearing into the walls?"

He didn't answer.

"Harlan, what is it?"

He was standing in front of a large circuit-breaker panel on one of the walls, looking back and forth between it and an electrical junction box above the door on the opposite side of the barn. Wires and a cable connected to the junction box were exposed. He nodded at it and said, "It looks like the cable coming into that box enters from outside, through the wall."

Roz stepped over to a window along the wall, opened it, and leaned out with her flashlight. She looked back at Harlan and nodded.

He joined her at the window and leaned out as well. A length of PVC piping, extending from the ground and up the wall, ended where the cable to the junction box entered inside.

Directly across the yard he saw a shorter length of PVC piping on the side of the house, extending from the ground to a point where the foundation ended. "And it originates there, in the house, transmitting power from there to this pole barn," he said.

"Apparently so," Roz said.

"Then what's the breaker panel for?" he asked as he traced the beam of his flashlight over some exposed wires connected to the light fixtures overhead. They ran not from the breaker panel, but from the junction box.

He returned to the other side of the pole barn and opened a window on the wall to which the breaker panel was attached. "I don't see anything coming through this wall to the breaker panel—no cable or wire, no PVC—nothing coming into this side of the pole barn from outside."

Roz joined him, stepped close to the wall, and tapped her knuckles on its drywall finish. "Sounds like there's plenty of space in there," she said, "enough for an independent cable coming up underground, inside the wall, where the rest of the circuitry could be. Maybe the line from the house to the junction box is an old one that's no longer used."

"But the ceiling isn't finished, and the only wires we see up there come from the junction box. Where are the ones from this breaker panel?"

"I dunno. It's a high ceiling. And there are lots of ways to hide a wire."

"Maybe," Harlan said as he reached for the breaker panel and began flipping switches to the off position.

When he had finished, the lights above still shone.

Roz raised her eyebrows and shrugged. "Either the breaker panel services the other outlets in here, or it's..."

She grabbed a small fan and walked it around the pole barn, plugging it into various outlets along the way. It ran in all of them, including an outlet directly beneath the breaker panel, while all of its switches remained off.

The two stood next to each other, studying the panel. "Twenty-two switches," Harlan said, "and not one of them goes to any of the lights or outlets."

Harlan walked over to a workbench and began shuffling through a mess of tools when Roz started laughing. "Pick up your head, Harlan. There's a whole row of screwdrivers hanging right in front of your face. We need a large flat-headed one."

She continued laughing as he returned. "I don't think I've ever seen such a sudden onset of *man eyes* before."

"Say what?" Harlan asked as he began unfastening the breaker panel. "What are man eyes?"

"It's a way of describing how a man can be looking for something, say, inside a refrigerator or pantry, and not see that the thing he's looking for is right there, directly in front of his face. Tell me that's never happened to you before."

"Sure, I guess it has. My ex-wife used to comment on it once in a while. What do you mean by a sudden onset of that?"

"Well, think about what you just did before your man eyes took over—all the things about this pole barn that were *not* obvious that you *did* see."

He glanced back at her and smiled, appreciative of what he took as a compliment but wondering if she still thought that his choice of clients made him a complete idiot.

After Harlan removed the last screw, they worked the breaker panel out of the wall. There was nothing attached to it, not a single wire.

Covering the hole behind the panel was a piece of cardboard taped on each end to vertical studs inside the wall. Harlan tore the tape away and, behind the cardboard, finally found what they were looking for.

It came in the form of neatly stacked bricks of something wrapped in brown paper, about the size and shape of small paperback books. Several fell to the floor as he pulled one out. He opened it. Inside was a compressed block of white powder that emitted a chemical smell when the paper was peeled back.

"Cocaine?" Roz asked.

"Not sure. It looks like a kilo of something with the right texture to be coke."

Harlan thought about the ten-million-dollar price tag Jimmy had quoted to Tank. If that's what this stuff truly was worth, a small sample probably wouldn't hurt him. Nevertheless, he had no intention of tasting it. Other than those seen on-screen, no cop or PI in his right mind would.

Bricks above the hole dropped down as they proceeded to empty the vertical gap in the wall, which eventually they could see had been created by removing a roll of thick insulation from between the studs and replacing it with a thin sheet of foam board pressed against the outer siding. Removal of bricks beneath the hole was made easy by a long-reach gripping tool conveniently left leaning against the wall only a few feet away.

"How many did you count?" Harlan asked after they'd emptied the space in the wall.

"Two hundred fifty," Roz answered.

Harlan's count was the same. He did some quick math and determined that Jimmy was expecting to fetch $40,000 per brick. His thoughts turned to what should be done with them when Roz pulled out her phone and started poking at it.

"What are you doing?" Harlan asked.

"Contacting the police, of course. We have to turn this stuff in."

"Hold on, Roz, let's think about this."

"Think about what?"

"About how I might be able to use this stash to do the job I've been hired to do."

"Finding Shotgun Gino?" Roz said, cocking her head. "How could it help you with that?"

"I don't know yet."

Roz returned to her phone.

"Please, Roz, don't make that call."

"Listen, Harlan, you may have lost your PI license, but I still have one. I have a duty right now to report this, and that's just what I intend to do."

"I get it, Roz. I do. And I have every intention of turning this over to the authorities. But not just yet, not while I might be able to use it to get leverage on the Grovers."

"How?"

Harlan paused to imagine various plays he might make on the dealers of these drugs. The problem, however, was that he simply knew too little about them at this point to formulate a plan.

"I just need a little more time. Can you give me that?"

"How much time?"

He thought for a moment and then pulled the number out of thin air. "Three days."

Roz stared at him for what seemed a long while before she said, "You have no idea how much time you might need, do you."

She seemed to be waiting for an answer. When he gave none, she said, "Okay, what do we do with it in the meantime? We're not putting it back where we found it—and where those Grovers might come looking when they see that their spy cam is out of service."

"Give me two minutes," Harlan said. "I'll be right back."

Harlan left Roz in the pole barn and went back to her SUV and her supply of PI gear. He rummaged through it until he found her spy cameras and grabbed a few. Before turning back, he paused at the sight of her GPS trackers, decided to grab a few of those as well, and stuffed them into the inside pocket of his jacket.

On his return to the pole barn Harlan found Roz filling garbage bags with the bricks of powder. "What are you doing?" he said.

"Well, like I said, we can't just leave them here."

"Sure we can," he said, as he crouched to the floor and tapped on it with his knuckles. "There's some space here too. We just need to pull out a few floorboards. Can I see that pry bar set of yours?"

"You're going to hide the Grovers' stash in the same pole barn where they hid it?"

"Why not? It'd probably be the last place they'd look if they thought someone ripped it off."

Before Harlan went to work on the floor, he handed Roz's spy cams to her and said, "Can you set these up to monitor this spot and the breaker panel?"

"Those look familiar."

"They should."

As she took the cameras, Roz said, "I'll take the keys to my car, too, Harlan."

He finished re-stashing all but seven bricks of the drugs; those seven he stuffed into Roz's backpack along with the Spartan gear that she had spilled on the floor earlier.

"Why are we taking that stuff?" Roz asked.

Harlan hadn't given up on imagining scenarios of various tactics he might employ going forward, and a vague outline of a plan for the Grovers was beginning to form. "The drugs might help with something I'm working on. As for the fan gear, you'd know why we're taking that if you checked your GPS app."

Roz poked at her cell phone as they walked back to her car; halfway, she stopped abruptly. Harlan stopped a couple steps ahead of her, looked back, and watched as she stared into her phone and learned the location of Randall Boggs' parked car.

Looking up from the phone, she asked, "Are you sending someone to East Lansing for tomorrow's game, undercover?"

He nodded. "Do you follow college football?"

"Enough to know it's a big game."

"Big? Are you kidding? The Buckeyes have been sitting at number one in the country since opening day, yet to be tested. An upset tomorrow night would put the one-loss Spartans back in the hunt for a Big Ten title, maybe even the national playoffs. The game is ESPN's primetime feature."

"And you think that for a home game of such magnitude Delta Grove might be crawling with Grovers, maybe even some from years gone by."

"Well, we know of one who's already there. And you saw for yourself, Roz, how rabid these guys are about Sparty."

Chapter 39

It was 1:30 a.m. when Roz dropped Harlan off where he'd parked the Range Rover earlier, about a half mile from Bert's place. She then continued on to join up with the others. He watched her taillights until they disappeared before allowing his thoughts to turn to his next destination, which had yet to be determined.

Inside his car, Harlan flipped on the dome lights and, hoping to get some ideas, opened the tourist magazine that he and Tank had picked up in St. Ignace. All Harlan knew was that at some point he'd have to deal directly with them—the so-called Grovers—and he wanted it to be at a place on this island where he would have every advantage.

Thing's more like a book, Harlan thought as he skimmed through the thick magazine. It contained a great many details about various sites on the island, each with a unique history and sometimes prehistory, but none at which he could imagine a plan of attack.

Until he came upon a description of one site that seemed to have potential—a *real* ghost town, Johnswood, and on its outskirts the ruins of a once-thriving lumber mill hidden in a copse of trees along Scammon Cove.

He paused over the name and said it aloud, "Scammon Cove." It seemed so apt, for if the Grovers would take the bait he had in mind, it would be just that—*scam on.*

He started the car.

Although the magazine described the mill's ruins as long forsaken, it told of a landmark—literally, a sign near the site—just off the road. And, in fact, there was one. His headlights caught it: "OWN THE HISTORIC JOHNSWOOD LUMBER MILL—FOR SALE!" Rotted and splintered, the sign looked like it could have been standing there since the mill had been shut down nearly a century ago.

Harlan followed the two-track road next to the sign to a point somewhere between the ruins of the old mill and the Scammon Cove shoreline. On foot, he opted first for the cove. The hike took him through an uneven terrain of dense vegetation that became increasingly marshy until he found himself at water's edge.

He stopped and scanned the cove's surface with his flashlight. Although his plan was still evolving, he imagined it would require a site accessible by boat, near big water. And there it was, as the map in his magazine had shown, extending beyond the mouth of the cove—Lake Huron.

Closer to shore, a group of pier pilings poked out of the water like needles out of a pin cushion. According to the magazine, they had survived a devastating fire in 1920. The decking did not, nor did a vessel moored there that day.

A couple other vessels were said to have sunk in the cove at other times, including one that would have been partially visible if he had been standing a quarter mile down the shore. With the aid of night-vision binoculars borrowed from Roz, Harlan looked in that direction and then around the cove's entire coastline. He saw nothing but woods and heard nothing but the sound of cicadas singing.

Solitude. That's good, he thought.

Harlan turned from the water and headed for the copse of trees, where the magazine had said he'd find the remains of the old mill itself. And he did—the naked concrete walls of a roofless edifice standing defiantly in the middle of nowhere, flanked by a fully intact chimney that poked into the canopy of towering aspen and birch. Standing before it, he felt for a moment as though he'd strayed from the woods of northern Michigan and into the site of ancient Mayan ruins camouflaged in the dense jungles of Central America.

He high-stepped through shrubs and weeds growing inside the main structure until he reached the chimney. Beside it grew a tall tree, so close that its branches bear-hugged the smokestack from bottom to top.

The branches were well spaced for climbing, Harlan thought, as he ran the beam of his flashlight over them. Recalling the sight of Roz perched up in a tree earlier that evening, he grabbed ahold of a low branch and hoisted himself up.

Harlan stopped about halfway up one of the chimney's massive walls, where there was a cutout through which he could insert himself and his flashlight for closer inspection of the dark interior. From the vantage point of the opening, the Mayan ruins had become a medieval tower housing a dungeon at its base. He imagined what it would feel like to be trapped down there, in an area about half the size of a one-car garage, looking up at four-story, concrete walls covered with odorous fungi.

A holding cell, he thought. *That might be useful. But how would you get prisoners down there?* A simple answer came to mind: *drop a rope down from this opening.* Keeping them down there would be even easier, he thought: *just remove the rope.*

Harlan climbed further up the tree, above the chimney, and, again with the aid of Roz's night-vision binoculars, peered as best he could through the treetops. Knowing that any ploy could bring out the worst in the Grovers, he searched the area for locations from which he might position himself for a clear line of sight—if he was a sniper.

As the magazine had promised, however, the inland topography offered no such vantage point. Its undulating hills achieved nowhere near the heights of the dolomite cliffs at Marble Head, an area he'd also considered until he read of that feature.

Harlan's elevated survey of the area narrowed to a lone structure that had managed to remain standing since the town of Johnswood had long ago ceased to be. It was a building that used to serve as the old mill's company store, the Wayfarers Mart, according to the tourist magazine. The hill on which it sat boosted its rooftop into the forest canopy, but not above it.

Harlan determined that a sniper would have to make ground-level shots, probably at close range due to the density of surrounding woods. And that's right where he'd want him. On the ground. Close. Perhaps wearing a ghillie suit of camouflaging vegetation, but right where Harlan's team would know to find him—or better yet, meet him when he arrived.

Harlan's attention returned to the lone structure and the use he had in mind for it.

• • • • •

The structure had received only a one-sentence description in the tourist magazine: *In what once was the heart of old Johnswood stands the town center's last ghost—the abandoned remains of the old mill's company store, known in its day as the Wayfarers Mart.*

Harlan scanned the area around Wayfarers with his flashlight, trying to imagine how it might have looked back in its day, a century ago, when Johnswood was crammed with the shacks and shanties of mill workers, whose families must have relied on the store for everyday provisions. According to the magazine, outlying lumber camps also had access to the town center via an extensive system of roads and rail, but none of it was here anymore; just the store, vacant and boarded.

Behind Wayfarers' main building was a small shed. Harlan decided to begin a closer inspection there. With a few tugs, boards nailed over the door came loose. He had to duck as he entered the cramped space inside, where he found a few yard tools, an empty five-gallon gasoline drum, and a generator still connected to a cable that ran into the ground.

The device couldn't be a century old, Harlan thought, as he ran his thumb through a build-up of grease and dirt around the on/off switch and then along the fuel line until it reached the carburetor. It looked intact, like it could still transmit power through the attached cable and on to whatever outlets and appliances it might reach inside Wayfarers' main building. He went there next.

Boards over a front window were easier to remove than the ones over any of the doors, so he went in through the window and into a spacious front room that he imagined must have once served as the retail area. It seemed that its most recent use, however, was as a dining room—or hall—as there remained in the center a long wooden table surrounded by over a dozen chairs.

Dust flew up into the beam of his flashlight as Harlan crossed the otherwise empty room and entered an adjoining one, where he found cupboards and cabinets that still contained cooking accessories, a space where he imagined there once was a refrigerator, or perhaps an icebox, and another space where there remained a vintage electric stove in reasonably good condition, he thought, for one manufactured around the time he was born.

That its most recent use was not as a retail store became even clearer as Harlan moved through other rooms in the building. Many had remnants of bedroom furnishings, including old dressers, bedframes, and the like, which, in light of the dining and kitchen accommodations, suggested to him that someone in the more recent past had tried to run the place as a small hotel or large bed and breakfast—though it was hard to imagine succeeding at such a business in this remote place. Apparently, they hadn't succeeded.

On his way out, Harlan stopped in a secondary entrance near the kitchen—a mudroom, he imagined—to look at something he hadn't seen on his first pass through. It was an interior door, smaller than any other, tucked in a corner of the room and partially obstructed by a coat stand that would have concealed it entirely had there been coats hung on it.

Through the door was a set of stairs that led to an underground cellar. Harlan went down, stood in its center, and turned full circle with his flashlight. It was empty. Then he made a second turn, more slowly, trying to visualize how the room might look if it were equipped for an operation that continued to take shape in his mind... a command center from which the operation might be directed... an operation he decided should have a name... *Scam on the Cove.*

Chapter 40

It was 3:40 a.m. when Harlan returned to Bert's place and located a key that had been hidden outside for him. Concerns about waking those inside ended as he opened the door to the discordant clamor of heavy snoring and high-spirited sex.

He stopped by the couch in the front room and considered quieting Tank, the fitful sleeper, but doing so seemed pointless in light of Bert and Morgan's lustful exhortations down the hall, which were much louder.

In the office, Harlan found Roz slouched in a chair at the desk, her head down, eyes closed, and breathing deep and rhythmic. She had changed clothes since he last saw her and was wearing a bedtime outfit that he thought looked more like Morgan's style of dress—revealing.

Harlan managed to divert his attention to a computer on the desk. With a slight nudge of the mouse, an unusual image was restored. It was a keg of beer standing on a hardwood floor next to a life-sized cardboard cutout of a muscular Spartan warrior, Michigan State's iconic mascot, Sparty. Above Sparty's head, suspended from the ceiling, was a digital timer displaying a countdown in progress, currently at eight hours, eighteen minutes, and a few seconds.

Is it streaming live from somewhere? Harlan wondered as he watched the few seconds wind down and the minutes drop to seventeen.

His train of thought was disrupted by what sounded like climactic outbursts signaling the end of Morgan and Bert's activities down the hall.

But in no time, they were right back at it.

"How can she sleep through that?" Harlan murmured, looking over at Roz.

"I can't," she complained as she picked up her head and opened her eyes. "They've been going on this way for I don't know how long."

"Seriously?"

"Yeah. It's unbelievable. I don't remember ever having that kind of drive, even at their age. Do you?"

"Well, I... uh..." Harlan stammered. "So... uh... what's up with Sparty and the keg of beer on the computer right now?"

"It's a countdown to a pregame tailgate, streaming live from Delta Grove. At noon they'll tap the keg. They do this for all the marque sporting events, like the football game today against Ohio State. That anti-frat house of theirs will be a zoo by mid-afternoon, and we'll be able to watch all of their antics online."

"How do you know?"

"Because you were right, Harlan. Delta Grove has a Facebook page. Their timeline goes back ten years, and so does their photo and video library. I've seen footage of some past tailgates."

"How about photos of the Grovers we're looking for?"

"One of them for sure."

"Randall Boggs?"

Roz nodded. "Cody Brown is his real name. They call him Kodiak, as in the bear, I guess because of his size."

"Any luck with Sully or Mike?"

Roz shook her head. "Kodiak's been tagged in so many photos, we can't narrow down who he hung with in those days. But we did learn something about Mike from another source."

"From Sam Boadle?" Harlan asked.

"It was a good hunch," Roz replied, smiling at him. "Sam's pretty sure that the photos of our blue-eyed guy Mike match up with the blue-eyed guy she met on the night of the storm."

As they spoke, Roz scrolled through the Delta Grove photo library. She stopped on a group photo that included Kodiak Brown and said, "Look at how young they were just a few years ago. They're still practically kids today, which makes me wonder how the ones we're after ever got involved with an old-school gangster like Shotgun Gino

Cruzano and his multimillion-dollar drug deal."

"The pharmaceuticals aren't turning that kind of profit," Harlan said defensively.

"I'm not talking about the pharmaceuticals."

"But you don't know whether Shotgun has anything to do with the other stash out at Bass Cove."

"Oh, please, Harlan. Be real. You said yourself that Jimmy expected forty grand a brick, times two hundred and fifty. Even if that's a significant markup, stockpiling it would have cost a fortune. Who do you think financed that?"

It was a question that had troubled Harlan too. There was no evidence to suggest that anyone beneath the man at the top of the pharmaceutical operation had the means to fund the other operation.

"Unless there's something about him we don't know, there's no way Jimmy 'the Leg' could have bankrolled the whole stash," Roz said, as if reading Harlan's mind. "I talked to Bert before he and Morgan took their reconciliation to the bedroom, and he says nobody was getting paid much on the pharmaceutical side of the business."

"Well, Bo Kitner was handling a lot of Shotgun Gino's money," Harlan said. "Maybe he and Jimmy were skimming."

"I don't think so," Roz said. "You remember your theory about Bo, as banker, being separated from the rest of the operation?"

Harlan nodded.

"According to Bert, you were right, and the method of delivering the money in the briefcase, he says, made it impossible for Jimmy or Bo to do any skimming."

"How so?"

"Bert says that they've made forty-some pharmaceutical runs since the operation started last spring, at around fifty grand per purchase. That comes to over $2 million flowing, he says, directly from Shotgun Gino to Bo Kitner in St. Ignace, and then to Bert here on Drummond in that locked briefcase, with the exact amount quoted by the Canadians for each purchase, usually one at a time, and never more than two."

"Did Bert say who took the price quotes from the Canadians?"

"That was my question, too," Roz said, smiling. "Bert says it was him, that he communicated directly with the Canadians via coded text messages he took on a burner cell phone in advance of each deal. Then he forwarded the price quotes directly to Shotgun Gino, who personally delivered the exact amounts needed to Bo Kitner."

If this was true, Harlan thought, it would make Bert a necessary player to any effort to rip off Shotgun Gino.

"And you don't think that Bert would have overstated those prices, allowing him or Bo to skim the difference," Harlan said.

"I'm pretty sure he didn't."

"Why?"

"Because he says that Bo Kitner came to him with just that kind of proposal, and he flat turned Bo down."

"When did that happen?" Harlan asked.

"Late last July, a few days before the Jeep Jamboree. Turns out that Bo never did any four-wheeling that weekend. He came here only to see if Bert would go along with his scheme."

"Did Bert come up with that time frame himself, without any prompting from you?"

"C'mon, Harlan. You think I don't know better?"

"And you believe Bert?"

Roz nodded confidently.

"The way I believe Eddy Chub?" Harlan said. "Based on intuition?"

"Yes, in fact, that is why I believe Bert. My gut tells me that he'd never skim from an employer, especially a dangerous one. And maybe Eddy Chub is the same kind of straight shooter. But hasn't it occurred to you, Harlan, that Eddy might not know all of what his boss, Shotgun Gino, has been up to?"

"What I know, Roz, is that Eddy says he was right there with Gino when the man reached out to bosses all along the Great Lakes—gangsters as old-school as he is—and promised them that his pharmacy wouldn't deal recreational drugs in any quantity, let alone 250 kilos. I don't see him breaking that promise. I used to work for these prehistoric bad guys. They don't like being a dying breed. And they will lash out at anyone who treats them like they are. Gino knows that better than anyone, because he's one of them."

"Maybe so, Harlan, but you still didn't answer the question: Who financed those 250 kilos? You know, as sure as you're standing there, that no drug lord would give Jimmy 'the Leg' Dillon that kind of stash simply on the basis of his promise to pay for it next winter."

They still didn't know all there was to know about the Grovers and their financial status, Harlan thought, but he decided to drop the issue and instead asked, "You're not thinking of bailing on me just yet, are you?"

"No, Harlan. I gave you three days, remember? And I'm following up with Eddy Chub and your other character witness."

"Doc Kimble?"

"Yeah. I left voicemails with both of them. The doc hasn't responded yet. Eddy Chub did, but not to me. He called Tank saying he didn't wanna talk to me—or anyone else—right now."

"Why?"

Roz shrugged and said, "All he told Tank is that he's too upset to talk about anything with anybody."

"Upset?"

"Yeah, you know, emotionally."

"About what?"

"I dunno. Whatever it is, Tank thinks it's serious. He says Eddy started crying over the phone."

"Crying? Wow," Harlan said. He then recalled the weight of Eddy Chub's personal challenges, and added, "Sounds like a man who may have been in need of group therapy on the day Bo Kitner went missing and that nerd showed up at the souvenir shop."

Roz rolled her eyes and said, "So tell me what you've been doing this evening, Harlan. Where did you go after I dropped you off at your car?"

"To a ghost town on Scammon Cove."

"What for?"

"To see if it will work for an operation."

"What kind of operation?"

"One that'll draw the Grovers into a situation where they'll talk."

"A threatening situation?"

"That, and disorienting."

"Sounds interesting. Tell me about it."

"Let me ask you something first," Harlan said as he sat down in a chair next to her and scooted close. "What can you tell me about the CDA?"

"The CDA from *Monsters, Inc.*? Why do you ask?"

"After what you told me about the names of the monsters—the ones the Grovers used as aliases—I did a quick search online to find out what I could about the movie, but I haven't had time to sort through any details."

Roz laughed. "You don't need to do that kind of research. I could tell you everything about that movie, scene by scene, if you'd like. It was my son's favorite. I can't even count how many times we watched it together on his DVD player."

"I figured as much."

"Okay," Roz said, looking excited to discuss the topic. "I assume you already know the movie's basic story line."

"Sure," Harlan replied. "There are these monsters who live in an alternative universe. But they're able to get here, to our world, through some special doors they have, doors that work like portals that let them into closets of kids here on earth. They come out of the closets at night to scare the kids because that fear releases a kind of energy…"

"Scream energy," Roz said.

"Yeah, scream energy, that the monsters somehow capture and use to power their world."

"Very good," Roz said. "But you realize, don't you, that the monsters are more scared of the kids than the kids are of them."

"I guess I didn't know that."

"Oh, yeah. The monsters are paranoid about the possibility of a kid slipping through one of their special doors and into *their* world. They think that kids are toxic. Even the slightest physical contact with a human child would kill them, they think."

"And the CDA… they…" Harlan said, trying to piece things together.

"It stands for Child Detection Agency," Roz said. "They're a government agency in the monsters' world, kind of like our CIA. They protect the monsters from the outside threat of toxic human children who might enter the monsters' world."

"Does that kind of intrusion ever happen?"

"It sure does."

"What does the CDA do about it?"

Roz laughed. "You should watch the movie and see for yourself what a CDA-style SWAT team does to a poor monster who returns from the human world with a kid's sock stuck to his back."

"Just tell me."

"No, it'd ruin the movie."

"C'mon, Roz. Please, just—"

"You two gonna jabber on all damn night?" yelled someone from the front room. "Some people in this house are trying to sleep!"

It was Tank. He said nothing else.

Harlan and Roz shared a stifled laugh, and then a long look.

The reconciliation down the hall had finished up a little while ago.

And the heavy sleeper up front had not yet returned to snoring.

The silence lingered.

He'd only known Roz for one day, but it felt to Harlan like something special between them might be happening, until it occurred to him that he didn't even know whether she already had a man in her life, or, for that matter, whether men were even her preference.

"Dibs on the guest room," Roz said, springing to her feet.

She touched him gently on his shoulder as she left.

It was a simple gesture, but one that led him gradually into an awareness of the rhythm of his own breathing… and a release of all else.

Chapter 41

A few hours later, Harlan woke to the smell of sizzling bacon and a lower back stiff from napping curled up on a love seat in the front room. He eventually followed the aroma to the kitchen, where Morgan was busy cooking and Tank, seated at the counter, was hunched over a freestanding mirror making a mess of his face with green and white paint that he applied with his bare hands.

"At least you remembered to lose the mustache and goatee," Harlan said.

"Morning to you too, Boss."

"Looks like Roz recruited you for the road trip to Delta Grove."

"She didn't have to ask twice."

"You're only going there for surveillance, Tank. No confrontation. Understand?"

"Got it, Boss. I'll blend in quietly with that crowd of tailgaters—all three hundred pounds of me—in my war paint and costume."

The costume, a spandex bodysuit, was draped over the back of another stool. "Does it fit?" Harlan asked.

"Like the gloves they tried to put on O.J. Simpson," Morgan said, her back to them as she worked with a spatula in one hand and a spoon in the other. "How do you like your eggs, Mr. Holmes?"

"Any way is fine, thanks. Is Bert up yet?"

"Yeah. He's in the utility room."

"Doing what?"

"Prepping for a dive."

"Why?"

"Don't know. You'll have to ask him."

Harlan looked at Tank, who whispered, "He's gonna check out the *EJ LaWay.*"

"The shipwreck where they did the drops? Why?"

"He thinks Finn Ramsey might still be there."

"At the bottom of the lake?"

Tank nodded and said, "That's where Bert thinks he might've been whacked by Randall Boggs, or… whatever the hell his real name is."

"Kodiak Brown," Harlan said as he started for the utility room. He stopped, however, when he caught a glimpse of Roz through a sliding glass door. She was in the backyard, on the phone, pacing. "Do you know who Roz is talking to?" he asked.

"Doc Kimble," Tank answered.

"So she returned Roz's call."

"Not really, Boss. The doc called in to your phone, a little while ago. I pulled it out of your pocket while it was ringing. You slept right through it. She wanted to check with you about talking to Roz. I told her it was cool."

• • • • •

Bert was working on some scuba gear when Harlan got to the utility room.

"Can I have a word, Bert?"

"What's up, Mr. Holmes?"

"I hear you're planning a dive at the *EJ LaWay.*"

"That's right."

"What for?"

"If you talked to Tank, you already know why."

"Finn Ramsey?"

"Yeah. Morgan says that the last time she ever saw him was when he was heading out to the *EJ* for a dive with Randall Boggs… or, uh, Kodiak Brown I guess his name is. That was Tuesday, Mr. Holmes, the day before Buck-Off Wednesday."

Recalling something he'd learned at his first stop on the island, Harlan asked, "Did Finn miss his usual Wednesday night of shooting pool at Chuck's Place?"

"Yes, he did, for the first time that anyone there can recall."

"Who'd you talk to from the bar?"

"Gerry and Candis were both there when I called. Neither saw him that night. Hell, they were even a little worried about him."

"But even if you're right, Bert, what makes you think that his body is still out there by the shipwreck?"

"A hunch."

"What kind of hunch?"

Bert stopped what he was doing, looked up, and said, "I trained four people for this dive, Mr. Holmes, and every one of them, except Morgan, ignored my advice against trying to penetrate the *EJ La Way*."

"You mean get inside the sunken vessel?"

"That's right. Finn and both Grovers, including this guy Kodiak, tried to enter it the first time I took them down there, after I specifically told them not to."

"Why would they do that?"

"You ever dive, Mr. Holmes?"

"No."

"Well, let me tell you. When you're on the bottom of a lake or ocean, the sight of something old and man-made can be alluring. It's natural to want to get close for a look, and inside if you can. But it's dangerous, especially when you're not trained for diving into an overhead environment."

"And you didn't train them for that."

"No, and I didn't equip them for it either. Wrecks can have sharp metal edges that can snag and cut ordinary gear, and they can have rigging and nets that can cause entanglement."

"And you gave Kodiak that specific warning?"

"Yes, I did, which means he knew when he went out there with Finn that entrapment in the *EJ* could look like an all-too-common type of accidental death."

Chapter 42

"What are you doing, Tank?" Roz complained. "You can't go to Delta Grove looking like that."

She must have finished her phone call, Harlan thought when he overheard the remark from the hallway leading to the kitchen. He paused before entering.

"Why not?" Tank asked.

"Because you look ridiculous. Now go wash your face and then let me help you with that paint."

As Tank left for the bathroom, Harlan stepped into the kitchen, greeted Roz, and asked, "How'd your conversation with Doc Kimble go?"

"As I expected," she answered curtly.

"Well, what'd she say about the operation—you know, about Shotgun Gino becoming a charitable bootlegger?"

"Do you even realize how you come across when you say something like that, Harlan?"

"But..."

"Oh, sure, she told me the same story you did about how the man was suddenly cured of severe depression by an inspiration to rectify the injustices of our nation's health-care system. And you know what, Harlan?"

"What?"

"I'm sure she really believes that, because I'm sure that Shotgun Gino Cruzano would have said anything necessary to get her to go along with his drug-trafficking scheme. I mean, c'mon, Harlan, you of all people should see a con game for what it is. Last night Tank told me about some of the stunts he's seen you pull to manipulate people. How could you possibly be fooled by this man's bullshit?"

"Well, you're not taking into account the fact that…"

"What the hell, Eddy?" Tank shouted into his phone as he returned from the bathroom. "Just how many bags of potato chips did you eat?"

Harlan and Roz stopped their conversation to listen to Tank's side of his.

"Cookies too? … How many boxes? … What do ya' mean, you lost count? … Come again… You don't know if it was one or two gallons of ice cream? Why not? … Food coma? What the hell is that?"

"Never mind, Eddy, I've heard enough," Tank said before handing his phone to Roz and saying, "He says he's ready to talk to you."

Roz took the phone and slowly raised it to her ear. "Eddy Chub?" she said tentatively. "Are you sure you can talk now? … Okay. Do you have FaceTime on your phone? … Good, I'll call you back using that."

After Roz stepped outside to make the call, Harlan turned to Tank and asked, "What was that all about?"

"Oh, Eddy went and blew up his diet."

"Why would he tell you?"

"Because I'm the one who put him on it. It's the diet I used in prison, along with weight and cardio training, to get myself ripped."

"Oh yeah, that's right," Harlan said. "You're training Eddy now."

"Well, I'm trying to. He needs direction on how to deal with his weight problem. And here I thought I was starting him on a simple program. Yet the man couldn't make it two lousy days."

"Food's on!" Morgan called out.

• • • • •

Roz had returned from outside and was at the kitchen counter moistening the face paints with a spray bottle, while Morgan retrieved some makeup brushes and sponges. At the other end of the counter sat Harlan, Tank, and Bert devouring platefuls of bacon, scrambled eggs, toast, pancakes, fried potatoes, and grits.

"Get over here, Tank, so I can paint your face," Roz said, once she had the brushes and sponges.

"Let me finish eating first."

"No. You're done eating."

"But I'm hungry."

"So was Eddy Chub. Now get over here already."

Roz began jabbing at his face with a sponge full of white paint as soon as Tank relocated himself onto a stool at her end of the counter. "Easy, Roz," he complained.

"Just sit still," she admonished.

"So, what did Eddy have to say?" Harlan asked.

"That somebody put him on a cruel diet."

"He said that?" Tank objected, jerking his face away from the sponge.

"No. *I'm* saying that," Roz answered. "Now stop moving around."

Roz pressed the sponge firmly into Tank's massive jowl, her strokes growing in length as she slathered on a base coat of white paint. "What the hell were you thinking?" she asked, "putting a five-hundred-pound man with an eating disorder on a zero-carbohydrate diet. No fruit, no bread, no pasta, no…"

"That's not quite true," Tank argued. "He was allowed up to twenty grams of carbs a day."

"Oh, so he could supplement his steady diet of meat and eggs with green beans and lettuce," Roz responded sarcastically.

"But that was just gonna be for two weeks to jump-start his metabolism—you know, the standard induction period for the Atkins diet."

Roz moved on to the green paint, and everyone remained silent for a few minutes, watching, as she worked precisely with brushes of varied sizes to combine swirls, dots, and stripes of green into an elaborate war-face paint design.

"Whoa, that's good," Morgan said when Roz was finished.

"Downright scary is what it is," Bert said. "And he doesn't even have the spandex on yet."

Harlan, impressed, simply nodded.

"Well, what do you think?" Roz asked as she placed a mirror in front of Tank.

He smiled broadly and said, "Damn, Roz, how did you do that so fast?"

"Glad you like it," she said. "And I'm sorry for getting a little chippy with you about the way you're handling Eddy. I know your intentions are good."

"Good intentions or not, I shouldn't have yelled at him. But I don't know what else to do."

"Can I make a suggestion?" Roz asked.

"Sure."

"Tell the man to stop letting people call him Eddy Chub."

"But he's been called that since he was a kid."

"I don't care how long he's been called *chub*. It has to stop, because he has to start thinking differently about himself."

Harlan, Bert, and Morgan all leaned in to listen as Roz continued.

"That's where a major life change always begins—in the mind."

"But he still needs a new diet," Tank said.

"Just tell him to eat healthy foods he likes, reduce the junk, and hit the gym."

Roz stared intensely at Tank and added, "But more importantly, tell him to *believe* in himself. And tell him that *you* believe in him—that you *know* he can reach his goal."

"But how's that gonna help?"

"Did you play any organized sports growing up?"

Tank nodded.

"You remember your favorite coach?"

Tank's nodding continued as he gazed off and said, "Oh, yeah, my high school football coach, Kyle Gaertner. We used to call him 'Coach G'… and all of us players were his G-men."

"Sounds like you have some good memories of Coach G," Roz said, "and I'm sure they include the way he could inspire you, fire you up, and make you give it your all."

She waited as Tank's expression grew serious, and then she added, "I'll bet you can still hear his voice, sometimes firm with you, sure, but always believing in you and motivating you to step up your game."

Again, she gave Tank a few moments to let the message sink in. His expression intensified further. Harlan had seen this transition before, when his partner was working himself up for physical confrontation. On this occasion, through the warrior paint, he took on more than just a game face. He looked savage.

"It's like Coach G is still with me, right here," Tank said, thumping his chest with a tight fist.

"Still standing by you," Roz said, "like he did when you were his G-man. And he did that win or lose, I'm sure, because he cared about you and wanted more than anything for you to realize your full potential. Am I right?"

"Absolutely."

"Don't you see, Tank? That's what *you* have to do now—for Eddy. You have to care about him. Believe in him. Coach him up, man."

Tank's eyes widened and his breathing intensified. "Coach G always told me to visualize myself—over and over—tearing through the O-line and blowing up plays in the backfield. 'Keep playing it in your head,' he'd say, 'and you'll make it happen on the field.'"

"And did you?" Roz asked, her eyes gleaming.

Tank hopped off his stool and snatched up the bodysuit with one hand and his phone with the other. "I gotta get on the road," he said, "and call Eddy."

Chapter 43

"That was pretty impressive," Harlan said after Tank had left. "I was getting all fired up myself."

"Why? Are you facing a life challenge right now?" Roz asked.

He didn't realize he was nodding his head, albeit slightly, until she said, "Maybe I can help you with that."

"With what?"

She scooted closer to him. They were alone, seated at the counter in the kitchen. "You're how old?" she asked. "Mid-fifties?"

"Smack in the middle."

"You have me by only a couple years, Harlan. I know what this stage of life is like, struggling to stay at the top of your game. And compounding that struggle for you, I imagine, is the uncertainty about where you're going to take your game next."

"What makes you think…"

"You don't talk about what you've been doing since you lost your PI license two years ago. Whatever it was, you're not going back to it. I can tell. But without that license, the only clients you could ever have going forward would be like the ones you're working for now—outlaws. Thing is, you're not one of them, which makes you feel conflicted about helping them. Oh, you're willing to do *some* wrong for these mobsters, if you can rationalize it away as somehow being right in the circumstances. But what are the odds of being able to do that the next time these guys call on you?"

Harlan was taken aback. The woman's insights were spot on. Curious, he asked, "How would you help me with something like that?"

"The way I used to when I worked as a life coach."

"Hold on," he said. "I thought you used to be a beautician."

"That was before I became a life coach."

"Which was before you became a PI?"

She nodded.

"Interesting career path," Harlan remarked. "How'd it come about?"

"It started with being a single mom," Roz said, shrugging, "and needing to find a way to provide for my son and me. One occupation just kind of led to another."

"How so?"

"Well, as a beautician, I gravitated to the part of the job that had me serving as an informal counselor, listening to clients tell their stories while I did their hair. And those stories, I came to realize, shared a common thread—a gap that all of us have, time and again through life, between where we are now and where we want to be. A life coach is someone who helps bridge those gaps."

Harlan thought for a moment about the gap he'd been stuck in for the past two years. The train of thought led him to ask, "How did work as a life coach lead you into private investigation?"

"It happened while I was working for a client who was navigating a gap between life with a domestic abuser and life on her own. During that process, she died. An accidental drowning, the authorities said. But every ounce of instinct told me they were wrong. I just knew she'd been murdered by her abuser. And I made it my business to prove it."

"And after you did," Harlan said, "you were hooked on doing private investigation for clients in that same gap, to prevent the same outcome."

"Exactly, though every once in a while the life coach in me makes an appearance."

"Like it did with Tank," Harlan said, "while you were coaching him up."

"So that he could coach up Eddy," she added.

"Yeah, poor Eddy Chub," Harlan mused, "caught in a gap between what he is now and what he wants to be."

"Is that why you take Eddy at his word, Harlan? Because he comes across as so damn pitiful?"

"I guess that's part of it."

"But it could all be an act, like the kind of theatrics you're noted for."

"Just what did Tank tell you about me?" Harlan asked.

"Plenty about the kind of mischief you got into with your last mobster client."

"Well… it really wasn't all that… uh…"

"And obviously you have more of the same in mind for your current one."

"Actually, what I'm planning this time is a little *more* mischievous," Harlan said, smiling.

"Go ahead, Harlan. You never did get around to explaining your plan last night. And I can see you're dying to tell me."

"Not until I know you're on board, Roz. And it doesn't sound like you're sold on Eddy Chub."

"Not yet. But I've seen enough to tell you I'm not going anywhere until I get word back on something I'm checking out about his story."

"What's that?"

"I have my secrets too, Harlan."

Chapter 44

Their tiny dinghy struggled, as did Harlan's stomach, with the choppy surface of Lake Huron's North Channel. He and Bert had traveled a mile into the waterway, and at this point they had Bert's Carolina Skiff in sight, right where Bert thought it might be, at the dive site for the *EJ La Way*.

Once on board the skiff, Bert suited up in a durable dry suit equipped for a cold-water dive while Harlan leaned over the side and waited to see whether breakfast might make a comeback appearance.

"You okay?" Bert asked.

Harlan straightened up and pretended to feel better.

Bert handed him a headset and directed him to the helm. "Take a seat here, Mr. Holmes."

A screen on the console flickered as Bert powered up a camera attached to the top of his mask. After he got the device working, Bert rolled over the side of the skiff and his view beneath the surface soon became Harlan's on the screen—a dark green cloud.

Harlan tapped at the screen with his fingertips. The cloud, however, remained. "I can't see a damn thing," he complained into his mic.

"I've seen it worse," Bert said, speaking with the clarity of a skilled ventriloquist through the breathing apparatus crammed into his mouth.

A few minutes later the blurry outline of an old steamer resting on the lake's bottom appeared on the screen. Then came a closer view of its algae-covered hull, which rearward from the cargo hatch looked largely intact, as Bert had said it would be.

The movement of the camera became jerky after Bert reached the hatch and presumably entered the wreck.

Seconds later, through Harlan's headset, there came a blast of unintelligible vocalization followed by something on the screen that said it all—the image of a bloated dead guy whose bulging eyes and purple mouth were frozen into place, wide open. In front of the catatonic face, somehow amplifying its ghastliness, hovered a mouthpiece attached to tubes stretching like tentacles over the guy's shoulders from a mass of equipment on his back.

Bert sounded like he might be hyperventilating as he maneuvered behind the dead guy and tried to say something. But no longer was he speaking with a ventriloquist's skill. Through the garble, Harlan thought he heard something about Finn Ramsey and a "pipe."

"Come again, Bert. Did you say that Finn is hung up on a pipe?"

"Yeah."

"Can you back up?" Harlan asked.

Bert did so, providing a wider-angle view that bought into focus a broken pipe, twisted ninety degrees, and Finn's body draped over it. But Harlan still couldn't see how Finn might be attached to it.

There was a prolonged silence during which the camera view returned to Finn's face. Bert's breathing slowed but remained far from normal. He was taking a long look at his lost friend, Harlan thought.

• • • • •

Several minutes had passed since Bert returned to the skiff. He'd spent the entire time sitting on the deck, still wearing most of his dive suit, head down. Finally, he looked up and began to explain what he was trying to say earlier when he was under sixty feet of water.

"Finn was hung up from behind on a busted pipe that was sticking out of the hull."

"How?" Harlan asked.

"One of his rebreather straps was looped over it and got twisted around it."

"Could that have happened accidentally?"

"It's possible, I suppose," Bert said. "He could've backed himself onto it without seeing it, and then made it worse by turning the wrong way to get off."

"And then what?" Harlan asked. "He just ran out of air?"

"I doubt that," Bert said. "The mouthpiece probably didn't just fall out after he died. It wedges too tightly into the diver's mouth to come out on its own. No, he either panicked and pulled it out himself, or it was no accident."

"Which do you think?" Harlan asked.

"The same as I thought before we got here—that he was drowned by that fucking monster, Kodiak Brown, who then staged it to look like Finn came out here alone and made the mistake of diving into an overhead environment without the right training and equipment."

Harlan turned his attention to the nearest stretch of the Drummond Island shoreline, Chippewa Point, and the mile of rough water in between. "But then Kodiak would have had to swim all that way back to shore."

"That would have been the easy part," Bert said.

"Through that rough water?" Harlan said.

"It's not rough down deep, Mr. Holmes, which I'm sure is where he stayed coming back. Our closed-circuit rebreathers can provide up to four hours of dive time down there, give or take, depending on the diver's level of exertion. And he wasn't exerting."

"What do you mean?"

"One of my underwater scooters is missing."

"How fast do they go?"

"Fast enough to tow him all the way back to Maxton Bay with plenty of time to spare."

Harlan scanned the coast southward, toward the bay, before turning back.

"You gonna be okay, Bert?"

"Just not sure what to do. Seems like we should call the police."

Harlan found himself agreeing, but he didn't want to say so.

Bert seemed to know why. "It's that plan of yours for the Grovers," he said. "It doesn't include going to the police, does it."

"Actually, it does," Harlan said, "but not this soon."

"And in the meantime, what? We're just supposed to leave Finn down there?"

Harlan thought for a moment before responding, "I can see my plan still working if you could limit any police report to simply saying that your boat and the guys who borrowed it for a dive went missing the other day. Cops might find him sooner that way, though I can't say for sure. It's up to you, Bert. If you have to play this straight, I understand."

"This plan of yours, Mr. Holmes, do you have me in mind for any part of it?"

"More than just a part, Bert. There's a central role in it for you—you and your skiff—if you don't mind us returning with it and anchoring the dinghy out here for the authorities to find instead."

"What kind of role?"

Harlan couldn't think of a way to answer the question honestly without offending Bert, and he wasn't going to lie to the man.

"Think about what these Grovers did behind your back, Bert, sneaking around with 250 kilos of drugs... and your girlfriend. They don't respect you. They can't imagine you ever being a step ahead of them. And we can use that against them."

"How?"

"By making you our point man on a deal we're going to propose, one that'll draw them into a trap. No offense intended, Bert, but if they think they're dealing with you, they're not likely to see it coming."

After a pause, Bert responded, "I don't know, Mr. Holmes, maybe they're right about me. I'm not feeling so confident right now, knowing that I'd be the one down there tied to that pipe, were it not for my woman cheating on me."

"I disagree, Bert. From what Tank has told me, you're perfect for the job."

"What'd he tell you?"

Harlan recalled Roz's demonstration of life coaching that morning and thought he might as well give it a try. He cleared his throat and said, "Tank says you had a granite jaw back in your boxing days, so hard you could even take *his* best punch. Oh, sure, a guy like Tank might knock you down, but you never stayed down. You always got up. I think you're in that kind of situation with these Grovers right now, Bert. They've knocked you down, but I can't believe they've knocked you out. And Tank doesn't believe that either. We think you can get back up and fight these guys—if you can believe in yourself. So, what do *you* say? Are we wrong about you? Have these Grovers beaten you?"

Chapter 45

"I can't take much more of this," Harlan said. Since returning to Bert's place, he had joined Roz by the computer to watch the live-stream feed of the Grovers' tailgate party. So far, the camera on site had remained pointed at the beer keg the same way it was during the countdown. The vantage point allowed them to see guests fill their beer mugs, including Kodiak Brown several times, but not much else.

"It's not so bad," Roz replied. "More interesting than the usual stakeout, if you ask me."

"I'm not talking about what we're watching," Harlan said, glancing away from the computer.

Down the hall, Bert and Morgan were back at it, having more exuberant sex. It had begun shortly after Bert and Harlan shared the sad news of Finn Ramsey's death.

"Apparently Morgan knows only one way to console her man when he's feeling down," Roz said.

Harlan thought about Bert's gruesome underwater discovery and wondered further about the cause of Finn Ramsey's death. Was it really a homicide, as Bert had said? Looking at the young faces on the live feed, Harlan found himself questioning the theory despite all the evidence supporting it.

"Have you learned anything about Kodiak Brown that could suggest he's capable of murder?"

"He's certainly capable of *some* misconduct," Roz said. "But murder, I dunno, that might be new for him." She reached for the computer mouse, began clicking through materials that she'd previously downloaded, and stopped on a document. "Delta Grove keeps bios on their former members," she said. "His is interesting."

Harlan scooted his chair closer to the computer. Beneath a picture of a wholesome face, captioned "Cody Brown," was a bio that went on at length about the young man's potential when he came out of high school as a four-star football recruit on full-ride scholarship at Michigan State. He was dubbed "Kodiak"—as in the big brown Alaskan bear—because of his size and ferocity at outside linebacker. The bio continued with other information about him, never returning to the subject of football.

"I follow college sports," Harlan said. "If he was such a stud on the gridiron, how come I've never heard of him?"

"Because he never played," Roz replied. "He was red-shirted his freshman year and got booted off the team a few weeks before the next season's opener."

"How do you know?"

"I did a little digging into some newspaper archives. There were lots of articles about all kinds of trouble he couldn't stay out of."

"Like what?"

"A couple minor in possessions, a DUI, and an aggravated assault and battery that he copped to disorderly conduct. But what ultimately did in his football career was performance-enhancing drugs."

"He tested positive?"

"Not just that. He dealt them to other guys on the team."

Fairly impressive rap sheet, Harlan thought, *but still far from murder.*

"And that's just what they know he did," Roz added, looking away.

Recalling the sexual assault Roz experienced at Chuck's Place, Harlan could imagine what she was thinking. What else had Kodiak Brown done? And to how many women?

• • • • •

"Harlan, wake up. You have to see this."

He had dozed off right there, in front of the computer, still alongside Roz. It was the time of day when he normally napped after getting home from his early morning shift at the gym. Roz smiled at him, seeming to understand his midlife need for a midday slumber.

"Wh-what's going on?"

"Check it out," she said, turning to the computer screen.

Tank, now in his green spandex bodysuit, was next in line for the keg at the Grovers' tailgate party.

Harlan, still coming to, squinted at the image and said, "What the hell is he doing?"

"Hey, isn't that Tank?" came a voice from the office doorway. Harlan looked back. It was Bert, wearing nothing but boxer underwear.

"I told him to keep his distance," Harlan complained as he turned back to the computer and watched Tank answer his phone.

"Hey, Roz, good timing for a call," Tank said into his phone. "I was beginning to think you forgot about me."

"Cool," Bert said. "They're streaming audio too."

"Is that Bert I hear?" Tank asked.

"Yeah, it's him," Roz replied.

"Whoa, hold on," Harlan said. "What's he doing there, inside the house?"

"What I told him to do," Roz said.

"What *you* told him to do?" Harlan responded incredulously.

"Boss? You're on the line too?"

"Gimme that phone," Harlan said.

"No," Roz answered. "Just chill out."

"Sounds like he's in a bad mood," Tank said.

"You think?" Roz replied. "Remind me not to wake him up next time he's asleep in the middle of the day."

"Sparty on, dude!" came a shout from a stranger at the party, who high-fived Tank while walking by. "Go green, brother!" Tank shouted back. A chorus of "Go white!" followed from what sounded like a room full of excited Spartan football fans.

"Looks like you're fitting in nicely," Roz said.

"You bet I am, thanks to my make-up artist," Tank answered as he took the beer tap from the person in line ahead of him.

"What the hell—he's drinking beer now?" Harlan complained.

Roz, ignoring Harlan, waited for Tank to fill his mug and step away from the keg, out of range of the audio feed. She then put him on speaker and asked, "So tell me, Tank, have you seen Kodiak Brown?"

"Oh yeah. He's in the front yard right now, playing bean bag toss. Got my name on the board for the next game."

"Good work," Roz said. "What name are you using?"

"Jimmy," Tank answered in a tone familiar to Harlan—his bagman growl.

"And is that helping you stay focused?"

"Sure is, Roz. Just like you said it would. I'm totally dialed in right now."

"Excellent. How about video or photos? Have you taken any?"

"Some video, I think. I've been walking around acting like I'm on the phone, trying to point the camera at people. But I haven't had a chance to check the quality of the recording yet."

"Have you noticed anyone of possible interest hanging with Kodiak?"

"I dunno, maybe his partner out there tossing bean bags with him. He's a crazy son of a bitch."

"How so?"

"It's like thirty-five degrees outside, and the dude's bare chested."

"Did he just say the guy's wearing no shirt?" Harlan said.

"That's right, Boss. He looks wilder than me, full of green and white paint from the waist up."

"What about his navel?" Harlan said.

"Well, gee, Boss, what kind of question is that?"

Harlan glanced at Roz. She smiled, placed the phone closer to him, and said, "Looks like you're finally dialed in too."

"Don't you remember what Bert and Morgan said about Mikey's navel?" Harlan asked.

After several seconds of silence, they saw a mass of green pass through the computer monitor. Next, over the speaker on Roz's phone, the background sound changed. "I'm outside, Boss, looking at him right now, still playing bean bag toss with Kodiak."

"And?" Harlan said.

"The guy has green and white circles painted on his abs. They get smaller and smaller, zeroing in on his navel… like it's a bullseye."

"Showing it off just the way Morgan said Mike does when he's around the house in front of people," Harlan said.

"Exactly," Tank said. "And it's an outie, Boss—the biggest, ugliest outie I've ever seen."

Chapter 46

"All right," Tank said, "looks like my game is coming up soon."

Roz still had him on her phone, set on speaker mode. Harlan and Bert pressed in close to listen.

"Do you have a teammate?" Roz asked.

"Oh, that's right, I'll need one. But who? Let's see… There's a guy watching the game up close, standing next to Kodiak right now. I'll try him."

"Remember what I told you about accent," Roz said.

"Got it, Roz," Tank answered. He then cleared his throat and spoke up, "Hey dere buddy… yah, dat's right, I'm talkin' to you, wouldn'tcha know, eh. Need a partner for dat game dere… yah, yah… Whatcha call it? … Yah, bean bag toss, dat's it. Up in da UP, we call it cornhole. But people downstate get da wrong idea. Minds 'r in da gutter down here under da Bridge. Know whud I mean, eh?"

"Why is he talking like that?" Harlan asked.

Roz pressed a finger to her lips, reminding Harlan that they were live on Tank's phone.

Hopefully he knows better than to have us on speaker, Harlan thought. But with Tank, he knew, commonsense precautions were not always taken.

"It's Yooper talk," Roz whispered. She smiled and added, "You betcha it is, eh."

Oh, for crying out loud, he thought. *She's worse at it than him, and she lives up here.* "Why'd you tell him to talk that way?" he whispered back.

Roz cocked her head and shot him a look that said, *Obviously, to keep him undercover.* Harlan rolled his eyes. *The size of the beast alone could blow that,* he thought.

The background voice of a stranger came through the speaker: "Holy crap, green man, you look like the Hulk."

"Pretty big fella yourself, dere... yah... dat ya'r, eh... Name's Jimmy."

"Jimmy what?"

"D'Reaper."

"Dreeper?"

"Close enough," Tank said. "And you?"

"Cody Brown. Friends call me Kodiak."

"You one a dese Grovers, Kodiak?"

"Hell yeah. Take it you're not."

"Nah, just partied wit 'em when I went to State. Class of '01."

"2001! And look at you, still all suited up for battle. You're my kind of guy, Jimmy. Welcome back."

"Appreciate da hospitality, Kodiak. Who's your partner down dere wit all da paint on his abs?"

"Eli Hubbard. He's a good ole Grover. Class of '14, like me—Ain't that right, Eli?" Kodiak finished with a shout.

There was no response.

Kodiak spoke up again, "Why don't you join him and toss from his end. The two of you would make a great picture, all green and white the way you are."

"Dat we would," Tank said. "Hey, how 'bout you take some photos of me and him wit my phone. My girl back in Escanaba would gedda kick oudda it."

"No problem, Dreeper."

"Quick, Roz, hang up," Harlan whispered, "before he gives him the phone."

"Hold on," she replied.

Another voice from a distance came through Roz's speaker. "C'mon, Kodiak! Send down some fresh meat!"

Roz then ended the call. She and Harlan both looked inquiringly at

Bert.

“That was Mike Wazowski,” he said.

“Sure was,” said Morgan from behind them. “Clear as day.”

Harlan turned to see her, standing in the doorway wearing, it seemed, nothing but an oversized men’s t-shirt. He looked back at Bert, still in his boxers, and said, “Why don’t you two put on some clothes and get back to work?”

Chapter 47

"The Delta Grove biography page has two guys listed under 'Hubbard' in the Grover class of '14," Roz said. "Eli and Jack."

Harlan looked up from a text just sent from Tank. "Two Hubbards? Are they related?"

"Not sure. I'm just getting into Eli's bio."

"Anything interesting?"

"Well, he's not just another pretty face."

Harlan stepped over to the computer to see the bio of Eli Hubbard on the Delta Grove Facebook page. It began with his photo, which looked like it could have been lifted from the cover of a *GQ* magazine. Beneath his jet-black curls were eyes almost as dark, a set of prominent cheekbones, and an angular jaw accented with a perfectly trimmed stubble beard.

And Roz was right. There was much more to him than good looks. According to the bio, Eli began college at age sixteen, a genius with a Mensa-tested IQ of 160. Over the next four years he earned undergraduate degrees in both math and physics and a graduate degree in propulsion engineering.

"Rocket science?" Harlan murmured.

"Apparently so," Roz said, as she continued scrolling down the screen. The bio ended with a reference to "Eli's big brother and fellow Grover, Jack Hubbard."

Roz moved the cursor toward the back button but stopped when Harlan said, "Wait. What are those links in the sidebar?"

"Term papers," Roz answered. "I've seen them in some of the other bios. Delta Grove keeps an online library of old term papers, I'd guess for use by future generations of Grovers to plagiarize from."

Harlan scanned down the headings of papers listed beside Eli's bio and stopped on the last one, described as a master's thesis and entitled, *The Aerosledge Reborn: An Amphibious Crossover Vehicle Like No Other.*

Roz stopped the cursor over the link as Harlan read it, apparently just discovering it as he was. She glanced at him before clicking on it.

The link took them to an eighty-page dissertation, which began:

"This paper will take you back in time to some long-forgotten propulsion technology developed in the Soviet Union during the Cold War—the Tupolev A-3 Aerosledge. An all-metal amphibious craft, this land-based missile was equipped with a powerful, single-pusher fan that could propel it, its passengers, and its cargo over every variation of snow, ice, and water encountered in the Siberian tundra.

"Production of the A-3 Aerosledge, however, ceased in the 1980s as a result of the more modern-day ATV and air-transport alternatives that were thought to be better. But newer isn't always better. As this paper will establish, the Aerosledge, with just a few design upgrades, can once again be a crossover vehicle of unsurpassed utility not only in the remote regions of Siberia, but also in some remote regions of our own, here in North America."

Beneath the introductory paragraphs was a photo of Eli Hubbard seated in a prototype of his reinvented aerosledge while it sat parked in the driveway of Delta Grove.

It was identical to the three amphibious vehicles that Harlan and Roz had seen at the pole barn back at Bass Cove.

Roz looked up from the computer and said, "He actually built the ones we—"

"That's his outtie all right," came Bert's voice from the doorway behind them. "Even uglier painted green."

Harlan turned to see Bert and Morgan, finally dressed, looking up from Bert's smartphone. They'd been copied on the text that Tank had sent Harlan a few minutes earlier. Attached to it were several photos of Tank and Eli playing bean bag toss at the Delta Grove tailgate.

"What's he doing in that one?" Morgan asked, looking at the

computer.

"Posing in a land-based missile he invented in college," Harlan said. "Eli Hubbard, AKA Mike Wazowski, is a propulsion engineer."

"A what?" Bert asked.

"A rocket scientist," Morgan said. "He once told me, but I thought he was bullshitting."

"Did he ever tell you about his big brother?" Roz asked after opening the Delta Grove bio for Jack Hubbard.

Morgan leaned close to the computer screen. A perplexed look set in as she said, "His brother… is Sully?"

"What makes you think that one is Sully?" Harlan asked.

"Because of that look on his face," Bert said, leaning in too. "It's obviously him."

To Harlan, it wasn't obvious at all. He'd seen some of Roz's surveillance photos of the red-headed, freckle-faced Sully. The guy whose bio they currently had on the screen looked nothing like him with his dirty brown hair, unblemished skin, and eyes of a different color.

"How can you tell?" Harlan asked.

Roz gasped before either of them could answer. "I've seen it before too!" she said excitedly. "It's that smirk of his… of Sully's… that cocky, shit-eating grin when he's, uh…"

"Being a jagaloon?" Harlan queried.

"A what?" Roz asked.

Harlan shook his head and turned to Bert. "Didn't you say something about him being the Grovers' leader?"

"That's right, Mr. Holmes. He did all the talking when they were together, as if what he thought was all that mattered. The mouthy little shit. Mikey acted the same way, a big talker too, but not when Sully was around."

"Do you mean like a little brother who's trying to be like his big brother?" Harlan asked.

Bert nodded slowly and said, "Now that I think about it, that might describe the way it was between them—a big brother/little brother thing going on. What do you think, Morgan?"

She was already nodding when he asked the question.

"Jack's also the Grovers' explosives expert," Roz said. "Check it out."

Harlan wheeled back to Roz and the computer. Most of Jack Hubbard's bio touted eighteen months of his life, between high school and college, when he served in the US Army as an explosive ordnance disposal specialist.

"What's that?" Morgan asked, reading alongside Harlan and Roz.

"He was on the bomb squad," Roz answered. "Says here that after Basic, he received forty weeks of advanced training to learn how to detect and neutralize ordnance—you know, bombs, like IEDs. And then he was deployed in Afghanistan for... look at this... six months, when he was discharged."

Roz looked up from the screen at Harlan and said, "Since when is a tour of duty done in six months?"

"After training him for a year," he replied, "it makes you wonder what kind of discharge."

"And then he enrolls at Michigan State, along with his little brother Eli," Roz continued after turning back to the screen, "only he opts for a course of study that's, well, not exactly rocket science. Leisure studies, it says here. What kind of degree is that?"

"Maybe it's for people who don't want to work for a living," Harlan said. "Like the kind of guy whose career after college is skippering a fishing boat."

"Which, as far as we know, was the last thing he ever did in his life," Roz said, "unless he's the one who wired the bowrider to explode and then bailed out before it did."

Chapter 48

It was dinnertime and Harlan and Roz, still at the computer, were working on a couple greasy burgers when his cell phone rang.

Tank's name popped up on the caller ID.

"You see what I'm seeing, Boss? On the keg cam?"

Harlan looked at the computer. Roz was using it at the time to search photos on the Delta Grove Facebook page, flagging those that tagged any of the three Grovers they'd identified to this point, in search of a fourth accomplice. The work was tedious, and their challenge was compounded by lack of information. They knew nothing about the fourth guy other than what little Roz and Morgan may have seen of him the day at Chuck's Place when four Grovers, camouflaged in fan gear and face paint, watched the Spartans' home opener against the Western Michigan Broncos.

"We're looking at something else," Harlan said. "What do you see, Tank?"

"The little son of a bitch is alive, Boss, and he's here, standing by the keg right now."

"Sully?"

"Yeah. If he's the one in the photo you texted, I'm looking straight at him—in the flesh."

"Roz," Harlan said, "switch back to the live feed, quick. Sully's at the keg."

"Jack Hubbard?"

No sooner had Roz said his name than Jack Hubbard appeared on the computer screen, standing near the keg among a small group whose conversation was barely audible over the background noise. Tank's voice, however, came through clearly as he stepped into the camera's view and spoke up.

"Name's Jimmy D'Reaper, friends. From da UP. How 'bout you folks?"

Jack Hubbard looked Tank up and down and replied, "*From* the UP? You look like you *are* the UP—you jolly green giant. What was that name?"

Tank let loose a hearty laugh before answering, "Jimmy."

"I caught that much," Jack said.

"D'Reaper," Tank added.

The wry expression seen in his Grover bio came over Jack's face. "That's one *hell* of a name," he said. "No pun intended. I like it. I'm Jack Hubbard. Grover class of '14. What about you?"

"Class of '01. But never was a Grover, sorry to say. Just partied wit you guys back in da day."

After glancing at a member of his group, Jack looked back at Tank and said, "That's cool, green man. My pal here did the same back in our day. Just came for the parties. Isn't that right, Zeppelin?"

• • • • •

Harlan shook his head once before returning his attention to the computer screen. Leaning in close, he said, "Did I hear him say, Zeppelin?"

"I think so," Roz answered. "Does that name mean something to you?"

Other than a seventies rock band and a World War I German airship, the name had only one meaning to Harlan. He slipped on his reading glasses and murmured, "Who else could he possibly be but…"

• • • • •

"Zeppelin Reed," the guy said, offering a hand to Tank. "Come from way under the bridge—Kalamazoo. But these days home is Traverse City."

"Traverse City, ya say, eh. I know some folks down dat way. Whaddya do dere?"

"I'm a state trooper."

"A cop? Really? You gonna bust any of da underage kids here at dis kegger?"

"No way, green man. I'm off duty—way off duty—here only to watch Sparty take those Ohio State Buckeyes out to the woodshed."

"I dunno," Tank said. "Dey say Sparty's a seven-point dog at home, wouldn'tcha know."

"Oddsmakers don't know shit, green man. We're gonna crush those—"

"Grover alert! Grover alert!" shouted someone from off screen.

Tank and Zeppelin looked away in the same direction, as did Jack Hubbard, who shouted back, "What's going on?"

"Buckeyes—swarms of 'em—trying to use Grove Street to get to the game."

"Buckeyes?" Jack shouted. "In front of our house?"

"That's right, man. Fucking Buckeyes think they can walk on our street."

"Like hell!" Jack shouted back. Then came his signature smirk as he looked around the room and shouted again, "What we need is a wall! A Grover wall! Let's move!"

Suddenly the scene online became erratic. Someone at the party had grabbed the camera and mic and was capturing random segments of what appeared to be a stampede of people erupting into action while chanting a phrase, louder and louder, as their numbers grew:

"Grover wall! Grover wall! Grover wall!"

The shaky camera settled somewhere outdoors, pointing at a mob led by Jack Hubbard. He positioned Kodiak Brown at a spot in the middle of the street and shouted, "No Buckeye passes this point! Are we clear?"

"Sir, yes sir!" many in the group shouted back, like wide-eyed recruits just arriving to basic training, as they assembled themselves on each side of Kodiak to form a human wall.

A thunder of howls and profanities from the wall soon followed. The verbal assault was directed at a small group of individuals dressed in scarlet and gray—the first Buckeye fans who had happened upon the barrier of Grovers dressed in green and white.

"Dreeper!" Kodiak shouted. "Get over here, man. Join the wall!"

The camera panned rapidly away from the wall and then stopped abruptly on a mass of green that turned out to be the chest of a giant. He must have been standing next to the camera operator, who slowly panned the camera up, skyward, until it reached his face, Tank's face, eyes glaring from sockets carved deep in an oversized brow covered with green and white war paint.

• • • • •

"Oh shit," Harlan said, fumbling for his phone while staring at the face that filled the computer screen. It was the same menacing game face he'd seen Tank wearing before departing Drummond earlier that day when the big man was recalling his high school gridiron days—and the way he used to blow up offensive lines en route to helpless ball carriers in the backfield.

Roz sprung to her feet, grabbed Harlan's wrist, and said, "No, Harlan. Let him work through this."

"What are you talking about, Roz? These guys murdered his friends. He's gonna light 'em up."

"I don't think he will, Harlan."

"Why?

"Because I told him not to."

"Oh, and you think he'll listen to you? The man never does a damn thing he's told to do."

• • • • •

"Didn't you hear him, D'Reaper?" Jack Hubbard shouted. "Get your big ass over here and shore up this wall!"

During a pause that followed the camera panned to the Grover wall—Kodiak Brown at its center, still taking orders from Jack Hubbard—and then back to Tank.

Tank's throat bulged as he swallowed hard. His game face, however, began to fade as he shook his head and said, "Not me… not in my Spartan Nation…"

He then turned and walked away.

"What the…" Harlan said. "How did you get him to do that?"

"Tank and I had a good talk this morning," Roz answered without looking up from the computer.

"About what?"

"Your scam on the cove."

"What about it?"

"I told him how I thought it would have a better chance of success if he could restrain himself on his mission downstate. So I gave him some advice about how to do that."

Roz's focus remained on the computer screen and, Harlan imagined, the man in the middle of it, Kodiak Brown, who had sexually assaulted her during her first day on the case.

"I would have thought you'd want to see that guy get what he has coming."

She turned from the computer and, staring sternly into his eyes, said, "I do. But I'm not so sure that you and I are on the same page when it comes to what that means. In this scam of yours, how badly do these Grovers get hurt?"

Harlan shrugged as he responded, "Physically, not so much. You want to hear more about it?"

She nodded tentatively.

Chapter 49

The game had ended a little while ago, not well for Spartan fans, and Harlan had gone outside alone. He stood at the bank of Maxton Bay mesmerized by giant shimmers of green and purple—the northern lights—dancing in the night sky as he waited for his client to answer his phone call.

"Holmes?"

"Hey Sawed-Off. What's up?"

"What do you mean, what's up? You just called me. What do you want?"

"Oh, yeah, I did. Sorry. I'm a little distracted right now. We've had some important developments here."

"Where are you at?"

"Drummond Island."

After a pause, Harlan added, "Michigan."

"In the UP? What the hell are you doing up there?"

"It's a long story, Gino. The short of it is that I may have learned who's behind the hits at Northport, and I have a plan for getting them to come to me and tell us whatever they may know of your parents' whereabouts."

"No shit. Who are they?"

"They call themselves Grovers."

"Grovers? What's that supposed to mean?"

"Like I said, it's a long story."

"What do you got on 'em?"

Harlan hesitated as his thoughts turned to the vulnerability of his cell phone, the security of which he questioned more and more since it began roaming to towers in Canada for a signal. But he knew when he placed the call that he'd have to get into some details before he could ask something of his client.

"The Grovers worked for your dad on the pharmaceutical side of the business. While doing that, they also somehow put themselves in a position to become a major exporter of another product, one I'd guess is made in South America. But now I control their stash—all $10 million worth—and they don't know that yet."

There was a pause before Gino responded, "Did I hear you right? Did you just say..."

"Yeah, it's cargo they've been moving through your father's infrastructure, maybe under his radar. I wanna use it as bait to lure them to a place I have in mind here on the island. But I need men—a lot of men—to pull this off."

"To pull what off?"

"The appearance of an overwhelming force of CDA agents."

"Of what?"

"Never mind that. Point is, I need at least twenty men and lots of supplies. You got a pencil?"

"Whoa, slow down, Holmes. I don't have the kind of manpower you're talking about."

"How many you have?"

"Just me and my crew. Six of us total. That's it."

Harlan had anticipated this problem and had a solution in mind. But he would rather not be the one to implement it. It required going to a former client, the Chicago underboss whose case had cost him his PI license two years ago.

"Can you ask Angelo Surocco?"

"I suppose I could try," Gino said, "but I haven't been on good terms with him. He was tight with my old man and wasn't too pleased when I, uh... took things over from him."

"Well, maybe he'll be more agreeable if you ask him to do it for your dad's sake."

"And maybe he'd be even more agreeable," Gino replied, "if *someone who once was his PI* asked him to do it for my old man."

The suggestion fueled Harlan's reservation. A favor from Angelo Surocco, Harlan knew, never came without the understanding, albeit unspoken, that the one asking for it would someday be called on for payback. But Sawed-Off was right, Harlan thought; it would go better coming from him.

"Okay," he said, "I'll call Surocco myself. But you need to step up here, too, Gino. This caper is gonna cost."

"How much, Holmes?"

"A lot, starting with another private eye who's already on your payroll."

"Another PI? Who?"

"Her name's Rosalina Cortez. Goes by the name Roz. You don't want to pass on her."

"Why?"

"She's from the UP. Works out of the Soo, mostly on domestic abuse cases. But she took an infidelity case on the island, and the client just happened to be your father's point man in the pharmaceutical business. She's been surveilling these Grovers, and incidentally learned a lot about their operation—including the location of their stash that we now control."

After a pause, Harlan added, "And she's good at, you know, private investigation."

"A chick detective," Gino said, sighing. "Sounds like you're warm for her form, Holmes. You sure this is business?"

"I want you to pay her the same as me," Harlan said, ignoring the accusation.

"Another ten grand a week? Seriously?"

"What's the matter, Gino. Haven't you ever heard of pay equity?"

"Pay what?"

"Look, we need her, and I'm already having a hard time convincing her to help me with the work I'm doing for the likes of you. The money's a must."

"What else does she know that's so important?"

"I'll tell you when you get here, along with your crew and the supplies we'll need."

"What kind of time frame are we talking, Holmes?"

"Not sure exactly. Few days maybe."

"That's not much notice," Gino complained. "Are we gonna need trucks for these supplies?"

"No, you're not to use ground transport for anything or anybody."

"No cars for the guys? Why not?"

"Because twenty goodfellas crossing over on the ferry won't go unnoticed."

"Then how the hell are we supposed to get there?"

"By chopper."

"Helicopter?"

"Yeah. Whatever day we plan it for, you'll be coming in the night before, landing on Bald Knobs."

"Bald what?"

"It's a secluded place here on the island. I'll arrange for an ATV escort of the men and supplies from there. Of course, that's gonna cost too."

"What the hell are you planning up there, Holmes? Some kind of paramilitary maneuver?"

"Look, Gino, if you don't wanna do what's required, I understand. But in my next text to your father, I'll have to explain why we broke off our search for him and your mother."

"Has he even answered any of your texts, Holmes?"

"No."

"So, you have no idea whether he's alive."

"No, but I'm hopeful."

"Why?"

"Because I'd like to keep your hundred-thousand-dollar Range Rover."

Chapter 50

"You got me a job? With him?" Roz complained. She'd come outside for a view of the northern lights. Their reflection off the bay was creating an illusion of colorful lightning bolts diving down behind the horizon.

"Well, yeah," Harlan said. "I thought you'd like to be paid for all the work you're doing."

"Not by your wiseguy client."

"But I can't pay you."

"Geez, Harlan. You and your man eyes."

"What's that supposed to mean?"

"That you can't see what's right in front of you."

"But I just thought—"

Her cell phone rang. "I have to take this," she said.

"Is that your source on Eddy Chub's alibi?"

"Might be."

As Roz stepped away to take the call, Harlan proceeded to place one he needed to make. For this call, he had a special phone—a CryptoPhone—that had been given to him back when he worked for the man he was calling, Angelo Surocco. When that case ended, Angelo insisted that Harlan keep the phone on the off chance that there might be some future call between them requiring encryption. That was two years ago. And this trip into northern Michigan was the first time since then that Harlan had resumed carrying the phone because he saw the off chance coming.

Angelo wasn't one for small talk.

"Whadaya want?" he said after they'd verified their confirm code.

"Hello to you, too, Angelo."

There was no response.

Harlan cut to the chase. "I take it you know about the attack on Shotgun Landing last Tuesday."

"Of course. Who doesn't? It's all over the news."

"And that you also know about Shotgun Gino and his wife going missing after it happened."

"Sure, I heard about that."

"Well, their son hired me to find them."

"That little tightwad, Sawed-Off Gino? Paying real money to find his old man?"

"Yes, he is, and I've learned who launched the attack at Shotgun's marina and at other locations where he was doing business."

"You did?" Angelo said. "Who do you figure, Holmes, one of the families? That's been the speculation down my way on account of, you know, the way those hits went down at the marina. Sure looked mob style to me."

"It was a family, all right, but not the kind you're thinking of."

"Whadaya mean?"

"They call themselves Grovers."

"What? What the hell is a—"

"I can explain later, Angelo. Bottom line is, I know who they are, where they are, and what they think their next move is gonna be."

After a pause, Angelo said, "Last time I heard you talk this way, Holmes, was when you worked for me and had some move of your own brewing. Just what you got going right now?"

"A play on these Grovers, a scam to shake 'em down for information about Shotgun Gino's whereabouts. Thing is, I need more guys to do it—a lot more guys. Whether these Grovers were working for or against Shotgun, I doubt they'll give in easily. That's why I'm calling. I need some outside help."

"You don't even know whose side these guys are on?"

"I'm afraid not," Harlan said as he heard what sounded like the laughter of another person, muffled as though Angelo had covered the phone. Eventually it stopped and Angelo returned.

"Believe me, Holmes, whoever these Grovers are, they're not

working *for* Shotgun."

"Says who?"

"Oh, just a friend of mine who happens to be here with me right now, listening in while you're on speaker."

"What friend?"

"Me, Mr. Holmes, Shotgun Giovanni Cruzano," came the answer, followed by more laughter. This time, the phone remained uncovered.

"Shotgun Gino?" Harlan said. "Is that really you?"

"Last time I looked in the mirror."

"And your wife? Is she..."

"Alive and well, Mr. Holmes. Appreciate you asking. The two of us have been staying with Angelo since we cleared out of Traverse City last Tuesday."

"You're in Chicago?"

"That's right, at the Suroccos' fine residence."

"Who knows you're there, besides Angelo?"

"Just his wife. She and mine are good friends. Nobody else knows."

"Why not tell Sawed-Off?"

"I don't tell that little shit anything, Holmes. He's dead to me after the way he forced me into retirement. Did he tell you about that?"

"A little. His side of it, I guess."

"Oh, I see. I'll bet he told you about money he thinks he's owed, the greedy little..."

"Look, sir, that's really not my business."

"All right, then, tell me about these guys you think are gunning for me."

"Or trying to frame you for mass murder, assuming they weren't working *for* you last Tuesday, all due respect, Gino."

"Respect? What the hell are you accusing me of?"

"Nothing. It's just... I don't know you."

"Well, you know Angelo Surocco. Former client of yours, as I understand. He'll tell you the same as me. I have no idea what happened at my marina. Ain't that right, Angelo?"

"Absolutely," Angelo said, speaking in the background. "Me and ole Gino, we got no secrets. If he's saying he don't know nothing, he don't know nothing."

"What do you know about the Grovers, Gino?" Harlan asked, ignoring the character witness.

"Nothing," Gino answered. "Never even heard the word before. What the hell is a Grover, anyway?"

"Some guys Jimmy hired last summer to work for you."

"Look, other than the ones I had regular contact with—Bo Kitner in St. Ignace and the guy in charge at Drummond, Bert Brydges—I couldn't tell you who Jimmy employed. Just some guys from his old bookkeeping operation is all he told me."

"Did he tell you about the 250 kilos of street drugs that he and the Grovers smuggled to Drummond, using your boat?"

After a long silence, Gino replied, "Shit, Holmes, what are you saying? What kind of street drugs?"

"Cocaine, heroin, I don't know. I didn't sample the stuff after finding it."

"You found it? Where?"

"Are you telling me that you know nothing about *those* drugs?" Harlan said. After a long silence, he added, "Oh, I get it, Gino. Or should I call you Shotgun? You're nothing but a retired gangster turned charitable bootlegger, whose only mission in life is to provide contraband pharmaceuticals to the poor and uninsured."

Harlan could hear the man sigh on the other end of the call.

"Listen, Holmes, you and I are getting off on the wrong foot here. If Jimmy and his guys have a serious stash up there, I can see why you might think what you do. But I'm telling you, that's not the way it is. It's got nothing to do with me."

"It's got everything to do with you, Gino. They're your crew."

"I'm telling you, if they did this, they went rogue on me."

"Bullshit, Gino. According to Jimmy, the stash is worth eight figures on the other side of the Huron. How does a broken-down old bookie finance that kind of transaction?"

"I don't know, Holmes. But I'm telling you, it's not my deal. You have to believe me."

"Why? What difference does it make what I believe? My job was to find you. And I just did. I'm done."

"Wait, Holmes, don't hang up."

Harlan stopped his finger just short of tapping the screen to end the call and slowly returned the phone to his ear.

"You there, Holmes?"

"Yeah."

"Did I hear you say that you got their stash?"

"Sure, I know where it is—and now they don't."

"And it's as big as you say it is—250 kilos?"

"Yeah."

Harlan waited through another pause, until Gino said, "That means you have leverage on these guys… these Grovers."

"Yeah, and I was going to use that leverage to find you. But that's not necessary anymore."

"Maybe you could use it to help me in another way."

"You're offering me a job?"

"Yeah."

"To do what?"

"To get me out of the deep shit I'm into if Jimmy 'the Leg' and these guys he hired, these Grovers, have been moving the kind of drugs you're describing."

"What kind of trouble, Gino?"

"If you've met my son and Eddy Chub, you already know."

"Are you talking about your arrangement with some of the families—your promise to limit your business on the Lakes to pharmaceuticals?"

"Of course I am. If these idiots are into the kind of drug trafficking you're describing, they're putting me at risk of going to war—*me*, with Eddy Chub as my only soldier—against every family in the Great Lakes region. If I don't get clear of that risk, I'm a dead man walking, you hear?"

"How am I supposed to help you with that?"

"You say you got these Grovers in your sights. And from what I'm hearing right now, you sound like the kind of guy who knows how to work a situation when he has the upper hand."

"I think I know where you're going with this, Gino, and I'll tell you right now, it's not going to work."

"Why not?"

"You want me to pin the street drugs on the Grovers. Make it so that the cops bust them—and only them—for trafficking *those* drugs, right?"

"Yeah, exactly, because that's the way it is. It's their deal, not mine, and the families need to know that."

"But the deal was run from *your* place of business, Shotgun Landing, by *your* man, Jimmy, who hired these wayward Grovers to work there and in the UP for *you*. Everything points at you, Gino, because you had them supplying your benevolent street pharmacy. What am I supposed to do about that?"

"I dunno. Maybe you can leave out the part about the pharmacy."

"Oh, well, that shouldn't be a problem," Harlan replied sarcastically. "We'll just pretend that those forty-some underwater transactions, at fifty grand a pop, never happened."

"I'd appreciate that, Holmes. In fact, when this is over, I'd like to go back to that business."

"Are you even listening to me, Gino? Because if you are, you can't be serious about going back to peddling those pharmaceuticals."

"But, I am. I mean, there are people who need those drugs. They're counting on me."

"Shit, man, you *are* serious."

"I sure am. I made a commitment to help some people, and I'm not gonna break it. Now listen up, Holmes. I'll pay you twice whatever fee my cheap-ass son has been paying for your services. And me and Angelo here, we'll put at your disposal whatever men and resources you may need. Anything, just name it."

More surprising than the offer was that Harlan found himself pausing to consider it. The case he'd been working for Sawed-Off was indeed over, which meant he was currently unemployed. His thoughts then turned to some big adjustments that would have to be made to his scam on the cove if he were to take this new case.

Harlan decided to explore the proposition.

"In addition to things that your money can buy, Gino, I'd need you to be directly involved."

"You want me up there?"

"Yeah, on the front lines, at my side, following my lead."

"Okay, no problem. I'll come up with Angelo's crew."

"No," Harlan said, "I'd rather bring you in myself. Nobody's to know about you until the time is right."

"What do you mean, until the time—"

"And I have two other conditions," Harlan said as he looked across the yard where Roz had been standing. She was no longer there. "I have a partner who gets paid the same as me."

"Guess I'm okay with that," Gino replied. "Go ahead and double that fee again, Holmes, and bring him along."

"You mean her."

"Him, her, it—whatever. It don't matter to me. What's your other condition?"

Harlan paused before answering, "You have to tell me how you got that name—Shotgun."

Chapter 51

Harlan woke to a familiar voice before he could will his eyes to open.

"Hey, Boss, you mind getting up?"

"What? Tank?"

"Yeah. Was wondering if I could have the couch."

"What time is it?"

"Late... or early, depending on the hours you keep, I guess."

Harlan clicked on a lamp as he sat up. Tank's face was now clear of all but a few smears of paint. He looked tired after having spent half of the last twenty hours driving and the other half finding Grovers.

"Nice job in East Lansing, Tank."

"Got lucky is all."

"No, you made all the right moves, and some I would have never imagined you making. Like the way you walked away from those guys when you had a chance to blow up their human wall. That was so... I don't know... unlike you."

"I just did what Roz told me to do."

"Which was..."

"She said that if I could get those guys in my sights—guys who killed my friends—but then let it go, it might make me feel better."

"Better than kicking their asses would've felt?"

"Yeah. Roz says she gives the same advice to victims of domestic abuse. She says that when you hang on to anger at people who've done you wrong, they keep hurting you. And you know what, Boss, I think she's right. It felt good to just walk away. Empowering, if you know what I mean."

Harlan found this hard to grasp, even coming from Roz. One of those Grovers had sexually assaulted her—a woman dedicated to fighting such abuse—yet her advice was to let it go. After struggling to wrap his brain around it, he asked, "Are you still up for the plan, Tank?"

"Sure, Boss. I still want justice. It's just vengeance I don't need."

"But you understand your role, right? I need you to be, well, the way you were before Roz got into your head."

"Before I what?" Roz said as she entered from the dark hallway leading into the front room.

Harlan could make out only her outline until she came into the glow of the lamp. Once again, she had borrowed one of Morgan's skimpy nighties. And, again, she wore it as well as Morgan, Harlan thought. Maybe better. He tried to keep his eyes on hers.

"You filled my bagman's head with all kinds of genteel ideas, Roz. I think you've ruined him."

"I'm sure he'll recover," she said. "He just needs some rest. You want the guest room, Tank? I won't be going back to bed."

Tank thanked her and left the room.

"What about you, Harlan? Ready for breakfast?"

"Why not? We can talk about our new client."

"We've already had this conversation," Roz said, shaking her head. "I'm not working for him."

"But it's not him anymore. We have a new, new client—for me too."

She looked confused.

They went to the kitchen, where Harlan explained the outcome of his phone call the prior evening to Angelo Surocco and, as it turned out, his new client, Shotgun Gino Cruzano. Roz simply listened as she whipped up two large bowls of oatmeal mixed with raisins and nuts.

Harlan continued talking as she ate. His food sat in front of him until he finished explaining the last of the adjustments he'd made to his plan for the Grovers.

"What's the matter?" Roz asked. "You don't like my cooking?"

It was like she hadn't heard a word he said.

"I'm just talking too much," he answered.

As he forced down a spoonful of the mush, he tried to read her reaction to what he'd said. But he found that he couldn't.

"I appreciate you looking out for my paycheck, Harlan. And I can tell you've given it some thought and come to believe in the justice of Shotgun Gino's cause..."

Everything before the word "but" is bullshit, Harlan thought.

"But—"

Harlan raised his hand to stop her and asked, "What would you have me do instead?"

"Give it all to the police, of course. We already have enough on these Grovers. We don't need to—"

"Not on Zeppelin Reed, we don't. All we have on him is that he's a cop assigned to surveil Shotgun Gino who happens to be a friend of these Grovers. That cop will walk if none of the others roll over on him. We need to draw him out."

"Look, Harlan, that's not your concern. You've done your job. You found the man you were hired to—"

"And then there's whoever financed the multimillion-dollar deal. If the Grovers got help on that, there's another bad guy who walks."

"I suppose Shotgun Gino told you he's not that guy."

"That's not all he said, Roz. He's willing to get directly involved in the operation to help nail whoever that may be."

"And you think he's being straight with you?"

Harlan nodded.

"Even so, I still don't like it," Roz said. "This plan of yours, it guarantees that you'll never get back your PI license. And so much as one misstep could land not just your client but you in prison, which is not where a middle-age ex-cop wants to live out his years."

He noticed that she was speaking only in terms of risks *he'd* face if *he* continued with the case. "Sounds like you've made up your mind, Roz."

"Please, Harlan."

"I appreciate your concern," he said. "And I can see why you have doubts about Shotgun Gino. But—"

Harlan stopped himself, realizing that he was now the one trying to ease gently into points of disagreement.

"Why are you doing this?" Roz asked. "Why not just be done with these hoods?"

As he reflected on the question, Harlan came to think that he was making more than a choice about whether to continue with the case. He was making a choice about whether to continue with her. But what would she want with him—and what would he want with himself—if he could no longer be a PI? That's what he was. And he'd never again have a license to be one, he believed, even if he did walk away from these wiseguys. They had become his only source of clients, and that source would also end forever if he bailed on them now.

He said none of this to Roz, however.

"I dunno. I guess I just have to see this through," he said. "If you don't feel the same way, I ask only that you not do anything to stop me."

Chapter 52

Harlan returned to the kitchen after a quick shower and change of clothes. He stopped at the window.

The sun still had not yet risen.

Roz had already left.

On the counter beneath the window, stacked neatly, were the few bricks of drugs that they'd stashed in her backpack the evening they first met.

She's washed her hands of it, he thought. *And of me.*

Not realizing that he was doing it to mask his sorrow, he let his mind drift into a false narrative: *We hardly knew each other. It wouldn't have worked. We're too different. And besides...*

The buzz of Bert's alarm clock snapped him out of it and back into the moment.

Minutes later, Bert entered the kitchen dressed only in his boxers, eyes squinting at the light.

"Don't you want to put on some clothes for this?"

Bert grunted in response.

Harlan took it as a no. "Then let's get started. May as well leave the bricks right where they're at and have you stand next to them."

Bert positioned himself as instructed, opened his eyes fully, and, with his cell phone, took a selfie of his face next to the drugs.

Harlan then took Bert's phone and attached the selfie to a text message addressed to Mike Wazowski, Randall Boggs, and Sully. Beneath the photo, Harlan wrote: "Hey, Eli Hubbard, look what I found in your pole barn. You guys been working some OT without me. We need to talk about that."

After clicking "send," Harlan paused, waiting for possible bounce backs. The numbers Bert had for them were probably linked to burner phones, Harlan thought, but he figured that so long as they hadn't accounted for Bert, at least one of them would hold on to his phone on the chance that Bert might reach out to them, as he was now.

None of the texts bounced back.

"You remember what to say, Bert?" Harlan asked.

"I got it, Mr. Holmes."

Harlan placed a phone call to Mike Wazowski, put the phone in speaker mode, and set it on the counter.

After a number of rings the call bounced into a voicemail box for "Mikey."

Harlan ended the call and tried again.

This time an answer came on the fourth ring.

"What the... B-Bert... Brydges?"

"Morning, Mikey," Bert said in an upbeat manner. "You sound a little under the weather. Tough loss to the Buckeyes last night?"

"What the hell... Bert? Is that you?"

"Damn straight it is, Mikey. You're talking to the guy whose woman you were fucking. But I don't give a shit about that. I got something that really matters on my mind."

"What do you want, Brydges?"

"Apparently you haven't checked your text messages in the last two minutes."

"Shit, man, you just woke me up."

"Well, then, check now. I can wait."

A minute later Eli Hubbard was back on the line. "How the hell did you find our stash, Brydges?"

"I like your choice of words, Mikey—*our* stash. Tell me something, *partner*, would you rather I call you Eli and our other associates Jack and Kodiak?"

"How'd you learn our names?"

Harlan raised a hand to stop Bert from responding.

The silence lingered.

"That private eye of yours?" Eli said. "The one who took those photos of Morgan and me? Is that how you got our names, and found *my* stash?"

Harlan kept his hand raised.

Another interval of silence passed.

"Dammit, Brydges, say something! Where's my shit?"

Harlan dropped his hand and nodded.

"I'll tell you where it is, Eli, in thirty minutes."

"Why not now?"

"In thirty minutes, you call me. And do it on Skype. I want to show it to you, all of you—Jack and Kodiak too. And I'll tell you something, Eli. If I don't see all three of you Grovers on that call, I'll dump the whole damn stash into a lake."

"What makes you think I can get ahold of those guys so soon?"

"Thirty minutes, Eli. Or you never see it again."

"But you can't expect—"

Harlan ended the call. "That was good," he said.

"Real good, Bert," Morgan said as she entered the kitchen.

Bert snapped his head around. "Morgan? How much of that did you hear?"

"All of it. I listened from the hall."

"And you're okay with it? Even what I said about, you know…"

"I'm fine with it, Bert. And I'm ready to do my part to stick it to these guys. Why don't you put some pants on and join me?"

Chapter 53

The Skype call came thirty-two minutes later. Bert took it outside on his laptop, down by the water where his Carolina Skiff was docked. He was seated at its bow on top of a large mound of something covered with a tarp. At the helm stood Harlan and Morgan, out of the laptop's camera range.

"Morning, Grovers, long time no see," Bert said. His demeanor was even more upbeat than during the earlier phone call.

"Cut the shit, Brydges," Eli said. "Where is it?"

"Right under my ass."

"I don't see it."

Morgan came up from behind the laptop, took it from Bert, and walked it back a few steps, widening the camera angle.

"Who's moving the camera?"

"I am," Morgan said, laughing as she leaned her head around to see the screen. "My, don't you boys look worse for the wear. Late night there in East Lansing, Eli, watching ole Sparty get his little butt spanked?"

"How would you know where we are?"

"I'm just hoping you didn't drive very far after getting shit-faced at Delta Grove last night."

There was a pause before Eli asked, "Is that something else his PI figured out?"

"Who gives a damn what they know about us," said one of the others. "Is that Maxton Bay I see behind you, Bert?"

"That's right, Kodiak," Bert answered. "We're just hanging out at home with our new retirement fund here."

Bert hopped to his feet and yanked the tarp aside, displaying 250 bricks of something individually wrapped in brown paper. All but a few were phony duplicates of the real bricks of drugs that Harlan and Roz had found in the wall of the Grovers' pole barn and relocated beneath its floorboards. Bert and Morgan had manufactured the duplicate bricks the night before, using a mix of dirt and clay scraped from the shoulder of an unpaved road.

Bert resumed sitting on the mound of bricks. Next to him, on top, were the few real ones. He picked up one of those and opened it.

"Mind telling me what this is?"

"You don't know?" Kodiak scoffed. "You're such a dumb ass, Brydges."

Bert extended the brick over the water and slowly poured the white powder into the bay.

"What are you doing, man?" shouted a third voice.

Must be Jack Hubbard, Harlan thought.

"I asked a question!" Bert shouted back. "What is it?"

"It's the Big C, dude," the third guy answered. "Quality shit. Not something you should be feeding the fish, Bert."

"That you, Jack?" Bert asked as he reached for another real brick. He opened it and scooped out a mound of powder onto three of his fingers.

"Sure is, friend. Hey, you be careful with that. You got yourself damn near a full gram of some potent nose candy there."

Bert smiled at the camera as he raised up the powder and took in most of it in one snort. He would have looked like an experienced coke user were it not for the huge smear of white residue that remained on his nose and cheek when he finished.

"Morgan, you gotta try some of this. Jack's right. It's good shit."

She promptly set the laptop down near the helm, still pointing at Bert, and joined him for a line.

Although using the stuff was not part of his plan, Harlan found himself enjoying the couple's improvisation, and even more the Grovers' reaction to it.

"What the hell!" Eli shouted. "I didn't call to watch you do my drugs. Now you listen up, asshole. You're gonna—"

"Oh, is this brick yours, Eli?" Bert said. "Beg your pardon." He then turned and dumped it into the bay, reached for another real one, and said, "Here, I'll do one of mine."

Jack laughed uproariously.

"What's so damn funny?" Eli shouted.

"You are, little brother. You act like you're the man here."

"You saying he is?"

"Damn straight, little bro. The dude's three hundred miles away messin' with a mountain of pearl, but at the same time he's gettin' right in your face, messin' with you, before he starts calling the shots. Ain't that right, Bert?"

Bert glanced up from the laptop, at Harlan, who now stood directly behind it. Rising to his feet and returning his attention to the screen, Bert asked, "Why aren't you dead, Jack, like my friends who were on that boat when it got blown to hell?"

Jack didn't respond.

"I know you were there, *dude*. I talked to Sam Boadle."

"Sure, I was there. But I'll tell you what, man, it's just shit luck that I survived. You remember the boarding ladder on that rig, the one for the swim platform that wouldn't stay fastened down?"

"Yeah. I told Pauly Russo a million times to fix that damn thing."

"Well, I'm glad he didn't. I was down low on the platform hauling that ladder in when the bowrider blew. About the only part of me exposed above board was my ass. Felt like a mule kicked it. Next thing I know I'm in the water, and there ain't no more boat."

"You got a bruise on your ass you can show me, Jack? Or should I call you Sully?"

"Listen, man, if you're saying what I think you are, you got it wrong. I was coming your way with your friends to bring all of you into the deal. Far as I'm concerned, you're an equal owner of the stash, along with the rest of us who dodged the bullet that day."

"Whose bullet, Jack?"

"Way I figure, it had to be Shotgun Gino Cruzano. He must've found out. Didn't Jimmy 'the Leg' ever tell you how he got that name?"

Bert nodded his head, but curled his eyebrows skeptically.

"Then you know Cruzano's a sociopath, man," Jack said. "That's why we were keeping the Big C under the radar—on Jimmy's orders—waiting 'til we had it all moved off the mainland. We were never planning to cut you out, Bert. I swear, we're partners in this deal… I mean, if you want in."

Bert stared into space as his expression began showing doubt. Either it was great acting, Harlan thought, or Bert was getting turned around. Harlan had seen it happen before—a player getting himself conned in the middle of his own con. *C'mon, Bert,* Harlan thought. *You must remember: Jack's the explosives expert, Eli's the nerd, and you figured out who murdered Finn Ramsey.*

"So what do you say, Bert, you want in?" Jack repeated.

Letting his expression relax, Bert responded, "I appreciate the offer, Jack. I mean it. But I don't want in. I want out."

"I get it, man. Guys getting whacked and shit. I didn't sign up for any of that either. But I don't see how we can cash you out. Every penny we got is into that stash behind you."

"*Now* you're bullshitting, Jack."

"What makes you think so?"

"Because you Grovers are barely out of school, still wet behind the ears. You didn't finance this shit. Someone else did. For all I know, it could've been Shotgun Gino himself, in on it all along with you guys, no matter what you're saying now. And maybe his dealing in this so-called Big C pissed off the wrong people, maybe even the mob that he used to belong to. Whadaya got to say about that possibility?"

Harlan smiled, relieved to know it was his guy, Bert, still running the con.

"I guess it's a theory," Jack said. "Some might even think it's a good one. But the truth is, Bert, I don't know where Jimmy went for the money. He was running things, just like he was with the pharmaceuticals, and we kicked in what we could, like I said. But where he got the bulk of the funds for this, I don't know. I really don't."

Bert glanced at Harlan, who returned a quick nod.

"Well, I'll tell you what," Bert said, "I'm sorry to hear about your financial situation, cuz if I don't get what I want, when I want it, this whole stash will end up in that bay behind me."

"What do you want, Bert?"

"Two hundred and fifty grand. By sunset."

Nothing was said for what seemed a long while. It was then that Harlan first noticed last night's crickets, still active, and a chill in the morning breeze hinting of a winter soon to come.

He nodded at Bert again.

"Go ahead, sweetheart," Bert said as he turned to Morgan. "Start feeding the fish."

Morgan grabbed an armload of the fake bricks and dropped them over the side of the skiff.

"Stop! For God's sake, stop!" Jack shouted. "We'll find a way to get you some money. Just chill, man."

Bert raised his hand to stop Morgan and asked, "How much?"

"Hold on, give me a minute," Jack said.

Harlan could hear their murmurs as the Grovers held a quick conference. When it ended, Jack said, "Okay Bert, look, what we think we can scrape together isn't what you asked for. Actually, it's only about half that much..."

"Okay, Morgan," Bert said, again turning back to her.

"Wait, Bert, let me finish."

Bert raised his hand again to stop her.

"Bottom line, man, and I'm telling you, it's the best we can do—a hundred and fifty grand, and you can take the amount we're short in product. You seem to like the stuff. Go ahead and keep a few kilos for you and Morgan, along with the cash. Seriously, bud, it's all we got. What do you say?"

Bert looked back at Morgan, who shrugged. Turning back to the laptop, he asked, "By sunset?"

"C'mon, Bert, be reasonable here. It's Sunday. We can't do it that soon. We need at least a few days."

Harlan held up two fingers.

Bert sighed deeply and said, "You got two. Tuesday night, you come to Drummond on the ferry leaving DeTour at 10:10 p.m. And you board that ferry on foot. No car. No weapons. Just the money. Got that?"

"Okay, yeah, I think we can manage that," Jack said. "Tuesday night, we walk onto the ferry with nothing but the money."

"All three of you."

"Sure, no problem."

"And only the three of you."

"That's fine. As far as I can tell, you and us three are the only ones still in this thing anyway."

"You're overlooking one, Jack."

"Who?"

"My partner. He'll be there Tuesday night when you come ashore. He's your ride to the place where I'll drop the stash."

"Wait, what partner?"

"Don't worry, he'll know who you are. And he'll take you where we'll meet, if all the money's there. But I'll tell you what, Jack, if you're so much as a penny short of 150K, you won't see me, you'll never see your cocaine, and my partner will unleash hell."

"Whoa," Kodiak said. "Who's this partner of yours?"

"Funny you should ask, Kodiak."

"Why?"

"Because you Grovers have already met him."

"Who?"

Bert paused to smile before responding.

"Jimmy D'Reaper."

Chapter 54

"What is it, Mr. Holmes?" Bert asked as he and Morgan stopped and turned. Harlan had come to a sudden halt on their walk back to Bert's place after the Skype meeting with the Grovers. Something that was said during the meeting was touching off a series of thoughts.

"The guy lied about so much," Harlan said, "from the way he survived the boat's explosion to who he said did all the killing. But something he said might have actually been true."

"Are you talking about Jack Hubbard?" Bert asked.

Harlan nodded and said, "It was after you told him your theory about how the coke was financed. Remember telling him that Shotgun Gino may have done that?"

"Sure, just the way you wanted me to, Mr. Holmes, to see how he'd react."

"And his reaction was telling," Harlan said.

"How so?"

"He balked at the theory and then said, and these were his exact words, '*But the truth is, Bert, I don't know where Jimmy went for the money; I really don't.*'"

"Okay..." Bert said uncertainly.

"Everything he said to that point was a lie," Harlan explained, "and then he makes that remark prefaced with the phrase, *the truth is.*"

"What are you saying, Mr. Holmes?" Morgan asked. "That Jack—a con man in his own right—was actually telling the truth about not knowing where the money came from, because he told us he was telling the truth?"

"What he told us, Morgan, was he didn't know *where Jimmy went for it.* There's an admission embedded in that denial—an admission to knowing that Jimmy in fact did go somewhere, or to someone, outside their circle for it."

As they resumed walking, Harlan said, "Roz told me what you said, Bert, about Bo Kitner coming to you with a proposal to skim pharmaceutical purchase money from Shotgun Gino."

This time it was Bert who halted the group as he replied, "And I told Bo *hell no,* Mr. Holmes. No way was I gonna cross Shotgun Gino. And not just because some people say he's a sociopath. The man came all the way out here to the island to meet me, by himself. And before he left, I could tell he trusted me, enough to introduce me to his Canadian connection and to tell them they could trust me too. I don't violate that kind of confidence."

"How about Jimmy?" Harlan asked. "Was he a straight shooter like you?"

"I… I always knew him to be," Bert said, his tone unsure.

"But Jimmy was in on Bo's proposal, at least that's what Bo said. In fact, I'll bet Bo told you it was Jimmy's idea, didn't he?"

"How did you know that, Mr. Holmes? I never told Roz that."

Because Jimmy knew that Shotgun would never defy the families and knowingly finance the coke, Harlan thought. *The money would have to be stolen from him, and for some reason, Jimmy was desperate enough to consider doing that.*

"If he couldn't get the money from Shotgun, who do you think Jimmy might have gone to?" Harlan asked.

"I can't think of anyone," Bert said. "I can't even imagine, because if Jimmy had that kind of source, he would've used it to restart his old business. The man had been booking bets for over forty years. That's what he knew and loved. He was never a drug dealer, not before this venture anyway."

• • • • •

Tank was finishing breakfast when they returned to the cabin. "How'd it go?" he asked.

"They crushed it," Harlan said, "like a couple hustlers who've been on the grift all their lives."

Tank smiled at the couple and asked, "When does Jimmy D'Reaper come for his due, Boss?"

"Tuesday night."

Much had to be done before then, Harlan thought, and some of it as soon as possible. In all likelihood, the Grovers would soon send someone to Drummond to scout ahead.

"I know I've been over this with you guys," Harlan said, "but I want to be sure that we're all clear. Bert, you know what you and Morgan are doing next, right?"

"Got it, Mr. Holmes. We're relocating to the Wayfarers Mart over on Scammon Cove and laying low there until things get underway."

"Good," Harlan said, "and you know what to do in the meantime, right?"

"Sure, get Wayfarers ready for the operation, the main issue being to restore power."

"Make sure to let me know if that gives you any trouble, Bert. The old generator for that place probably needs more than just gas and a new spark plug to get it up and running."

"Don't worry, Mr. Holmes. If it's functional, I'll get it going. Like I said before, I do all the engine work on the boats and vehicles around here."

"Right. And the rope we'll need to access the old mill's chimney—you said something about having that too."

"Better than a rope, sir. There's a rope ladder for a deer stand in the woods. Hunting season is still a month off. Nobody will miss it."

Harlan paused before continuing. Most of the supplies and equipment would be choppered in Monday evening along with a crew from Chicago. But there was one more important detail that Harlan had in mind for Bert and Morgan, by far their most challenging task. "What about the chickens?" he asked.

Bert smacked his forehead. "Oh, dang it, that's right."

"What chickens?" Morgan asked.

"I forgot to tell you about them," Bert said. "We need to get at least twenty live chickens for the operation."

"What the heck for?"

Bert shrugged and looked at Harlan, who answered, "I'll explain later. For now, just make sure to get those chickens in time for dinner on Tuesday. And make sure we have everything needed to pluck, clean, and roast every one of 'em."

"Okay," Morgan said, nodding slowly, "but why can't we just pick up frozen chickens at the supermarket?"

"No," Harlan said. "That's no good. They have to be live birds. At least twenty. Can you get them?"

"We'll try to figure out a way," Bert said.

"Trying isn't good enough," Harlan said. "First thing tomorrow, you let me know whether or not you have a line on those chickens. If you don't, I'll find 'em myself."

Harlan then turned to Tank, who began speaking before questioned. "I know my job, Boss. I'm gonna set up some spy cams on East Channel Road, where the ferry comes in, and some at Bass Cove to keep an eye on Mikey's house and pole barn."

"And you're to find a place at Bass Cove to locate yourself for a stakeout," Harlan said.

"Right, Boss. And if a Grover shows, I'm supposed to attach one of Roz's GPS trackers to their car."

Harlan then realized that he hadn't seen any of Roz's spy cams or GPS trackers left behind that morning, only the few bricks of cocaine that they'd placed in her backpack. "Is her backpack still here?" he asked.

"I haven't seen it, Boss, but I think she left some stuff in a grocery bag I saw in the guest room when I woke up."

"What's in it?"

"I don't know. I didn't look. There's an envelope on it addressed to you. Thought it best to leave it. Probably a love letter."

"I can assure you it's anything but that," Harlan shot back, rolling his eyes. "That woman wants nothing to do with me. And as far as I'm concerned..."

"Oh, please," Morgan interjected. "When the hell are you gonna wake up, Mr. Holmes, and jump that woman's bones? For crying out loud, it's obviously what the two of you want—and need."

Harlan opened his mouth to speak, but he didn't know what to say.

"She's right, Boss," Tank added. "The two of you, the way you are around each other—it's obvious. Maybe you should go read that letter and see for yourself."

• • • • •

The letter consisted of two short sentences: the first, nowhere near what Tank had predicted; the second, however, just a near miss.

Dear Harlan,

You'll find the things you need in this bag and on the kitchen counter. In another time or place, maybe it could have been. Best,

Roz

Chapter 55

The following morning Harlan was at his self-assigned place of deployment, outside Bert's cabin, peering between tree branches, when his cell phone vibrated. He glanced at the caller ID. It was Bert, calling first thing as instructed with an update on the chickens, or so Harlan hoped.

"Yeah, what's up?"

"I just checked a voicemail, Mr. Holmes, left maybe ten or fifteen minutes ago by the deputy sheriff, saying he wants to see me."

"About what?"

"I'm not sure. He just said it was urgent and that he wants to meet with me right away. I figure it's probably about my boat, you know, the dinghy I reported missing, along with Finn Ramsey and Randall Boggs. Cops must've found the boat and maybe…"

During a pause, Harlan heard a vehicle traveling on Maxton Road, getting louder. It was only the second one that morning.

"What do you think, Mr. Holmes? Should I call him back?"

Harlan continued listening to the approaching vehicle. It now sounded like two.

"Mr. Holmes?"

The first one turned onto Way Winx Road and sped toward Bert's cabin.

"I think they found Finn Ramsey's body," Harlan said.

"How do you know?"

"Because that deputy wouldn't be making a personal visit right now just to tell you about your dinghy."

Harlan ended the call and watched as a patrol car for the Chippewa

County Sheriff's Department locked up its brakes in front of the cabin. The second vehicle, following close behind, was a Coast Guard SUV. It also stopped in front of Bert's cabin. A uniformed officer emerged from each: a lanky guy from the county sheriff's car and a heavyset woman from the Coast Guard's. The sheriff's deputy held a piece of paper in his hand.

A search warrant, Harlan thought.

The officers met at the cabin door, knocked hard, and announced themselves. After trying again and waiting, the sheriff's deputy went around back. A few minutes later the front door opened and the Coast Guard officer entered the cabin through it.

• • • • •

A half hour had passed before the Coast Guard officer exited the cabin. She made her way around the neighborhood, knocking on doors of other cabins and learning what Harlan already knew—everybody was gone for the season. She'd soon learn the same about the resort next door, Harlan thought, as he watched her walk over to its office.

His cell phone vibrated again. This time it was Tank.

"I got company, Boss."

"At Bass Cove?"

"Yeah, some hippie driving a VW van."

As Tank said this, the ping of an instant tech alert came through Harlan's cell phone. The motion detector for a spy cam in the pole barn had activated. Harlan scrolled to his phone's app while talking with Tank on speaker.

"Did you say hippie?"

"That's right, Boss. Long hair, big beard, tattered jeans—the whole nine yards. Showed up in some old van, like Rip Van Winkle just getting back from Woodstock. He's in the pole barn, as we speak."

Harlan then saw this for himself on his cell phone. It felt surreal, like he'd been transported back to his early childhood and was watching on TV one of those freethinking peaceniks that his dad used to poke fun at, except this one wasn't there to promote love over war. He was removing the screws from the fake circuit box in the pole barn to confirm whether the space behind the box had been emptied of 250 kilos of cocaine.

Recalling the distance from the floor to the circuit box, Harlan estimated the hippie's height to approximate Zeppelin Reed's. And his physique probably matched as well—a compact, muscular mesomorph—though it was hard to tell for sure beneath the loose-fitting jean jacket and bell bottoms.

"Have you gotten to the van?" Harlan asked.

"Not yet, Boss. He drove that VW clear down to the pole barn, straight away, and parked right outside the door. There's no way I can get close enough to attach one of the trackers."

"All right, keep your distance. And stay on the line."

The Coast Guard officer had returned from the resort's office to the porch of Bert's cabin, where she seemed to chat idly with the sheriff's deputy. Harlan tried to imagine what they were looking for besides Bert Brydges. If it was evidence of a crime, their warrant was supposed to specifically describe not only what it was, but also their grounds for probable cause to believe it was inside. Of course, he well knew how creative cops could be with facts in order to meet that standard. Whatever it was, hopefully they were giving up their search for it. The hippie would be here soon, no doubt.

"Hey, Boss, he's on the move."

Harlan glanced at his phone's screen. Sure enough, the hippie had left the pole barn.

"Okay, Tank, listen up. I want you to—"

"Hold on, Boss. He's stopping by the house."

While Harlan waited for Tank to continue, he watched the officers return to the driveway, shake hands, and head for their respective vehicles.

"Looks like I might get a shot at the van after all," Tank said.

"How so?"

"He went into the house."

"Can you tell what he's doing in there?"

"Well… looks like he's on the first floor, turning on lights… from one room to the next."

"Searching the place?"

"Maybe."

"Let me know when he goes upstairs."

A few minutes later, Tank said, "He just got up there."

"Okay, where are you right now?"

"Not far from the van."

"You say it's old?"

"Yeah."

"Did you see him hold the handle when he closed the door or stick the key in after?"

"No, I don't think so."

"Try to get inside."

"Seriously?"

"Yeah. It sounds like he left it unlocked."

A few seconds later, Tank said, "You're right. I'm in."

"Just check the glove box for registration or proof of insurance—something that might have a name or address."

As Harlan watched his visitors drive away, Tank returned to the phone. "Got it, Boss. Looks like it's registered to a George Sanderson, from Cross Village, Michigan."

Harlan repeated the name, "Sanderson… George Sanderson." He'd heard or read it somewhere, recently.

"You know him, Boss?"

"Kind of," Harlan said, making the connection. "He's one of the monsters from that Disney movie." *The one who had the run-in with that knockoff federal agency, the CDA,* Harlan recalled Roz telling him.

"Another one?" Tank said.

"I'll tell you more later. Just put a tracker on that VW and get back in the woods."

Chapter 56

Harlan broke off his stakeout and took up surveillance of the hippie, following the GPS signal transmitting from his van as it toured the island. The only time the hippie stopped was at Bert's place, which of course got him nowhere near Bert.

Eventually the hippie returned to where his tour had begun and settled into in an empty campground located a few miles from Bass Cove. By then it was about an hour before sunset and Harlan needed to be elsewhere.

• • • • •

The dirt road that Harlan took into the island's interior eventually vanished, and he completed his journey on foot to the highest point on Drummond Island, an area known as Bald Knobs. The view of the setting sun remained spectacular for a few minutes after he reached a clearing near the summit.

Still standing in the middle of the clearing, Harlan finally dropped his gaze from the horizon and resumed the task at hand. He turned full circle slowly, studying the area's even terrain and tree-lined perimeter. Bert was right, he thought. It was a perfect landing site for visitors due to arrive soon.

As Harlan removed some supplies from his backpack, he heard the distant hum of motorized vehicles resonate across the landscape. Barring an unusual coincidence, those were ATVs being driven by Tank, Bert, and Morgan to a point as far as the dirt trails would take them; from there, they'd hike in as he had.

Twilight was giving way to night by the time his companions approached on foot.

"Sorry about running late," Tank said when they arrived. "The hike was longer than I expected."

"That's okay," Harlan said. "We still have some time, and we need a location like this, something out of the way."

"Out of the way? Are you kidding, Boss? This place feels like it's on the end of the planet. How are they gonna find us out here?"

Harlan smiled in response as he began setting up signal lights around the perimeter of the clearing. "Anything to report?" he asked.

"Not really, Boss. I've been keeping an eye on all the cameras, like you asked, and haven't seen anyone suspicious since that hippie got to the island."

"What's been happening down by the ferry dock?"

"Just what you'd expect, I guess. People coming and going like they always do. Mostly Islanders, I suspect, running errands on the mainland. Nobody who ended up at Bert's place or the Grovers' house on Bass Cove."

"How about the Wayfarers Mart?" Harlan asked, turning to Bert.

"I think it's good to go, sir. Morgan and I got that generator working like new, put in some lights, and got everything needed for dinner tomorrow, except… uh…"

"Except the main course," Morgan added, "those live chickens you wanted."

"I heard, but that's okay," Harlan said, turning his head to search the sky for the source of a faint sound that was growing louder. "They'll be here soon."

• • • • •

They stood clear of the rotor downdraft as a large utility helicopter set down to deliver, it was promised, twenty-plus men, tactical gear, weapons, communications equipment, and two dozen live chickens.

As soon as the door opened there came a shout from inside the chopper's cabin, "Let me the hell outta here, away from these fucking birds!" It was the voice of his client's son, Sawed-Off Gino Cruzano. He stepped out first and directed his cold stare at Harlan before his second foot touched the ground.

"Quick, Tank, run some interference for me, would you?" Harlan said.

Tank did as instructed and engaged Sawed-Off while Harlan looked among the disembarking wiseguys for a soldier whom he'd specifically requested that Angelo Surocco send along. The man, Phoenix Wade, was Surocco's go-to guy for challenging assignments. Harlan had worked closely with him in the past and came to believe that, of all the badasses he'd ever encountered, Phoenix was second only to Tank.

He was easy to spot among the crew, as he was the only person of color Harlan had seen since his arrival to the island. The way he carried himself also made him stand out, Harlan thought, as he watched Phoenix refuse to remove his mirrored sunglasses despite the overtaking darkness.

The shades were part of his cover, his way of not letting on that, inside the six-foot frame packed with lean muscle, was a man who could outthink most others. Especially those who bought into his cliché street-kid routine.

"Yo, Holmes!" Phoenix shouted as he approached. "What it is, brotha?"

"Shit, Phoenix, how can you even see me through those shades?"

"Because you're fluorescent, man. Don't you ever get your white ass outside?"

"Truth is, I don't. I've been working indoors the last couple years."

"So I hear. They say you been runnin' some trendy health club for hot chicks in tights—dawg."

"I wish."

"And now what, you're back in the game, old man?"

"Something like that. Appreciate you coming along."

"Hell, you think I was gonna miss this? No way, man. This scam you got goin' here is already legend back in Chi-town."

"What're they saying?"

"That you're taking down some homicidal cop who's trying to pin a drug rap on ole Shotgun Gino. Tell you what, man, that cop picked the wrong mark. Every boss with business anywhere near the Lakes is backing you on this play."

"Seriously?"

"You didn't know? Shit, man, wait 'til you see what we brought along, besides those chickens you asked for. What's up with that, anyway?"

They both looked at the crates of squawking hens that had been unloaded from the chopper. Sawed-Off was still complaining about them to Tank.

"Tell you about that in a minute," Harlan said as he pulled an iPod out of his pocket. "Want to talk first about a particular job I have in mind for you."

Harlan powered up the iPod and opened an app that displayed the signal transmitting from the GPS tracker on the van of the hippie, AKA George Sanderson. It was still parked at the campsite near Bass Cove.

"That the cop?" Phoenix asked.

Harlan nodded, handed Phoenix the device, and said, "I think it's him. We don't actually have hard proof of that yet. To get it, we need someone on him for the next twenty-four hours."

"Does that someone get to take down his sorry ass?"

"Yeah, but not until they get video evidence of who, and what, he really is."

Phoenix removed his sunglasses and said, "I suppose you want him alive."

"Can't ask him questions if he's not."

"You think you're gonna get answers?"

"That's what the chickens are for."

• • • • •

Eddy Chub was the last of the crew to step down from the chopper. He joined Tank and Sawed-Off and said something to them before Harlan got to within earshot.

"The hell with that, man, I'm not waiting," Sawed-Off replied to Eddy.

"What's the problem?" Harlan asked.

Sawed-Off shot a hostile look at Eddy and said, "What do you think? The bane of my existence—Eddy Chub."

Looking away, Eddy dropped his head and poked out his lower lip.

"Hey!" Tank shouted. "I don't give a damn who you are, Sawed-Off. You call Eddy that name one more time, and I'm gonna bust you up."

"What name?" Harlan asked. "The one he's been called since he was a kid? Eddy Chu—"

"Don't say it, Boss. Eddy don't like it no more."

Harlan recalled the advice that Roz had offered about the name. If Eddy was going to lose weight and get in shape, it was important, she thought, that he change the way he and others thought about him—beginning with his name. Harlan turned to Eddy and said, "Sorry about that, Eddy."

Still pouting, Eddy looked up. "It's okay, Mr. Holmes."

"No it's not," Harlan replied. "I wouldn't like it either. As a matter of fact, I wouldn't like any of the nicknames you wiseguys call each other. Why do you guys do that, anyway—Sawed-Off?"

"Well... uh," Sawed-Off stammered, "you gotta call a guy something. And just look at the fat slob. Can you think of any better name than—"

"Don't you go there," Tank growled. "You know damn well what he's to be called from now on."

"Yeah, right," Sawed-Off said, rolling his eyes. "Humvee Eddy. Like that works for him."

"Humvee Eddy?" Harlan said, looking at the obese man.

Eddy nodded and said, "Yes, sir. Hummer for short."

Another military vehicle, Harlan thought, glancing at Eddy's new life coach, Tank. "Okay, I get it... Hummer. Now why don't you tell me what the problem is here."

Eddy looked at the chickens as he spoke. "It's them, Mr. Holmes. They've been packed tight in those crates since we left Chicago. It's cruel. I was just saying to these guys that we should get them back to the Wayfarers Mart right away and find somewhere to turn 'em loose."

Tank nodded and said, "I was thinking maybe in the shed, Boss."

"Can you even believe these two?" Sawed-Off said. "It's gonna take a bunch of trips to get all of us and the gear back to the Cove, and they wanna take these fucking birds first. Shit, they're gonna be dinner tomorrow."

"Don't mean they should suffer between now and then," Tank said.

"Okay, you guys, that's enough," Harlan said. "Let's just figure out a way to work this out. Gino, why don't you join them on the first trip back, along with the chickens?"

"No way, Holmes. I'm not spending another minute with those stinkin' birds."

Taking notice of Tank's expression, Harlan replied, "Then, as far as I can tell, you'll have to make a choice: wait, or walk."

Chapter 57

Harlan's next morning began with a road trip back into the Lower Peninsula, to Traverse City, where he'd scheduled a meeting for later that day. By midmorning he was driving south on US-31 with still a ways to go when his virtual assistant, Siri, spoke out from his cell phone—

"In a quarter of a mile, turn right on Levering Road."

Siri was taking him on a planned detour west, to the rural community of Cross Village. From there, she directed him a short distance south on M119, through the area's famed Tunnel of Trees, and then onto a back road. It was the road on which the hippie, AKA George Sanderson, lived, at least according to the registration for the VW van that Tank had found.

"You have arrived," Siri said. "Your destination is on the right."

"What?" Harlan replied, stopping in front of a dilapidated farmhouse—the quintessence of the small farmer's plight—on what otherwise was a picturesque stretch of country road.

"You have arrived. Your destination is…"

"This dump?"

"I'm sorry. I don't understand what you mean by, this du…"

Harlan shut off the app, got out of the car, and approached the shambles on foot, trudging through weeds and around junk strewn about the yard—the rusted shell of a fifty-year-old Plymouth Fury, vestiges of household furnishings, and other garbage in various stages of decomposition.

He made his way to a doorway that had no door. It was on the side of the house over which the roof had not yet collapsed. He stepped through, slipped on a pair of plastic gloves, and found a kitchen with more junk inside.

Could this possibly be the right place? he wondered, hoping that something in the mess might tell him who made it.

It didn't take long. Among the trash was junk mail. About half of it was addressed to George Sanderson and the other half to James P. Sullivan, known at this point to be Jack Hubbard.

A joint investment? Harlan wondered. *What the heck for?*

Harlan's thoughts turned to the reason he'd come there. He was looking for something, anything, that might identify George Sanderson, no doubt the fourth Grover, as Zeppelin Reed, the state trooper whom he'd met a week ago at the scene of the Northport massacre. Such evidence would be helpful for Harlan's meeting later that day.

Even more helpful, if he could find it, would be evidence that might shed light on the backstory of these Grovers, especially the cop who seemed so earnest about his duty to protect and serve when Harlan first met him. How did the young man and his college buddies ever get themselves involved in mass murder and the trafficking of cocaine in a quantity larger than any ever seized by law enforcement in northern Michigan's history?

Harlan found nothing of interest, however, until he reached the last of the rooms not yet buried beneath the sinking roof. In that room was a fireplace. He paused, trying to recall whether he'd seen a chimney when he was outside the house. He went back out for another look. The closest thing he could find was an exterior pipe for the wood stove in the kitchen.

A wood stove with an exhaust system, Harlan thought, *but a fireplace without one.* He recalled the phony breaker panel in the Grovers' pole barn back at Bass Cove and how it was used to conceal illegal drugs. *Are phony built-in appliances a modus operandi?*

If they were, he thought, then so too might be the use of security cameras to monitor them, as the Grovers had done back at Bass Cove.

Suddenly Harlan felt exposed. He got out his cell phone and called Phoenix Wade, the wiseguy watching the hippie back on Drummond Island. After explaining his situation, Harlan asked, "What's he doing right now?"

"A lot of nothing, man."

"You sure?"

"Yeah, I'm sure. After you left this morning, he took another one of his drives over to Bert's place. Then he came back to the same campsite he stayed at last night. He's not exactly roughing it in the wild, though."

"What do you mean?"

"He's been lounging in his van all day, watching TV. Right now he's got ESPN's Sports Center blaring inside there."

"How close are you?"

"Not too close. I'm hearing it with a listening device we brought along yesterday."

"You hear anything else more interesting?"

"Just some conversations with his homeboys, mostly about the money. Nothing about any trespasser at George Sanderson's place. And he's not acting like he knows you're onto him."

"He hasn't made a sweep of the van?"

"Not that I've seen."

"Or the campsite?"

"Nope."

"All right, let me know if he does anything like that."

Harlan returned to the fireplace. On closer inspection it aroused even more suspicion. Inside there was charred wood, but the walls to the firebox containing it were clean, as if the wood had been burned somewhere else and then placed inside. He began pushing and pulling randomly at various parts of the fireplace—its mantle, header, pillars, trim panel—to see if it might move on an unseen hinge or pivot. It didn't.

Next, he removed the wood and grate from inside and continued probing—pushing and banging on the walls of the firebox. Still there was no movement. Stepping back, he scolded himself—*think, Harlan*—as he studied the fixture. *It's a modern appliance that's never been used… in this shithole.*

He reached inside again, this time to find somewhere to dig in his fingertips, and pulled. He thought he felt it move, the whole thing. He pulled harder. It did move. Eventually he worked the entire fireplace insert away from the wall and found that it wasn't connected to anything in back.

At the base of the cavity left behind was a chunk of metal about the size and shape of a manhole cover. With some effort, he was also able to slide it out by hand, revealing just what one might expect to find underneath—a manhole.

Harlan leaned into the breech with a flashlight and discovered a chamber below. Its cramped configuration reminded him of an old-fashioned Michigan basement, but those were usually dank cellars with earthen floors and walls made of dirt and field stone. This one had a smooth concrete floor and walls neatly bricked and mortared.

Harlan scanned the light over some shelves that were stacked along its perimeter. From top to bottom they were packed with items assembled, it seemed, to support basic human needs: cans, boxes, and jars of nonperishable food; large drums of water; containers marked "salt," "sugar," "coffee," etc.; piles of linens; crates of fishing and camping gear, hand tools, and small appliances; and toilet paper. Lots of toilet paper.

They're preppers, Harlan thought, *doomsday preppers, getting ready for the end of the world as we know it.*

Harlan recalled a cousin whom he hadn't seen for a while, Stan Ellerbrook, and how he had become a member of the same survivalist counterculture after a stunning turn of political events resulted in the election of a loose cannon as president of the United States. The way Stan described it, he and people like him took steps, often extreme, to ready themselves for some future upheaval—an end to social and political order—caused by environmental or manmade disaster. They call themselves preppers, Stan had once said, because that's what they do. They prepare places of retreat, like this remote bunker, for postapocalyptic survival.

Harlan turned the beam of his flashlight to the spot directly beneath the manhole, where there stood a small file cabinet. It was perfectly positioned for use as a platform onto which he could lower himself into the chamber.

After he did that, Harlan opened the cabinet and perused files inside.

All were geared toward the purpose of this place—survival. They contained maps of the area's trails and waterways; information about where, when, and how to harvest the area's various fish and wildlife; and some general materials on gardening techniques, edible plants in the wild, and herbal medicine. Much of this information was still in envelopes addressed in some cases to James P. Sullivan and others to George Sanderson.

Harlan paused over a file marked, "Floorplans." There were drawings inside detailing an architectural design for the space above ground. It called for knocking down the old farmhouse and replacing it with a fortress constructed of reinforced concrete and steel. Sketches of the interior showed double sets of half-ton doors creating mantraps that would keep intruders from the facility's core. Airborne toxins would also be blocked from the core by an ultraviolet radiation chamber designed to filter all air coming into the facility.

This bunker is just the beginning, Harlan thought as he dug further into the cabinet... *the beginning of something that'll cost a fortune... like the fortune that their stash of cocaine is worth.*

Upon reaching the bottom drawer, he found two items that, unlike everything else, were not intended to support survival after the apocalypse. They were photo albums intended, it seemed, to preserve memories from before. And some of what they preserved was exactly what he'd come there in search of.

Chapter 58

It was a few minutes before 6:00 p.m. when Harlan stepped off the elevator and into the Low Bar, a subterranean cocktail lounge with a speakeasy-feel in downtown Traverse City.

"Just you?" asked the hostess.

He waited for his eyes to adjust to the lack of lighting before answering, "No, I'm expecting three more. We'd like something private."

"That's all we have," she said before showing him to a corner high top.

His order, a cheese board and four ice waters, arrived just ahead of a text message. "They're here" is all it said.

A minute later Captain Martin Nash and Detective Riley Summers of the Michigan State Police entered the lounge. The text announcing their arrival had been sent by one of several Chicago wiseguys who'd been tasked with tailing the officers for the past twenty-four hours. It was just a precaution. Harlan couldn't imagine either of them being a part of Zeppelin Reed's extracurricular activities, but he wasn't taking chances.

The officers took some time, as Harlan had, to get their bearings in the dimly lit bar.

"Water?" Nash complained after they joined him. "C'mon, Harlan, I'm thirsty, not dirty."

It was a goofy remark that Harlan recalled the captain making a few times in the distant past when, as young officers, they went out to eat after shifts on highway patrol. Recalling also the captain's usual beverage, Harlan caught the table server's attention and added a Bell's Two Hearted Ale to the order.

Riley waved the server off before he could ask what else she might want. Then she got down to business.

"Let me guess, Harlan. You have something to tell us about the murders at Shotgun Landing last week."

He took a sip of water and nodded, hoping he could make her believe his answers when the questions got more pointed.

"Have you had contact with Tank Lochner?"

"He called last night."

"So he's alive."

"Uh huh."

"And was that the first you've heard from him since the murders?"

"Yeah," Harlan said, beginning the lies. He had to be especially careful with her, his trainee during his last year on the force. She knew him well.

"What did he say?"

"He's figured out who did it. Says it's a crew that includes one of yours."

"One of ours? You mean, a state trooper?"

"That's right," Harlan said. He turned to the captain and, inviting a change of interrogator, added, "One of *yours*, Marty."

The captain, however, said nothing. He sipped his beer and let Riley continue.

"Who?" she pressed.

"Zeppelin Reed."

"What do you have on him, Harlan?"

"Nothing. Tank's sending someone who knows the details."

"Someone who's meeting us here?"

"Yeah."

"Who?"

"He didn't say."

"And you didn't ask?"

"I didn't want to know, and he didn't want to tell me."

"Then why did he call you at all?"

"Because he wants me to provide his contact with a couple cops who can be trusted."

"Trusted to do what?"

"Observe some kind of sting operation he's working on."

"And just what kind of—"

"That's it, Riley. That's all I know. Tank says he's been working this case since last week. And he says he's got all the perps—including your guy Reed—set up for a fall. He just needs a couple honest cops to arrest 'em when it's over."

"Who are the other perps?"

"I don't know."

"When is this bust supposed to happen?"

"Don't know that either."

"How about a location?"

Harlan shrugged.

"Oh, c'mon, Harlan. Your guy Tank got himself caught up in the middle of a mass murder, and he doesn't turn to *you*—a close friend and skilled detective—until *he's* fully investigated the matter?"

"Well, I guess he knows my license was—"

"And then, when he does reach out, he doesn't tell you shit?"

"That's right."

"And you don't ask?"

"Where the hell is he?" Harlan murmured, looking at his watch for refuge from her glare, but more so for another purpose.

That was the signal.

"I see what's going on here," Riley said.

"What?"

"You've been investigating this case yourself, Harlan Holmes—without a PI license. That's a felony in this state, and you know it. So now you're trying to tell us that your muscle-headed bagman, who doesn't know squat about police work, is the one who—"

Nash gasped on a swig of beer and his eyes bulged as he looked toward the entrance.

Harlan and Riley both turned. "You know him, Marty?" Harlan asked.

"Are you saying you don't?" Riley said.

Her stare remained fixed on an elderly man at the entrance taking, it seemed, much longer than usual to adjust to the dark environment. Harlan shrugged casually and continued lying, "I've never seen that guy in my life."

"What? That's Shotgun Gino Cruzano," Riley said, her teeth clenched.

"You mean the Shotgun Gino who owns Shotgun Landing?"

"Hell yeah, that's him. I thought you used to work for the Chicago mob. How could you not know him?"

"I worked for the Surocco family. Never crossed paths with any of the Cruzanos. What do you think, Riley, could he be the guy Tank sent here to meet with us?"

"You're asking me? Dammit, Harlan, stop messing with us here."

Chapter 59

The hostess led Shotgun Gino toward them, but he stopped short, looking confused as he squinted at something on his cell phone. After looking for herself, the hostess directed him to Harlan's table.

"Harlan Holmes?" Gino said before taking the open seat.

Harlan extended a hand and replied, "Yes, I am. This is Captain Martin Nash and Detective Riley Summers from MSP. And you would be..."

"Oh, for God's sake, Harlan," Riley complained, "knock it off already. You know damn well who he is. And he knew who you were long before he and the hostess looked at whatever the hell is on that phone of his."

Gino plopped into the open chair, snatched up a cracker, and dug it into one of the cheese dips on the board. After stuffing it into his mouth, he asked Harlan, "What's her problem?"

"She thinks I should know you."

"Why?"

"Because she thinks I'm running this gig."

Cracker crumbs flew out of his mouth as Gino laughed. "What, like you're my boss?"

"Interesting choice of words," Riley said. "That's exactly what his bagman calls him—Boss—if memory serves."

"I don't know nothing about that," Gino said.

"What *do* you know?" Nash asked.

"About what?"

"Guess."

"Zeppelin Reed?"

"Yeah."

After cramming more food into his mouth, Gino answered, "Well, let me see, I'll bet he called in sick to work the last couple days, unless he's been in two places at the same time."

The officers shared a look and an almost imperceptible nod, to which Gino reacted with a *gotcha* smile riddled with chunks of cheese and crackers stuck in gaps between his stained teeth. He picked at a chunk with his pinky and added, "And I know that he's a damn good shot with a rifle. Probably one of the best you got at Post 71, wouldn't you say?"

"Maybe he is," Nash said. "So what? I thought you came here to tell us something we didn't already know."

"Oh, I see, you want new information. Why didn't you just say so?"

Gino reached into a briefcase he'd brought with him. "You recognize this guy?" he asked as he placed a photo on the table. It was an enlarged head shot of the hippie who had shown up on Drummond Island the day before.

Both officers stared down at the face, studying it at length, until Riley said, "Those are his eyes and nose, and that might be his jawline beneath the beard."

"That's *your* guy all right," Gino said, "showing up yesterday right where a drug deal's going down tonight. He's scouting ahead for his Grovers, incognito. *Capisci*?"

"No, I don't understand," Nash said. "Who the hell are the Grovers?"

"His drug-smuggling crew, man—the ones whacking my employees and fucking with me."

Gino slapped another two photos down on the table. One was of the hippie beside his VW van; the other was a snapshot of the registration that Tank had found in the van's glove box the day before.

"George Sanderson?" Nash said as he scanned the vehicle registration, looking clueless.

"That's right," Gino said. "That's his alias, and it has something in common with the aliases all these Grovers used when my guy, Jimmy, made the mistake of giving them honest jobs."

"What aliases?" Nash asked.

"Mike Wazowski, Randall Boggs, and James P. Sullivan."

Nash still had no clue. But Riley did. It was obvious from her expression that she was trying to recall something.

"What is it?" Nash asked her.

"It's those names. I know them from somewhere... from when I used to babysit my niece. They're from a movie we watched together a few times, a Disney movie."

"What movie?" Nash asked.

"*Monsters, Inc.*," Gino answered.

"That's it," Riley said.

"What's it?" Nash asked.

Gino smiled and said, "All the Grovers used aliases from that movie, including your guy Reed."

"They were the monsters," Riley said, continuing to recall the movie. "The monsters who—"

"Hold on," Nash said, his expression becoming stern. He turned to Gino and said, "You say he showed up somewhere for a drug deal. What deal?"

"The one Tank Lochner infiltrated. He's even got a recording of a Skype meeting with the Grovers when they worked out the details for the transaction tonight."

"Where's it going down?"

"Far eastern end of the UP. I can get you there if you wanna see for yourself."

"You're offering me a ride?"

"No. A flight. Got a chopper waiting for you right now."

Nash began staring down at his beer bottle.

"Captain," Riley said, "you're not actually thinking of—"

"No. Hell no," Nash answered, lifting his head. He turned to Gino and said, "What makes you so sure that Zeppelin Reed's been killing your guys and messing with you?"

"Tank Lochner can answer that question better than me, but it all adds up. Reed was one of your lead cops surveilling me, and he shows up at the right place in the middle of nowhere a day ahead of the Grovers, who we can prove used my business facilities in Northport and

St. Ignace for a drug operation made to look like it was my doing."

Nash returned his stare to his beer bottle. He wasn't denying Harlan's guess, which Harlan had passed along to Gino, that Reed was indeed one of the cops whom Nash had assigned to surveil Gino—one of the cops referred to as "newer recruits" by Riley's partner when Harlan ran into them a week before at the scene of the massacre and asked who was on the case.

"If you ask me," Harlan interjected, "I don't think it adds up at all."

Both officers turned to him. They looked more than a little surprised by his unsolicited input supporting what perhaps seemed more like their side of the exchange.

"What?" Harlan said defensively. "It's just that I've met Officer Reed. And he didn't seem like the homicidal, drug-trafficking type, if you know what I mean."

"You've met him?" Riley said.

"Sure, the day of the attack at Shotgun Landing, right after I saw you guys there. I ran into him on my way out. Struck me as an eager young cop. I'll bet his record is squeaky clean."

Nash nodded.

"Well, there you go," Harlan said, trying not to show how much fun he was having. "You tell me, Riley, what's the motive? Why would a good young cop go so bad?"

"How about the root of all evil?" she said. "Money."

"Wait a minute," Nash said. "Harlan has a point here. I know Reed, quite well in fact. He's a damn good cop. Trustworthy. If he's at the scene of some drug deal—and that's a big *if* as far as I'm concerned—there must be some other reason, like maybe he's angling for a bust. Worst case, that makes him a cop with too much ego and not enough good sense, trying to fly solo."

"You know what," Harlan said, "maybe this whole thing is a bad idea."

"What thing?" Riley asked.

"Calling you guys here for this meeting. You're probably right, Riley. Tank Lochner doesn't know squat about investigating crimes, and he's got something seriously miscalculated here. It's probably not a good idea at all for the two of you to—"

"Hold on," Gino said. "You want more proof? I got that right here."

Gino reached into the briefcase and pulled out two photo albums. They were the ones Harlan had found earlier at the dilapidated farmhouse near Cross Village. He'd delivered them to Gino personally earlier that day when he prepared the elder mobster for this meeting.

As he slid one of the albums across the table, Gino said, "It was found at the address listed for George Sanderson on that car registration."

Nash leafed through a few pages of the album, stopped on one, and asked, "Who am I looking at?"

"Well, that's Zeppelin Reed in his Army days with his soldier buddies overseas," Gino said, leaning in for a glance.

"I can see that," Nash said. "But who's this other guy, the one always circled in blue ink? I take it you did that to draw my attention to him."

Gino smiled and said, "Oh, that guy. He's one of Reed's partners in crime."

"One of these so-called Grovers?" Nash asked.

"That's right. Go back to the first one of him again. It should look familiar."

Nash turned back to the photo and stared down at it. In this one, the guy circled in blue ink wore the signature smirk of Jack Hubbard. That didn't seem to help Nash, however.

Gino tried to nudge him along. "C'mon, Captain, by now your team must've enlarged the images on that video of the bowrider—including all those frames recorded for a full thirty-three seconds before the boat blew up."

"Like this one," Gino added, reaching into his briefcase for an enlarged photo of the bowrider twenty-four seconds before it blew. It captured the face of the skipper—the last image of him on board before the explosion—walking toward the stern with the same smirk on his face.

As he looked at the photo, Nash's reaction did indeed show recognition, as did Riley's. But it lasted only until they each scanned back and forth a few times between the smirking face of the red-headed, freckle-faced skipper, whom they seemed to recognize, and the smirking face of the brown-haired, clear-skinned soldier, whom they didn't. The smirks were spot-on identical, but nothing else was.

Gino reached into his briefcase again. "Here's another one of your guy with his smart-ass friend," he said, "taken at a party in East Lansing the other day."

Again, the smirk was a perfect match.

It took a while longer, but eventually Riley began nodding her head. "Zep talked about plans to go downstate for that game," she said to the captain, "along with some old friends of his. And if you imagine this old Army buddy having red hair…"

"Maybe," Nash replied. "But even if that's him with the guy, that doesn't mean he's, you know, *with* the guy when it comes to…"

Harlan cleared his throat and said, "You're right, Marty. Hanging out with a bad guy doesn't make Reed one. In fact, none of these photos comes close to answering my initial question about this squeaky-clean cop. Why would he be involved in mass murder and major drug trafficking? It makes no sense."

"Well," Gino shot back, "maybe it would if you let me finish."

"Whadaya got," Harlan scoffed, looking at the other photo album still closed on the table. "More old photos?"

"In fact, I do," Gino said. "Even older. Family photos of your guy Reed, back when he was a kid."

Gino slid the second album across the table to Nash, who opened it immediately to the first few pages. Riley scooted closer. "That's him," she said. "You can see him in the kid's face. Zep, around age five or six."

"Was this one found with the other photo album?" Nash asked.

"Yeah, at the same farmhouse," Gino said. "And did I mention that they were found hidden in a secret bunker under the house?"

"A bunker?" Nash said. "You mean like a bomb shelter?"

"Not exactly. More like a doomsday hideaway for end-times, when zombies roam the earth eating everybody in sight."

"A survivalist shelter?" Riley said.

"That's right. I'll tell you what, your boy Zeppelin Reed is a full-on whack-job."

"Lots of people do that sort of thing," Riley said. "Doesn't make him whacky, assuming it's even true. If this is all you got, Mr. Cruzano—"

"Just keep turning the pages, Detective. There's more. A lot more. You'll see."

Harlan, of course, knew what was coming, but he scooted his chair over and looked on curiously as though taking it all in for the first time.

Chapter 60

Zeppelin Reed was around age seven in the last of the photos, but that wasn't the end of the album. Next came newspaper clippings and some loose journal notes explaining how the intimate family to that point—Mom, Dad, and Zeppelin—had come to a tragic end. The media at the time reported it the same as the police did. Zeppelin's dad, they said, was gunned down along with other drug dealers in a shootout between them and the police during a raid of a crack house in Kalamazoo, Michigan.

The journal notes, however, told a different story, one based on Zeppelin Reed's recollection of events at age seven, there at the scene, waiting in a car on the street for his dad to return from a visit to the crack house. Clearly discernable from the child's account was that his father was a drug addict—not a drug dealer—in search of a fix in the wrong place at the wrong time. The man ended up getting shot in the back, unarmed, as he ran from the police. And officers continued shooting the man—over and over, the notes said—as he lay on the ground, lifeless, beneath the passenger window through which the youngster watched.

But the police didn't use body cams in those days, and nobody took the word of a traumatized kid over theirs. Except his mother. Who was also a junkie. She lost custody of Zeppelin not long after the shooting, and they never saw each other again.

Nash and Riley shared a blank glance before continuing to the last few pages of the photo album. They contained recent printouts from various doomsday blogs and websites that offered different versions of how the world as we know it will soon end. Most predicted misery, at best, for survivors of catastrophic events like nuclear annihilation, pandemic disease, or cosmic collision.

Some bloggers, however, were more optimistic, including one named "George Sanderson." He spoke of an end by economic and governmental collapse and a better world for survivors afterward in a stateless society—a life of real freedom, he predicted, like that of our ancestors for hundreds of thousands of years, unburdened by law.

"He's an anarchist," Riley said.

"But not the type who advocates the violent overthrow of government," Harlan said. "Look how he describes himself here, as an anarcho-pacifist, waiting for government to bring itself down under the weight of its own corruption, which he seems to think will reach critical mass if our country's current president is reelected."

"Why the hell would a guy like that become a cop?" Nash asked.

"He's not a cop," Riley said. "He's an anti-cop."

"What the hell is that supposed to mean?" Nash complained.

Riley reflected before responding, "When I was kid and people asked me what I wanted to be when I grew up, I always said, a police officer. What about you, Marty? How old were you when you knew?"

"Young, I guess. So young, I don't even remember anymore."

"Just imagine," Riley said, "at age seven, being made to feel just the opposite—hating everything to do with the law—because those charged with enforcing it destroyed your family and then called you a liar when you spoke the truth about it."

"What are you saying—that our fellow officer spent his life working his way onto the force, just so he could take a shot at us in retaliation?"

"Why not? From his perspective, his dad was murdered by cops who got away with it by falsely accusing him of being a violent drug dealer. Why not become exactly what his father was wrongfully accused of being, and get away with murder just like those cops did, wearing a badge, as a way of saying F-you to the system in its last days before it crumbles under its own weight."

Nash sighed deeply as he murmured the term that Riley had coined, "anti-cop..."

"Just like he's an anti-frat boy," Gino said.

"What are you talking about?" Nash asked.

"Him and the guys he hung with at Michigan State," Gino said, "including his Army buddy, Jack Hubbard, after his dishonorable discharge. They were all members of an anti-frat—their term, not mine—in a house off campus. Reed partied with 'em in those days. Still does, like he did this past weekend."

"At the tailgate for the Ohio State game," Nash acknowledged, sighing.

"He told you about it, Marty?" Riley said.

"Just that he needed the weekend off to go to this thing, a reunion tailgate with old college buddies at some place he called… uh…"

"Delta Grove," Gino said.

"Yeah, that's it."

"And that's where Tank Lochner first saw him—together with his Grover buddies—and started putting it all together."

"Putting what together?" Nash asked.

"Lochner sees it the way I think your partner is starting to see it. Zeppelin Reed's been planning this gigantic fuck-you-to-the-system for a long time, maybe since he was seven. And he found himself some Grovers who'd go along with him for the job, guys with his kind of mindset—anti-everything—and talents that might be useful… an explosives expert, a rocket scientist, and a Kodiak bear."

Nash turned his stare back to his empty beer bottle and began picking at its label.

"I know what you're thinking, Marty," Riley said. "But you can't go with him. He hasn't even told you where this sting is supposedly happening."

Gino placed his briefcase on the table, opened it, and said, "There's a car in the alley waiting to give you a ride to the chopper. Put your cell phones and radios in here if you're going."

"He's trying to walk us into something blind, Marty, with no backup," Riley said.

Nash continued peeling the label from the bottle. Not looking up from it, he asked, "What do you think happens if we don't go, Harlan?"

"We?"

"I'm not going there without you. You know this guy Lochner. He trusts you. I think there's half a chance we control the situation if you go. I mean, if it is what Cruzano's telling us, and we do nothing, more people are likely to die, don't you think?"

"Well, I'm certain that Tank's no killer. But if we're getting the story straight here, I'm also sure he's plenty pissed at these guys for murdering his friends and trying to do the same to him." Harlan turned to Gino and said, "And you must be pretty pissed off too, if they're really trying to frame you for it."

Gino stared back and replied, "Why you looking at me that way, Holmes? You think I'm a killer?"

Nash stopped messing with the beer bottle and asked, "Just how did you get that name, Shotgun?"

"Enough talk," Gino said. "Are you going, or not?"

Nash paused to look at Riley and then at Harlan. Neither offered an answer.

"Don't worry," Gino said. "I won't be there. In fact, Lochner's got another crew on the scene—the same guys you used to work with, Holmes."

"Angelo Surocco's men?" Harlan asked.

"Yeah. Bunch of pussies if you ask me. Going along with some mind game Lochner wants to play on these Grovers."

"What do you mean, mind game?" Harlan asked.

"Oh, I don't know. Some kind of bullshit sit down where they're gonna mess with these Grovers' heads. If it were up to me, there'd be no fucking discussion."

"How'd Surocco get involved?" Harlan asked.

"After I told Lochner how I thought these guys should be dealt with, he reached out to Surocco for men and supplies needed for the job. I guess Surocco thought it was in his interest to help out."

"How so?"

"Because he still works on the Lakes, and this shit that went down at my marina looks old-school Mafioso, which isn't good for business."

"And Surocco's guys are okay with involving the cops?"

"All I can tell you is that so far they've been following Lochner's lead."

"His lead," Riley scoffed. "Bullshit. If it's a mind game, I know who's running it."

Chapter 61

It was well after sunset by the time they completed their hike from the clearing on Bald Knobs to a Wrangler Rubicon that was waiting at the trailhead. The driver pretended not to know Harlan, but snuck a silent greeting in the rearview mirror as they got underway.

Their serpentine ride via ORV trails sliced through the island's wooded interior. Dolomite boulders along the way presented the biggest challenge, at times requiring the Jeep to three-wheel rather than four.

They finally arrived, frazzled more by the drive than the preceding flight and hike.

"What is this place?" Nash asked.

"The Wayfarers Mart," the driver answered. "There's a door around back. Someone should be waiting for you there."

"Who?" Riley asked.

Harlan could have told her, but he let the driver answer.

"I don't know."

As they approached, a light above the back door turned on, illuminating the yard and, in it, feathers scattered everywhere. Ahead, surrounding a large tub, the feathers thickened into a layer that covered the ground completely.

They stopped by the tub. Harlan tried to look as surprised and appalled as his guests at what they saw inside—the blood, guts, and other remains of recently slaughtered chickens.

"Harlan Holmes!" someone in the doorway exclaimed. "Welcome to the party!"

It was Vincent Surocco. He'd put on a few pounds since Harlan last worked with him and now looked even more like his father, Angelo, whose crew would someday be his.

Harlan greeted the heir apparent and then asked, "Did your dad make the trip?"

"No, but I'm sure he would have if he knew that his favorite PI was coming. What are you doing here, anyway? Thought this was Tank Lochner's show."

"Sure," Riley said, rolling her eyes.

"What's her problem?" Vincent asked.

Harlan shrugged and said, "Oh, she just thinks I'm a duplicitous con man working for mobsters who are up to no good."

"Sounds like she knows you."

Vincent led them through the largest room in the Wayfarers Mart—an open, ground-level area that once served the company store's retail customers from the town of Johnswood. It currently was serving as a banquet hall for twenty-some Chicago mobsters, each of whom feasted, Viking style, on his own roasted chicken and an assortment of sides.

Sawed-Off Gino and his crew of five sat in a corner, like youngsters at the kids' table. The rest were seated at a long table in the middle of the room. They were Angelo Surocco's men. Many offered nods as Harlan passed. It had been over two years since he last worked with them. Apparently he'd been missed.

None of this was missed by Riley. "Maybe you should pull up a chair and have a bird with your boys," she said, "you know, use this opportunity to walk 'em through your game plan one last time."

Vincent led them to a secondary entryway and opened a door to a set of stairs that went underground. After flashing a smile, he said, "Command center is down there. Check it out. It's state of the art."

Tank and Eddy were in the cellar down below, glued to one of several monitors lining a workbench. The image on the screen also drew Riley and Nash close. They looked first at it, then at each other. It was the hippie whom they'd seen earlier that evening in the photo.

Nash flashed his badge and said, "MSP. What's his location?"

Tank's knuckles whitened as he squeezed the handset of a two-way radio before speaking into it.

"Still on the north side of Channel Road, near the Humms turnoff, right?"

"Yeah, just like I said before," the voice of Phoenix Wade answered.

"Right here," Eddy said, pointing at a map of the island on a wall. A pin had been inserted at the point just described. It was a quarter mile from the dock where the DeTour ferry landed once an hour, 24/7.

"What's he doing?" Tank asked.

"Same damn thing you've been watchin' him do for the last thirty minutes," Phoenix responded. "A whole lotta nothing, bro. Relax, would ya? He's going nowhere 'til his Grovers come ashore."

Tank sighed deeply as he lowered the transmitter. He looked stressed, as if suffering the burden of unwanted leadership. A bead of sweat broke free of his brow and streamed down the side of his face. He wiped it clear and then extended the sweaty hand to Harlan.

"Glad to see you, Boss."

"Uh huh," Riley interjected. "I'm sure you are."

This was the glitch in the plan that Harlan didn't have time to properly fix. Someone else had to appear to be in charge. Harlan previously had a perfect operative for the role—a PI he valued for reasons both personal and professional—but she had bailed on him. Now it was going to be a guy he'd met only once in the past and tried to coach up the evening before, a hustler recommended by Angelo Surocco.

It was time for Harlan to cue the hustler's arrival.

"The detective is right," he said to Tank in a raised voice. "It's obvious you're not running this scam. How about telling us who is?"

The response came from the top of the steps.

But it was not the voice of the hustler he expected.

Chapter 62

"What the hell are you still doing here?" Roz hollered as she rushed down the steps leading into the cellar. She went straight to Tank, got into his face, and shouted again, "Your big ass is supposed be down by the dock already! What are you waiting for?"

"This guy right here," Tank answered, nodding at Harlan. "He just arrived."

Roz and Harlan looked each other up and down. His reaction—shock—was more real than it could ever have appeared to be if they had merely rehearsed the encounter, which of course they never had the opportunity to do.

He offered a hand and said, "Glad to meet you. I'm—"

Her glare cut him short. The anger and annoyance behind it were also real. She let the hand hang as she turned back to Tank and said, "You tell me. Who is he?"

"A friend of mine, Harlan Holmes. I've been meaning to tell you about him. He's a PI, just like you."

"What's he doing here?"

"Thought we could use his help."

"Why? You don't like my work? You'd rather have *him* take down the Grovers?"

"Listen," Harlan said, "I'm not here to—"

"Does it I look like I'm talking to you?" Roz admonished, glaring again at the man who'd put this scam ahead of their feelings for each other.

"I guess not."

"Then shut the fuck up."

"I don't know who she is," Riley said to Nash, "but I like her."

Roz turned to Riley and said, "The name's Roz Cortez. *I'm* his PI."

"Tank Lochner's?" Riley asked.

"Yeah, or at least I thought I was. Who are you?"

"Detective Riley Summers, state police. And this is Captain Nash."

Roz wheeled back to Harlan. "Cops!" she shouted. "You brought fucking cops?"

"Because I asked him to," Tank said.

"You did?" Roz said.

"Yeah. You said the plan was to turn the Grovers over to the police once we got 'em. And I figured that my friend Harlan here, being an ex-cop himself, could—"

"I meant *after* we got the Grovers, Tank. Do you realize what you've done, bringing cops here before we get statements from these guys?"

"I… guess not."

"What about you, Inspector Holmes? Do you realize what you've done bringing state troopers into the mix?"

"Actually, I'm not an inspector. I kind of lost my license."

"Why am I not surprised?" Roz said, shaking her head. "How about you, Detective Summers? Something tells me that you see the problem."

Riley nodded slowly as she gazed around the room. Harlan watched her take it all in, the various equipment he'd assembled for the job: assault rifles, ballistic shields, body armor, helmets, and other tactical gear, including dark jackets with large block letters printed on the backs—"CDA."

If she's seen Monsters, Inc., Harlan thought, *she knows what those letters mean.*

"What problem?" Nash asked.

"State action," Riley answered.

Exactly, Harlan thought. He continued to study her as she processed the issue. The equipment down here was for the wiseguys upstairs, feasting on chicken in advance of a major SWAT-type maneuver that they—posing as the Child Detection Agency—would soon make on the Grovers. No doubt the police tactics they'd use to produce incriminating statements—deceit, coercion, perhaps even torture—would be unlawful if done by *real* police. After all, even bad guys have constitutional rights—rights against *state* overreaching. And, of course, evidence obtained in violation of those rights could never be used against them in court.

"That's right," Roz said. "Everything we get from these Grovers will be inadmissible in court if it looks like any state cops—like you and your captain—had a hand in what we're about to do here."

When a burst of maniacal laughter upstairs subsided, Riley said, "I take it that your team's tactics are going to deviate some from standard police procedure."

"Quite a bit, I expect," Roz replied, "which means I have to do something with you and your captain, Detective. Something that prevents any semblance of state sanction."

"Like what?" Nash asked.

Roz kept her focus on Riley and said, "I think I like you, too, Detective. I hope you understand what has to happen here."

"I get it," Riley said as she turned, placed her hands on the wall, and spread her feet.

"What are you doing?" the captain asked.

"Assuming the position, Marty, as should you."

"I'll do no such thing."

"Oh yes you will," Roz said. She nodded at Tank and Eddy, and the two behemoths promptly overtook him and relieved both officers of their weapons.

As he effortlessly restrained the captain with an arm wrapped around the man's head, Tank asked, "What should we do with 'em, *Boss*?"

Roz answered, "Put 'em in the hole."

Nash struggled to ask, "The hole? What the hell is that?"

It was the chimney for the old Johnswood Mill, which had been adapted to serve as a holding cell for these officers while they witnessed, by live stream video, the CDA's bust of the Grovers. But that was not how Roz described it.

"Well, it was supposed to be an accommodation for your fellow officer, Zeppelin Reed," she answered, lying.

"You can't lock us up," Nash argued.

Tank tightened his grip and said, "Just shut up, man, and this'll go a lot easier on you."

"Ease up, Tank," Roz said. "Let him talk."

The captain straightened up and stretched his neck after Tank released him.

"You just added a second felonious assault of a police officer to your rap sheet, Mr. Lochner. And as for you, Ms. Cortez, do you have any idea what kind of time you'll be doing if you kidnap the detective and me?"

Roz smiled and responded, "Why, it's not kidnapping at all, Captain."

"Then what is it?"

"A citizen's arrest."

"How the hell do you figure?"

"Take a minute, Captain, and think about it. Who's my main target for the bust going down here tonight?"

Nash glanced at the hippie still on the monitor. "Him," he answered, "Zeppelin Reed."

Roz stepped closer. "And what is he?"

"Well, you think he's a murderer."

"I fucking know he's a murderer. A cold-blooded assassin. And I *will* prove that."

"So what if you do. That still doesn't—"

"And who are *you*—Captain Martin Nash—in relation to him?"

"I'm... his captain."

"That's right, his *boss*. And here you are, along with another of the assassin's fellow officers, showing up on the very night that he's gonna appear in the middle of nowhere to whack more people during a major drug transaction. You tell me, what am I supposed to make of that?"

"Well, your own client, Tank Lochner, just told you. Harlan Holmes brought us here."

"And who the hell is Harlan Holmes?"

Roz raised a hand before the captain could answer and said, "Wait, I'll answer that." She looked at Harlan with contempt before returning her glare to the captain. "At best, he's a complete dumb ass for bringing you here. But I can't assume that he's just a dumb ass—because he's a fucking ex-cop himself. Another one of *yours*, I'll bet."

"You actually think that we… uh…" Nash stammered.

Roz's stare was so fixed, and her voice so steady, that she actually *did* seem to believe what she said next.

"I'll tell you what I think, Captain. Bottom line. Your guy, Zeppelin Reed, is a bad cop in the middle of spree of violent crimes facilitated by the undercover work he does for you, which gives me reasonable cause to suspect that you and your fellow officers are a part of his criminal enterprise."

"That's an outrageous accusation. And you—"

"I don't have to be right," Roz continued calmly. "For a citizen's arrest, I only have to have reasonable cause to believe that you're engaged in the commission of a dangerous felony. And I have plenty of cause to believe that's just what you're doing, right now, considering your relationship with Reed and the timing of your arrival. And by the way, Captain, if you're here on official police business, where's your backup?"

"Now wait a minute. I can explain that…"

"Lock 'em up, boys."

"Hold on, Ms. Cortez," Riley said. "I understand where you're coming from. And I could even see myself doing the same thing if I was you. I just want to know that we'll be okay in this lockup of yours, that there won't be any undue restraint or mistreatment."

"We'll make sure you're comfortable, Detective. Right, Tank?"

"Got it, Boss."

"We'll even let you witness the bust for yourselves, in the event you are on the level," Roz said.

"You want some equipment set up in the hole, Boss?" Tank asked.

"Yeah. Give 'em live feeds."

"On which cameras?"

"May as well be all of them."

Riley's expression eased but remained serious as she turned her stare to Harlan. The look on her face reminded him of the days when they worked closely together on the force and could sometimes communicate without speaking. The message he was now getting was mixed: She still wasn't buying the ruse, but as long as the captain was, she'd roll with it.

Riley turned back to Roz and asked, "What are your plans for the stool pigeon here, Inspector Holmes, the one who got the captain and me into this shit storm?"

"Oh, I've got something in mind for him," Roz said. She looked at Tank and added, "When you get upstairs, tell Surocco to send down a couple of beefy soldiers. Mr. Holmes is gonna answer some questions I have about him and his cop friends."

"Wait a minute," Harlan said. "You can't—"

Roz grabbed his arm, spun him around, and slammed him into a wall.

"Shut up and spread 'em, Holmes!"

She then frisked him more aggressively than Harlan could recall ever having done himself to even the hardest of criminals.

"You their informant?" Roz asked as she groped his inner thigh.

"No! Hell no! I'm just a pain in the ass to them."

"Well, you've become one for me too," she complained.

The door upstairs closed behind Tank, Eddy, and the officers.

Roz grabbed Harlan again. This time she pulled him away from the wall, and close to her. So close that half the breath he took was hers.

"Why did you come back?" he asked.

"How many times do I have to tell you to shut up?"

She buried her face into his, kissing him hard. A little too hard, perhaps. Blood oozed from ruptured scabs that had formed where she busted his mouth a few days before, during their first encounter.

Chapter 63

Harlan and Roz were in the cellar watching monitors when his phone rang. The caller ID said it was Tank. Harlan turned to Roz before picking up.

"What do we have, maybe twenty minutes?"

Roz nodded as she continued staring at the live feed streaming from the body camera of an undercover soldier on the mainland. It showed the Grovers in line for the 10:10 p.m. ferry out of DeTour Village.

Harlan stepped away to take the call. If Roz had to use the two-way, he didn't want to be overheard by the cops in lockdown, who were able to listen in on all radio communications.

"How you doing, Harlan?" Tank asked.

"Oh, so now we're on a first-name basis?"

"What can I say? I can only have one boss at a time, or I'll get confused. And let's face it, that woman of yours *is* in charge."

"What are you talking about?"

"Oh c'mon, man. Tonight's the second time she's whipped your ass. It's obvious who's wearing the pants."

"Very funny, Tank. What'd you call for, anyway?"

"To talk to Eddy. He's not answering his phone."

"Hold on."

Harlan went upstairs and found Eddy alone in the kitchen, wolfing down another round of roast chicken straight from a cooler that was serving as a make-shift refrigerator. He winced when Harlan caught him in the act.

Harlan covered the phone and said, "It's okay, Eddy. Are you able to talk to Tank?"

Eddy sleeved some chicken grease off his face before responding, "You won't tell him, will you, Mr. Holmes? Tank's got strict rules for my training. One of 'em is that I don't eat straight from the fridge. Technically, I figure this cooler isn't one, but I think he'd see it differently."

Harlan smiled as he kept the phone covered. "Don't worry, Eddy. I got your back."

Eddy then reached for the phone but stopped short at the sight of his greasy hand. "Maybe you should hold onto it and just put him on speaker."

"All right, Tank, he's on the line," Harlan said after switching phone modes.

"Eddy?" Tank said.

"Yeah."

"Listen up, man. Got something important to tell you."

"About what?"

"The thing we're doing tonight. Our part of the scam on the Grovers."

"Don't worry, Tank, I got it memorized."

"Not this part, you don't."

"What part?"

"A little something extra I'm planning just for you, to cap off your training."

Eddy turned to Harlan, who shrugged in response.

"Well, what kind of extra thing is it?" Eddy asked.

"Can't say or it'll ruin the effect. I just want you to know that no matter what I say or do to you tonight, it'll be for your own good."

"Hold on, Tank. I don't like the sound of this."

"I'm not asking for your approval, Eddy. I'm trying to tell you something here."

"What's that?"

"That changing your name from Eddy Chub to Humvee Eddy was only the beginning, partner. Tonight, you *become* the Hummer."

"What the hell are you talking about?" Harlan said.

"That you, Harlan?"

"Damn straight it is. What are you planning for Eddy?"

"Sorry guys, like I said before, I can't explain."

Harlan switched modes and brought the phone to his ear. "All right, you're off speaker. Now tell me what the hell is going on."

"Sorry, but I can't trust you with the information. It's like that detective said, you're a bit of a stool pigeon."

"Dammit Tank, you listen to me. You need to stick to the script. You understand? No improvisation."

"Sorry, no can do. I'm gonna have a prime teaching moment with Eddy, and I can't pass it up."

"Now you listen here!"

"Later Harlan. I'm out."

Harlan returned to the cellar. Along the way, he tried calling Tank back, but there was no answer.

"What was that about?" Roz asked.

"I don't know for sure. Tank's got something in store for Eddy, off script. Won't tell me what it is. I swear, the guy never does a damn thing I tell him to do."

"Oh, that's why he called," Roz said. "Don't worry about it. It's just part of Eddy's training."

"How would you know?"

Roz ignored the question as she leaned in close to a monitor.

"C'mon, just tell me what the—"

"Never mind that, here comes the ferry."

Chapter 64

Vincent Surocco stepped out of the shadows and into the path of three individuals walking along East Channel Road, alone, a short distance from where they had come ashore. Their ferry had already reversed course for the mainland, and the taillights on the last of the few vehicles it let off had just disappeared.

A wire worn by Vincent and several night-vision cameras in the bush streamed the encounter live to Harlan and Roz at command center and the cops in the holding cell.

"I'll take the cash, Grover," Vincent said, looking at Kodiak Brown, who carried a briefcase. All three stopped and stared back.

"Who the hell are you?" Eli said.

Two of Vincent's men stepped out of the shadows, each with a hand in a coat pocket, and flanked the Grovers.

Kodiak and Eli looked at Jack. He had become the Grovers' spokesman when negotiations via Skype with Bert Brydges got tricky, Harlan recalled. Apparently they expected him to take over again.

"No offense," Jack said, "but we're here to meet someone, and you're not him."

"Well, I'm here to meet you, Jack," Vincent said. "That is your name, right—*Jack*?"

"Yeah. Who are you?"

"Oh c'mon, Jack, how do you know I'm not Bert's partner, Jimmy D'Reaper? Wasn't he wearing a costume the day you met him?"

"He's twice your size, man. And he talked like a Yooper. Ain't no way you're him. And Bert never said nothin' about bringin' anyone else into this but D'Reaper."

"What about you, Jack? Did you bring along any other Grovers besides these two?"

"No. We're it."

"You sure about that?"

Jack nodded.

"All right then, I'll take that briefcase and everything else you're carrying."

One of the guys flanking the Grovers dug his hand deeper into his pocket, making more pronounced the gun he held.

"Easy," Jack said, showing his empty hands and nodding at his partners to do the same. "We came here in good faith to do business with Bert Brydges—nothing else."

"Like the kind of business you did last week at Shotgun Landing?" came a shout from the shadows, followed by a giant.

"Is that you, Dreeper?" Kodiak shouted back.

As the giant neared, Jack Hubbard resumed, "You're Jimmy D'Reaper?"

"Well, who else would I be?" Tank said, towering over everyone as he stopped alongside Vincent.

Jack looked up, into Tank's undisguised face, and said, "Holy shit. You're him, the big guy with the mullet who I met at the marina last week right before all hell broke loose… the one they keep showing on cable, Tank Lochner. Aren't you supposed to be dead?"

"Should be," Tank said, scowling. "But I kicked the real Reaper's ass and came back for the sons of bitches who killed my friends that day. And I'm thinkin' it might be you, Jack, the only survivor on the bowrider, and whoever your partner was that day onshore with the rifle."

"No way, man. You got it wrong. Listen, the way I see it—"

"You can tell me your story on our way to meet Bert—after you give my guys your money, guns, and cell phones."

• • • • •

Vincent Surocco's wire continued to transmit Tank's conversation with the Grovers as their vehicle began its GPS-monitored journey to

Scammon Cove. So far, Jack had merely repeated the story he told Bert two days before about his "shit luck" survival of the Northport massacre and his theory that it must have been ordered by Shotgun Gino.

Tank must not have appeared receptive to the recitation.

"C'mon, Lochner," Jack said, "you were there. The way that marina got lit up, shit, that was Mafioso for sure. Wouldn't you agree?"

"I don't know, Jack. I just spent a couple years in the joint. Saw a lotta gangland hombres in there, but never any Cosa Nostra. You're talking like this Shotgun Gino is some kind of real-life Tony Soprano, still making moves."

"Your man Jimmy sure thought he was the real deal—real enough to want to hire you to help us move the dope into Canada. He said you're the best damn bagman on the planet."

"That's because I am."

"Well, if that's so, we could still use you, if you want in for more than a measly 150K, which I'll bet you're gonna have to split with Bert Brydges and these other guys you brought along."

"A cut of the $10 million?" Tank said. "You're still willing to let me in on that?"

"Sure I am. We all are. Hell, that's what Jimmy was trying to tell you when he got himself whacked."

"Bert told me about you making that offer to him too."

"And I meant it, big man. Right now Bert's got this whole thing all twisted around, thinking that us Grovers are somehow to blame for shit going sideways. Man, I'm telling you, like I told him, that's not the way it is. Isn't that right, boys?"

"Hell yeah, that's right," Eli said. "Bert's got everything all messed up in his head, probably for good reason."

"And what would that be?" Tank said.

"Well, you know, because of what I was doing with his woman."

"You mean fucking her behind his back?"

Eli sighed before responding, "Look, I know that wasn't cool. And now I can see how it's messing with Bert's perspective about us Grovers. He's thinking he can't trust us because of that. But it's like Jack says, when it comes to real business, we're stand-up guys."

"And what do you have to say, Kodiak?" Tank asked. "Does Bert have you Grovers all wrong?"

"You must know he does," Kodiak replied, "if you really are the Dreeper who partied with us at Delta Grove. You saw us there and who we really are—fun-loving guys and all. You really think us goofy Grovers could be assassins?"

As Harlan and Roz listened, they kept an eye on the GPS signals transmitting from both Tank's car and the hippie's VW van. The movement of the van, they noted, didn't begin until well after Tank's car had passed, which suggested that the hippie must have also had a tracker going on his guys, hidden somewhere on them or in their briefcase. Another such device on Phoenix Wade's car showed him bringing up the rear.

"Money's all here," Vincent said, back in Tank's car. "A hundred and fifty grand, on the nose."

"Damn right it's all there," Jack said. "I'm telling you, Lochner, we're on the level."

"I must say, he's pretty convincing," Harlan said to Roz back at command center.

She looked at him with a hint of the anger she'd displayed earlier. "He's almost as convincing as you can be."

"What do you mean by that?"

"It's just an observation."

"But the way you said it, Roz, it sounded to me like—"

She raised her hand to cut him short. The lead vehicle's GPS signal was slowing down.

Chapter 65

The GPS signals on all three vehicles stopped near Scammon Cove: Tank's along the turnoff for the old mill, the hippie's short of the turnoff, and Phoenix Wade's shorter still.

"You getting this?" Phoenix said over the radio as his video feed came online. The hippie was scanning the landscape with the scope of his rifle. "He's looking for a position with a good sight line, maybe something elevated."

But he won't find it, Harlan thought, recalling the flat, wooded terrain he saw when he previously checked out Scammon Cove. *He'll have to work from the forest floor, up close.*

The hippie returned to his van and minutes later emerged in a ghillie suit covered with shed vegetation that would blend him into the nighttime woods.

Roz squeezed on the transmitter button. "You know what we need, Phoenix."

"Yeah, video evidence of him setting up."

"Stay close, but not too close."

"We've been over this, Roz. I know."

"And don't let him get too far along. He's dangerous."

"What the hell you think I am?"

"I know, Phoenix, you got this."

• • • • •

There was a muffled cry as the screen went dark.

Nash and Riley turned to each other. They were in the holding cell and had been watching a live stream of the hippie sniper take up a position in the woods until the blackout.

"They have better night-vision camcorders than we do," Riley said.

Nash stared at the monitor, his expression as blank as it was. "Maybe we're wrong about this hippie, maybe it's not him. I just can't believe that he would..."

The screen suddenly rebooted in Nash's face; on it was a very different image of the sniper, this time gagged, groggy, and minus his fake hair and beard.

"Got him, Roz," said a triumphant Phoenix Wade.

"So I see. Good work. You know where to take him, right?"

"Oh yeah, same place where we're holding that cop lover, Harlan Holmes."

After Phoenix and Roz signed off, Nash said, "How the hell did I not see this?"

"You can't blame yourself, Marty," Riley said, though she had a hard time feeling bad for him. A few years before, he had blamed her and some other veteran officers for getting played by Harlan Holmes the first time he'd become entangled with the mob. Indeed, that was the captain's reason for rejecting his veteran officers in favor of newer recruits—rising stars like Zeppelin Reed—for surveillance of any further mob activity in Traverse City.

"Fucking ironic," Nash said, continuing to beat himself up.

Riley turned to a table full of food that had been set up in the holding cell along with the communications equipment. She began gnawing on a drumstick while holding a plate full of fries and coleslaw.

"Maybe you should eat something, Marty."

"Are you kidding? How can you have an appetite while we're trapped inside this hell hole?"

She looked up at the four-story, moss-coated walls, dimly illuminated by lanterns, and shrugged. "It's not so bad."

Nash's eyes bulged. "What are you talking about? We're inside a fucking smokestack for crying out loud."

"Well, look at it this way, Marty, it sure beats the holding cell back at the station. Good food and drink, blankets, and all kinds of equipment for us to watch and listen to everything that's—"

"Got a visual on the candy man," came a voice through a speaker.

Chapter 66

Riley and Nash turned their attention to another monitor that had booted up. They saw a portion of Scammon Cove's shoreline where bare pilings that once supported the old mill's pier rose out of the water. Further out was a fast-approaching boat.

"Who's he again?" Nash asked. "Bert something?"

"Brydges," Riley said. "The seller."

In the foreground onshore awaited the Grovers and their escorts, Tank, Vincent Surocco, and Vincent's two soldiers.

Bert pulled his boat in all the way to shore and tossed out a line. After tying it off, Vincent hopped into the boat and helped remove a piece of tarp covering neatly stacked bricks wrapped in brown paper. The wire he wore picked up his breathing as he worked.

Tank waited until the goods were fully revealed before tossing the briefcase into the boat. "It's all there," he said. "They even thought to make it small bills."

"Appreciate that, boys," Bert said, smiling at the Grovers. "Feel free to come aboard and start unloading your dope. Don't wanna be here all night."

"And then what?" Jack complained. "You guys leavin' us a car so we can move it?"

"Don't remember that being part of the deal," Bert said.

"Then what the hell are we supposed to do with it out here in the middle of nowhere?"

"That's your problem, Jack. You boys have ten minutes to get this cargo off my boat, or I'm leaving with it—and the money."

The Grovers hesitated, looking first at each other and then around at the dark woods beyond.

"You expecting someone?" Tank asked.

"N-no… course not," Eli said, his eyes still scanning the woods. "It's just… uh…" He turned to Jack.

"It's just… that we hear a chopper," Jack said, "coming this way."

All of them looked up to search the sky, except Vincent and his two soldiers. The soldiers drew their guns and Vincent flashed a badge as he shouted, "CDA! Hands on your heads!"

"What the hell, Jankowski?" Tank shouted as he wheeled to face Vincent and the pistol he stuck in Tank's face.

"That ain't my name, Lochner."

Tank's mouth fell open.

"That's right, dumb shit. I'm CDA. Now get your hands on your head. You too, Hubbard."

Jack Hubbard was the last to comply with the demand. As he did, he looked at Tank and said, "This guy told you his name is Jankowski, and you believed him? Shit, man, he's about as Polish as Al Pacino."

"How was I supposed to know, Jack? Guy I knew in the joint told me they were cool. I had no idea they were… Who'd you say you are?"

• • • • •

For Riley and Nash, the volume of the helicopter's approach was amplified by the hollow of the chimney they were inside of. Another sound, however, suddenly overwhelmed it.

"Break 1-9 for Sky Guy, you copy?" came Roz's voice over the radio. "Come on, Sky Guy, talk to me. Where are you? You're late."

"Right here, Roz, comin' in low and hot. Be there inside fifteen seconds. Over."

"All right, be ready boys… Sky Guy, we go on your count. Over."

"Copy that, Roz… and five, four, three, two, one…"

"Go! Go! Go!" Roz shouted.

Just then every monitor in front of Riley and Nash lit up with flare-illuminated images of the shoreline from different angles, including a chopper-cam overview of heavily equipped men in CDA jackets pouring in from the woods onto the scene—their cryptic imperatives flooding the airwaves.

"23-19! 23-19!"

"Move! Move! Move!"

"Red alert! Red alert!"

"Duck and cover people! Duck and cover!"

As the meaningless banter continued, Nash stepped closer to one of the screens and said, "They've already made the collar. Why are they doing all this?"

"For effect," Riley said.

"But they can't possibly think they sound real. 23-19? What the hell is that supposed to mean?"

"They're not trying to sound real, Marty. That would be impersonating the police."

"Then what are they doing?"

"They're impersonating a scene from *Monsters, Inc.*"

"The Disney movie?"

Riley nodded and joined the captain by the screen. The Grovers were huddled together with Tank and Bert, surrounded, trying to shield themselves from the relentless downdraft and blinding floodlights of a helicopter hovering overhead.

"But why go to all this trouble?" Nash asked.

"It's that devious PI, Roz Cortez. She's messing with their heads."

As if necessary, a voice boomed from the chopper: "This is the CDA! You're under arrest!"

Riley and Nash watched closely as soldiers pretending to be CDA agents handcuffed the Grovers, Bert, and Tank and took them into custody.

"I don't know," Nash said, "that sure looks like impersonating the police to me."

"It can't be," Riley said.

"Why not?"

"Well, as you know, Marty, the crime of impersonating a police officer requires a specific intent on the part of the accused."

He thought for a moment and responded, "Sure, an intent to deceive."

"That's right. And there's no way that Ms. Cortez is trying to deceive those Grovers right now."

"You mean, they know that someone is messing with their heads?"

"And Ms. Cortez knows that they know," Riley said, nodding with approval, "because they were the ones who started it when they used those monster aliases."

"That's pretty twisted."

"I like her more all the time."

The scene on the monitor ended with a radio transmission that could only have been for the benefit of observers who'd seen the movie: "Situation on the ground is niner-niner-zero… I repeat, niner-niner-zero. All clear."

Riley smiled, recalling that line from her teenage years when she watched the movie while babysitting her young niece. And her smile broadened as her thoughts scrolled forward to more recent times and some of the other stunts she'd seen pulled by her former mentor, Harlan Holmes.

Chapter 67

It was almost midnight by the time most of the uninvited guests of the Wayfarers Mart had returned to the room that earlier served as their banquet hall. The room's configuration, however, was no longer suited for that purpose. The enormous dinner table abounding with food had been removed, and in its place, surrounded by CDA agents, were the five perps arrested lakeside—Bert, Tank, and three of the Grovers—tied to chairs arranged side by side.

Pointed at the suspects, from up high in a corner, was a camera. In a chair directly beneath the device sat Harlan, like an offscreen director, as it transmitted his view of the lineup to the officers in the holding cell.

Also offscreen was a short, double-barreled shotgun of the break-open type—a *lupara*—lying across Harlan's lap. The style of firearm had intrigued him enough to search Google for the name's literal translation—"for the wolf"—which he learned was based on its traditional use by shepherds in the high pastures of Sicily.

Harlan looked up from the gun and nodded at one of the CDA agents, who responded with a shout, "Ready, Boss!"

A door flew open and in stormed Roz. Without saying a word, she headed straight for Kodiak Brown and unleashed a crushing right hook to the side of his face.

"You remember me, *Randall*?"

He took a while to shake off the cobwebs before answering, "What?"

She hit him again and then stepped back and watched him struggle against his restraints, blood gushing from his nose and into his mouth. It sprayed everywhere as he stammered, "L-Listen… I don't know wh-who you… you…"

He paused as his eyebrows curled.

"Give you a hint," Roz said. "It was halftime during Sparty's home opener against Western."

Still confused, he replied, "Chuck's Place? Is that where we met?"

"No, asshole. That's where you sexually assaulted me. And ever since, I've been watching you and your Grover friends. *Always* watching."

"What the hell are you doing, Roz?" Bert shouted.

"You know her?" Kodiak said.

Bert, feigning confusion, ignored the question and stared at Roz, waiting for one of the Grovers to figure it out.

Eli did. "She's your fucking PI," he said, "the one you hired to spy on Morgan and me."

Slowly nodding, Bert said, "What do you think you're doing here, Roz? I hired you to—"

"What makes you think I was *ever* working for you?"

Bert looked around the room at the men surrounding him. "Who are these guys? What's the CDA?"

"Ain't no such thing, dumb ass!" Jack shouted. "She's working for somebody else, man. Probably whoever's on the other side of that camera. Do you even realize how big you and your bagman fucked up here?"

Bert's look of confusion, however, slowly faded and was replaced with a smile that widened as he said, "Not as big as you think. Isn't that right, Tank?"

Tank paused as if reflecting on the situation, and then he began smiling along with Bert.

"What's so damn amusing?" Jack asked.

Roz stepped close to Bert, leaned over him, and seethed. "I know what you think is so damn amusing, Brydges."

"What is it?" Jack asked.

"The dope you just paid $150,000 for," Roz said as she turned to Harlan. He reached under his chair and retrieved one of the bricks of drugs that had been onboard Bert's boat.

"What about it?" Jack said.

Roz took the brick from Harlan and tore open the paper. "They're all just like this one," she said as she poured its contents onto the floor in front of the lineup.

It was nothing but dirt.

A silence lingered after the last of it hit the floor.

Wait for it, Harlan thought.

"Damn you, Brydges!" Eli shouted. "What'd you do with our—"

"Hold on," Jack said, flashing his signature smirk. "Don't you see, little brother? That's the only dirt they've got on us."

"It gets even better than that, Jack," Bert said.

"How so?"

"You still got your dope, dude."

"We got no dope," Jack said defensively, glancing up at the camera.

"Sure you do," Bert said. "I left it right where you Grovers stashed it in the first place."

"That's bullshit, Brydges."

"I mean it, Jack. It's in the same pole barn, just not in the walls anymore."

"The pole barn?" Eli said. "Still?"

"Shut the hell up, both of you," Jack said. "You're just talking out your ass, Brydges, about shit that makes no sense."

Roz leaned over Bert. "What are you saying? That you know where the real shit is?"

"Yeah, right, like I'm gonna tell you… you treacherous b—"

Roz unloaded another vicious right hook, this one to the side of Bert's face. But this time, there were no cobwebs to shake off.

Harlan and Tank shared a look as Harlan recalled what Tank had previously said about Bert having a jaw that, back in his days in the ring, withstood beatings from heavyweights.

"Pretty good punch for a little woman," Bert responded calmly. "You mind hitting me again, maybe a little harder? It brings back fond memories."

"Don't antagonize her, man," Jack said.

"Oh, don't worry, Jack. I'm not gonna tell her where your pole barn is."

Roz struck again, this time bloodying Bert's nose.

"Yes you are," she insisted.

Bert opened his mouth and licked the blood streaming down from his nose. "Tastes good," he said. "Appreciate it, detective, but I'm still not telling you shit. You don't work for me—remember?"

"Listen, if you don't tell me where that pole barn is, you're gonna meet who I work for. And I assure you, he won't be as nice as me."

"Whatever you got, Roz—bring it."

She looked over at the lupara in Harlan's lap and said, "You should be more careful about what you ask for, Bert."

Chapter 68

Shotgun Gino entered the room on the heels of Roz's warning. He stopped short of the Grovers, turned his head, and, licking his lips, stared longingly at the lupara still in Harlan's lap.

Roz reached over to steer him away from it.

"Not yet, Mr. Cruzano. Only if we have to."

Gino struggled against Roz's intervention, holding for as long as he could a wistful gaze at the weapon. The longer he hovered, the more wildly his tongue moved as it continued moistening his lips. Its eventual frenzy reminded Harlan of a rock star from his youth—an orally well-endowed bassist named Gene Simmons—made famous by the dexterity of his oversized appendage.

The eyes of their hostages widened as Gino completed his turn, tongue waggling, and stared them down before shouting—

"*You goddam Grovers wanna fuck with me?*"

The air went dead, until there appeared on Kodiak's crotch a soggy patch of urine. The stench of it spread quickly throughout the room, causing lips to curl and noses to wrinkle among CDA agents who randomly voiced objection.

"Oh, for god's sake, man!"

"Are you shittin' me? Did he just..."

"All right, you guys," Roz said. "Get over it."

She then directed Gino's attention to Bert.

"This one here says he knows where they're hiding it. But he won't tell. Thinks he's a tough guy. Used to be a boxer."

"Got the face of one," Gino said. "Maybe we *should* use the lupara after all, Roz. You know, blow off a kneecap and see if that don't get his mind right."

"No, there has to be a better way. I was thinking maybe that guy who works for you, the big one. You know who I'm talking about?"

"Yeah, I know, but that might be even more cruel."

"It's what this meathead wants," Roz said, shrugging.

Gino nodded and then cupped his hands to his mouth and shouted again—"Gimme Eddy Chub!"

Following the shout there came a collective gasp from surrounding CDA agents as Eddy made his entrance, head down and lower lip protruding. He looked more like a dejected kid than the tough guy whom he was scripted to play.

C'mon, Eddy, get with the program, Harlan thought. *You're supposed to be the man's enforcer.*

"What's wrong?" Gino asked, genuinely confused.

"We don't call him that no more, Cappy," said one of the agents.

"Don't call him what?" Gino said. "Eddy Chub?"

Looks of dismay deepened among the agents. A few even cringed.

"What don't I know here, Eddy?"

Eddy slowly lifted his head and responded, "It's that name, sir. I don't like it no more."

"The name Chu—"

"Please, sir, don't say it. It's demeaning."

"What meaning?"

"No sir. I said, *dee*-meaning."

"Oh, that kind of meaning," Gino said, pondering the situation. "I see. Guess I never thought about it that way. Always liked calling you that. Thought you liked it too. You know I'd never *dee*-mean you on purpose, don't you Eddy?"

"Of course, sir. Over these past couple years, the two of us basically being our own crew, I've come to think of you more as a friend than a boss. I know you mean no harm by it."

Eddy glanced at Roz, who gently nodded her head with approval.

Are you kidding me, Roz? Harlan thought. *Get these guys back on script.*

"Feeling's mutual, Eddy," Shotgun said. "But what am I supposed to call you now? A man in our line of work should have a special name, you know, a handle he goes by that says something about who he is. You tell me, what should that be for you?"

Eddy smiled and said, "Humvee Eddy, sir. Hummer for short."

Gino repeated the name, "Humvee Eddy… Hummer," mulling over it as though his approval was necessary before it could be official. "Okay," he eventually said as he turned to the surrounding CDA agents. "You hear that, boys? Man's got a new name. Anyone call him different, he'll be dealing with me. And by me, I don't mean Giovanni Cruzano. I mean *me. Shotgun* Gino. We clear?"

Gino's tongue-waggling and look of bloodthirst returned like a reflex action in response, it seemed, to his self-identification with the word that had come to encapsulate his personal brand.

"So, what'd you want, sir?" Eddy asked.

"These guys we got all tied up here—you know who they are, right?"

"Sure, the ones who've been trafficking cocaine through our marina and killing people, now trying to pin it on you and me and make everyone think we're the ones who lit up the marina."

"That's right, Hummer. That's who they are. And this one here, with the lopsided head all beat to hell, he knows where the dope is but won't tell Roz. She gave him her best shot, but he just smiles about it. Crazy son of a bitch says he likes getting his face punched."

"And you think he won't like it so much with me."

"I know he won't, big man. So, what do you say? Can you gimme a pass on what I've been calling you all these years and do me the favor of dropping the Hummer on this guy?"

Eddy peeled off his outer shirt, down to a tank tee stretched so tightly that it fit his blubbery torso like a string bikini top.

Whoa, Harlan thought, *that's way too much information.*

"Cut him loose," Eddy said to a CDA agent.

Chapter 69

A clock overhead had just finished striking midnight as Roz joined Harlan in the corner of the room. Together they watched Eddy go to work on Bert. It was more like watching a silverback gorilla play with a rag doll.

The finale to the beating occurred at the feet of the Grovers, where Bert lay, it seemed, unconscious on the floor while Eddy repeatedly jumped straight up in the air, made a half turn, and landed his five-hundred-pound frame, backside first, on top of him. All the while, a fist-pumping Shotgun Gino led the CDA agents in a chant—

"Hummer! Hummer! Hummer!"

"You sure Bert's okay?" Harlan asked Roz.

"Oh, yeah. The guy's like a two-hundred-pound chunk of leather. This is exactly how they rehearsed it."

"But he looks so… dead."

Roz smiled at Harlan, squeezed his hand, and said, "Time for me to get back to work, Dear."

• • • • •

"What the hell, Eddy?" Roz shouted. "You haven't even asked him where the pole barn is. And look at him. He's useless."

"Sorry, Roz. Guess I got a little carried away with all the cheering from the boys."

Shotgun cleared his throat to gain their attention. He had returned to Harlan, and the lupara. With his back to her, he said, "Please, Roz."

It seemed that even Bert, who groaned at that moment, knew what

Shotgun wanted.

One of the CDA agents seconded the request: "May as well let Mr. Cruzano finish giving him his due. It's like you said, Roz, he's useless now. And besides, from the way these Grovers were talking, they all know where this pole barn is."

Shotgun Gino remained fixated on the lupara as his snake-like tongue action resumed. *But why?* Harlan wondered. *His back is to everyone else in the room, including the Grovers. There's no reason for it unless... maybe... it really does have some hold on him.*

"All right," Roz said, sighing. "Go ahead. But take it outside."

• • • • •

"So, which of you Grovers wants to tell me about the pole barn?" Roz asked after Eddy and Shotgun Gino dragged Bert out of the room.

"We don't know nothing about it," Jack said.

"Let me rephrase the question, gentlemen. Which of you would prefer dealing with me rather than the alternative?"

"What alternative?" Jack said.

At that moment, just outside the door, there was a deafening shotgun blast.

Kodiak started to cry. It was the reaction of a classic bully. *Just like pissing his pants was,* Harlan thought. A tough guy when preying on a lone woman or a handful of fans for an opposing team when he had the numbers. But all just a cover for what he harbored deep inside—a coward.

"What's the matter with you?" Roz said. "Did that hurt your ears?"

"You... c-can't d-... d-do this. It's—"

Another blast rang out.

Kodiak screamed, "Oh my God! We're gonna die!"

"Get ahold of yourself, Cody," Jack shouted. "They're staging this shit. They didn't just shoot Bert Brydges. I'm sure of it. There's no way in hell that they're—"

The door flew open and in walked Shotgun Gino, blood splattered all over his face and body—and tongue writhing like an alien parasite feasting on an earthly host.

Oh crap, Harlan thought as he noticed something stuck to Gino's shoulder blade. It was the foot of one of the chickens that had been slaughtered earlier for dinner. Fortunately, Eddy followed close behind and saw it too. He subtly removed the foot and another chunk of chicken guts while Gino snapped open the lupara and dumped out the used shells.

"Gimme another!" he shouted.

"Slow down," Roz said. "We got one here who wants to talk to Humvee Eddy."

"Which one?" Eddy asked.

"The one who looks like he's about to add a load of shit to his pants."

Kodiak trembled as Eddy approached.

"Please, Mr. Hummer, sir, I'll… t-tell you everything. I swear. Just … d-don't—"

"Shut up, Cody!" Jack shouted. "Don't you see the camera? They're messing with us, man, just trying to make us talk."

"Is that what you think, Jack?" came the voice of one who'd remained silent to this point.

Not now, Tank. Not when we got one about to crack, Harlan thought.

Tank turned to Eddy and continued: "Whatever it was you just did to Bert Brydges, why don't you get your *lard ass* over here and try it with me—Eddy *Chuuub*."

Eddy, stunned by the malevolence of Tank's departure from the script, looked to Harlan, as did every CDA agent in the room.

Like there's anything I can do about this, Harlan thought.

"What are you looking at!" Tank shouted. "I'm over here—Eddy *Chuuub*."

Eddy turned to face Tank.

"That's right," Tank said, "You heard what I called you. Because that's what you are—*Chuuu*—"

"Enough of that!" shouted Shotgun Gino. "How 'bout what I said, asshole, if anybody ever called him that name again. Did you hear that?"

"Way I see it, Cruzano, I'm dying here today. So what the hell, I'll call my killers whatever I want. And this fat man of yours ain't no *Hummer* to me."

Gino turned to Harlan and said, "C'mon, man, gimme a couple shells. I'm gonna waste this bastard."

"Hold on, Gino," Roz said.

Finally, Harlan thought, *somebody's going to put an end to this.*

"This is Eddy's fight," she said.

You can't be serious, Roz.

"Cut Lochner loose!" she shouted.

Now it was Eddy who trembled as a CDA agent drew a knife and applied it to Tank's restraints.

"It's okay, Eddy, you can do this," Roz said.

She then joined Harlan again, this time for the evening's main event.

"What do you think you're doing?" Harlan said to her.

Roz's eyes popped wide open.

"I'm getting the hell out of the way—move, Harlan!"

Chapter 70

Harlan made it to his feet, but only in time to see what hit him—an eight-hundred-pound human freight train careening toward a wall and picking him up en route.

Sandwiched between the wall and the grappling Neanderthals, Harlan felt the last of his air being squeezed from his lungs.

"Get off me!" Eddy shouted.

Get off you? Harlan thought, struggling for air with his face smashed into Eddy's sweaty back.

The pressure intensified to the point of suffocation as Harlan heard Tank speak.

"C'mon, man, fight me."

"I can't," Eddy said.

"Then to me, you'll always be Eddy *Chub*."

Desperate, Harlan used the last of his breath to utter the only words he thought might save him: "Please, Eddy, be the Hummer."

In his next conscious moment, Harlan found himself lying on the floor gasping for air. Roz knelt at his side. She was saying something that he couldn't hear over the chant—

"Hummer! Hummer! Hummer!"

Harlan propped up on an elbow in time to see with his own eyes something he otherwise would have never believed happened—Eddy, dropping the Hummer on Tank one last time before dragging his unconscious body outside.

Shotgun Gino followed.

Two lupara blasts later, Harlan was breathing slower.

Soon after, Eddy and Gino returned.

Eddy stopped in front of the Grovers, a mix of sweat and chicken blood streaming down the sides of his massive face. "Gimme that one," he said, pointing at Kodiak Brown.

Chapter 71

"Hold on," Eddy said to the CDA agent who was about to free Kodiak. "I think he's got something he wants to tell me first."

"I'll tell you everything," Kodiak said. "Just please, Mr. Hummer, d-don't—"

"Get ahold of yourself, Cody," Jack said. "They got nothing on us if we stay quiet."

"Is that so," Eddy said, glancing at Roz, who stood ready with a remote-control device in hand. She pointed it at a monitor that was suspended from the ceiling in position to be seen by the lineup of Grovers. Via wireless transmission, what it played would also be seen by the officers in the holding cell.

Soon the monitor showed a silent video recording of the hippie assassin setting up for an attack on Scammon Cove. Roz paused the presentation and zoomed in for a close-up view of the assassin's undisguised face after he'd been caught.

"You know him?" Eddy asked.

"Don't answer," Jack said.

"I asked you a question, Kodiak," Eddy pressed.

"Y-yes… That's Zep."

Jack let loose a loud exhale as he threw himself back in his chair. Eddy stepped in front of the chair and stared down at Jack, while continuing to speak to Kodiak.

"Full name?"

"Zeppelin… Zeppelin Reed."

"Same sniper who was at Shotgun Landing last week?"

"He wasn't even there," Jack said, staring back at Eddy.

"We'll get to what he was doing," Eddy said. "But that was the plan, wasn't it, Cody? That your buddy Zep would be the shooter on shore at the landing?"

Kodiak nodded.

"I can't hear you," Eddy said, still looking at Jack.

"Yes, sir. Th-that was the plan."

Roz then forwarded the video to a scene showing the bowrider's last voyage the week before, paused it at a point thirty-three seconds before the explosion, and zoomed in on the face of the person at the helm.

"That's Jack, right?" Eddy said. "Disguised as Sully."

Kodiak looked at Jack, who glared back not at him but at Eddy.

As Kodiak silently nodded, Eddy turned his stare to him. Kodiak responded, "Yes, yes. That's him. Jack disguised as Sully."

Roz resumed playing the video until moments before the explosion and then pressed pause.

Eddy stepped over to the monitor, looked up at it, and then looked back at Jack. "Gee, Jack," he said, "where'd you go?"

Jack looked away.

"I mean, one minute, there you are at the wheel, the captain of the ship. And then, poof, you're gone."

Roz played the recording a few frames forward to the explosion, paused it, and then returned to the spot a few seconds before.

Eddy said, "C'mon, Jack, tell us where you went."

Jack remained silent, looking away.

"How about telling us where you told Bert Brydges you were when the bowrider blew."

In response to Jack's silence, Roz fast-forwarded the video to another scene—one of the Skype call between the Grovers and Bert two days before. She turned up the volume and played back the part when Jack had told Bert of his "shit-luck" location on the swim platform, hauling in the loose ladder, when the bowrider blew. His butt, he had said, was all that was exposed above board.

Roz returned to and paused on the scene just before the explosion.

"Shouldn't your butt be right about there?" Eddy said, pointing at the stern.

Jack looked at the monitor and scoffed, "The camera angle ain't right to see it. Hell, the videographer was damn near a quarter mile away."

"Doesn't matter," Roz interjected. "Your story doesn't hold up. The explosion originated below deck—in the hull." She punched the remote and said, "See for yourself."

As the explosion played in slow motion she explained, "Look how the deck—and everything on it—blows up, vertically. The bomb was underneath. The only safe place to be was beneath it, underwater. Which is where you were."

"That's nothing but speculation," Jack said.

"What do you think, Cody?" Roz replied. "Do you agree with Captain Jack? Am I just speculating about him—the former military explosives specialist—abandoning ship?"

Kodiak stared blankly at the monitor and then at Roz.

"Answer me," she said. "Did Jack blow up that boat?"

As Eddy took a step toward him, Kodiak answered, "Yes, yes. Jack set the bomb... and he... h-he jumped off the boat before it blew."

"That don't mean nothing!" Jack shouted. "He's just saying whatever that fat monster wants him to say about stuff he wasn't even there to see."

Jack was right on both counts, Harlan thought. Kodiak was under severe duress, confessing to murders he'd never witnessed. Such a statement would never prove Jack's guilt beyond a reasonable doubt. But it could help create reasonable doubt about Shotgun Gino's guilt, a subject that Harlan knew was going to be explored next.

Eddy stepped alongside Roz and asked, "How about me or my boss, Mr. Cruzano? Aren't you gonna claim that we're the ones who lit up that marina after we learned that Jimmy and you guys were dealing drugs out of it?"

"Why would I do that?" Cody said.

"Because that's what your buddy Jack has been telling people," Eddy replied. "And that's how you Grovers tried to make it look in St. Ignace when you nabbed Bo Kitner."

"But... I... w-wasn't even there," Kodiak stammered as he looked to the other side of Jack, at Eli Hubbard.

Eddy turned to Eli and said, "You been pretty quiet here tonight. Bet you're Jonesin' for a stick of gum by now, aren't you?"

Roz handed Eddy a pack of gum. It was Eli's brand. Eddy popped a piece into his mouth and chomped on it a few times before asking, "Sure you don't want some? You've been looking pretty uptight all evening, like you think you might be in a little bit of trouble."

"I don't know what you're talking about," Eli said.

"That's right," Jack said. "We don't know nothing about the lies Kodiak is spewing right now."

"Zane Hertz!" Eddy called out, "you got something you wanna say about what happened at St. Ignace that day?"

"Damn straight I do," said a CDA agent as he came forward. "Something to say to this fucking nerd."

Eli looked up at Zane, who approached, saying, "That's right, it's me, the guy you shook down at the souvenir shop, after you got to my Uncle Bo."

"I've never seen you in my life," Eli said.

"Bullshit, man, I hear him in your voice—that fucking nerd who came to the shop. Same voice as the guy who called me before on my uncle's phone, claiming to be someone else."

"I never called you."

"Zane," Roz said, "why don't you tell him about the timing of that call. Maybe refresh his memory."

"It came in after the marina got hit," Zane answered. "Still got it logged in my phone at 11:04 a.m. that day. Guy calling said he had my Uncle Bo and that I'd never see him again if I didn't answer his questions about some cargo that Jimmy 'the Leg' was moving outta Shotgun Landing."

"Who'd he claim to be?" Roz asked.

"Gino's guy, he said—Eddy Chub."

Several CDA agents gasped.

"It's okay, boys," Eddy said. "He's just repeating a name Eli Hubbard called himself that day, back when everyone still called me that."

"That's a lie," Eli said. "I never made that call." Eli looked up at the camera and continued, "Can't you see what's going on here? It's obvious who the homicidal maniacs in this room are. It's *these guys* who are trying to frame *us*."

"Is that right," Roz said. "Well, maybe we should get to the bottom of this. What do you say, Eddy? Did you make that call?"

"Oh, c'mon," Eli complained, "like he's gonna admit it."

"Go ahead, Eddy," Roz said. "Tell us whether or not you made that call."

"That morning? When they attacked the marina?" Eddy said. "No way. I couldn't. I was in Traverse City… uh… busy with something that… uh…"

Eli shook his head and laughed. "You call this an alibi? He's trying to make it up as he goes along. And he sucks at it."

"Go ahead, Eddy," Roz said, "tell us what you were doing."

"Well, I was… uh…"

Eddy looked at Shotgun Gino, the only other mobster in the room who knew. Shotgun nodded and said, "It's okay, Eddy. If anybody gives you shit about it, they'll be dealing with me."

"Oh, c'mon, this is ridiculous," Eli said. "Obviously these two murderous gangsters have fabricated a—"

"I was at a support group meeting for… for… f-fat people… getting help with my weight problem," Eddy said.

Eyebrows rose and jaws dropped throughout the room as CDA agents exchanged stunned looks in reaction to the admission. But none dared to comment.

"Sure, an anonymous support group, I'll bet," Eli scoffed.

"That's right, it was," Roz said. "An anonymous support group that meets at the college in Traverse City—and is run by a professor who happens to be a friend of mine."

"Oh, I see," Eli said. "Now *you're* gonna vouch for him."

"Not me. A videotape will do that, one that the professor made as part of a study she's doing at the college. She checked it for me, and it shows Eddy sitting there that morning the whole time, from 10:30 'til 11:20 a.m. He never left the room. And he most certainly made no phone calls."

Harlan recalled Roz mentioning a way she might have to fact-check

Eddy's alibi, but she'd never told him the specifics. He wondered now how they'd ever get any of the specifics about the ultimate disposition of Bo Kitner. A confession from Eli seemed doubtful.

Zane stuck his face within inches of Eli's and seethed as he asked, "What'd you do to my Uncle Bo, you son of a bitch?"

Eli looked past Zane and responded directly to the camera: "Whoever the hell you are, I'm invoking my right to counsel right now. And then we'll see just how much of this bullshit can be used against us in court."

"Right to counsel?" Roz remarked, laughing. "What are you thinking? That there are cops on the other side of that camera who are running this shakedown? Think again, Eli. Fact is, you're in *my* custody, undergoing *my* interrogation, and *I'm* no cop. Which means you have no rights right now. But you're welcome to remain silent while your accomplice continues incriminating your sorry ass, starting with telling us about his underwater murder of Finn Ramsey—at *your* direction."

Chapter 72

As Kodiak confessed to Finn Ramsey's murder, Vincent Surocco and one of his men led Zeppelin Reed into the interrogation room, shackled and battered. Vincent joined Harlan after sitting Reed down in the lineup.

"He won't talk," Vincent said.

"I see you guys asked nicely," Harlan replied.

"By our standards, we did. Don't see what good it's gonna do bringing him in here."

Roz stood over Reed and stared down at him, though she continued directing her questions to Kodiak.

"Let's talk about the drug trafficking," she said. "When did you Grovers get involved?"

"Last summer," Kodiak said. "Middle of July."

"How?"

Kodiak looked at Zeppelin before responding, "Zep arranged it with Jimmy 'the Leg.'"

"Arranged what?"

"A meeting in Northport at his fishing business."

"Tell me about it, from the beginning."

"Well, it was at night, after business hours. A text from Zep told us to let ourselves in—Eli, Jack, and me—and come around back to the office..."

• • • • •

Zeppelin and Jimmy were already there, seated across a desk from one another. On top of the desk were photos that Zeppelin had taken during his police surveillance of Jimmy's activities at the marina.

"My, oh my, check that out," Jack said after stepping around the desk, behind Jimmy, and looking down over his shoulder. "All those photos of the same tourist going fishing with your employees—for days—and never coming back with any fish. What's up with that, old man?"

Jimmy remained silent, head down, as Jack reached over his shoulder and picked up a few zoomed-image photos of Jimmy's men returning from points unknown with mystery goods in garbage bags.

"He won't say what they're moving," Zeppelin said.

Jack perused more of the photos, pausing over a few of Jimmy, alone, taking the garbage bags east on the bass boat. "Where do you take them, old man?"

"Like I'm gonna tell you," Jimmy answered calmly.

Jack elbowed him in the face, hard, but Jimmy held firm. Then Jack leaned over him and spoke directly into his ear, "I hear you're real cool under pressure, old man. Goes back to your days as a professional gambler. And right now I bet you're thinking you still got some cards to play, don't you? You figure these photos don't amount to much. Just circumstantial. But all of us in this room, we know you're moving something in those bags."

"Whadaya want?" Jimmy said.

"For starters, we want in."

Jimmy laughed and said, "In on what? The peanuts I'm making?"

"C'mon, old man. Don't make me hit you again. Just tell me, what are you into?"

Jimmy rolled his eyes and said, "Pharmaceuticals, for crying out loud."

"What?"

"You heard me. Pharmaceuticals."

"Like the kind you get at Rite Aid?" Jack said, frowning at Zeppelin.

"You wanna see for yourself?" Jimmy said.

"You got some of your goods here right now?" Jack said.

"May I?" Jimmy asked as he scooted his chair back a few inches.

Jack let him get up from the desk and go to a closet in the same room. He returned with a black garbage bag and removed what was inside—a clear PVC tube packed with layers of pills.

Examining the tube, Jack asked, "What kind of value does this shit have?"

"None, unless you got the ailments those pills cure."

"What about pharmaceuticals that could be moved on the street, like medical marijuana or opioids? You ever get any drugs like that?"

"Sure, but never in quantities worth the effort."

Jack continued to study the goods. Each layer of pills was labeled. "These words mean anything to you?"

Jimmy shook his head. "I'm no doctor."

"Who do you sell this to?"

"You'd have to ask my distributor."

"And who's that?"

Jimmy stared at Jack and calmly said, "I don't give names."

Jack swung a backhand but stopped it short of Jimmy's face, barely. Jimmy didn't flinch. He held Jack's stare.

Jack smiled and said, "So you have a distributor somewhere east of here, who gets this shit to sick people who can pay."

"Something like that."

"And your supplier?"

"Canadian."

"Any points in between?"

Jimmy paused for a long while, giving it some thought before responding, "St. Ignace and Drummond."

"Drummond?"

"An island up north in Lake Huron, by the border."

There was another pause. This time it was Jack giving some thought to the progress of their meeting. Eventually he said, "You're being straight with me, aren't you?"

Jimmy nodded. "Best cards I can play in the circumstances."

Jack nodded back and asked, "You ever think about doing anything in the other direction?"

"You mean selling into Canada?"

"Uh huh."

"I got nothing to move that way."

"But if you did..."

"Guess it would depend on what it is."

Jack looked at Zeppelin and said, "Go ahead."

"You sure?" Zeppelin said.

Jack nodded.

"Cocaine," Zeppelin said.

"How much?" Jimmy asked.

"Two hundred-plus kilos."

"You're holding that much coke?"

"Well, not yet. But I have a connection."

"From all the good police work you're doing, no doubt," Jimmy said.

"Something like that," Zeppelin answered.

"And how does your connection want to do business?"

"Four drops. Cash on each delivery."

"Whose?"

"Whose what?"

"Whose fucking cash?" Jimmy said.

Zeppelin didn't respond.

"Oh, I see," Jimmy said. "You think I'm gonna pay for it, even though I told you just a minute ago that I'm not making shit here."

Zeppelin remained silent, his stare turning blank.

"Un-fucking believable," Jimmy said. "You jokers want me to buy the dope, then sell it, and then, if I'm getting your gist, let you take all the profit."

"Easy, Jimmy," Jack said.

Jimmy cocked his head and looked sideways at his four visitors. "You've never done anything like this in your lives, have you? You're just a bunch of kids."

"Guilty as charged," Jack replied. "But we're willing to learn, especially from an old pro like you. And while we're at it, we're gonna help you with the pharmaceutical side of the business."

"How so?"

"You can't keep using the same crew, over and over, to move that shit. It's getting obvious. Isn't that right, Zep?"

Zeppelin smiled in response. This part of the plan was his idea. The

Grovers would insert themselves into Jimmy's pharmaceutical business and, wearing disguises, use his facilities to run their cocaine so that if things ever went sideways, they could simply disappear, leaving suspicion to focus on Jimmy and his gangster boss.

"And what if I don't want your help?" Jimmy said.

"That's not an option," Jack replied, "because then we'd have to turn those photos over to certain people, which would put you in some deep shit—along with the guy you're working for."

"What guy?" Jimmy asked.

"I know," Jack said, smirking, "you don't give names. That's something I actually like about you. But you know who I'm talking about. The owner of this marina. And the same guy who can help us with our little financing issue for the coke."

"He'd never go for it, even if you were gonna cut him in for a major share. The man can't do that kind of business any more, especially on the scale you're talking."

"Why not?"

"Because Shotgun Gino's not the gangster he once was."

"What do you mean?"

"It's a long story."

"Well, he's backing the pharmaceuticals you're into, isn't he?"

Jimmy stared down at the tube of meds on the desktop as he gave the question some thought. His stone-cold expression unchanged, he finally answered, "I'm backing this stuff. Got every penny I ever saved tied up in it."

"Are you shittin' me?" Jack said. "You're running drugs out of a marina owned by a full-on wiseguy, and you're cutting him out? I don't believe it. You're lying, old man."

"If you think it's his gig, why aren't you busting *his* chops right now?"

"Cuz we got no fucking pictures of him, not anywhere near the shit. He knows well enough to keep a distance."

"Uh huh," Jimmy said. "He's at a distance all right. I'm telling you, the guy's retired."

"Well, I'm sorry to hear that," Jack said, "because one month from now, the first shipment of that coke is showing up right here, at Shotgun

Landing, and the guys delivering it don't take credit."

"What?" Jimmy said.

"You heard me, old man. We start our new business in a month—you, me, and my fellow Grovers here."

"Your what?"

"Never mind. You just worry about the financing."

"But I just told you—"

"Enough," Jack said. "I can tell you're a resourceful guy. You'll figure out a way."

Chapter 73

All eyes were on Shotgun Gino, whose grin could be no broader. Jimmy had covered for him on the pharmaceuticals, and now it was the word of a dead man who could never be cross-examined.

After Roz resumed her interrogation of Kodiak, Harlan got Gino's attention and they left the room together.

Vincent followed as they headed into the kitchen.

"You mind?" Harlan said to him.

"He's okay, Holmes," Gino said.

"But I have something to discuss with you, my client."

"I know you do. And the answer is no—Jimmy never came to me for the money."

Harlan found himself believing this as he thought about Jimmy's failed attempt to skim Gino's money rather than ask for it. That happened late last July when Bo visited Bert on the island to propose the plan, Harlan recalled, not long after Jimmy's meeting with the Grovers.

"Who else would Jimmy go to?" Harlan asked.

Gino shrugged.

"Seriously?" Harlan replied, "you'd been working with this guy for months, and you have no idea?"

"You calling me a liar, Holmes?"

"No, I'm just saying that you seemed to be his only connection. Maybe you introduced him to somebody at some point, someone he might have turned to."

"Not a chance," Gino said. "I was as unconnected as he was. Remember? I was forced into retirement too. The only made guy still in the mix who'd even talk to me was Angelo Surocco, and that was only because we knew each other since we were kids. I think he pitied me more than anything."

Harlan looked at Vincent, who seemed to read his mind. "Wasn't my old man who Jimmy reached out to. I'm sure. It's like Gino said, my dad felt bad about the situation. He wouldn't stab his old friend in the back that way."

Vincent's last remark triggered a connection. *He's right,* Harlan thought. *It's one thing to stand by and watch the man get run out of Chicago; it's quite another to finance a major cocaine operation, run out of his marina behind his back, knowing what the other families would do to him if he got busted for it. Who would do that to him?*

"Where's Sawed-Off?" Harlan asked.

"What?" Shotgun Gino said. "You think my own son would..."

"Why not?" Harlan said. "He's the one who forced you into retirement two years ago, when he stopped being your son."

"But then why would he hire you to find me?"

"I'm starting to think that he wasn't looking for you, Gino."

"Then who was he looking for?"

"Whoever killed off your crew and, as far as he could tell, probably you too."

"Why would he go after them?"

"To protect his investment."

"Investment? You mean the coke?"

"Where is he right now?" Harlan asked, turning to Vincent.

"Not sure, but I'll find out."

After Vincent left, Harlan said, "I assume you never introduced Jimmy to Sawed-Off."

"I didn't meet Jimmy until after my retirement," Gino said, shaking his head, "long after Sawed-Off was outta my life." Gino paused and added, "It's kind of funny how things sometimes come about."

"How's that?" Harlan asked.

"It was *you* who I was hoping would introduce me to Jimmy after I got the idea about trafficking meds. You remember that day at the gym?"

"Sure, the day you showed up with Angelo Surocco, unannounced, and he asked me if I could join you guys for a tour of the town."

"That's right, except all I wanted to see were guys who might be willing to join me in my new pharmaceutical business. I told Angelo about what I was planning and how I needed a new crew—you know, bad boys local to Traverse City. He told me about your history with a bagman who used to work for a down-and-out bookie, Jimmy 'the Leg' Dillon. We thought maybe you could hook me up with Jimmy and some of his old crew."

"But I blew you off."

"No big deal. I got to meet him anyway."

"Did you ever say anything to Jimmy that might've given him the idea that he could go to Sawed-Off behind your back?"

Gino looked off, thinking about the question. "I might have, the first time we met, when I was making my pitch. He thought I was still some big-city mobster and couldn't understand why I was coming to him. So, I told him."

"You told him what?"

"The truth..."

• • • • •

Shotgun Gino and Jimmy stood at the end of the pier at Shotgun Landing, looking out at the mouth of the bay where it blended into the big water of Lake Michigan.

"I don't get it," Jimmy said.

"Well, it's a pretty simple operation," Shotgun replied. "Like I said, after your crew crosses the Straits from the Huron into those waters out there, it's a clean shot to where we're standing here on the mainland. And then from here—"

"No, that's not it, Gino. I get what you're saying. What I don't get is why you're saying it to me."

"What's there to get? I need somebody to run it, and you still have guys who'll work for you."

"An old one-legged bookie and what's left of his ragtag crew—that's who you want running your drug ring? I thought you were a major player."

"I guess I once was."

"So, where's *your* crew?"

There was a long pause before Shotgun responded, "You got any kids, Jimmy?"

"No, not my own anyway. I do have a niece who's like a daughter to me. She used to work for me back when I ran the book. We're real close."

"Close enough to bring her along if you were to run this gig for me?"

"I'd want to. Sam's a good kid. And someone I can trust with my life."

"What if Sam thought you owed her money—a lot of money—and maybe she's right, but you won't give it to her. You got your reasons, but she doesn't understand. Could you imagine her turning on you—turning your whole crew against you—and running you out of town?"

"Sam? Treat me that way? Never. Not over money."

"And then you come up with a plan for a new operation in your new hometown, like the plan I'm telling you about—would Sam try to block it if you didn't give her a piece of the action?"

Jimmy shook his head.

"Well I have a son, my only child, who did all that. And now I have no crew."

Gino waited for the confession to settle in, and then closed the deal. "Tell me something, Jimmy, how do you like being retired from the life?"

"It sucks."

"I hear that."

• • • • •

Vincent had returned from his errand and seemed to be growing restless as he waited for Shotgun to finish his story.

"What'd you learn?" Harlan asked.

"Sawed-Off and his crew are supposed to be on the perimeter," Vincent said, "keeping lookout for unexpected visitors. But they haven't reported in since the raid. And they're not answering now. Can't get 'em on the radio, cell phones—nothing. I sent some guys out to check, but it looks like they bolted."

Harlan tried calling Sawed-Off on his cell phone. There was no answer. He had a bad feeling and decided to pull up the app for the spy-cams at Bass Cove that he and Roz had planted to watch over the cocaine stashed in the pole barn. No activity had been recorded on any of the cameras all day, but that still didn't settle his uneasy feeling.

Chapter 74

After checking the spy cams, Harlan texted instructions calling for the release of the hostages in the holding cell. He then headed out the backdoor, nodding as he passed a CDA agent stationed outside. Something caught his attention, however, and caused him to stop and turn back. The agent was smoking a cigarette.

"Did you want one?" he asked.

It had been twenty years since he'd broken the habit, yet Harlan found himself at this moment craving a smoke as if he were in the grips of withdrawal all over again. It was the same kind of flashback urge he had endured a few years ago when he lost his job on the force, and again more recently when he lost his PI license. Both times, however, he found other ways to deal with the stress. Not so this time.

Harlan accepted the cigarette and then walked a short distance away—far enough to be alone, but close enough to see inside the interrogation room through a window.

Detective Riley Summers soon entered the room and immediately began questioning those present. She focused first on Tank Lochner, who had returned sometime after his fake execution. Bert Brydges, of course, had not. Harlan took a moment to imagine where the man might be.

• • • • •

Bert was at the wheel with the throttle wide open, jumping waves somewhere on Lake Huron. He had everything he needed to start a new life: his boat, his woman, and sustenance from the Grovers in the form of a briefcase full of cash and a few kilos of cocaine.

Morgan was hanging all over him, running her hands everywhere. She stopped when a trickle of blood, which still ran from his nose, gushed at the jolt of a six-foot swell.

"We should do something about that nose!" she shouted over the roar of the boat's engine.

Bert shook his head, stuck out his tongue, and licked his upper lip clean.

It still tasted good.

• • • • •

After finishing the cigarette, Harlan got out his smartphone and again accessed the cameras hidden in the pole barn. Captain Nash had not yet arrived. "C'mon, Marty, would you get there already?" Harlan murmured.

A few minutes later the captain did, and he began his search right where Kodiak Brown had said he last saw the cocaine—in the wall behind the circuit box.

Harlan continued watching the scene at the pole barn until he was distracted by the blare of sirens to the north. Police backup units were coming to shore and no doubt would soon arrive at both Scammon and Bass Coves.

A few minutes after returning his attention to the phone, Harlan was distracted again, this time by the slam of the back door. Tank was coming. Harlan quickly popped a mint into his mouth to kill the cigarette odor on his breath. The measure, however, probably wasn't necessary. Tank was too excited about something to have noticed.

"Guess what, Boss."

"What?"

"Got me a new job, man."

"Really. Tell me about it."

"It's with Shotgun Gino. You heard what the Grovers said about the pharmaceutical business. Jimmy gave no names. So Gino figures he can keep it going by just changing up the locations. And he wants me to join him and Eddy. Gonna put us in charge—Eddy downstate and me somewhere up this way."

Harlan tilted his head and looked sideways at Tank.

"I know what you're thinking, Boss, it being illegal and all. But it's for a good cause. I'll be helping sick people get better."

"Uh huh. Tell me something, Tank, you have PADI certification?"

"Who's Patti?"

"I'm talking about scuba diving credentials, Tank. The operation on this end happens underwater, remember?"

"Yeah, but how hard can it be? I mean, you put on the gear and swim down to the bottom. Don't even have to hold your breath."

As silly as it sounded, Harlan could tell that Tank was serious. He was ready to move on. Harlan wasn't, because he felt he had nothing to move on to. That reality became even clearer when he tried to make Tank a better offer.

"I don't know about this, Tank. I thought maybe we would... you know, that we'd..."

"It's okay, Boss. Besides, I can't keep hanging with you now that you got yourself a woman. I'd be a third wheel."

Harlan sighed deeply. Tank's remark was a reminder of the original source of his moodiness and urge for a smoke. "I'm not so sure about her," he said.

"Oh, c'mon, Boss. You can't still be in doubt—not after she came back for you the way she did. That woman put everything on the line for you. In fact, she still is."

Through the window, Harlan could see Roz. She was now the focus of the detective's interrogation.

"It may look that way," he said, "but I'm not so sure it was me she came back for."

"What are you talking about? Who else could it be?"

Harlan looked down at his cell phone again. The captain hadn't gotten to the pole barn's floorboards yet.

Tapping and scrolling further on his phone, Harlan switched into his text messages and opened one marked "urgent." He had sent it to Sawed-Off Gino Cruzano insisting that Gino call ASAP. There still had been no reply by phone or text.

Looking up, Harlan asked, "Don't you find her initial involvement in this case a little curious?"

"Roz's involvement?"

"Yeah, that night we first met her, some of the things she did, like the way she conducted her search for the drugs at Bass Cove."

"What about it, Boss?"

"She spent what, maybe twenty minutes, tops, searching the house before she went outside, straight to that pole barn. And in the middle of the night, through a window, she spots a camera lens that's the diameter of a number two pencil from a hundred feet away, using a flashlight and a little spy glass."

"You saying she'd seen it before?"

"I'm saying that I could barely see that thing when she held the light on it and told me right where to look."

"Well, she is a PI, you know, paid to be observant."

"So am I, remember?" Harlan said defensively. "And what was she being so observant about on past occasions at Bass Cove when she took photos down by the water?"

"Just what she told us," Tank said. "She was checking things out and came across the bowrider."

"But she was supposed to be spying on Morgan and Mikey at the time. Where do you think the young lovers were while she was down by the shore taking pictures—a lot of pictures?"

"I dunno, back in the house, I guess."

"Which you can't see from the dock down by the water. She told me that herself when I wasn't able to see the dock from a window inside the house."

Tank went silent.

Harlan continued.

"She had all the tools she needed to get into the pole barn that night, including a fully assembled rifle to take out the camera. And she wasn't the least bit concerned about getting caught, like she knew it was the only camera, and knew it had a monitoring distance short of the window she used to make the shot."

"What are you accusing her of, Boss?"

"Of not really working for Bert," Harlan said. "You ever talk with Bert about how he found her in the first place?"

Tank slowly nodded his head and replied, "Yeah, but I never gave it a second thought."

"What'd he tell you?"

"He said it was kind of a chance meeting they had a while back."

"They just happened to bump into each other somewhere, when he happened to be in need of a PI?" Harlan said.

"That's basically how Bert described it, I guess."

"Tell me exactly what he said, Tank."

"It happened at the Northwood, the bar and restaurant at Four Corners. You remember. It's the first sign of civilization when you get off the ferry and come inland. Bert and Morgan went there for a burgers and beer one night and..."

• • • • •

Bert glanced around the bar after Morgan had left their table to use the restroom. He noticed an attractive, middle-aged woman sitting at the bar alone. She caught him looking and came over, staring back at him like a lonely heart on the prowl.

"All due respect, ma'am," Bert said, "I'm already taken."

Roz laughed. "Oh gosh, you've completely misread me. Not that I wouldn't have those intentions if I was twenty years younger."

"You think you're that much older than me?"

"At least. But, hey, I didn't come over here looking for flattery."

"Well, then, what can I do for you?"

Roz sighed as she glanced in the direction of the women's room. "It's none of my business," she said, "but in my line of work, I get paid to see things, you know, be observant. And it's a hard thing to shut off when I'm not on the job."

"What's your line of work?"

"I'm a private eye. And I can't help but remember seeing that woman you're with tonight, right here in this bar not long ago, being all cozy the way you two are tonight—with another man. They were sitting right over there by the…"

Bert struggled to process what she'd just said. "What other man?" he asked.

"I couldn't tell you a name," Roz said as she shrugged. "But he was a pretty boy. Blond hair and blue eyes. Kind of a slight build. Maybe mid-twenties. Like I said, it's none of my business but…"

Bert looked at the door to the women's restroom. "Can't be true," he said before returning his attention to Roz.

"Look, I'm sorry to be telling you something like this. My name's Roz Cortez. Here's my card. If you think you need to, give me a call when you have more time to talk."

• • • • •

Backup police units arrived as Tank completed the story. Harlan barely noticed them rush by.

"You okay, Boss?" Tank asked.

He didn't have to tell Tank what he was thinking: *Not one, but two chance encounters with Morgan Pierce, in a public place, being all cozy with the different men in her life.*

"You don't like coincidences, do you, Boss?"

"There's nothing to like or dislike," Harlan said. "I just don't believe in them."

"So, what do you think?"

"That maybe she runs a scam better than me."

Harlan looked again at his phone to check on the cameras at Bass Cove. Backup units had arrived there too and were moving the search along, at that point into the rafters.

The back door slammed again. It was Vincent Surocco this time.

"Don't know about you guys," Vincent said, "but I'm starting to get a little antsy with all these state troopers around here. Would it be okay with you if me and my guys hit it?"

"That's fine," Harlan answered. "Just one thing. Have you gotten any word from the guys you sent looking for Sawed-Off and his crew?"

"Yeah, they checked the whole perimeter, and then from Township Park clear down to Bass Cove."

"And?"

"Nothing. No sign of them anywhere. My guess is they went back on the same ferry that all these cops came in on."

After Vincent left, Tank asked, "What do think is up with Sawed-Off, Boss?"

Harlan returned to watching his camera views of the search of the pole barn while explaining to Tank, point by point, his concerns about the junior Gino Cruzano. The police had finally begun pulling up floorboards.

Chapter 75

Humvee Eddy came bounding out of the back door to tell them what Harlan already suspected and would have known for sure, had his cameras at the pole barn not been discovered and confiscated by the police.

"That detective got a call," Eddy said, short of breath, "and then all of a sudden she started questioning the Grovers about the coke—like the cops didn't find it in the pole barn."

"It wasn't there?" Tank said.

"That's how it sounded from her questions," Eddy answered, "and from what I overheard some cops saying after she kicked me out."

"What'd you hear?" Harlan asked.

"Talk about a BOLO out on Bert Brydges, like they think he got away with the coke."

"What are the Grovers saying?"

"Nothing. They're not talking. Not even Kodiak."

That's it, Harlan thought. *There's no doubt about it now.*

Somebody got into the pole barn and left with 250 kilos of coke, and Harlan never received so much as a single alert from any of the cameras' motion detectors.

Roz's cameras, he thought. *The ones programmed with her app, which only she, Tank, and I had password access to. Who else could've muted them while Sawed-Off raided the pole barn?*

Harlan looked at the window. The detective stood in front of it talking on the phone—and staring out at him. Harlan stared back until the back door slammed again.

Roz was coming.

"Let's go, Eddy," Tank said.

"Where?"

"Anywhere. Just not here."

Tank paused before leaving and said, "Give her a chance, Boss. There must be a reason."

Harlan and Roz studied each other as she approached. Their nonverbal cues advanced them to the middle of the conversation by the time words were exchanged.

"It's not what you think," Roz said.

"Oh, it's exactly what I think," Harlan replied. "It's that thing you accused me of the night we met—situational ethics. I just don't know what the *situation* is with you and Sawed-Off Gino Cruzano."

"No, you don't."

"Hell, I don't even know you."

"That's not true, Harlan."

"But you got to know me—a broken-down ex-PI whose future holds nothing but getting old alone—and you used it to play me."

"I'm telling you, Harlan, that's not—"

"*Everything* was a lie."

Just then the detective stepped away from the window and left the interrogation room.

"She's coming out here to talk to you," Roz said, "to fact-check my statement. I can tell she trusts you, despite all your shenanigans."

"Don't worry, Roz. You think I'm gonna tell her how you managed to dupe me into giving 250 kilos of cocaine to your scumbag client?"

"Look, Harlan, you're right about me helping him. But there's a lot you don't know. Please, let's talk about this."

The back door slammed again. As predicted, it was Detective Riley Summers.

Whatever Roz's reasons might be, Harlan thought, she couldn't explain them in the few seconds they had before Riley arrived. He sighed deeply and said, "There's a place on the other side of the channel, right where you get off the ferry. Dinghy's Diner. It should be open for breakfast by the time the detective is done with me."

Chapter 76

On one of the diner's paneled walls hung the head of a moose overlooking a seating area with only enough room for a dozen or so small tables. Each was neatly set with paper napkins and placemats, coffee mugs, and four vinyl-padded chairs pushed in all the way. Roz and one other customer there must have been the diner's first two that day.

She sat at a table by a window, her hands wrapped around a cup of coffee in front of her.

The other customer sat on a stool at the front counter chatting with a young woman wearing an apron. The woman held up a pot of coffee and raised her eyebrows at Harlan when he entered. He nodded back and then joined Roz.

There was no greeting. There wasn't even eye contact until the waitress had poured his coffee and left. Then, as soon as her eyes met his, Roz started in with a story that seemed to come out of nowhere:

"It was a few years ago, when I lived in Chicago and was new to private investigation. One of my first clients was a woman who'd found her fifteen-year-old daughter's diary. In it were some graphic accounts of the kid either having sexual relations with a teacher from school or fantasizing about it. The mom hired me to find out which it was. And I did.

"I caught the teacher taking the kid home—to his house—after school one day. I'm on my way to that asshole's front door, on the phone with the kid's mom, and she asks for the address, saying she wants to call the police. I told her I'd make the call. But she insists. As distracted as I was, I just gave her the address and started banging on the front door.

"The asshole opens the door—his fucking shirt unbuttoned—and I barge in, yelling and screaming shit that makes no sense. He and the kid are trying to play it down, telling me to relax and have something to drink. It was surreal. I didn't know what to do, except rant and rave and lecture the asshole about the meaning of *consent*, until the cops showed up.

"And when they finally did, it got even more weird. They don't knock and announce, show badges, or do anything real cops do. They just bust right in, three of 'em in plain clothes. Two of 'em grab the teacher and haul his ass, squirming and screaming, to another room where all of a sudden he goes quiet. Meanwhile the third guy and the girl are arguing. She's using a name—Uncle Alphonse, she calls him—begging him not to hurt her boyfriend.

"At some point Uncle Alphonse cuts her short and says her father wants her home right away. And then he looks at me and says I'm supposed to take her there."

Roz paused the story for the waitress as she provided refills and asked if they wanted to order food.

"We're good with just the coffee for now," Harlan said.

Roz stared into space for a while after the waitress left. "I was so stupid," she said.

"No you weren't," Harlan replied, forgetting for the moment the reason for their meeting and finding himself, instead, wanting to defend her actions in the story she'd told. "You just lacked experience. I mean, what the hell, you went from cutting hair and life coaching to chasing down sexual predators and child molesters—on your own. You were bound to make mistakes."

"This one got worse," Roz said.

"You took the girl home?"

"Yeah."

"You didn't call the police?"

"I know I should have, but I just wasn't thinking straight. I felt like an accomplice."

"What happened at the house?"

• • • • •

The front door opened as Roz and the girl came up the walk. Roz's client stepped out and met them on the porch. Looking at the girl, she said, "You and I are going for a ride while your father talks to Ms. Cortez."

The girl shook her head. "Listen, Mom, I'm not going anywhere until—"

"He's in the dining room waiting for you," the girl's mother said to Roz.

Roz remained on the porch long enough to watch the girl and her mother drive off. A curtain to a nearby window moved as she turned back to the door. She paused again. Whatever fate befell the asshole teacher, she knew that the author of it was on the other side of that curtain, and he wouldn't be the kind of person who'd let her just walk away from it.

She let herself into the house and found the dining room, where two men were seated at a long table. After looking back and forth between them, she settled on the one who looked about forty, the right age to be the spouse of her client. The other one was around seventy.

It didn't hit her until she said the name out loud, to him.

"Mr. Cruzano?"

Her thoughts raced. *Who was the guy with that name? He was in the news... indicted for something, but never convicted...*

"Yeah, Gino Cruzano, Junior," he replied. "You've probably heard of my father."

She nodded slowly, recalling local news reports about some of the alleged antics of the elder mobster.

Turning to the other guy, Gino said, "What's that saying about the apple, Joey? That it doesn't fall far from the tree?"

The older guy nodded, never taking his eyes off her.

"All along, I've been working for you?" Roz asked.

"No," Gino said, "I didn't know about any of this until after my wife called the police."

"The police? Just how stupid do you think I..." She paused, calmed herself, and opted for a sarcastic reply. "Oh, I guess I didn't realize that Uncle Alphonse and his men were officers of the law."

Gino rose from his chair and stepped toward her, his nostrils flaring and lip curling. "That sick pedophile was fucking my little girl's brains out!"

"Okay, look, Mr. Cruzano," she replied, now trying to calm him. "I understand your anger; believe me, I do. Predators like him, they deserve whatever you've done to him, or are doing right now. But sir, I can't be a part of it."

Gino's expression eased as he stepped back. "That's fine," he said, "because you've already done your part. And I appreciate it. That's why I wanted to meet you. Truth is, my wife never told me about any of this until today, right after you called from that bastard's house."

Gino reached back to Joey, who handed him a large envelope. "This is for you," Gino said. "A little bonus. Actually, a big one. There's fifty large in here. It's yours for a job well done."

Roz understood her choices: take it, and he might believe he could let her live; or turn it down, and he'd know he couldn't.

"You may as well take it," Joey said. "You can't go to the authorities with this anyway. Under state law, a private investigator owes her client a duty of confidentiality."

"Not when the PI finds out she's been used to perpetrate a crime," Roz said.

"That's not how I read the law."

"Who are you?"

"Why, Ms. Cortez, you know me. I'm your attorney, Joey Elias. And, on advice of counsel, you're going to keep everything you know about this case confidential."

"You're not my attorney. I've never seen you in my life."

"Of course I am. I've been your family attorney for years."

"Your *whole* family," Gino said, "including your son, Philip."

"My son? What the—"

"Yes, your son," Gino continued. "I understand he just graduated from Illinois State last spring and took a job as a loan officer at a bank right here in Chicago. A good job. Wears a suit and tie every day. Today it's a blue suit with a plaid tie. Next time you talk to him, though, you might tell him that his shoes could use a shine."

She looked away, wondering how he could possibly know anything about Philip, her only child.

As if reading her mind, Joey said, "Social media, Ms. Cortez. It's something I would advise against for someone in your line of work."

She took the envelope.

Chapter 77

"Are you sure you want all that?" the waitress asked.

Business was picking up at Dinghy's Diner, and Harlan felt guilty about monopolizing one of the establishment's few tables while consuming nothing but coffee. Though not the least bit hungry, he'd just ordered enough food to feed himself all day.

"Yes, please," he said, "and could you get me started with a mess of bacon and a large OJ?"

He turned to Roz after the waitress left. "Obviously that wasn't the last time you dealt with Sawed-Off Gino."

"No, it wasn't. After that day, he started calling on me for PI services, like he thought he had me on retainer."

"Did he?"

Roz leaned back in her chair and sighed.

"What kind of services?" Harlan asked.

"Typical stuff, you know, record checks, asset research, surveillance. Nothing illegal on its face. I hated every second of it, but what was I supposed to do?"

"Is that why you moved to Michigan?"

"Yes. I thought, what work could he possibly have for me up here, five hundred miles away in the UP?"

Harlan considered leaving at this point. What else could she say? She'd been lying to him since the day they met and covering her tracks with all her bullshit concerns about the work that *he* was doing for the wrong people.

Roz must have sensed his train of thought. She leaned forward and launched into the more recent half of the story:

"It was just like you figured, Harlan. Jimmy went to Sawed-Off for financing on the coke. It was supposed to be a high-interest loan that Jimmy would pay back in February after he closed the deal with the Canadians. But Sawed-Off had something else in mind. He was gonna steal the coke for himself and, through the outstanding loan, own Shotgun Gino's lead player in the pharmaceutical ring. All along, Sawed-Off was looking for a way to get his claws into that business."

Harlan nodded as he recalled his first meeting with Sawed-Off. The man's resentment toward his father was palpable; at bottom, it was about money he thought he was owed.

Roz continued:

"The main challenge was finding the coke, which as you know was being moved by boat. Sawed-Off's guys weren't mariners and lacked imagination. They never learned more than what Jimmy had said in the first place—that it was coming in four installments and would be stashed somewhere in the eastern UP, in the vicinity of the pharmaceutical operation. So Sawed-Off was in the market for a PI up this way. You can imagine his reaction when he found me in Sault Ste. Marie. I became his hope to find the coke and learn all the ins and outs of his father's pharmaceutical business."

She paused when the waitress arrived with Harlan's OJ. After she left, he asked, "How did you find it?"

"Easy. I went fishing."

"With Jimmy's crew?"

"Yeah. You ever see those online photos of Jimmy's Charter Fishing?"

Harlan nodded.

"I'm in a few of those with the crew, Paul Russo and Chase Banwell, and a monster pike. Of course, you probably wouldn't recognize me without my grey hair and wrinkles."

"Did you put one of your GPS trackers on the bowrider?"

"I sure did, and it led me to Bert Brydges on Drummond Island. His girlfriend's affair with Eli Hubbard, AKA Mike Wazowski, led me to Bass Cove. And after spending some time there, I was able to find the most likely location of the coke—a pole barn inside of which was the only security camera on the premises. I never actually saw the coke until the day you and I went inside. But I had a strong hunch that it was there."

Harlan's bacon showed up, still sizzling. He slid the plate aside. "Why did Sawed-Off wait to steal the coke?"

"Because I told him that I couldn't find it. If I could avoid it, I wasn't going to be an accomplice to drug smuggling. As far as he knew, I had the location narrowed to somewhere on the premises of either Bert's place at Maxton Bay or the Grovers' place at Bass Cove, but nowhere more specific. I told him that finding it would take a serious search—digging holes, busting into walls, that kind of thing. And I convinced him to wait to do that until Bert and the Grovers broke off the pharmaceutical trafficking for the season."

"How did you know when they would do that?"

"I was also working for Bert, remember? He never realized it, but he gave me some insights into the pharmaceutical side of the business that helped me keep Sawed-Off at bay."

"But you were never going to give him the coke."

"No, my plan was to delay him until I could figure out a way to turn it over to the police without it looking like I was the informant. What I never saw coming, though, was all hell breaking loose."

"You mean, the Northport massacre?"

Roz nodded and said, "Sawed-Off never saw that coming either. He called me that day, panicking about the coke, of all things. Not the fact that his parents went missing. No, he thought for sure that whoever took down the drug dealers at Shotgun Landing would come north for the coke. But I told him there was nothing going on up here, other than Bert Brydges getting his heart broken."

"Who did Sawed-Off think might be coming for the coke?" Harlan asked.

"He had no idea."

"How about his northernmost PI? Did you—"

"I had no clue either. That's why he hired you, to see if you could figure out who was behind the hits downstate. It was never about finding his parents. He assumed they were dead."

"It sounds like Sawed-Off told you about me."

"A little. He said you were recommended by some of his Chicago associates, but that you probably wouldn't help if you knew about his dealings with Jimmy and how they ran contrary to his father's interests."

"Is that why you didn't tell me?"

"That's why I *couldn't* tell you."

"So you knew who I was the day we met, when you put a gun to my head and—"

"What I knew, Harlan, was that you were making some kind of move on Morgan, while I was keeping an eye on her for Bert. I mean, c'mon, what was I supposed to do after seeing you sneak in through the back door as your gigantic bagman went through the front. You're lucky I didn't put a bullet in the back of your head."

Two table servers arrived with three trays of food. Roz waited until they had finished cramming it all—waffles, pancakes, toast, and eggs—on their table and then she continued:

"But then you turned out to be just what I needed—I mean, aside from the personal thing between us—once it became clear that you were going to do the right thing with that coke and bring *real* cops into your scam on the cove. Or at least I thought you were just what I needed, until..."

"Until what?"

"Until the personal thing started between us, and you went and messed everything up."

"I messed everything up?" Harlan said a little too loudly. The remark raised eyebrows throughout the diner.

"Yes, you," Roz whispered. "That night, after we figured out the real identities of the Grovers and started arranging for CDA agents and supplies, do you remember who you called first?"

"Well, yeah, my client, Sawed-Off."

"And do you remember the big *favor* you did for me, after I specifically told you to keep me out of whatever arrangements you made with him?"

"I... uh... got you a job working for him."

"That's right, Harlan. You got me a job with the guy I was already working for. And do you remember how you persuaded him to hire me—again?"

"Well, I… kind of told him you helped find the coke."

"No, Harlan, you told him that I led you right to it."

"Oh, yeah. I guess I did."

"After that, the little pip-squeak knew I was holding out on him. You remember what happened next, following your phone call to him?"

"Sure, I told you the good news about your new client, except, from your perspective, the news wasn't so good and the client wasn't so new."

"I mean after that, Harlan. What happened after you fed me that shit sandwich?"

"I made another call… to Angelo Surocco because we needed more CDA agents and… and…"

"And I got a call from Sawed-Off. In fact, you saw me take the call, there outside, not far from where you ended up talking to your new client, Shotgun Gino, who happened to be with Surocco. I'm on one side of the backyard getting lambasted by *my* client, *Sawed-Off,* while you're on the other side of the yard making plans with *your* client, *Shotgun.* Remember?"

How could he not remember? He'd stumbled upon Shotgun Gino, and that changed things. He still planned to trap the Grovers using the coke, but the goal had gone from finding Shotgun to clearing him of all the drug trafficking.

"That's right, you had a new client and a new game plan," Roz said, "and you stuck me with our old client and his game plan—and a little conflict of interest with my new boyfriend, if you know what I mean."

Harlan stared down at the table full of untouched food. *How did this get to be my fault?* he wondered. *She's the one who gave the bad guys the drugs.*

"How did you do it?" he asked as he looked up.

"How'd I do what?"

"You disabled push notifications from the cameras back at Bass Cove, so Sawed-Off and his guys could get in and out of there without me knowing. But when did you ever have time to do that? You conducted the entire interrogation."

"That was a little tricky, but made easier with all the distraction caused by Eddy Chub's transformation into the Hummer, part of which you were unconscious for."

"But wouldn't it have been easier for you to just..." Harlan stopped himself before completing the question and started answering it for himself. *It would have been a lot easier, and safer, for her to have helped Sawed-Off from a distance*, he thought, *and wash her hands of the scam on the cove.*

"You could have gotten yourself into all kinds of trouble, Roz, and you still might, for making that citizen's arrest of those cops and torturing the Grovers."

She responded with a long look, one that reminded him of what happened between them the first time he asked her why she'd come back. From that memory, he worked backward through other memories of their time together over the last five days... not so much what they did, but how it felt. Finally, he let himself lean into those feelings.

And then he pulled out his cell phone and began tapping at it.

"You *do* understand why I had to help him," Roz said, "don't you?"

As he continued tapping at his phone, Harlan recalled what she had said about Sawed-Off's threat to her son Philip. "I get it, Roz. I have a daughter who's about the same age as your son. I told you about her when we were in the pole barn."

Harlan stopped tapping at the phone and looked up. "There's nothing I wouldn't do to protect her," he added as he slid the phone across the table to Roz.

On the phone there was a map of Michigan's Lower Peninsula, which looked like a gigantic mitten. In the middle of the palm was a tight cluster of blinking dots heading south on US 127.

Roz looked at it curiously. "Are you tracking somebody?"

"Yeah, with your GPS trackers."

"Mine?"

"Remember me going back to your car to get those spy cams after we found the Grovers' stash in the pole barn?"

Roz nodded slowly.

"That's not all I borrowed from you. And cocaine wasn't the only thing in some of the bricks I put under the floorboards of the barn while you installed the cameras."

She stared off, processing this new information. Her eyes eventually returned to his. Smiling at him, she said, "You didn't tell me about planting trackers in the stash, which means you must not have fully trusted me."

"How dare I."

Her smile broadened. "And there's something else you're not telling me right now."

"What?"

"You're still on the case, aren't you?"

He nodded, imagining that she knew what he was thinking. Her next remark confirmed that she did.

"You're dreaming up some kind of scam for him, as we speak."

Harlan tried to hold a deadpan stare back at her, but he couldn't.

"C'mon already," Roz said. "I can see that you're dying to tell me. What kind of scam?"

"The kind that'll get the little pip-squeak out of your life for good."

About the Author

John Marks is an attorney in mid-Michigan who provides legislative counsel to lawmakers at the state capitol. He previously practiced law in California and has taught Constitutional Law and appellate advocacy at Western Michigan University, TMC Law School. He and his wife, Dena, have traveled much of the world but continue to enjoy most exploring the woods, waterways, and wildlife of northern Michigan with their children and grandchildren.

CPSIA information can be obtained
at www.ICGtesting.com
Printed in the USA
FSHW020758070419
56969FS